SONGS IN THE STORM

Wind River Chronicles Book 2

KATHY GEARY ANDERSON

Copyright © 2021 by Kathy Geary Anderson

All rights reserved.

No part of this book may be reproduced in any form or by any electronic or mechanical means, including information storage and retrieval systems, without written permission from the author, except for the use of brief quotations in a book review.

Edited by Kristin Avila and Marjorie Vawter

Cover by Carpe Librum Book Design

This is a work of fiction. Where real people, events, establishments, organizations, or locales appear, they are used fictitiously. All other elements of the novel are drawn from the author's imagination.

Scripture quotations are from the King James Version of the Bible.

ISBN 978-1-7369207-2-5 (paperback)

ISBN 978-1-7369207-3-2 (ebook)

www.kathygearyanderson.com

For Mom, who first taught me to love stories, especially family stories. I know you are smiling from Heaven to see this one finally in print.

"If I take the wings of the morning, and dwell in the uttermost parts of the sea; Even there shall thy hand lead me, and thy right hand shall hold me." Psalm 139:9-10

Chapter One

Newark, New Jersey, May 1900

Maddie Skivington's gaze locked on the white fabric of the handkerchief marred now by bright, scarlet splotches. A wave of cold swept through her, numbing her fingers, her mind, her very soul.

Blood.

How could this be? Rob had coughed. That's all. Simply coughed. And then, *blood?*

Her eyes met her husband's, reading the chagrin there.

"Has this happened before?"

Rob glanced away, carefully folding the stains into the handkerchief and tucking it back into his pocket. As if folding the evidence away would make everything better.

"Only once. About a week ago."

"And you didn't tell me?"

"It wasn't much. A few drops is all. I didn't want to worry you. Herb said it was nothing to be concerned about unless . . ."

"Unless?"

"It happened again." Rob's voice dropped to nearly a whisper.

Maddie sank into one of the chairs at the kitchen table. Silence stretched between them. She couldn't believe he'd told her older brother before he told her. Granted, Herb was a doctor and had been a godsend to them during Rob's illness, but surely a wife should know these things before a brother-in-law.

"You should have told me."

"I'm sorry. I honestly thought it would be nothing. I'm still fairly certain it's nothing to worry about. I've lost more blood in a nosebleed."

"That's not the point. A nosebleed is normal. Coughing up blood is not."

Rob took the chair next to her and wrapped his hands around her own clenched tightly in her lap.

"Sweetheart. This is precisely why I hadn't told you about the earlier episode. Herb wasn't concerned, so I didn't want to worry you. I feel fine. You know I do. I'm convinced I'm getting better, not worse. If it will help, I'll make another appointment with Dr. Waite. I'm sure he'll tell us the same thing."

He *was* doing much better than last fall when they first visited Dr. Waite, the specialist Herb had recommended. A weakness of the lungs, the doctor had said then, brought on by a bout with bronchitis and long work hours. Nothing a little rest wouldn't cure. Since then, they'd moved out of the city, and Rob had cut back on his work.

The change had taken effect. Rob's cough had improved. He'd gained back his weight. She looked at his face, no longer haggard but as healthy and handsome as the day they met. Rob was right. She was worried probably for no reason.

"Promise me you'll see Dr. Waite as soon as possible."

"I promise, as long as you promise not to worry. I'll be fine. You'll see." His breath caught in another cough, but this time blood spilled out of his mouth and down his chin. Maddie leaped up and grabbed a basin by the sink. As Rob spat blood into it, she knew. And he knew. This changed everything.

∽

Two days later, Maddie sat rigid in the hard wooden chair in Dr. Waite's office.

"I have the results of your sputum test and your x-rays here, Mr. Skivington, but after your recent hemorrhage, I'm sure you already know what I have to tell you. You have tuberculosis."

The word clanged like the lid of a coffin. It was one thing to suspect a verdict, quite another to hear it confirmed.

Tuberculosis.

Please, God. No. Not Rob.

Maddie closed her eyes. Dr. Waite's voice droned from a long way off, a mere hum beneath the pounding in her ears. She couldn't do this again—watch another person she loved slip away from her. *Why, Lord? Why must it always be the ones she loved the most?* Was she cursed somehow?

She forced her eyes open, trying to focus on the shiny mahogany of the doctor's desk. She needed to listen. She knew she did. For Rob. For both of them.

Breathe. Just breathe.

"You might say this early hemorrhage was a blessing in disguise," Dr. Waite was saying. "The earlier we begin treatment, the more likely you'll enjoy a full recovery."

Maddie relaxed her grip on the arm of her chair and latched onto that word. Recovery. If the doctor was talking recovery, then maybe Rob's condition wasn't as bad as she feared.

"What do you suggest?" Rob leaned forward, resting his elbows on his knees.

Dr. Waite rocked back in his chair. Steepling his fingers, he tapped them against his thick, gray mustache. "We have a couple of options. First and foremost, you must get out of the city."

Rob glanced over and caught her eye, then cleared his throat. "We did move out of the city last fall, sir, on your recommendation. We have a small cottage in Morris where we've spent the winter."

"You haven't been in the city at all?"

"Only to visit family and take care of business matters."

"And how often is that?"

"Twice . . . maybe three times, a week."

Dr. Waite shook his head. "It won't do. The cold, damp air of our New Jersey climate is bad enough, but mixed with the foul and polluted air of the city, it's literally poisoning your already damaged lungs. If you want to survive this disease, you'll have to make a bigger move."

"How big?" Maddie wished her voice didn't sound quite so panicky.

The doctor turned his gaze in her direction. "Your husband's recovery will require great sacrifice on both your parts."

"I'll do anything within my power to see that my husband recovers, Dr. Waite."

His gaze softened. "I have no doubts about that, my dear."

Rob shifted in the seat beside her. "What type of sacrifice are we talking?"

The doctor pursed his lips. "Well, obviously, your choices depend somewhat on your financial resources. As a business owner, am I to assume you have access to enough money to sustain you for a while?"

Rob gave a short nod. "My partner has mentioned an interest in buying me out."

"Good."

Good? Dr. Waite had no idea what Rob's business meant to him. How he had poured his time and energy into building it. How he was finally beginning to make a name for himself among the high-end jewelry stores on Maiden Lane. How could Rob selling his life's dream ever be good? She blinked against the tears that threatened, not wanting either man to see her distress.

"Let's say I have the means, doctor. What would you recommend?"

"I'm sure you've heard Dr. Trudeau is doing good work in Saranac Lake. You might consider checking yourself in there for six months or a year. Maddie could remain with her family here in Newark."

"No! No institutions."

If Rob's vehement response surprised the doctor, he did a good job of hiding it. With only the slightest lift of an eyebrow, he continued. "Well, then. What I'd recommend instead is a total change of climate. Dry air. High altitude. Somewhere you can be outdoors as much as possible."

Dr. Waite leaned forward and studied them across the surface of his desk. "I had a patient who came to me two years ago in much worse shape than you are right now. He took my advice and went west. Settled somewhere in Wyoming—Laramie or Lymore or—well, it's no matter. The point is, he's enjoyed great success. I talked to his uncle just last week. He tells me the young man is in excellent health. Recently married, in fact."

Rising, Dr. Waite went to a tall cabinet against the wall and pulled out a folder. "Ah, Lander is the name of the town." He copied the information onto a slip of paper and handed it to Rob. "Here's his name and address. I suggest you get in touch with him. Go out to Wyoming. Get into farming, ranching—anything that will get you outdoors. Hard work won't kill you, but if you stay in this city, in this climate . . ." He let the words trail off.

Rob studied the paper for a minute before tucking it into his suit pocket. "I don't suppose they have a need for jewelers in Lander?" One corner of his mouth tipped up in a rueful grin. "I'm a city boy, doctor. I'm afraid I don't know much about farming or ranching."

Dr. Waite peered back at him with a sober face. "Even if they did need jewelers, I wouldn't recommend following your same line of work. When I said get outdoors, I meant it. Many of my colleagues recommend their patients *sleep* in the open air, even in the dead of winter. Believe me, Mr. Skivington, if you are to survive this disease, you'll need to start over. Adopt an entirely different lifestyle."

Fear stabbed the pit of Maddie's stomach. Wyoming? All she knew of Wyoming was what she'd read in her brother's dime novels. According to those lurid tales, Wyoming was wild and barren, a haven for outlaws and Indians. But that was all fiction. The only thing she knew for a fact, Wyoming was hundreds of miles from New Jersey.

What about her family? Her sisters? What would Hazel and Edie do without her? More importantly, what would she do without *them*?

And then there were Father and his new wife Fran, and the boys, and all of Rob's family. No. It was too much to ask. She opened her mouth to say so but quickly shut it, remembering her brave words just a few minutes earlier. *I'll do anything within my power to see that my husband recovers, Dr. Waite.*

But Wyoming? *Dear God, please, don't let it come to that.*

Chapter Two

❧❧❧

"You don't have to come with me today if you're not feeling up to it."

Rob felt soft fingertips brush the hair off his forehead and opened his eyes to see Maddie, her pretty face puckered with concern, bending over him. Puzzled, he looked around and saw the book he'd been reading upended on the floor beside him. Drat! He'd fallen asleep in the chair again.

Sitting up, he pushed away the cotton throw Maddie must have wrapped around him while he slept. If only he could slough off his exhaustion just as easily. Ever since the hemorrhage, he'd been weak as a kitten.

He shook his head, trying to clear it. Where was it they were going again? Oh. Right. No. Staying home wasn't an option, as tempting as it might sound.

"Of course, I feel up to it. I wouldn't miss my wife's birthday dinner for the world." He looked up at her with what he hoped was a convincing smile.

He could tell she wasn't fooled. She cocked her head and studied him, lips pursed, eyes squinted. "Truly, Rob. There's no need for you to go if you're feeling too tired. My family will understand. We can celebrate my actual birthday together, just the two of us, on Tuesday."

He pushed to his feet and picked his suit jacket off the end of the bed where he'd laid it when they came in from church. "We'll celebrate today *and* on Tuesday. You know I don't like you riding into the city alone. And your family certainly won't understand if they have to have a birthday celebration without the guest of honor."

She moved to the bureau and picked up her brush, looking back at him over her shoulder. "I already thought of that. Mrs. Peabody told me at church this morning that she plans to catch the two o'clock to visit Ellen today. I'm sure she won't object to my company."

Rob pulled on his jacket and adjusted his cuffs. "If I didn't know better, I'd think you didn't want me to come."

"Of course, I do. It's just . . . well, if you're not feeling up to it, maybe you should stay home this time."

Ever since their visit to Dr. Waite's, she'd been treating him as if he were made of spun glass. "I'm fine. Besides, today might be a good time to talk to your father about Wyoming." The silence that greeted his words was almost palpable, but he forged ahead anyway. "What do you think?"

Maddie turned from where she was fussing with her hair at the bureau mirror. "I thought we weren't going to make any decisions until we heard back from Mr. Westraven."

"Actually, I received an answer from him on Friday." Stepping around her, he avoided eye contact by rummaging through his bureau drawer for a tie. Pulling one out, he joined her at the mirror and began working it into a bow around his neck.

She caught his eye in the mirror. "And when were you going to tell me?"

He should have told her yesterday, had meant to, but somehow couldn't bring himself to bring up the subject. They'd not talked about Dr. Waite's advice after that first day when they'd both agreed to wait for an answer from Ted Westraven.

And somehow, even after having heard from the man, it was so much easier not to broach the subject at all. Talking about it made it real. But they couldn't avoid the inevitable. If they were going to act, now was the time—before his disease got worse.

He mustered a sheepish smile. "Now, I guess."

She turned back to fussing with the soft brown curls along her forehead. "What did he have to say?"

"He was very encouraging. Couldn't say enough about the climate, the people, the opportunities . . . He seems to think I'd have no problem hiring myself out to some farm or ranch and pretty much confirmed what Dr. Waite said. The climate out there has been a lifesaver for him.

"Oh, and he also mentioned if we are serious about coming, to let him know. He has a sister in Newark who's been wanting to come out to visit him, but their uncle won't let her travel all that way by herself. Could be some good company for you for our trip, should we decide to go."

Maddie began poking through her jewelry box. "Are you . . . have you . . . have you given any more thought to Saranac Lake? Maybe it would be wise to put yourself under a doctor's care rather than trying this on your own."

The sanitarium? Why was she even considering that? She knew how he felt about institutions. He ran a finger along his starched collar, suddenly overheated. Besides, the thought of being away from her for who knows how long was more than he could bear. After three years of marriage, the thought of living life without Maddie by his side was like considering severing his right hand. Not something he'd ever do voluntarily, that much was sure.

"I can't, Maddie. You know I can't. The walls . . . the confinement . . ." He struggled for air. "It would kill me as sure as this disease can."

She turned. Placing her hands on his shoulders, she forced him to meet her gaze. "It's not an asylum, Rob. You'd be free to leave at any time."

"Only if the doctor agrees. Think, Maddie. It could be months, maybe years, before Dr. Trudeau deems me well enough to leave, and then what? Should I come back to the same poisonous air that put me there in the first place? Best to make the break now, take charge of our own destiny."

She let her hands drop from his shoulders and turned back to her jewelry box. Picking up the garnet and opal brooch he'd made her as a wedding gift, she pinned it to the lace on her collar and surveyed the effect for a minute.

He bit back his impatience at her continued silence. "So, what do you say? Do we talk to your father tonight?"

She let slip a small sigh, then turned to face him again. "I suppose it wouldn't hurt. Herb will be there. We could get his opinion, as well. Maybe he could recommend an alternative treatment to what Dr. Waite suggested, something not so far from home."

He doubted it. Herb had been the one to recommend Dr. Waite to them in the first place. It wasn't likely he would offer a dissenting opinion. Still, Maddie obviously wasn't ready to accept Wyoming as their only option.

He wished he could give her the time she needed to adjust to the idea. Leaving her family—leaving *both* their families—would be hard, but time wasn't something he had much of. Something in his gut told him if they didn't go soon, they'd miss the opportunity to go at all.

"But let's not bring up the topic right away." Maddie's eyes pleaded with his. "I'd hate to ruin everyone's day if we can help it. Promise me you'll wait a bit before you tell them?"

He wrapped his arms around her, pulling her close until her head settled just beneath his chin. "Tell you what. You're the birthday girl. I'll let you bring up the subject whenever you feel it's best."

∽

HE'D TOLD FATHER. SHE COULD TELL BY THE GRIM SET OF Father's shoulders and the silent appeal in Rob's eyes when he caught her gaze after coming back up from downstairs. What happened to letting her be the one to break the news? They hadn't even had cake yet.

She should have known Father would weasel the news out of Rob the minute he invited him down to his lair. Other fathers had their dens and libraries. Her father preferred a trip to his workshop in the basement. Ostensibly the invitation was always an offer to show off his latest project—a bookcase, a chair back, a gracefully turned table leg. Everyone in the family knew by now, though, that Father was after far more than admiration of his skill with a lathe.

She should never have told Father about Rob's impending doctor's visit. Of course, he was going to ask about it. And stronger men than Rob had cracked under her father's skillful questioning. No, she couldn't blame Rob, but that didn't mean she was ready to discuss their move with the rest of the family.

"Let's take a walk over to the river, Edie." The words flew out before she had time to think and seemed to startle her sister as much as they did her.

"Don't you want your cake?" Edie said.

Of course. The cake.

Hazel bounded over, braids swinging. "Wait till you see it, Maddie. I made it all by myself. Edie only had to help me a little bit, with the stirring 'cause my arm got tired, and we decorated it with the prettiest bunch of posies. Just wait till you see it."

Maddie pulled the girl into her lap and gave her a quick squeeze. "You made it all by yourself? That's mighty impressive for an eight-year-old."

Of all her siblings, she would miss Hazel the most. In fact, the thought of leaving Hazel was almost as hard as the thought of losing Rob. Almost.

Sixteen years separated them, and if Mother had been well when Hazel was born, they probably wouldn't even be close. But

Mother had not been well. She had never truly recovered from Hazel's birth. As the oldest daughter, Maddie had fallen into the role of surrogate mother to each of the younger Long children: Edie, Les, and Hazel. But especially to Hazel. From the moment she first held her baby sister, when Hazel's tiny hand wrapped itself around her finger and somehow also around her heart, the girl had been hers.

Then Mother had died, and Father withdrew into his grief, leaving Hazel entirely to Maddie's care. Only recently, when Father had married Fran, and Rob had become so gravely ill, had Maddie relinquished that care to others. Fran was a wonderful stepmother and an answer to their prayers for Father, but Maddie missed her role in Hazel's life. The move to Morris had been hard enough, allowing her to see Hazel only once a week. A move to Wyoming was nearly unthinkable.

"Ouch, Maddie. You're squeezing me." Hazel wiggled in her lap, pushing against her arms.

"Sorry." She let Hazel slide from her lap. She had to stop thinking about Wyoming, or she'd never make it through the day.

"Who's ready for cake?" Fran walked in from the kitchen, cake held high.

Her youngest brother Les, who'd been lying on his stomach shooting marbles over by the window, hopped to his feet. "Thunder and Moses, Hazel. Whatcha put all over that cake? Weeds?"

"They're not weeds. They're posies. I think they're beautiful."

"Look like weeds to me."

Maddie stepped between the two before Hazel had a chance to deliver the kick she was aiming Les's direction. "I think it's a perfectly lovely way to decorate a May birthday cake. And, Les, if you want a piece of it, you might want to mind what you say."

He took the hint, scrambling into his chair without another

word. Father and Rob and her other brothers drifted in from the parlor.

"And I tell you, Bryan is never going to win the White House." Father's voice rang clear as they entered the room.

"Now, Henry. Enough man talk for now. It's time to celebrate Maddie's birthday." Fran set the cake on the table.

"Who says it's man talk?" Percy slid into the seat next to her and poked her with his elbow. "Maddie may want to bone up on her politics, with her moving to Wyoming and all. I hear the women out there are allowed to vote."

He told Percy? Had he told all her brothers, then? She didn't even try to stem the accusatory glare she shot across the table at Rob.

"You're moving to Wyoming?"

The soft query drew Maddie's eyes to the end of the table where Edie stood cutting the cake, knife suspended midair. Had she looked so peaked and worn earlier? Dark circles smudged her lower eyelids, her fragile bone structure more prominent than ever. She could strangle Rob for breaking the news this way. Well, to be fair, Percy had broken the news. She'd strangle them both.

"Nothing's settled. Dr. Waite suggested it, is all," she said, throwing a warning look in Rob's direction.

"Whoa! Wyoming? Like in Buffalo Bill and Deadwood Dick?" Les's eyes glowed.

"Yes," Rob said. "Though I doubt it will be anything like the stories in your dime novels. My contact out there tells me Lander is quite the modern town with electricity and everything."

"Can we not talk about this now?"

An awkward silence settled in the room at her words. Father raised an eyebrow. Les looked expectantly between her and Rob. Edie seemed about ready to burst into tears. Quietly, Fran passed around slices of cake. Maddie could hear the ticking of the clock in the parlor.

Oh, good heavens. She hadn't meant they couldn't talk at all. Taking a deep breath, she bit off a piece of cake and dredged up a smile. Swallowing, she turned to Hazel. "This cake is wonderful, sweetie. You did a marvelous job for your very first one."

Hazel looked back at her with serious eyes. "Wyoming is an awfully long ways away, isn't it, Maddie?"

Not much hope for it, was there? Letting loose another sigh, she capitulated. "Yes, honey, Wyoming *is* a long way away. But the doctor thinks the air out there will help Rob get better again. Besides, it's not like we'll have to travel all that way by horse and wagon. We'll go by train, and if you ever needed to come see us, you could get on a train too and be there in no time."

Rob cleared his throat. "Actually, we can get *most* of the way by train. The railroad doesn't go all the way to Lander yet."

How did he know so much more about all of this than she did? Apparently, unlike her, he hadn't spent the last ten days ignoring Dr. Waite's words and hoping this would all go away.

"Then how will you get there?"

Hazel's question was a valid one.

"They have a daily stagecoach service between Rawlins and Lander. We'll travel the old-fashioned way and go by stage."

"A stagecoach? Bully! Do you think you'll have a holdup?"

"Les. Mind your slang." Fran said. "And no one's going to be held up. You read entirely too many of those novels."

Maddie set down her fork and stood up. She needed air, and she needed it fast. "How about that walk, Edie?"

Edie was halfway out of her seat when she paused and glanced over at their stepmother. "Oh, but maybe we should help clean up first."

"Go. Both of you." Fran waved them toward the door. "I have plenty of helpers here. Don't I?"

The expression on the faces of those helpers was anything but enthusiastic, but Maddie refused to let them sway her today. After all, this was her birthday celebration, and if she wanted a walk with her sister after dinner, she was going to take it.

They took the same path they always did, past O'Reilly's Corner Market, then up Hamilton to Grant, making sure to wave to Granny Higsby settled in her front porch rocker. Then, bypassing the shortest route to the river up New Street, they opted as usual for the trip up Reynolds past the rows of workers' cottages from Carter's Mill and the larger houses of the superintendents.

The Morris and Essex Branch railroad rumbled across its tracks overhead on its way into the city, making speech impossible. No matter. They rarely talked until they reached the river anyway.

Edie was not the sister-friend of her childhood, the sharer of secrets under the bedclothes and tea parties under the lilac bushes in the back yard. Katie Alice had held that position and probably always would. But Katie Alice was gone.

Edie had come along a mere three months after Katie Alice died. "The Lord giveth and the Lord taketh away," Mother had said. To her own six-year-old self, the Lord had seemed mighty unreasonable taking away her favorite playmate and replacing her with a tiny, wrinkly, squalling nuisance who did little more than sleep and cry all day.

But, as Edie had grown, so had Maddie's love for this sweet, quiet sister. Exactly when Edie made the transition from charge to confidant, Maddie couldn't say. But she was almost certain it had occurred sometime during Mother's last, long illness, and she was equally as sure that these walks to the river played a large part in it.

They settled into their spots along the bank, feet tucked up under their skirts. Edie plucked a few blades of grass and let them drift on the wind. The muddy waters of the Passaic reflected the clear spring sky above. Maddie followed the course of a three-masted schooner as it glided slowly past and under the overhead railroad bridge.

"Was Walter able to get that job you told me about?" She glanced over at Edie.

"Yes, but Father thinks he shouldn't take it."

"Whyever not?"

"He says hauling for a brewery is just as wrong as making the liquor itself."

"What does Walter think?"

"He says a job is a job and that he hauls all sorts of things he never plans to use—from corsets to cannons—and he's not about to turn down a paying job just because he doesn't like the cargo."

Maddie bit back a smile. Her brother-in-law's Irish Catholic upbringing often clashed with Father's Methodist convictions, probably always would. For the sake of family harmony, the sooner Edie and Walter could save enough to buy a home of their own, the better.

She studied her sister's pale profile. "Have you been getting enough sleep? You look tired." And fragile. More fragile than usual, that is. None of the Long sisters were of sturdy build, but Father had always told her that she had the look of her mother's family but the constitution of a Long. Meaning, she supposed, what she lacked in stature and girth, she more than made up for in grit and gumption.

Not so with Edie. She was her mother's daughter through and through. She was delicate in both looks and nature and easily susceptible to illness.

Edie offered a wan smile. "I *am* tired, but not for lack of sleep. Fran says I'll be fine."

"*Fran* says. How about Herb?" Shouldn't a doctor's opinion matter more than their stepmother's?

"Herb, too. I'm fine. Or I will be, come December."

"What do you mean?"

A faint blush stained Edie cheeks. "I'm . . . we're . . . Walter and I are . . . in the family way."

"Edie!" Maddie threw her arms around her sister and drew her close. "Why didn't you tell me sooner?"

"There's hardly been time, with the party and all."

Something in Edie's voice made Maddie pull out of their embrace. Still holding Edie by the shoulders, she searched her face. "But you're happy about this, right? You and Walter?"

"Of course we are."

"Edie?"

"Truth be told, Maddie. I'm scared. Silly of me, I know. Women have babies every day. But I keep seeing Mother, how hard it was for her with each new baby. Besides . . ."

"What?"

Edie broke from her grasp. Tucking her knees up under her chin, she stared out over the river. A few minutes of silence passed before she spoke again in a low voice. "I thought you'd be here. I'm not sure I can do this without my big sister."

"Oh, Edie. Nothing's settled yet. I told you that."

"But if a move to Wyoming is the only thing that will help Rob, I can't see how you can stay."

Maddie scanned the city skyline sprawled out before her on the opposite bank of the Passaic. Though the day was bright and clear, a perfect spring day in fact, the sky was marred by plumes of dark smoke from hundreds of smokestacks belching their fumes into the Newark air. She turned her head to look behind her. Why, Clark's Mill alone had at least five of the beasts. Even in this lovely setting, the poisonous air Dr. Waite warned would kill Rob surrounded them. Edie was right. How could they not go? Much as she loved her family, Rob came first and always would. If Wyoming was what he chose, then she would choose it too.

Chapter Three

Rob signed his name to the bottom of the document, then laid down the pen.

"Congratulations, Mr. Johnston," Mr. Francis Lawton of the law firm Bigglesby, Lawton, and Marsh, turned to shake Harvey's hand. "J&S Jewelry Manufacturing is now officially yours." He turned back to Rob, handing him a cashier's check. "And congratulations to you, as well, Mr. Skivington. You've earned yourself quite a tidy profit."

Rob looked at the amount penned on the check, signifying everything he'd worked for in the past eleven years. Ten thousand dollars. A goodly sum, yes. And, frankly, a bit more than he'd expected for his part in their fledgling business. Coupled with the money they'd made on the sale of their cottage in Morris, he and Maddie should have plenty to help them make a fresh start in Lander.

So why did it feel as if he'd just severed his right arm? He supposed he should be happy that Harvey had been able and very willing to buy him out when he approached him about it. Still, the transition from Rob Skivington, business owner, to Rob Skivington, invalid, was painful to the very core of his being.

When he'd asked Maddie to marry him, he'd promised her

their future would be bright. And he'd believed it. J&S Jewelry was finally turning a profit, with its margins growing every year. All the hard work of his and Harvey's early years—the scrimping and saving to put money back in the business, grow their clientele, put out product—was finally paying off. They were well on their way to a comfortable life. They'd hoped to build a home here. Raise a family. They both wanted children. Scads of them, he'd often joked. But now, a mere three years later, all he had to offer Maddie was an ailing husband and the opportunity to join him on what might be a futile chase for a cure.

He folded the check into the inner pocket of his suit coat and pushed to his feet. He needed air. He was halfway to the door when an arm fell across his shoulders. Rob turned to look down into Harvey's gray eyes, brimming with concern through his gold-rimmed spectacles.

"You going to be all right?"

Rob dredged up a smile. "Sure. I'm tired, is all." It wasn't a lie. He was always tired these days. "I appreciate what you did today, Harvey. And the buy-out price . . . it was very generous."

"No more than you deserve. I couldn't have built this business without you, and I'll be profiting from your designs for some time yet. Did I tell you I sold your line of seed-pearl brooches to Billings last week?"

Chester Billings? They'd been trying to sell to him for years. He didn't even try to bolster his slipping smile. Life was moving on . . . without him.

They reached the busy sidewalk, teeming with Newark businessmen hurrying to and fro. A few months ago, he would have numbered himself among them. But not today. He felt like a boat set loose from its moorings without a rudder.

Harvey engulfed his hand in a hearty handshake. "I'd best be off. Lewis is smelting today and is liable to burn the shop down without me there to oversee him."

Rob managed a feeble grin.

"Will you and Maddie come to dinner tomorrow night?

Helen and the kids would like a chance to say goodbye before you leave."

"Thank you. We will."

Harvey nodded, then, with a wave of his hand, hurried off down the street. Rob watched until his brown derby was swallowed by a throng of other derbies. And that was that. Eleven years of planning, dreaming, building, and designing gone in less time than it took to set a line of diamonds in a necklace.

A woman, laden down with shopping bags, jostled his arm as she brushed past him on the sidewalk. Rob squared his shoulders. No use dwelling on what might have been. He had errands to see to if they were to leave on Monday. Turning, he made his way up Broad Street toward the First National Bank of Newark.

Half an hour later, Rob caught the trolley at Market and Broad. Settling into a window seat, Rob stared out at the bustling mass of pedestrians, horses, wagons, cyclists—all darting and dodging in and out of the trolley's path. The vibrant activity around him left him feeling all the more drained.

What would their new home be like? Apart from the few months they'd lived in Morris County, he'd only ever known the city—London, when he was very young, and then Newark. Ted Westraven had described Lander as a town of less than eight hundred people. Eight hundred. Watching the teeming humanity around him, he wouldn't be surprised to learn eight hundred souls were gathered on this portion of Broad Street alone.

A sliver of his old self buried deep beneath his lethargy stirred at the thought of the adventure that lay ahead. Maybe in the new climate with his tuberculosis on the mend, he would discover again the strength and energy necessary to take on that adventure. Maybe he'd even start again. Build another business. Give Maddie the life he'd promised. The life she deserved. Maybe. Right now, all he sought was a nap. He rested his head on the back of the high trolley seat and closed his eyes. *Please, Lord, grant me the will and the energy to begin again.*

~

When he switched trolleys at Pennsylvania Avenue, he caught sight of a familiar head of black hair near the front. Making his way up the aisle, he dropped into the empty seat beside the young man.

"Durand's let out early today?"

The look of startled guilt on his brother's face almost made him laugh. How many times had he caught the boy with just that same expression?

"Oh. You're playing hooky, then?"

"No." Fred's tone was defensive. "Orders have been slow this month. Old Hodgkins said half of us could leave at noon."

Rob cocked an eyebrow at his brother but held his peace.

"You know how it is. Hodgkins favors the married men when days are slack."

Yes, he knew how it was, but he also knew he'd never let Hodgkins bully him into taking time off and had risen through the ranks much quicker because of it. To be fair, he'd had a lot more riding on his success than Fred ever had. At sixteen, he'd had his mum and five younger siblings to support. Fred, being the youngest, had only himself to think of. Still, the boy had such potential, it was hard to sit back and watch him squander it.

"Are you enjoying stone setting?"

Fred shrugged. "It's all right. I'd rather be doing what you are, though."

He chuckled. "Give it time. You don't become a designer overnight. It takes years of working in each of the departments. I was twenty before I became certified."

"I don't mean what you *used* to do. I meant what you're doing now."

"I'm not doing anything now." Funny how much the truth of that hurt.

"You're going west. Think of it, Rob—mountains, ranches,

cowboys, wildcats, bear. I'd give my right arm to be heading into all that."

And he'd give a lot more than that to have even half of his brother's enthusiasm again. He let out a soft snort. "Wildcats? Bear? George got you reading dime novels again?"

"Not a dime novel. Roosevelt's *Ranch Life and the Hunting Trail*. Have you read it?"

"Can't say as I have."

"Well, you should. I can't believe you're going to see all those things—live on a ranch, hobnob with cowboys and Indians—and you haven't even read about it."

He shrugged. "There hasn't been a whole lot of time."

"George and I were talking. Maybe we should come to Wyoming with you."

"And do what?"

"Same as you. Work for a rancher or a farmer."

"What I need you to do is stay right here with the jobs you have. I need you to take care of Mum while I'm gone."

"She has Alice and Peachie."

"Peachie's a great son-in-law to Mum, but we're her boys. We have the responsibility to care for her. Not Peachie."

"Billy and Harry are her boys too. They'll still be around. I'd think that'd be enough."

"Billy and Harry have their own families to care for. Besides, I don't even know what type of work I'll be able to find. It's not like Newark with a factory on every street corner and jobs for the taking. No sense all three of us leaving behind good-paying jobs for jobs that may not even exist."

"But once you get out there and see that there are jobs, can we come?"

He heaved a long sigh. He didn't have the energy to fight this battle today. "We'll see."

He glanced out the trolley window to see Jackson's Park passing on the right. Pushing forward, he picked up the satchel he'd set at his feet.

"Best get ready."

Two blocks later, they hopped off the trolley in front of a modest, red-brick row house. Fred bounded up the steps ahead of him and almost bowled into Peachie, who opened the door a mere second before Fred reached it.

Peachie side-stepped just in time. "Steady there, Fred. Where's the fire?"

"Sorry. Any dinner left?"

"Oh, I think we managed to leave you some."

Peachie's dry response made Rob chuckle. Keeping his two youngest brothers fed was no easy task. If he weren't pitching in with a monthly stipend to help toward his family's room and board, he might feel a bit guilty. Not that Peachie asked anything of him. Had even insisted Mum and the boys move in with him and Alice shortly after the two were married. But still. Since dad's accident, his family's care had been his responsibility. Sharing it with someone, even a man as capable and willing as his brother-in-law, was difficult.

"Nice talking to you too," Peachie called to the empty doorway as Fred disappeared inside. Then, with a shake of his head, he came on down the steps. "Were we ever that hungry?"

"I'm pretty sure we've both had our days." Though his days of feeling hungry seemed mere figments of the past—his past before tuberculosis, that is. Breakfast had been hours ago, but he still felt no need to eat.

"And I, for one, have the belly to prove it." Peachie patted his ample girth, then looked Rob over. "So, how'd it go today?"

The obvious sympathy shining in his brother-in-law's pale blue eyes was almost his undoing. Swallowing hard, he looked away. If anyone understood what this day had cost him, Peachie would. At his own father's death fifteen years ago, the man had taken over a small warehouse and built it into a thriving provision's dealership.

Rob cleared his throat. "It went well. Harvey insisted on paying more than I had even asked."

"Good. Good. You worked hard to build that business. You deserve to turn a good profit. So, you all set to leave, then?"

He gave a nod. "Monday morning, as planned."

It was Peachie's turn to clear his throat. "I haven't wanted to say this in front of the ladies . . ." His beefy fingers toyed with the black derby he held in his hands. "I guess it goes without saying. You *do* know your mother and the boys all have a place with us for as long as they need it?"

"Yes. And I appreciate that."

"What I mean is . . ." Peachie looked up and locked gazes with him. "You don't need to be worrying about sending money each month." He held up a hand when Rob opened his mouth to protest. "No. Hear me out. With the boys and me all working, we have plenty to support your mother. Drat. I'm saying this all wrong. I *want* to support your mother. So far as I'm concerned, she's my mom too."

He knew Peachie meant well, but at his words, he felt another piece of himself being torn away—his health, his business, his responsibilities. *What's left, Lord?* Soon he'd be stripped of everything but a shell of his former self and this blasted disease.

He wanted to dig his heels in and stubbornly refuse to relinquish his hold on one more thing, but instead, he forced a weak smile and spoke the words he knew Peachie wanted to hear. "I understand. And thank you. But when we get settled . . ."

No. He couldn't quite let it go.

Peachie reached out and squeezed his arm. "When you get settled, I'll hang on to Mum, but I may just send the young scamps back to you. How's that?"

Rob laughed. "Fair enough."

"And here comes my trolley. We'll talk more tonight." Stuffing his derby on his head, Peachie jogged toward the approaching trolley and hopped aboard.

Rob waved him on his way and headed into the house. Maddie met him in the front hallway.

"I wondered where you'd got to. Fred told us you were on the trolley with him."

"I was talking with Peachie."

He pulled her into an embrace, marveling anew at how tiny and delicate she was, how good she felt in his arms. He was wrong before. He hadn't been stripped of everything. He still had this, and this was enough. She nestled against him for a minute, then pushed back, scanning his face. Powerful eyes she had, not only in their beauty—emerald flecks on a bed of golden velvet—but also for their ability to commune with his very soul.

"The morning went well?"

"As well as can be expected." He was saved from saying more by Mum, who bustled out of the kitchen a glass full of frothy milk held high.

"There ye be. We've been a wonderin' what was keepin' ya. Oive got yer milk right here. Don't dally now, or yer meal'll get cold." She brushed ahead of him into the dining room in a flurry of black serge.

"Yes'm," he called to her retreating back. He and Maddie exchanged smiles before following after.

Fred sat alone at the table, sopping up the last bits of gravy from his plate with his bread. On the table beside him was a plate heaped high with potatoes and roast. Mum set the milk beside it and stepped to the side, clearly expecting him to sit down and dig in the way Fred had. With a sigh, he took his seat and picked up his fork. Why was it that the doctors' main prescription for a disease that left him with no appetite was food, food, and more food? The women meant well, he knew, but the day he conquered this tuberculosis would be the last day he ever drank another glass of milk or downed another egg.

Mum sat down next to him, and Maddie took an empty seat across the table.

"So ye've sold the business, then?"

"Yes, it's sold, and the money's on its way to a bank in Lander."

"Ye'll be leavin' on Monday for certain?"

"Yes."

Alice bustled in with two large pieces of apple pie, which she set by each of their plates. Fred was digging into his before it even reached the surface of the table.

Rob took a few more bites of meat and potato, feeling the eyes of each of the women resting on him. It was no use. He pushed the plate aside, deciding to concentrate instead on getting the milk down.

"You gonna eat that?" Fred's fork was poised for an attack.

"Fred!"

"It's all right, Alice. Leave the boy alone. At least *he* has an appetite."

Fred pulled the plate close and began shoveling in the food before anyone else could object. Not that anyone did. The women had suddenly all become very quiet, making him wish his last comment hadn't sounded quite so bitter.

After a few minutes, Mum broke the silence. "Ye be coming with me on Visiting Day, then?"

Visiting Day? He hadn't thought about that in months. There was a time when he'd accompany her every Sunday like the dutiful eldest son he was. But with his marriage and then this illness, he'd let the practice slide.

"This Sunday?" He met Maddie's eyes across the table. "No. We'd planned to spend the day with Maddie's family since it's our last day."

"Samuel Robert Skivington, never tell me ye plan ta go all the way out ta Wyoming without so much as a 'by yer leave' to yer father."

He had planned to, or rather, hadn't planned at all. Simply forgot. Not that it would matter to Dad. He glanced at Fred, who sat staring at him, fork suspended halfway to his mouth, then over at Alice, who surveyed him with wide eyes.

He sighed. "I'll have to go tomorrow, then. Could you move your visiting day up this week and come with me?"

"On a Saturday? But who will do the weekly baking? Besides, I'll 'ave nothing to bring your father." Every week like clockwork, Mum took Dad a basket of his favorite fresh baked goods. Visiting Dad on any day but a Sunday was suspect. Visiting him without that basket was out of the question.

"I'd be glad to help Alice with the baking if you want to go along with Rob," Maddie said.

"And we could make Dad's baked goods this afternoon if you'd like, Mum," Alice added.

Mum studied the two women for a minute, then gave a decided shake to her head. "That's what we'll do then. We'll make Saturday our visiting day this week. Superintendent 'inckley won't know what to think."

Chapter Four

❦

The next morning, he and Mum took the Caldwell branch of the Erie Railroad to the small township of Verona, disembarking at the Overbrook station. Silently, they made their way up the road toward an imposing red brick building that lay halfway up a small hill, partially shrouded in the early morning mist. Essex County Hospital for the Insane. The words alone sent a shudder through his frame.

As they drew closer, he had to admit the building with its pretty white trim and wide porticos was a far sight better than the crowded wards of the hospital in Newark where Dad had been housed until two years ago. He'd only visited this facility a few times and not at all in the past six months.

He saw the framework for a new wing abuzz with activity this Saturday morning. The ring of hammers and the rasp of saws cut across the crisp spring air.

Glancing down at his mum trotting along beside him, he marveled at her serenity. Dressed in her second-best gown of black bombazine, wearing her best hat—a large black monstrosity that stuck out in front of her like the prow of a ship—she looked the very picture of a respectable widow. One would never suspect she was on her way to visit an ailing husband who, even on his best days, she was not allowed to see. Not truly a widow, not really a wife, he wondered again how she managed to cope.

"Do you ever wish Dad had died in that accident?" The words slipped out without his thinking, and now, judging by the shocked expression on Mum's face, he wished he could somehow take them back.

"Why, Samuel Robert! What a 'orrible thing to say."

Horrible? Maybe, but also honest. Surely even she had entertained the thought at least once in the past fifteen years.

"Would it really be so horrible, then? Him being in heaven instead of here?"

"'Tis no such a bad place," she said, looking around at the buildings and trees.

"No, but it's not heaven."

Her face softened. "No. That it's not."

They walked in silence for a few minutes before she continued. "I don't know why the Good Lord did no' take your dad those many years ago. I don't know why 'e allows 'im, and all the others who are 'oused 'ere to live as they do with their addled brains." She paused for a minute as if in deep thought. "Or even why he allows my big, strong son to get a disease that wastes 'im and takes 'im miles away from 'is family." She looked up at him from beneath the brim of her hat. "I only know what 'e told us in the Good Book. 'is ways are not our ways, and 'e works everything together for our good. Ain't my place to know all the reasons, but tis my *duty* to trust 'e knows best."

He wished he had even a small measure of his mum's deep faith. He had faith, at least he thought he did. But he also had this insatiable need to understand. To know why. He didn't know if he'd ever be able to just let it go as she did. He remembered well those dark days after Dad's accident, how hard they had prayed and how joyful they'd been when the doctors assured them of Dad's full recovery.

What they hadn't realized—hadn't even suspected—was the

man who returned home from the hospital that day was not the same Dad they'd always known. The railroad beam that felled him had taken their father as surely as if it had killed him, leaving a morose, volatile stranger clothed in Dad's body instead. Their quiet, easy-going, hard-working father became a man who could no longer hold a job due to his inability to get along with others or control his temper.

But worst of all were the delusions, the unreasonable suspicions, and accusations—mostly directed at Mum—that tore their family apart. The names he called her, the vile acts he accused her of committing. Mum. Who never had an unkind word or thought for anyone. Then came that fateful day, when drawn by Alice's screams, he and Billy had run into the kitchen to find Dad chasing Mum with a butcher knife. He'd have killed her that day, the woman he'd once loved more than life. He'd have killed her for certain if they hadn't been there to wrestle him to the ground and subdue him until the police were called. There was no help for it, the doctors had said. He had to be committed.

For the first time since Dad was sent to the asylum, Rob found himself empathizing with the man. He now knew what it felt like to have everything in his life stripped away through no fault of his own. But he had more choices than Dad. He didn't have to leave Maddie all alone, neither wife nor widow, like Mum. Though it hurt him to take his wife away from everything and everyone she loved, at least they still had each other. He had to believe that together they could face anything. That's why he wouldn't voluntarily choose a sanitarium. He didn't want their fate to be the same as Mum and Dad's.

As they reached the branch hospital, Rob let Mum go ahead of him up the front staircase and in the main doors. The attendant at the reception desk informed them that Superintendent Hinckley was in today and could consult with them about their relative if they so wished. Apparently, Mum wished.

After a twenty-minute consultation with the superintendent where they learned Dad's condition had not changed, Rob headed out the back of the main building to the kitchen gardens where he'd been told he'd find his dad. Mum stayed behind in the kitchen, able to see her husband through the window but unable to have any contact. The sorrow of that fact stung more than usual today.

He wasn't surprised that Dad would be in the garden. Dad had always loved to garden. Though Mum was a city girl, born and raised a mere block or two from Big Ben, Dad had grown up in the country just outside London where his father worked in the garden of a rich man's estate. Rob couldn't remember a time his father hadn't had a small plot of earth to work in. Even on Mulberry Street, where their backyard plot had been tiny, he'd managed to plant a few tomatoes and beans.

As he slipped out the back door, he gulped in huge breaths of the clean spring air. The sun had burned away the earlier mist, bathing the day in bright, warm sunshine.

Several yards ahead of him, stretching hundreds of feet in all directions, lay a kitchen garden, busy today with a half dozen men hoeing along the rows of newly emerging plants.

He caught sight of Dad's distinctive shock of thick gray hair and made his way toward him, halting when he came within a few feet.

"Morning, sir," he said.

Dad looked up briefly, then turned back to his work.

After a few minutes, Rob tried again. "How've you been?"

Silence, then a few words mumbled under his breath. Rob barely caught the last phrase. "H'ain't seen ya in months."

"Yes, sir. I'm sorry. I've not been well."

Dad showed no signs of having heard him.

Rob watched the rhythmic chopping of the hoe against the weeds for a few minutes, then cleared his throat and looked around. Now what? He was used to wordless visits with his father, but they'd always been conducted in a private room indoors. He felt rather foolish standing here watching the man work.

In the shadows near the building, he could see the white coats of two attendants who must be supervising the patients while they worked. One of the men laughed, the sound ringing out over the quiet of the garden.

"These weeds won't come out by themselves."

Rob turned back. "What?"

"Don't just stand there, son. Grab a hoe."

Those words transported him to his childhood when they'd worked together in Mum's garden. His father had stopped his work and looked at him with eyes as clear and brown as his own. Then, with a gesture of his head, he pointed him toward where a pile of garden tools lay propped near the base of a tree.

Well, why not? Hoeing sure beat standing here in silence. Making his way to the pile, Rob stripped off his jacket and hat and rolled up his shirt sleeves. He grabbed a hoe from the pile and returned to his dad, setting to work on a row next to him.

They worked in silence down their rows and up two more. Muscles Rob hadn't used in months began to ache and burn. A blister formed on one finger. Stopping a minute to wipe the perspiration from his brow, he marveled at Dad's stamina. Not a wonder, really. Though fifty-seven, Dad had always had the strength of an ox, whereas Rob was only a few weeks off a major hemorrhage. That he was able to work at all was a small miracle and boded well for the future. If he were to hire out to a local farmer upon reaching Wyoming, today's work might be good practice. Maddie would have his head, though, were his fever to spike up again tonight.

At the end of the next row of potatoes, his breath caught in a coughing jag. Pulling out the new sputum flask Dr. Waite had given him, he was careful to spit into it, replacing the lid and returning it to his pocket. Glancing up, he caught Dad's eyes trained on him again.

"Best take a break," was all he said.

Rob nodded. They made their way over to the tree where he'd left his jacket and hat. Spreading his jacket on the grass, he sat on it, glad to feel a cool breeze dry the dampness around his scalp. He leaned back against the tree's trunk and closed his eyes. Maybe he wasn't as strong as he'd hoped. Three rows of potatoes had about done him in.

"Ya got the consumption?" Dad's voice cut into his thoughts.

"Yes." He didn't open his eyes. Didn't want to see Dad's reaction or lack thereof. He wasn't even sure which would be worse.

His dad's mild oath answered that question. He was almost shocked at how good it felt to know he cared. Could still care.

Glancing up, he saw the concern etched in his father's face as he leaned above him, hands resting on the handle of his hoe.

"This may be my last visit for some time. The doctor says I need to move to a better climate. I don't know when I'll be back." He didn't say *if*, wouldn't say it, but they both knew it was implied. "I'll send word through Billy. He'll let you know how I get on."

Dad nodded and looked off into the distance. "Be ye leaving soon?"

"On Monday."

Silence stretched between them.

"Are you happy here, Dad? Don't you sometimes miss your old life? Miss Mum?"

All the softness drained from Dad's face. He spat out a string of words that would have earned Rob the strap had he ever said them in front of his father back in the day.

"Miss her? Why would I miss the woman who wants me dead?" Hefting his hoe over his shoulder, Dad stomped back into the garden and began attacking the weeds again. Rob swallowed at the lump that threatened to close off his throat. Fool. He knew better than to think the glimpse he'd seen of the old Dad was anything more than that—a glimpse of what had been but was no more.

Rob pushed to his feet, pulled on his jacket, and set his hat back on his head. With one last glance at the angry man in the garden, he made his way back toward the door of the kitchen. Some things he was glad to leave behind.

Chapter Five

❦

"Do you suppose those men are real cowboys?"
Maddie had to laugh at Jenny Westraven's wide-eyed excitement. You would think the girl was viewing her first aborigine rather than a group of ordinary men in western style hats. "Judging by the size of the stockyards in Omaha, I would think the whole population of Nebraska must be cowboys," she said.

"Oh, don't remind me." Jenny wrinkled her pert little nose. "I know one thing, cow and sheep smell much better on the plate than they do in the stockyard."

Maddie had to agree. In fact, the roast beef she smelled as they wended their way down the swaying aisle of the Pullman dining car was making her stomach growl. A white-aproned waiter led them to a table, pulling out seats for her and Jenny. Rob settled into the seat across from them.

Shaking out the white linen napkin folded beautifully on her plate, she laid it in her lap and glanced around appreciatively. Mellow light from the gas lamps danced against the carved mahogany paneling of the train car and flickered across crystal and china. She was glad their days on the train were drawing to a close, but she would miss these evening meals. She'd rarely eaten in such luxury and knew the fact she did now was due solely to her pretty new friend.

When Jenny's uncle had asked them to chaperone his niece, he had insisted on paying the difference between their standard fare tickets and first-class. She knew his generosity was for Jenny's benefit alone, but she was thankful for the unexpected comfort the gesture had provided. Even with the luxury of first-class travel, the last three days had been taxing on Rob. She could tell by the drawn look around his eyes. And his quiet demeanor.

"There. What did I tell you?" Jenny, who'd been scanning the menu, turned it for her to see. "Leg of mutton, roast sirloin, and veal cutlets. After passing those stockyards, I shouldn't even want them, but I do. Very much, in fact. Am I not the most unfeeling woman you've ever met?"

"Well, if you are, I must also be. In fact, I want all three."

In addition to the first-class tickets, Miss Jenny Westraven herself had been a godsend. Within five minutes of meeting the younger girl, Maddie had felt like they'd been friends for a lifetime. She knew Rob sometimes tired of the girl's lively chatter, but for her, it provided the distraction she needed to keep her mind off that final scene at the train station when everyone had gathered to see them off. If she let them, the faces would surface again in her mind. Father's had been grim and stoic. Mother Skivington's, as always, was full of hope and love. And then there were her sisters. Edie had been teary-eyed, but Hazel . . . . Well, she could hardly stand to remember how little Hazel had stood, lower lip trembling but chin squared in an effort to be brave. No, Jenny's chatter could never be tiresome if it kept her mind off that.

"Do you mind if I join you, folks?" The words cut into her thoughts as a dapper gentleman with close-cut gray hair and a salt and pepper mustache stopped beside their table.

"No. By all means. Have a seat." Rob waved to the empty chair next to him.

In the three days they'd been on the train, they'd rarely had a meal where some unaccompanied gentleman did not join them. Maddie suspected Rob enjoyed these moments of male companionship more than he would admit.

The man reached out to shake Rob's hand and nodded to both her and Jenny. "I'm R. J. Taylor." The way he burred the r's in his name reminded her of Father's Scottish friend, Mr. McKinzie.

Rob introduced them all around, then asked where the man was heading.

"I'm heading home. I have a ranch not far from Grand Island. Should be able to rest in my own bed tonight," the man said with a quiet smile.

"You have a cattle ranch?" Jenny leaned forward, face aglow.

"Some cattle, yes, but mostly sheep."

"Oh."

Mr. Taylor seemed unfazed that Mr. Taylor, shepherd, had far less appeal in Jenny's eyes than Mr. Taylor, cowboy. "And you folks? Heading home or away from it?"

"Heading to a new home," Rob said. "We're on our way to Lander, Wyoming. Miss Westraven will be visiting her brother there, but my wife and I hope to make it our permanent home."

"Wyoming? Ah. Ye can't go wrong with Wyoming. Greatest place in the nation to raise sheep. I got my start there back in the '80's," Mr. Taylor said, picking up the menu and looking it over. "Still own a bit o' land out in Natrona County. Are ye aiming to start a business there?" He glanced over at Rob.

"Not really. My doctor recommended a change of climate for my health. I'm hoping to hire out for work, maybe on a ranch or a farm. Something outdoors, if possible."

Maddie waited for the inevitable response that always followed Rob's declaration that he had come West for his health. Was he consumptive? Or, more often as of late, was he a lunger? As if Rob was little more than a symptom of his disease.

But Mr. Taylor didn't even look up from the menu. "You should get into sheep ranching."

Well, she'd give the man one thing. He certainly loved his sheep.

Rob gave a short laugh. "I don't think I'm ready to buy into any ranches."

"Aye, but ye don't need a ranch. That's the beauty o' Wyoming. All ye need is a wagon and a band o' sheep. The land's perfect. Plenty o' open range with sage as far as the eye can see. Anyone can use it."

"But if you don't need a ranch, where do you live?" Maddie asked.

"Some live in tents, but most sheepherders live in their sheep wagons. A blacksmith in Rawlins came up with the idea a few years back. It's a small covered wagon with a bunk and a cookstove that's much better at keeping ye warm and tidy during the cold Wyoming winters than a tent." His eyes twinkled at them across the table. "No, sir. Ye can't beat sheepherding for getting ye out in the open. And it's a great way to make your fortune. I started out with a wee band of six hundred sheep and now have close to a hundred thousand."

A hundred thousand sheep! Surely, she hadn't heard him correctly. Even his "wee" band of six hundred seemed an enormous amount. How could anyone possibly keep track of a hundred thousand sheep?

The waiter returned to take their orders, and the conversation flowed to other topics.

Soon she was digging into a plate piled high with roast, mashed potatoes, and cauliflower. The roasted sirloin turned out to be an excellent choice. So tender she could cut it with a fork, the meat fairly melted in her mouth.

Across from her, Rob picked listlessly at his veal cutlet.

"You should try a bite of this roast, Rob. The flavor is excellent."

He nodded absently, then turned to Mr. Taylor. "How much capital would a man need to get started in sheepherding?"

Sheep again? Surely Rob wasn't giving the man's suggestion any credence.

"No' that much, really. Three hundred dollars should buy ye a good wagon and all your gear. Fifteen hundred head o' sheep will run ye aboot three thousand dollars. But if ye don't have that, ye can always borrow. I took a loan for my first band and had it paid back within three years."

"And the rangelands? How far are they from Lander?"

"Depends on the time of year. You could be as close as fifteen miles or as far as thirty. Winter grazing is on the plains closer to the towns and ranches, but summer grazing is in the mountains."

Thirty miles from town? Any town? "I can't see how that would ever work for us, Mr. Taylor. Rob needs to be near a doctor, and we need easy access to good, fresh food . . . eggs . . . milk . . . plenty of fresh vegetables. Our doctor told us that diet would be a major component to Rob regaining his health."

She caught Mr. Taylor glancing at Rob's plate, still almost full compared to the rapidly depleting plates in front of the rest of them. Rob flushed and sent her an exasperated look before stabbing at another forkful of meat. She knew she deserved it for sounding like his nursemaid, but even he must admit this sheepherding idea was preposterous.

Mr. Taylor laid his fork across his own empty plate and took a sip of water. His eyes met hers over the rim of his glass. "I beg your pardon, ma'am. I dinna mean to press my opinion on ye and your husband. But I hope ye won't dismiss the idea completely. My foreman came to this country a verra sick mon, but after just one year o' sheepherding, he completely regained his health. That was twenty years ago."

It was Maddie's turn to flush. She shouldn't have been so vocal in her dismissal of the man's proposal. He couldn't help but champion the profession that had brought him so much success. "I do appreciate your desire to help us, sir. And Rob and I will certainly keep your suggestion in mind." There. She'd been very diplomatic.

"In fact, if you don't mind, I'd like to learn a bit more from you before you leave the train tonight." Rob's words cut into her complacency. "Would you mind if I picked your brain a bit after supper?"

"Not at all. In fact, if ye're finished, ye can follow me back to my car now. I'll be glad to answer any questions ye have."

As the men took their leave, Maddie did her best to keep the dismay from showing on her face. Surely Rob wasn't serious about pursuing sheep ranching. Helping out on a ranch or farm was one thing, but tackling it on their own? They'd be foolish to even try.

"So, Maddie. Do you fancy yourself as a shepherdess out here in this wild west?" Jenny said as they settled into their seats back in the sleeping car.

"To be honest, no. I didn't even know they herded sheep out here. Cows, of course, but not sheep. Rob and I wouldn't know where to begin."

"That Mr. Taylor made it all sound so exciting, though. Following sheep on the open range . . . living in a sheep wagon." A misty look came into Jenny's eyes. "Now that I think on it, I wish Ted had taken up ranching when he came out here instead of going back into banking. Why, just imagine. I'd be on my way to a real live ranch instead of a house in town. Soon, I'd be hobnobbing with cowboys, roping calves, riding horses. Why, I bet if I practiced, I could ride as well as one of those trick riders you see in the Wild West Show."

Maddie laughed. Had she ever been that young? So many times on this trip, she'd had to remind herself that Jenny was actually a year older than Edie. But Jenny was nothing like Maddie's soft-natured, soft-spoken sister. No, her new friend jumped into life with both feet, and, as had happened often on this trip, she felt drawn into the younger girl's enthusiasm.

"You could always find yourself a handsome rancher who'll

set you up on his ranch as his wife," she said, going along with Jenny's daydream.

The girl pulled a face. "I'm not looking for love. I'm looking for adventure. Don't get me wrong. I wouldn't mind flirting with a handsome cowboy or two or three, but I'm not out to marry anyone."

Maddie looked out the window to where a three-quarter moon was lighting the gentle hills of the rolling prairie. Adventure? Had she ever sought adventure? If Rob hadn't become ill, she'd have been quite content to live her whole life in her pretty cottage in New Jersey, raising their children and spending her Sunday afternoons and holidays with her family in Newark.

"It's not that I don't want what you and Rob have. Love. Marriage," Jenny said. "It's just I haven't found anyone I'd want to spend the rest of my life with yet. At least, I don't think I have. How did you know it was Rob for you? Was it love at first sight?"

"Not at first sight, no. But it did happen fairly quickly. Rob and I met at a dark time in my life. My mother had been an invalid for many years, especially after my youngest sister was born. I was used to being a caregiver for my younger siblings. But when Rob and I met, she was dying. We'd just come off a very long, cold winter. I was spending all of my time nursing Mother plus taking care of the house and Hazel and Les. I'd hardly been out of the house for months.

"My friend Betsy finally convinced me to join her one evening for choir practice at her church. They were planning a special number for their Easter service and wanted extra voices. She knew I loved to sing, so between her and Father, they convinced me to go."

"And Rob was there?"

"Yes. Actually, he was the choir director."

"Really? I would never have guessed. I didn't even know he sang. So what happened? Did he ask to see you home?"

"No. Not that night, but he kept looking at me. I know I was new to the choir and all, but it was rather disconcerting. I've told him since then how rude it was to stare at a person like that. I didn't know if I had a stain on my shirtwaist or something caught in my teeth to keep him looking back at me so often."

Jenny laughed. "So it was love at first sight for Rob."

Maddie chuckled. "Maybe." She could pretend she'd found his attention irritating, but really she hadn't. He'd made her feel seen after months, maybe even years, of being next to invisible. "I might have minded more if he hadn't been so handsome. Those soulful brown eyes of his are hard to resist. But what I fell in love with first was his voice, his singing voice especially. It's such a rich baritone, and with that British accent of his. . . . Well, like I said, it didn't take long for either of us.

"He brought music back to our household. We'd always loved music as a family, but with Mother so ill, a lot of that had slipped to the wayside. Then Rob started coming around. Because of Mother's illness, much of our courtship took place at my parent's home. We had an upright piano. Rob would sit down at it and start playing and singing, and before we knew it, we would all be gathered around joining in. I can remember Mother lying on the chaise lounge in the parlor and smiling to hear us all sing."

"Do you sing together now? I'd love to hear you."

"No. Rob's tuberculosis has affected his larynx. The doctor says he probably won't sing much ever again." She swallowed against the tightening of her throat. She didn't think she'd ever be able to say those words aloud and not want to bawl.

Jenny reached over and squeezed her hand. "I'm sorry."

Maddie fought the gathering tears and dredged up a smile. "Rob and I were married two months before Mother died. God gave him to me just when I needed him most. Like I said, he was my light in a very dark time."

And now she needed to be there for him. She couldn't allow her fears about the unknown to hold him back. He was her rock. Now she'd be his. If that meant taking on something as unfamiliar as herding sheep, so be it.

Chapter Six

Maddie couldn't remember the last time she'd seen a tree. Had there been any trees since Omaha? Maybe in Laramie. She couldn't say. They'd passed through in the dark. Certainly not in that dusty, rain-deprived city of Rawlins. At least not the trees she was used to—large, leafy oaks and maples like the ones that shadowed their little cottage in Newark.

She'd never imagined a landscape could be so bleak or that she could see so far and still see . . . nothing. No farms. No towns. No trees. Nothing but miles and miles of sand and sage brush.

She was five when her family moved from Canada to New Jersey. She could remember very little about the sea voyage that took them to Newark except for a few vague sensations: excitement tempered by fear and an overwhelming sense of insignificance. Today's stage ride brought those emotions back in buckets. The rocking of the stagecoach was not unlike the rocking of that ship, the vast stretches of rolling plains differing from the sea waves only in color.

Would this new home bring sorrow and death like the one in Newark?

The sigh escaped before she could catch it, but she managed a bright smile at Rob's questioning glance. A lift of his eyebrows told her he wasn't fooled, but he said nothing.

Buck up, girl. So what if Wyoming was nothing like what she'd dreamed her life would be with Rob? This was their reality now. For Rob's sake, she needed to be content with it. She was here to help him, not make his life more difficult with the burden of an unhappy wife. If living in the middle of nowhere is what it would take to make him well, she'd pay the price and gladly.

It wasn't as if she needed trees. The little ranch house they'd seen at their last stage stop sat in the most desolate spot she'd ever seen. Yet, the tea roses and ivy the rancher's wife had planted around the door and windows gave it a homey appeal. And that's what she'd do. If their new home had no trees, she'd plant roses and ivy.

The stage splashed across a creek and rattled to a stop. Maddie's eyes traced the words on the sign above this next stage station as the horses pulled in. Lost Soldier Station. Wyoming sure seemed to have an abundance of place names with the word "lost" in them. Lost Soldier. . . Lost Cabin . . . Lost Creek. Not an especially comforting thought.

The stage stop itself looked none too comforting either, consisting of only two small wooden buildings and a corral. Maddie scrambled out of the door after Jenny, anxious for the chance to stretch her legs and find an outhouse. They would have just the time it took to change the four horses before the stage set out again. The vast empty stretches of land were almost threatening outside the safe confines of the stagecoach. The sky, a bowl of blue above her, felt limitless. Wrapping her arms across her chest, she hugged herself close, wishing for the comforting embrace of trees, buildings, *anything* to block out the enormity of it all.

She and Jenny made use of the crude facilities and hurried back toward the stagecoach. Looking down the road to the west, she could see a rim of rocky cliffs and, off in the distance, a hazy blue ridge promised that the Wind River Mountains near Lander were at least within sight now. By her estimation, they were only halfway through their stage ride. She hated the thought of eighteen more bone-jarring hours on the road, but she hated this feeling of vulnerability this wide, empty land engendered even more.

Soon the driver signaled he was ready to depart, and they all clambered back into the coach.

"Was there really a lost soldier, or is it just a name?" Rob asked Mr. Willoughby as the horses picked up speed. The rancher had been the only other passenger to board the stage in the early morning hours when they left Rawlins. After snoring in his seat for about an hour, he'd awakened and proved to be a veritable font of information about the area. Rob and Jenny had peppered him with questions. His garrulous friendliness made him a welcome addition to their group.

The older man had settled once again on the bench across from them, stubby legs outstretched, arms folded over his plump belly. Though her own legs were pulled as close to her seat as possible, the edge of his boots still rested against her ankles.

"Well, now. Funny you should ask that question." Mr. Willoughby pursed his lips and looked at them from beneath the brim of his wide Western hat. "Folks'll tell you different stories, but best as I can tell, there really was a lost soldier. They say, back in the Indian times, a group of travelers was on their way to Lander and hired a couple of soldiers to guard them on their journey. They'd made camp by that crick back there, and one of the soldiers went and wandered off and got hisself lost."

Maddie shuddered at the thought of anyone lost in that vast emptiness.

"What happened to him?" Jenny asked.

"Well, the story goes, he wandered around in circles for a while, then ended up just east'a here at Tom Sun's ranch.

Nobody was home, but Tom had left the latch string out on his door. Instead of using it, though, what'd that soldier do but take apart the window and climb through. Then he fixed hisself some supper and went to bed. Tom come home the next morning to find his window panes leaning up against his cabin and the soldier asleep in his bed. Says a feller who don't have enough sense to use a door what's left open deserves to get lost."

Maddie chuckled along with the others.

Rob leaned forward, elbows on knees. "That reminds me of a story we tell back in Newark. Seems there was a country gentleman who came to the city wanting to see the sights. He gets off the train and sets out to see the city, but after turning a few corners and walking several blocks, he realizes he's hopelessly lost. Pretty soon he comes upon a young newsboy lounging on a corner and asks him, 'Do you know the way to Washington Park?' The boy replies, 'No sir, I don't.' 'Well,' the man continues, 'do you know where I can go to get a good, cheap meal?' 'No sir, I don't,' the boy says. 'Well,' the man tries again. 'Do you know how I can get back to the train station?' 'No sir, I don't.' Frustrated, the man yells. 'You don't know much of anything do you?' 'Mebbe not,' the boy answers," Rob paused a moment, then delivered the punch line. "'But I ain't lost.'"

Mr. Willoughby threw back his head in delight and slapped his knee. "That's a good one, that is. I'll have to remember that one to tell the wife."

Soon he and Rob were trading jokes like lifelong cronies. Watching Rob, hands gesturing, dark eyes flashing, exchanging story for story, laugh for laugh, she would never have suspected that a month ago he'd had that awful hemorrhage.

She knew the signs now, though. Eyes a little too bright, cheeks a little too flushed. What most people would take to be high spirits and health, she'd learned to interpret as signs the fever had returned and a relapse might be imminent. If they'd been alone, she'd have felt his forehead and cheeks for fever.

Maddie shook herself from her worried thoughts, willing

herself to concentrate instead on the men's jolly banter. Mr. Willoughby seemed to have an endless supply of tall tales and anecdotes that soon had them holding their sides and wiping their eyes. When the stage again slowed and turned, Maddie looked out the window in surprise to see a low, wooden fence and a one-story ranch house. They'd reached their supper stop already? Surely the last three hours could not have passed that quickly.

Grasping Rob's outstretched hand, she stepped out of the stage and looked around. This stop was by far the most prosperous of any of their previous ones. The long, rambling log house featured a porch that ran the house's length, sheltered by the building's lean-to roof. Beyond the house, Maddie could see several more log buildings, including a large barn.

"Harris' Road Ranch," Mr. Willoughby said as he hobbled down the steps behind her. "I recommend you part with the fifty cents it'll take to get a meal here. It'll be well worth your money."

Maddie didn't see they would have much choice. They'd long ago used up the hamper of food she'd packed at their journey's outset, and they'd not stopped long enough in Rawlins to replenish their supplies. Still, it had been hard to part with thirty-five cents apiece for a bit of cheese, a hard roll, and some stewed apples at their lunch stop earlier that day. Thank goodness their journey was nearing its end.

Ducking into the ranch house's dim interior, she saw a tall man step from an adjoining room to greet them. Jenny stopped short in front of her, gazing in fascination. Not surprising. He looked like someone off the cover of one of Les's dime novels with his high-topped riding boots and flowing hair.

"Welcome, folks," he said. "Grab yourselves a seat. Supper will be out in just a minute."

Mr. Willoughby introduced them all around, then led the way to a long, gingham-topped table that ran the length of the room. "I'm telling you, folks, you're in for a treat tonight. Sadie's one of the best cooks in the county."

The meal did indeed live up to his praise. Savory beef stew and flaky, sourdough biscuits were washed down by large glasses of ice-cold milk. She smiled to see her husband dig into a second helping with as much enthusiasm as Mr. Willoughby. Maybe the change of climate was already working its magic.

She'd just dipped her fork into a sweet slice of apple pie when a trio of grimy young cowboys burst through the doorway and made their way to the bar along the far wall.

"Sparrowhawk," one of them yelled at the man who had come out of the kitchen carrying a coffee pot. "Ya got any whiskey?"

"This isn't a saloon, Jake. You know we don't serve liquor here."

"Give me some coffee then, but I want it black as sin, hot as heck, and stirred with a pistol."

Never blinking an eye, Sparrowhawk poured coffee into one of the tin cups sitting on the bar, then pulled out his pistol and let it hover over the cup.

"You want some smoke in it?"

The young man laughed and picked up the cup. "Naw, just wanted to see if you were still packing that thing."

"Oh, I'll be packing it as long as the likes of you keep coming around."

"Hear that, boys?" The man looked back at his companions. "If I didn't know better, I'd say we wasn't exactly welcome at this here eating establishment."

"If you're here to eat, Jake, then you know the procedure. Show me your money, and I'll see that you get your plate. In the meantime, I need to get back to our other customers."

For the first time, the young men seemed to notice them.

"Well, well, what have we here?" The one called Jake sauntered over to them, subjecting her and Jenny to a leer that studied them from head to toe. She saw Jenny blush under his gaze and felt her own cheeks grow hot. The young man stood so close behind their chairs, he blocked any hope of escape. So close, in fact, she could tell it'd been several days, maybe weeks, since he'd spent any time with a bar of soap. She discreetly raised her napkin to her nose and did her best to ignore his presence.

"Cy, aren't ya going to introduce us to your friends here?"

Mr. Willoughby gave the young man a measured stare before answering quietly, "If you'll mind your manners. Jake McCreedy, this here's Mr. Rob Skivington, a jeweler from New Jer—."

"Jeweler, huh? Well, I don't know much about jewelry, but I sure do like the looks of his two jewels." He placed a hand on Maddie's shoulder and leaned forward between her and Jenny until she could feel his breath on her cheek. "Get yourself a ruby-haired one, Jeweler, and you'll have quite a collection."

She pulled to one side, withering the young man with what Percy always called her Queen of England glare. Before she could react further, Sparrowhawk stepped up and yanked the young man back by his collar.

"Son, I'm afraid you've made the mistake of many young men who don't know their heads from a hole in the ground. You've treated two respectable ladies like a couple of dance hall girls. Mistakes like that could hurt you." Maddie glanced over at Rob who had pushed to his feet and now stood on the other side of the table, face dark with anger, hands balled into fists. As Jake backed away, swaggering over to the bar where one of his friends chortled and slapped him on the shoulder, Maddie jumped to her feet and intercepted Rob before he could follow the young man.

"Let it go," she murmured, grasping tightly to his arm as he tried to push past her. "They're just boys. Not much older than George or Fred."

"You're comparing my brothers to these hoodlums?" Rob's eyes sparked. "They knew better than to treat a woman with such rudeness long before they were half that age."

"Of course, they did. Because they were blessed with a very

wise mother, who, if she were here now, would be the first to say, 'Let. It. Be.'"

A whistle from the driver confirmed that the stage was indeed ready to leave. Maddie breathed a sigh of relief when Rob, with one last glare at the men at the bar, turned and followed Mr. Willoughby out the door.

Back on the stage, Jenny was bubbling with excitement. "Wasn't he magnificent?" Adoration glowed from her eyes.

Maddie had to admit Sparrowhawk definitely lived up to the image he was trying to portray. Or were all men in the west truly like the heroes of dime novel fame?

"Well, now, I dunno as I'd call him magnificent, but Sparrowhawk's a smooth one, I'll give him that."

"That's certainly the last time I'll let anyone introduce me as a jeweler, at least here in the West." Rob's anger had abated some, but his color was still high. "From here on out, I'll tell folks I'm a sheep man and let it go at that."

Mr. Willoughby shook his head. "Now, don't think I didn't think of that, cuz I did, but in this case, I figured it was the lesser of two evils. Those McCreedys are a bad lot. Jake's father owns a cattle ranch up on the Sweetwater. Been ranching in these parts twenty years or more. Though he uses the free-range just like everyone else, he seems to forget that free-range means it's free to everyone, not just him.

"He hates sheepherders, and he don't mind telling you. Been a lot of bad blood between him and the sheep ranchers in this area. Not as bad as the trouble out in Johnson County, but close. And his men ain't just mean. They're dangerous. Rumor has it a couple of 'em are members of the Wild Bunch Gang hiding out after that train robbery last spring." He shook his head again. "Nope, I know it don't seem that way, but that deal back there could'a been a whole lot worse."

He glanced over at Maddie. "But don't worry none. If you stick to ranching around the Lander area, you should do just fine. McCreedy's got no need of range land that far north."

Maddie tried to muster a smile to assure him she wasn't worried, but she couldn't even convince herself. What were they doing here? How could they fool themselves into thinking they could handle an environment where men wore guns to supper, outlaws were your neighbors, and the nearest railroad was one hundred and thirty-five dusty, body-numbing stagecoach miles away?

Chapter Seven

❧

His cough woke him. Always the cough. For the past eighteen months, as reliable as the sunrise, his cough had been his morning alarm, signaling a new day, a new round in his fight with this dratted disease. Rob sat up and reached for the sputum flask he'd placed on the bedstand the night before, spat and examined the specimen with the objective eye of a doctor. Not a great amount, green but no streaks of brown, no tinge of pink, and best of all, none of the bright red that signaled the hemorrhage—the one that had sent them on this desperate two-thousand-mile chase for a cure.

As quietly as possible, he eased himself from the bed before another round of coughing spasmed through his body. No need to wake Maddie. He made his way to the dresser, dug into the small traveling bag they'd set there last night, and pulled out the tonic Dr. Waite had prescribed. Nothing would stop the cough completely, but a spoonful of the tonic each morning at least helped quiet the cough for a time. He checked his pocket watch that lay beside the bag on the dresser. Six a.m. He'd slept a full fourteen hours, no night sweats, no coughing jags. A good sign.

He continued his morning inventory. Appetite? None. Not

unusual, but still a bit troubling given their last meal had been at noon on the previous day.

Tired? Yes. Even after fourteen straight hours of sleep, but nothing like last month after his hemorrhage when he couldn't even muster the strength to tie his own shoes. He glanced over at Maddie, who lay curled into the feather mattress, her long brown braid spread across the pillow behind her. She hadn't even stirred at his coughing, which told him his own fatigue could be as much a result of the journey as it was the disease.

That last leg—the thirty-six hours on the stage—had been brutal. He'd barely had the strength to check into the Lander Hotel yesterday and carry their bags to the room before collapsing on the bed.

No. The fact he was up at all this morning was promising. Very promising.

He walked to the window. Pulling back the heavy curtain, he gazed out over the wide, main street of the town and off to the west where the Wind River Mountains rose purplish-blue against the lighter blue of the morning sky.

I will lift up mine eyes to the hills, from whence does my help come? Familiar words from a favorite psalm. His help came from the Lord, but would those mountains be the vehicle God used? He prayed so. The exhilaration that had been building since they had first stepped off the train in this wild country of vast open spaces threatened to bubble over and spill out. This place would be his salvation. He knew it. He felt it.

Maddie stirred in the bed behind him.

"What time is it?"

"A little after six." Letting the curtain drop back into place, he turned toward her as she sat up and stretched, smiling at the picture she made with her sleep-tousled hair. His Maddie would never be caught in public with a single hair out of place, which made these casual moments for his eyes only all the more intimate.

"Hungry?" He sat down on the bed beside her and pulled her close until her head nestled just under his chin.

"Famished. Did you say it was after six? In the morning? Have we truly slept through dinner and all through the night?"

He laughed at her astonishment. "We have. A pity, too, since Cy said the hotel's restaurant is one of the best around. We won't miss breakfast, though. I can guarantee that."

She reached up to brush a lock of hair from his eyes, her hand lingering against his cheek in a gesture that was both a caress and her subtle way of checking his temperature. He covered her hand with his.

"Cool as a cucumber," he said, letting her know her ploy had not fooled him.

Her eyes searched his. "And you slept well? You're hungry?"

He dropped a kiss on her nose, not wanting to quench the hope he saw in her eyes. "I'll race you to the breakfast table."

An hour later, he pushed away his breakfast plate, hoping he'd downed enough scrambled eggs and potatoes to satisfy his wife. Two years ago, if anyone had told him he would someday struggle to find pleasure in food, he would have called them a fool. Today, his appetite was just one item in a long list of things this dratted disease had robbed from him.

Across from him, Maddie set aside her own completely empty plate, then broke open and buttered another biscuit.

"So, what are your plans for today?"

"I thought I'd head over to the bank to talk with Ted Westraven, make sure he received the money I wired him. If we were to buy into a sheep ranching outfit, we'd need a pretty big outlay of money to get started."

"You truly plan to follow through on the sheep ranching idea? What about the other options we discussed?"

Ever since his talk with Mr. Taylor from the train, he'd been drawn to the idea of sheep ranching. It was the only option he'd heard so far that would allow him to own his own business, be his own boss, and still spend the time outdoors that Dr. Waite had recommended. Maddie obviously wasn't on board yet. He noted the spark of panic in her eyes and tempered his answer. "I don't know for sure. Thought I'd run the idea by Mr. Westraven while I'm over there. I'd like to know more about how he went about finding the cure. He may have an opinion on what would be the best way to go. Also wouldn't hurt to find out who he uses as a doctor. Whatever he's done, it sure seems to have worked."

Maddie nodded. "I'd never have suspected him for a consumptive if Jenny and Dr. Waite hadn't confirmed it."

They'd met the man briefly the day before when he came to meet Jenny at the stage office. He certainly hadn't looked like an invalid to Rob either.

"It sure gives me hope. You can hear a hundred stories about people who've found the cure, but to actually meet one . . ." His throat tightened. "Well, it means a lot."

Blinking rapidly, Maddie reached across and squeezed his hand.

He cleared his throat. "Anyway, Cy wanted me to meet him down at the livestock barn today also. Sounds like a couple of men brought in a string of wild horses, and they're having an auction. He said it'd be a good place to meet some of the ranchers, get a better idea of the types of jobs that might be available. I'd have you come along, but I'm not sure how many women will be there. Will you be all right on your own?"

"Oh, I'll be fine. I have letters to write, and Jenny said she'd try to stop by. You go on. Get your errands run. You can tell me all about it tonight."

He reached over and clasped her hand, gently stroking her soft skin with his thumb. "I promise I won't make any final decisions without discussing them with you first."

∼

LATER THAT MORNING, ROB STRODE DOWN MAIN STREET, heading to the southwest edge of town where Ted Westraven had told him he'd find the horse auction. He'd enjoyed the hour he'd spent with Ted. The man was as likable as his sister with an easy-going charm and an eagerness to help. He'd had much to say about his own quest for the cure, but as Rob mulled it over, he wasn't sure how much would apply to his own situation.

For starters, Ted had been alone. Rob had Maddie to consider. Also, as an heir to a banking fortune, Ted hadn't had to worry about how to support himself in his search for the cure. Rob did not have that luxury. Though the sale of his business had given them the funds to get out here and get established, he could not afford to wait a year or even six months without some sort of income.

From what he'd gathered from their conversation, Ted's cure had started with a lot of bed rest followed by occasional camping trips of two-to-three-day duration into the mountains when the weather was fine. Ted also recommended sleeping in the open air but had seemed skeptical about Dr. Waite's maxim that heavy exercise would not hurt him. Apparently, that young man's most common outdoor exercise consisted of his wielding either a fishing rod or a hunting rifle with plenty of rest in between.

Rob reached the end of Main Street, where a few small cottages scattered along the town's edge. Maybe he and Maddie should look into buying or building a small cottage like these. They'd be close to town and a doctor. He could hire out to one of the nearby ranchers. Didn't seem fair to drag Maddie away from all civilization on account of his own needs. And yet . . . he turned his gaze once again to the mountains on the horizon. He couldn't deny their pull.

He struck out across an open field toward a pole barn where a crowd of men had gathered. Most of the men were clothed in what he'd come to recognize as typical western gear. Large hats, boots, and canvas pants. Only a few, like himself, had on the more formal suits and derbies.

Several men leaned against the log fence of a wooden corral, looking over the string of horses. Others stood talking in small groups. Rob spied Cy up against the fence, talking to a thin man with a long gray beard. He headed their direction winding his way through the crowd.

Neither man seemed to notice as he drew near. Cy had his back to him, and his companion looked none too pleased. He caught the words " . . . nursemaid to some ailing tenderfoot" before the dust from the arena made him cough, drawing both men's attention. The chagrined look on Cy's face was all he needed to confirm he was indeed the "ailing tenderfoot" in question.

"Rob!" Cy hurried forward to grab his hand and slap him on the back. "You made it. I was afraid that stagecoach ride would keep you in hiding for a few days."

Did he really appear so frail?

Cy gestured toward his companion. "This here's T.J. McCallister. He's been in ranching since they first opened these lands to the whites and has one of the biggest spreads around. I've been telling him about your situation."

With rave reviews, apparently.

Rob sketched a polite bow and forced the words "Pleased to meet you" while the man eyed him skeptically from head to toe.

"Ever worked cattle before, Mr. Skivington?"

Rob clinched his jaw. He hadn't felt so lacking since he was a schoolboy with a missing assignment. "No, sir, I've lived in the city all my life. London first, then Newark. We don't see many cows in the city—live ones anyway." The man didn't even crack a smile.

"So, what is it you think you could do for me?" The question was a direct attack.

"Well, sir, I don't know if I'll be able to do anything." Rob tried to keep his tone neutral. "I told Cy I might be interested in hiring myself out to do odd jobs—chopping wood, hauling water, driving a team—anything that was needed. You may have nothing for me, and that's fine. I can look elsewhere."

"You're wanting chore work? You'll have to talk to the

Missus. She's the one in charge of seeing that stuff gets done." The man's tone was condescending at best.

Heat rose in Rob's chest. Between this man and those rude bozos at the stage stop, he was getting pretty fed up with Westerners. He got his first paying job at fourteen, was the sole support of his mom and brothers by age eighteen, and owned his own business at twenty. He knew how to make quality merchandise, balance his own books, and haggle with the best merchants on Maiden Lane. In the last ten years, he'd built a successful business which he recently sold for a tidy profit. Just because he couldn't wrangle a steer or drive a cow, didn't mean he wasn't as much a man as they were.

A squeal in the arena behind them drew everyone's attention to the ring. Rearing up, a giant black stallion broke loose from the men who were holding him and galloped wildly to the far end of the corral. Something in the wild horse's attitude resonated deep within Rob. His illness may have taken a lot from him, but it wasn't going to steal his independence. If he'd wanted someone telling him how to run his life, he'd have stayed home and gone to the sanitarium.

He turned back to Mr. McCallister. "Thank you for your time, sir, but I don't think I'll be needing any odd jobs after all. I've been considering buying into an outfit of my own, trying my hand at sheep ranching. I'm beginning to think that may be my better option."

McCallister spat at the ground near Rob's feet. "If it's sheep you're wanting, no use talking to me. I'm a cattle man and always will be. You should talk to Bunce or"—he jerked his head in the direction of the canvas pole barn—"talk to Baldwin over there. He's into sheep now."

Cy pounced on his suggestion. "Baldwin's the one I told ya about in the coach. I didn't see him come in earlier, but he's the one to talk to, all right. Come on, I'll introduce ya." Cy practically dragged Rob away from Johnson.

"Sorry about that," Cy said once they were out of earshot. "I forgot how ornery T. J. can be. He's a great rancher, but as people around here say, he gets along better with his cows than he does people."

So it was the man and not Westerners in general. Must have been a string of bad luck on his part to run into so many "ornery" ones in such a short amount of time.

They found Mr. Baldwin with a group of ranchers inside the pole barn. A stocky man with sandy brown hair, intelligent blue eyes, and a close-cropped goatee, Baldwin looked to be in his mid-forties. Cy wasted little time with the introductions and quickly went on to explain Rob's situation.

"Ever been around sheep before?" Baldwin asked.

Great. Another cross-examination. "No, sir. I'm afraid I'm just a city boy, born and bred."

Baldwin nodded. "Well, sheep aren't too tough. All you need is patience, a lead sheep or two, and a couple of dogs. Tell you what. My camp tender, Jackson Garrity, will be heading out to one of my camps tomorrow. Why don't you ride along and see what you think? He can show you how a camp is run. Fill you in on the business. If you still think it's what you'd like to do, come see me. I'm short a herder this spring and have about two thousand head I need to either sell or divvy up among my other herders. We might be able to work out a deal."

Finally, someone was willing to give him a chance. He reached out to shake Baldwin's hand. "I appreciate that, sir."

"Shall I tell Jackson to meet you at the livery tomorrow morning?"

"I'll be there."

Chapter Eight

"I'm so glad you agreed to come with me today, Maddie. I would have died if I had to be the new girl all by myself." Jenny squeezed Maddie's arm as they walked along one of Lander's narrow side roads.

Maddie smiled back at her friend, so pretty in her straw boater and raspberry red dress. "Don't be silly. You'd have a new best friend ten minutes after walking through the door."

Jenny laughed. "Maybe, but I'd still much rather be going in with you."

They were headed for the weekly meeting of the Lander Ladies' Aid Society. Jenny's sister-in-law, Grace, and her mother, Clarice Parkhurst, walked a few paces ahead of them. Maddie surmised from her conversation with Jenny the day before that where Grace's mother went, Grace and, by default, Jenny was expected to follow.

Maddie also got the impression Jenny's relationship with her new sister-in-law was not progressing as Jenny had hoped. The fact that Grace and her mother had said very little to either one of them and that they were walking ahead rather than beside them seemed to lend credence to that possibility. Still, Jenny had said nothing, so Maddie didn't bring it up. It was early days yet. Maybe Grace didn't make friends as easily as Jenny. Oh, who was she kidding? *No one* made friends as easily as Jenny.

Though she initially hadn't wanted to join Jenny today, Maddie was glad now she'd agreed to her friend's pleas that she come. She'd been missing home all morning. Hopefully, meeting some of the town's women and forming new friendships would help keep her mind off Edie and Hazel and life back in Newark.

They caught up with Grace and her mother at the gate of a small clapboard house painted white with black trim. Young ivy vines grew along the front windows, seemingly the decoration of choice for housewives in this arid environment. Two tiny trees planted in the front and side yard told Maddie the home was newly built. It would be years before the young trees offered much shade. Still, it reminded Maddie of the little cottage she had left behind in New Jersey. She blinked against the tears that pricked at her eyelids.

No. She wouldn't let herself dwell on what had been. Now was the time to look to the future. Maybe she and Rob would have a home like this one soon, here in Lander. Maybe some of the women here would be her new neighbors. Today was a day for making new friends.

"Mrs. Drew Johnson is hosting our Ladies Aid meeting today," Mrs. Parkhurst turned to inform them as they walked up the path toward the front door. "Her husband is the proprietor of the Lander Meat Market."

Mrs. Johnson, or Emma, as she called herself when she greeted them at the door, was a pretty young woman around Maddie's age. She took their hats and gloves, then led them into a small parlor where several women were stretching a brightly colored quilt on a frame balanced between two ladder-back chairs.

"We're quilting our signature quilt today," Mrs. Parkhurst said as they entered the room. "The signatures alone have already brought in twelve dollars, and we hope to raise even more money when we auction it off at our ice cream social next month."

"Ladies." She called the attention of the six other women who were milling about the room. "We have visitors today. Grace's sister-in-law, Jenny Westraven, and her traveling companion, Mrs. Skivington, have graciously agreed to help us. I think with the turnout we have today, we can safely say we'll have this quilt completed by the time we leave."

Several of the ladies clapped, and a cheery, robin of a lady came over to greet them, arms outstretched. "Jenny and Maddie, am I right? I'm Eliza Willoughby. Cy has already told me all about you." She tipped her head to one side as she looked them over. "Yes, as pretty and sweet as Cy said you would be. I'm so glad to meet both of you."

Jenny dimpled and gave the woman a hug. "Oh, and we're so glad to meet you. You're exactly what I pictured when Cy talked about his wife."

Maddie had to agree. This bright, friendly woman seemed the perfect complement to the garrulous and kindly Mr. Willoughby.

"Your husband has been so good to us." Maddie shook the woman's hand. "We're so glad to have met him on the stage into town."

"Bless you, child. He's the one who benefited from your company. Cy never does like to do things alone. Usually, I go with him on his trips to Rawlins, but I couldn't get away this time. Our cook up and quit without a minute's notice last week, and somebody had to stay and see that the hired men were fed."

Mrs. Parkhurst bustled up to their group, cutting into their conversation. "Since we have so many ladies present today, we'll take turns on the quilt," she said. "Eliza, I'm putting you on the first shift. Jenny, why don't you and Mrs. Skivington help the ladies in the kitchen for a while? Grace can show you the way."

They entered the cozy kitchen to find Emma, their hostess, busy stirring something on a shiny, new cooking stove. The toddler, who had been balanced on her hip earlier, was now attached to her leg, sucking on his thumb. Maddie smiled at him, and he quickly ducked his head into his mother's skirts.

Another young mother sat in a rocker in the corner, nursing an infant. Grace dropped to a seat next to a dark-haired girl at a table near the door, and the two were quickly engaged in a whispered conversation. Seeing that Grace had no intention of introducing them to the other ladies in the room, Maddie turned back to Emma.

"Mmmm. It smells wonderful in here. Can we be of any help?"

Emma turned with a bright smile. "If you'll stir this sauce for a minute, I'll see if I can get Gertie to take Alan." She picked up the toddler who had squeezed himself between his mother and the stove and walked over to the back door.

"Gertie!"

A few minutes later, two young girls appeared at the back door. Emma thrust Alan into the arms of the taller of the two girls. "Take your brother to see the kittens or keep him busy outside. He's going to get himself burned if he stays in here."

"You've got the easy part now," she told the woman in the rocker as she headed back toward the stove. She gestured toward the baby in the woman's arms. "Wait 'til she starts walking."

The young mother sighed, lifting the baby to her shoulder and patting her back. "Maybe, but I feel like all I do is feed her. About the time I put her down to sleep, she's up again wanting food."

"How old is she?" Jenny walked over to the rocker and lightly touched the baby's head. "She's so precious."

"Six weeks." The woman pulled the baby from her shoulder, allowing them to see her tiny little face. "She was born on May Day. I wanted to call her Fleur for the May flowers, but Tom said he couldn't get his mouth around any French name. He wanted May Belle, but that made me think of our old milk cow when we were growing up, so we settled on Bella Rose. Bella for short."

"Why, Bella's a perfectly beautiful name," Jenny said. "Is your name just as pretty?"

Emma turned from where she was pulling a loaf of bread from the oven. "I'm sorry. I forgot you two hadn't been introduced yet. This is my sister Julia . . . Julia Petersen. She and her husband Tom ranch northwest of town, so she doesn't get to come to our meetings very often. But she and Bella have come to stay with us for a few weeks while Tom's busy with spring roundup."

Emma glanced over at Grace and her companion. "That's Stella Jones there with Grace. Julia, this is Jenny Westraven and Mrs. Skivington."

"Please, call me Maddie."

"They've arrived from New Jersey just this week." Emma smiled at Maddie and Jenny. "I'm so glad you agreed to come today. Gives us all a chance to get to know you right away."

Julia looked up at Jenny. "You're Ted Westraven's sister? I should have known. You look just like him. Well, just like him if he were a girl, I guess. You look enough alike to be twins."

"Teddy and I are only eighteen months apart in age, so people have often mistaken us for twins. I know I couldn't feel closer to him if he were my twin. You have no idea how happy I am to be with him again."

A barely smothered laugh drew their attention to the table by the door. Without glancing their way, Grace and her friend rose and exited the room, heads together, Stella giggling at something Grace whispered in her ear.

"Well," Emma said, cocking an eyebrow at Maddie and Jenny. Then she shrugged and turned back to her sister. "Are you going to be able to help me with the sponge cake, or should I go ahead and start it myself?"

Julia looked down at her daughter, who was still wide awake in her arms.

"I could hold her if you'd like," said Maddie, moving the

sauce, which had now thickened, to a cooler portion of the stove and wiping her hands on a towel.

"Thank you," Julia smiled. "She usually goes to sleep as soon as she eats. But wouldn't you know she'd choose today to stay wide awake?"

Maddie lifted the small bundle into her arms and smiled down into the tiny face. "That's a baby for you. They rarely sleep when it's most convenient."

"Do you have children, Maddie?"

"No, not yet, but plenty of nieces and nephews. And younger brothers and sisters, so I've held my share of babies." She took Julia's place in the rocker while Emma set Jenny to work beating the custard. Gently rocking, she smoothed little Bella's downy head and kissed her soft fingers.

There had been a time not so long ago when she had thought the next newborn she held would be her own. She and Rob had both come from big families and, even before they married, they'd talked of the children they wanted. Rob had told her he wanted scads of them. They'd even picked out a few names. But the children hadn't come. Then Rob's illness had put that dream on hold—had put so many of their dreams on hold.

Tears pricked at her eyelids once again. Why was she such a watering pot today? She gave her head a little shake. Now was definitely not the time to dwell on what might have been. Today was a day for new beginnings. She tuned her ear to the conversation by the stove until Grace called them to join the others in the sewing circle.

∽

THE REST OF THE MORNING PASSED QUICKLY. WHEN MADDIE and Jenny took their turns at the quilt, they found themselves seated between a Mrs. Jones and a Mrs. Hornecker. They were discussing the latest ranching news. She listened with interest as they exchanged stories about the spring roundup and the challenges of feeding all the men involved.

"But listen to us go on about ourselves. We have two newcomers we haven't really met yet. They're going to think us very unsociable." Mrs. Jones turned to her and smiled. "We know Jenny has come to Lander to visit her brother. What brings you and your husband here, Mrs. Skivington?"

"Rob's health has not been good this past year. We are hoping the dry, clean air out here will change that."

"Oh yes," Mrs. Hornecker said. "I've known any number of people who have found our climate to be most beneficial. There's Mr. Westraven, of course. I can still remember the first summer he was here, poor boy, so pale and thin. Why, he was barely able to walk down the street. But look at him now. Healthy, and strong, and newly married." She beamed across the quilt frame at Grace. "And do you remember Mrs. Reynolds when she first arrived? No one thought she would last through that first winter, but she's well into her fifth year here and doing quite well."

"And whatever happened to that nice man from Boston—Mr. Phillips, was it?" One of the ladies from across the quilt chimed in. "You remember him, don't you, Sally? He came out a year or so ago and . . ." Her words faded away as she caught Mrs. Parkhurst's eye.

An uncomfortable silence settled over the women.

"Well, I'm sure your husband will do quite well," Sally Hornecker said after a few minutes. "Clarice tells me he is a jeweler. Will he continue in the jewelry business here in Lander?"

"Well, no. He's hoping to find an occupation that will allow him to be outdoors as much as possible. His doctor said that would be best. He's been looking into ranching of some sort." Maddie said. "In fact, he's gone to visit a sheepherder today to see if that might be an option for him."

"You can't be serious!" Grace addressed Maddie for the first time all day.

Maddie looked at the young woman in surprise. Well, of course, they were serious. How could you not be serious when life and death were on the line? Surely, Grace of all people could understand. Maddie bit her lip to keep the angry words from spilling out.

"Why? What's wrong with herding sheep?" Jenny tossed the question at her sister-in-law like a loaded grenade.

"Nothing's *wrong* with it, of course. It's just that sheepherders are so . . . well, they're . . . "

Mrs. Parkhurst broke in. "I think what Grace is trying to say is sheepherding is not a profession for a gentleman. Most sheepherders are uneducated, unkempt, and uncivilized after spending months alone with no company save large herds of smelly sheep. Why, any of them I've ever known were either crazy or drunk or both."

"Oh, they're not all so bad as that," Sally Hornecker said. "And there have been a few gentlemen much like Mr. Skivington who have taken up sheepherding for health purposes. Why I know of a sheepman over by Douglas who has an English nobleman as one of his herders. Fancy that! A duke in a sheep wagon."

"Surely, Mr. Skivington doesn't expect you to live in a *sheep wagon*," Grace said.

Maddie didn't know how to answer that having never seen a sheep wagon in person. But, from the horror in Grace's voice, she surmised living in one would be little better than living in a barn.

"That would be entirely out of the question," Mrs. Parkhurst answered for her. "If Mr. Skivington does decide to pursue sheepherding, Mrs. Skivington will have to find a nice family to board with here in town. I heard Amanda Winter is looking for boarders now her husband has passed on. That would be just the thing."

Maddie felt her back stiffen. Why is it some people always thought they knew what was best for everyone else? She hadn't come all the way out here to abandon Rob when he needed her support the most.

"Don't sheepherders generally have their wives with them?"

Mrs. Jones let out a sharp bark of laughter. "Sheepherders don't have wives."

"Generally, they don't," Mrs. Hornecker said, "though we have a few Basque herders near us who have their wives with them. One even had a new baby last winter."

"Oh, well, foreigners." Mrs. Parkhurst's voice fairly dripped with contempt. "There's never any telling what one of them will do. I've seen families of ten or more foreigners all packed into a one-room cabin. But, as a general rule, you will not find a woman in a sheep wagon. And certainly not a lady. No, you'd be much better served if you and your husband were to find a nice little cottage here in town. Your husband could hire out to any of the nearby ranchers as day help if he wants outdoor work."

That had been their original plan, of course, but the idea of owning their own enterprise, one that would allow Rob to be out in the dry, open-air day after day, had seemed so attractive when Mr. Taylor had described it to them. And Rob had come back from the horse auction after talking to Mr. Baldwin so full of hope. But hearing these ladies' reactions to that idea now filled her with misgiving. There was still so much about this strange new area she and Rob did not know. Maybe it would be wise to listen to the advice of those who had lived here for a while.

"Dinner is ready." Emma stood in the doorway.

"Give us five minutes to finish the quilt blocks on this row," Mrs. Parkhurst said, "and we'll have this quilt completed."

Maddie pushed her anxious thoughts to the back of her mind, focusing instead on the quilt block in front of her. There'd be time enough in the days ahead to make their decision. Take their time. Weigh the options. No need to fret on it now.

Chapter Nine

Rob breathed in, the crisp morning air cooling his throat and filling his lungs. Holding the breath as long as possible, he slowly let it escape, then slowly inhaled another. Surely air this thin and pure would bring the cure Dr. Waite had promised. If only all the doctor's tonics were this sweet to take. He wanted to fill every cavity, every corner of his lungs, and purge the disease from his body forever.

The morning had dawned clear and cold, but the strength of the sun's rays already promised a warmer day ahead. A covey of quail rose from the grass in front of Rob, spooking his hired mount. He gentled him with a firm tug on the reins. It had been years since he'd ridden a horse. Luckily, the livery had given him a very gentle mount, and the young giant who was his guide today seemed in no hurry.

Baldwin's camp tender had been a surprise. Just shy of six foot himself, Rob rarely felt short. Still, meeting young Jackson Garrity at the livery this morning made him feel like a Lilliputian to this Wyoming Gulliver. Young Garrity was a bear of a man who bested him by six inches and at least thirty pounds. If all of Wyoming's sons were made this hardy, he could well believe in the health of its climate.

They had reached a beautiful valley where lush green grasses grew along the banks of a narrow river. A wall of scarlet sandstone flanked the valley to the east and drew his gaze. He wished they had time to explore those cliffs at closer range. However, Jackson had told him the sheep camp they were visiting lay in the mountains. He turned his mount westward into the sage-covered buttes that flowed in waves toward the distant Wind River range. After several minutes, he realized the grayish-white rocks he saw scattered across one of the buttes ahead were moving. Sheep.

Rob drew abreast of his partner and nodded toward the distant flocks. "Are those Mr. Baldwin's sheep?"

"Naw, those are Bunce's. Range land here is public, so lots of ranchers use it."

"How do you know where to find Baldwin's sheep?"

Jackson's teeth flashed white against his tanned face. "They'll be where I put them, or close to it. The herder doesn't move camp 'til I move him."

"How often does that happen?"

"'Bout every ten days or so."

Rob surveyed the treeless hills stretched out for miles ahead of them. "How do you know where to put them?"

Jackson shrugged. "Depends on the season. In the summer months, we'll keep moving 'em higher and higher into the mountains. Cooler there, and more water. Winter range is down here in the buttes. Wind blows the snow off the ridges so they can graze pretty much year-round. Also keeps 'em closer to the home range for lambing and sheering."

"Does Mr. Baldwin have many herders?"

"Six. I'm in charge of three, and my brother Louis has three."

Rob calculated quickly. Mr. Taylor from the train had told him that most western herders were responsible for between fifteen hundred to two thousand sheep. That would mean Baldwin probably owned around twelve thousand head. That's a lot of mutton. With that many sheep, he could see how the man could sell him a thousand or more and not really miss them.

They traveled for several hours, climbing ever higher, passing two or three more sheep camps along the way. Rob soon began to recognize the sight of a herder's wagon with their white canvas tops and the tinkle of sheep bells that signaled the approach of each new band.

True to its earlier promise, the sun beat down upon them with increasing intensity as the day progressed. He wished he'd left his suit coat at home and eyed his companion's casual broadcloth shirt and trousers with envy. But about the time Rob was ready to shrug out of his tight jacket, Jackson turned in his saddle and said, "Tavis's camp should be over that rise."

Sure enough, they crested the next rise to see the now-familiar, canvas-covered wagon parked beside a narrow stream. Thousands of sheep, some standing in small bunches, others drinking at the stream, spread out through the narrow valley. A ribbon of sheep flowed out from a fringe of trees about twenty yards away. The flow soon narrowed to a trickle, then a couple of black and white dogs and a grizzled little man popped out of the tree line behind them. Spotting them, the man threaded his way through the mass of sheep to greet them.

"Thought ye might be by today," the man said to Jackson, then nodded a greeting to Rob. A question formed in his eyes, but he didn't ask it. Instead, he turned to Jackson. "Saw cat prints in the sand this morning. Good time to be moving on."

"Cat?" Jackson took off his hat and scratched his head. "Might be hard to move you far enough to get out of its territory. Lose any lambs?"

"No' yet. Best to be moving on, though."

Jackson nodded, then hooked a thumb at Rob. "This here's Mr. Skivington. Wants to learn all about sheepherding. Mr. Baldwin said to bring him out to meet you. Said nobody knows more about sheepherding than you, Tavis."

The old man's weathered cheeks darkened under the praise.

"I dunno aboot that, but ye're sure welcome at my camp, Mr. Skivington."

"Call me Rob."

"Ye lads want some dinner?" Tavis motioned them toward his wagon.

For the first time in days, food actually sounded like a good idea. This fresh air must be a powerful tonic indeed.

Rob slid off his horse and tethered him next to Jackson's along the side of the sheep wagon. Then, following Jackson's lead, he stepped onto the tongue of the wagon, braced his hands on each side of the doorway, and pulled himself up and in. Tavis clambered up behind him.

Though small, the wagon's interior was bright and cool. Light filtered through the white canvas of the roof and in at the small window over the bunk which ran crossways across the back of the wagon. Benches with hinged lids lined both long sides of the wagon. Rob caught a whiff of a pot of fragrant stew bubbling on the wood stove to the right of the door and felt his stomach rumble a response.

Jackson draped his length onto the bench opposite the stove, so Rob found a seat on the other bench, careful to avoid the big man's knees which filled most of the space in between. As soon as Rob was seated, Jackson reached between them to pull out a thick slab of wood from a slot under the bunk. Swinging a gate leg down from the underside of the slab, he formed a table. Soon, Tavis set out three bowls of the stew, a loaf of bread, and three mugs of cold water. Then he squeezed onto the bench beside him.

Once the simple lunch was over, Jackson rose and banked down the stove while Tavis rinsed the stew pot and bowls and placed them inside the bench Jackson had vacated. Not knowing how else to help, Rob returned the table to its position beneath the bunk. Then he did his best to stay out of the way as Tavis scurried to and fro gathering canisters, cups, and even a shaving mirror off the wall, stuffing them into compartments under the benches.

Jackson straightened from his job at the stove, caught Rob's eye, and grinned. "Want to help me hitch the horses?"

Finally! A job he understood. Inching past Tavis, he followed Jackson out of the wagon and set off to fetch the sheepherder's horse grazing a few yards away. Jackson led his own horse over, and they soon had them harnessed to the wagon's tongue. Meanwhile, Tavis had emerged from the wagon and was busy rounding the sheep into a large moveable mass.

Now what? Rob looked to where Jackson was wrangling a three-legged stool from a hook beneath the wagon. Pulling it out, he placed it just inside the doorway of the wagon. Then he grabbed the horses' reins and climbed into the wagon, shutting the bottom of the wagon's two-part Dutch door behind him. Mounting the stool, he was now as ready to drive the wagon as any Newark teamster. Clever.

Soon they were off, Jackson leading the way, Rob following on horseback, and Tavis bringing up the rear behind the sheep. Once set in motion, the sheep seemed to have little trouble moving as a pack. The dogs patrolled the edges nipping at the heels of any stragglers, and the whole mass moved steadily along, like an undulating snake stretching out behind the wagon with Tavis a lone dark tail at its end.

Rob reined in his horse to allow the stream of sheep and dogs to pass, dropping back behind Tavis to watch how he got the sheep to trail. As far as he could tell, the man merely walked along behind the sheep allowing the dogs to do the work. A series of whistles, a sharp "Come bye, Danny," and the dogs would effectively cut off any stragglers and veer them back toward the herd. Rob marveled at their intensity, their attention fully focused on the band in front of them.

"Can they keep up this pace for long?" Rob asked Tavis, who was now walking at his side.

"Oh, aye. An hour or two, for sure. The lads'll earn their

supper tonight, though." He spoke with the quiet pride of a father, and Rob could see how dogs would be indispensable if he were to try sheepherding for himself. Tavis let off another series of whistles and one black-and-white border collie shot after a lamb that had branched away from the herd.

"Your whistle told him to do that?"

"Aye, they hear the whistles better than the commands when we're trailing. If they're close enough, the command'll do."

This may be more complicated than he thought, but if he could learn the whistles, it would save his voice. His throat was hoarse enough without adding the strain of calling out commands all day.

"Are there many to learn?"

"A dozen or more. A good pup'll learn 'em by the time he's a year."

Surely he was smarter than a pup. But then, he wouldn't have the luxury of a year's time to learn them. A few weeks might even be too long.

"Teach me some. Which ones do you use the most?"

"Ye truly be wanting to herd some sheep then, lad?" Tavis' eyes were kind but skeptical.

"I'm thinking about it. My doctor tells me working out in the fresh air would be good for my lungs."

Understanding dawned in the man's eyes. "Ah, chasing the cure, are ye? Get aboot one new herder every odd year or so, that'a way."

"The cure works, then?"

"Dunno. Most don't stay long enough to find out."

Not very encouraging.

"So, could you teach me some commands?"

Tavis was a willing teacher, and by the time they reached Tavis's new campground, Rob had learned several commands and whistles. The old shepherd even let him try his hand at herding the sheep by himself the last few miles, though Rob secretly suspected the dogs could have handled the job on their own.

The sheep fanned out into the mountain meadow where Jackson had stopped. Tavis and the dogs kept a close eye to see none ventured too far from the camp. Jackson was busy finding a level spot for the sheep wagon, so Rob found a seat on a large rock and took in the scene.

A temperate breeze kept the sunny day cool. Only the occasional bleat of a lamb or trill of a bird disturbed the peace of the valley. He leaned back against the hillside and pulled in another deep breath of the thin mountain air. The cloudless sky was a bowl of blue above him. Rob followed the flight of an eagle gliding on wind currents no eye could see, his heart soaring in response. One more deep breath and a slow exhale. He could do this all day. He chuckled at the thought. If he were to buy his own band of sheep, he *would* do this all day.

Somehow, he felt at home here. He shook his head at the thought. He, Rob Skivington, born and bred to the streets of London and Newark, feeling at home on the side of this mountain in Wyoming? How the boys back home would laugh at that. He was more used to catching a streetcar than a horse.

But maybe this was where God was leading them all along. The pieces had all seemed to fall into place. Meeting Mr. Taylor on the train, then Mr. Willoughby with his connections to Baldwin—could they all be markers from the Lord leading him along a trail to a cure?

His gaze settled on the spot where Jackson was securing Tavis's home on wheels. The sight caught him up short. Sure, *he* felt the pull to step out and try this new life, but what about Maddie? That wagon was an incredibly clever contraption—compact yet equipped with everything a man needed to make a home in the wilderness, but was it enough for a woman? More to the point, would it be enough for his city-bred wife, who was used to a house of her own and the companionship of a large family and many friends?

He glanced over at Tavis, who had taken a seat a few feet to his right. "Do you get to town often?"

"Town? Oh, aye, aboot once a year. Most of us herders'll try to take a short holiday in the fall once the lambs are sold."

Once a year! How could he even think of asking Maddie to spend an entire year with only himself for company? And what if he were to have a setback? Days like those after his hemorrhage when he'd barely had the strength to get out of bed? Could Maddie handle the work on her own? Was it fair to ask her to?

He coughed and spat into the flask he always carried in his pocket. Cough and spit. Cough and spit. How he longed for the day when those two actions no longer governed his life.

He considered his options. Dr. Waite had said to spend as much time in the open air as possible. Sheepherding would certainly accomplish that. Or they could find a house in town, and he could try to find work at someone else's ranch, but who knew if any of the ranchers would be willing to hire him without any experience? If Mr. McCallister was any indication, they wouldn't.

From what he could tell, sheepherding wasn't terribly strenuous. Not like the chores he'd be expected to do as a farm or ranch hand. And with a sheep wagon close by, he could always rest if he needed to. Besides, any mistakes he made would be at his own expense, not theirs if he owned his own operation. He hated to ask Maddie to make such a sacrifice, but sheepherding continued to look like their best option.

Maybe it wouldn't take a whole year to find the cure. Maybe six months would be enough to cleanse his body and heal his disease-laden lungs. Then they could get back to the life he'd promised her. He had to give it a try. Surely Maddie would understand.

Chapter Ten

Setting down her pen, Maddie looked over her letter. Somehow, being able to share her day with her sisters, describing to them the ladies she had met at the quilting bee, had eased her homesickness a bit. She had been missing them so all day. Watching Julia and Emma in the kitchen had reminded her of the many times she and Edie had prepared meals together back home, and little Gertie with her long brown braids was about the same age as Hazel. How Hazel would have enjoyed playing with her and the other children.

Of all her family, little Hazel had been the hardest to leave behind. The bond between them, forged by Mother's illness and early death, had proven costly, maybe too costly. Maddie could still hear her little sister's sobs, feel the tight hug of her arms around her neck when they said their goodbyes at the station.

The tears that had been threatening all day spilled over, and this time Maddie let them come. How long had it been since she'd allowed herself to have a good cry? Too long, considering how fast the tears were flowing now. She dropped her head into her hands and gave in to the sobs.

After several minutes, she pulled out her handkerchief, mopped her cheeks, and blew her nose with determination.

Enough of this. Rob would be home any minute, and he certainly didn't need to find her wallowing in self-pity.

She turned her thoughts instead to the little frame cottage Mrs. Parkhurst had shown her on their walk home today. According to Grace's mother, the property had recently come up for sale and would be about perfect for her and Rob. The house was small, only a little over half the size of their home in Newark, but it boasted a spacious front porch, and pansies grew in the window boxes flanking the front door. Maddie couldn't wait for Rob to come home so she could tell him all about it.

A rosy glow from the setting sun filled the hotel room. Maddie leaned back in her chair, watching the rose slowly fade to gray against the papered walls. She should get up and turn on a lamp, but she couldn't muster the energy after her crying jag. Boots sounded on the stairs, and her heart raced as a merry whistle wafted down the hallway.

Rob was back.

Since the tuberculosis had made him too hoarse to sing, Rob had taken to whistling everywhere he went. "The music will out," he'd say with a shrug whenever Maddie would comment on it.

"Sitting alone in the dark, Maddie-girl?" Rob said as he came through the door.

"It's only just become dark." She lifted her face to his kiss as he bent over her chair. She hoped any traces of her tears would be hidden in the fading light.

He gave her shoulders a squeeze and walked over to the bedside table to turn the key on the lamp.

"So, how was your day with the ladies? Did you find some new friends?"

"I believe so. The hostess and her sister were especially nice. Oh, and I met Mrs. Willoughby, who was exactly as I pictured her. She's such a dear."

"And Grace and her mother? Still frosty, or are they beginning to warm to you?"

Maddie wrinkled her nose at him. "Now, don't be mean. I'm sure they'll improve with time."

"Whatever you say," Rob sat down on the bed and began to pull off his boots.

"But what about your day?" She walked over to sit on the bed beside him. "Do you still think there's promise in the sheep-herding business?"

Rob dropped his second boot to the floor and settled himself upon the bed with his back against the headboard, pulling Maddie up beside him.

"You should see it out there, Maddie. So open . . . so free . . . and the air so thin, a man can literally see for miles. The camp was right on the edge of the Wind River Mountains." He leaned his head back against the headboard and turned his gaze to the ceiling. "I don't know how to describe those mountains to you, Maddie. You'll have to see them. All I know is, I got the strongest sense that this was it, this was where God was leading me . . . leading us." He turned and looked into her eyes. "I'm going to get well out there. I know it. I don't know how I know. I just do."

She reached out and traced his cheek and mustache with her fingertips. "I pray it's so, darling."

He pulled her fingers to his lips and kissed them. "Sing with me."

"What?"

"That song. It's been going through my head all day. Sing it with me."

What song? Had the sun damaged his brain somehow?

Rob paid no attention to her perplexed look. Instead, he began to sing, his voice hoarse and deep, *"He leadeth me . . ."*

Of course. The song he was whistling as he came up the stairs.

"Sing with me?" His eyes pleaded. *"Oh, blessed thought . . . ,"* he continued, eyes still intent on hers.

A million excuses came to mind: the neighbors, his throat,

79

the lateness of the hour, but she was ever a sucker for those puppy-dog brown eyes. Softly she joined in. *"Oh, words with heav'nly wisdom fraught . . ."*

"Wh—" Rob's voice caught, and he went off into a spasm of coughing. Clearing his throat, he tried again, *"Whate'er I do . . . , wh—"*

Maddie placed her hand on his chest and shook her head. "Rob, stop. You'll hurt your throat."

"Then sing it for me, Maddie. Be my voice." He pulled her onto his lap, her back pressed against his chest, skirts draped across his legs. His mustache tickled as he whispered in her ear, "Sing it, Maddie. Please?"

She drew a breath and sang, feeling his warm breath on her ear as he whispered the words along with her. *"Whate'er I do, where'er I be, Still 'tis God's hand that leadeth me."*

Maddie had always said music had brought them together—not only in their meeting but throughout their courtship. She relished the times they sang together, their voices blending, melding, creating together a sound they could not accomplish alone. But this—this took that intimacy to a whole new level. She closed her eyes and felt the rise and fall of his chest beneath her. The words he whispered in her ear spilled into her lungs and out her throat—not fully hers nor fully his but somehow a mystical mixture of the two.

"Lord, I would place my hand in Thine,
Nor ever murmur nor repine;
Content, whatever lot I see,
Since 'tis my God that leadeth me."

The words she was singing suddenly hit home. Had it truly only been a brief half-hour since she had wallowed in tears of self-pity? When Rob had suffered his last big hemorrhage, she'd pleaded with God: whatever it takes, Lord, show us what to do. Was she so weak that she was buckling under the pressure already?

"His faithful follower I would be, For by His hand He leadeth me."

The final words to the song hung in the air around them. Rob pulled her closer. "Thank you," he murmured. She could feel his warm lips move against the tender flesh on her neck and jawline. How she loved this man!

If Mrs. Parkhurst had never seen a lady in a sheep wagon, she'd better sit up and take notice because one was about to move in.

Chapter Eleven

"So, what do you think of it?"

Maddie gazed at the vehicle in front of her. A sheep wagon. Rob had practically dragged her into the livery yard to show her. He was that excited. The wagon's box was painted a bright green, and its curved canvas top reminded her of a miniature prairie schooner. Very miniature. The entire wagon was barely as wide as Rob was tall.

"It certainly is compact." Compact was an understatement. Maddie wasn't sure how they'd both fit inside without tripping over one another. The tiny cottage Mrs. Parkhurst had shown her on Main Street was a mansion compared to this.

"You'll be amazed at how cleverly these things are put together. It has everything you'll ever need for keeping house, yet it's small enough that it's easily pulled by a couple of horses." Rob hopped up into the wagon's doorway and extended his hand. "Climb on up. I'll show you."

Maddie gathered her skirts in one hand and allowed Rob to help her onto the wagon's tongue and into the doorway. Careful not to brush against the woodstove that took up a good portion of the entry, she followed Rob into the wagon, taking in the narrow bunk and wooden side benches. Rob lifted the lid on one of the benches.

"You can store everything you need in these . . . blankets, linens, clothes, food. And there's more storage space under the bunk. Oh, and look at this." Rob pulled the table from its hidey-hole and gestured for her to take a seat with the flourish of a maître d'.

Maddie smiled at her husband's enthusiasm and sat on the bench he'd indicated, letting her eyes scan the wagon's interior. A navy oilcloth patterned with tiny white flowers covered the walls above the bed and behind the stove. It provided a cozy contrast to the white-painted cupboards and benches. If she added a brightly colored quilt to the bunk and some lacy curtains to the window, the wagon would feel quite homey. It reminded her a little of the playhouse her father had built for her and Katie Alice when they were little girls.

Excitement bloomed in her chest. Maybe this sheepherding venture wouldn't be such a bad option. If it truly was where God was leading them, maybe it was time she set aside her fears and stepped into the adventure.

"I know it's small," Rob sat on the opposite bench and leaned toward her, intensity glowing in his deep brown eyes. "but we'll really only be in it to eat our meals and sleep. Most of the time, we'll be outside, and you should see it up there in those mountains, Maddie. So beautiful and peaceful. It'll be like having the whole world as our living room."

His enthusiasm was catching.

"And housekeeping should be a snap. Five or ten minutes every morning, and my work will be done for the day. Why, I'll be so spoiled I may never want a traditional house again," she said.

Rob took her hand in both of his, "It will only be for a little while. I promise. Just until I get better."

Maddie nodded. "Of course, it will. And think of the stories we'll have to tell our children someday."

He rose to his feet and pulled her up into his arms. "I don't deserve you, Mrs. Skivington." Cupping her face with his hands, he bent and brushed the gentlest of kisses against her lips. Any remaining doubts she may have had vanished at his touch. She closed her eyes, breathing in the fresh scent of his shaving cream, and leaned into his lips, deepening their kiss with her response. Rob pulled away first, setting her back from him with a shake of his head.

"Best save that for when we're alone on that mountain," he grinned.

Heat rushed to her cheeks. The open door! The sheep wagon was parked in the yard of a busy blacksmith shop right on Main Street. Anyone walking by could look in and see them. For all practical purposes, they might as well be embracing on an open street corner.

Rob touched her cheek. "Don't worry. No one saw us. Come on. Let's go make this sheep palace our own."

"Maaaad—die!" Jenny's voice wafted across the carriage yard as Rob helped Maddie down from the wagon. Turning, she saw her friend hurrying toward her from Lander's main street, Grace and Mrs. Parkhurst following more sedately behind. Goodness. Had they walked by a few minutes earlier, they would have caught her shamelessly kissing her husband in public. The thought sent a swath of heat back up her chest and face.

"Looks like we've got company." Rob's knowing smile told her he knew exactly what she was thinking.

She elbowed him in his ribs. "You behave."

He winked. "I think I'll just go settle things with Mr. Oldenburg while you talk to the ladies."

With a tip of his hat and a quick bow to the oncoming trio of women, Rob took off in search of the blacksmith. Coward.

"Maddie, I'm so glad we ran into you." Jenny's smile faded as she took in the wagon behind them. "What's this?"

Mustering a brave face, Maddie flourished a hand toward the

vehicle behind her. "This is a sheep wagon." Her brightness sounded forced even to her ears.

"So he's going through with it?"

Maddie wasn't prepared for the panic she saw in her friend's eyes. She searched for words that would soften the blow.

Grace had caught up with Jenny and was surveying the wagon as one might a large spider that had crept into one's bedroom. Mrs. Parkhurst bustled up behind her.

"Good morning, Mrs. Skivington. Were you able to tell your husband about the cottage I showed you yesterday?"

"I'm afraid we won't be needing that cottage, after all, Mrs. Parkhurst. Rob's in with Mr. Oldenburg right now putting an offer on this sheep wagon."

Mrs. Parkhurst pursed her lips, then nodded. "Well, if your husband's set on trying this silly experiment, I guess there's nothing you can do to stop him. We'll have to go with my earlier plan. I'll talk to Mrs. Winter today. I'm sure she would welcome a paying boarder."

"No. You don't understand. Rob is buying the sheep wagon for both of us. I will be going with him."

Mrs. Parkhurst raised her eyebrows so high they all but disappeared behind the brim of her hat. "Going with him? Child, did you hear nothing I said yesterday? A sheep camp is no place for a lady. Frankly, I'm surprised your husband would even suggest it." She tapped a finger to her lips and squinted her eyes. "Maybe I should have a talk with him."

"No," the word came out much louder than Maddie had intended. She struggled to modulate her voice. "Mrs. Parkhurst, I'd really appreciate it if you would not do that. Rough as it may be to live in a sheep wagon, I simply cannot let Rob do this on his own. If he were to become ill again . . . out on the mountain, all alone . . ." Maddie looked away, swallowing back her tears. Taking a deep breath, she continued. "I must be there with him. He needs me. It's why I'm here."

Mrs. Parkhurst stepped back a pace, raising one hand. "If you do not want my advice, you only have to say so. I'm merely trying to say what I'm sure your own mother would say if she were here today. I'm certain she raised you to be a lady."

Maddie thought of her delicate mother, born and bred to English gentry, who, when the time came, disregarded the advice of her own family to follow her fiancé across the ocean to an entirely new life.

She raised her chin and looked Mrs. Parkhurst in the eyes, "You're right. She did raise me to be a lady . . . but she also taught me to follow my heart. So forgive me if I believe I can do both."

The older woman let out a heavy sigh and shook her head. "You truly have no idea what you are getting yourself into. Well, don't come crying to me when you find out I am right. Come along, girls. We have more shopping to do." Mrs. Parkhurst turned and walked quickly back toward the boardwalk, Grace at her heels.

Jenny took Maddie's hand and squeezed it. "Don't mind her. No plan is a good plan unless it's hers. I'm sure you and Rob are making the right choice. I just wish you didn't have to leave town to do it. How soon do you leave?"

"Rob hopes to head out early next week."

Tears sprang to Jenny's eyes, but she quickly flicked them away. "Don't mind me. It's just . . . I've only just found you and you're leaving already. It's . . . I've . . ."

Maddie pulled the girl into a hug. "I know. I'm going to miss you too." Seemed like her life these days was nothing more than one goodbye after another. "We still have a few days, though. Come by tomorrow. You can help Rob and me shop for the supplies we'll need for our sheep camp."

"I'd love that." Jenny glanced over her shoulder. "I'd better go. It simply won't do to keep Mrs. P. waiting." Then, with a quick wave toward Rob, who had just stepped out of the blacksmith's office, she scurried off after the Parkhursts.

Chapter Twelve

Maddie clung to her horse's reins and tried not to think about how high she sat off the ground. The head of the black beast beneath her shied and whinnied at her clutch. *Loosen the reins, Miss Long.* The voice of Miss Amelia Jenkins of Miss Jenkins's Riding School for Young Ladies rang in her ears. She could almost feel the gentle tap of her teacher's riding crop across her fingers. *A lady's balance is determined by the firmness of her seat, never by her hold on the reins. An accomplished rider should be able to hold her seat without ever touching the reins.*

Well, she had never claimed to be an accomplished rider and this morning's ride was proof of that. But what could she expect? Other than those days at Miss Jenkins's school, she could count the times she'd been on horseback on the fingers of one hand. Up until today, she would have claimed the money her parents spent on those lessons had been a waste, but now small tidbits of those long-ago lessons filtered back to her.

Legs together, toes down and in, torso square with the horses' back, Maddie checked through the list and firmed her seat. Really this wasn't so bad . . . if she didn't look down. She swallowed and focused her attention squarely between her horse's ears. A gentle, sweet mare, Mr. Grimmett at the livery had called her. Maybe, but she was certain those ponies at Miss Jenkins's had never been half this tall.

Maddie stiffened as the mare started down another rocky embankment. *Ladies are not made of cast iron.* Another of Miss Jenkins's axioms came rushing back to her. *Keep your upper body flexible, like a willow in a storm.* She closed her eyes and willed her body to sway in keeping with her horse.

"Are you all right?" Rob was waiting for her at the bottom of the gully. "Relax. You look as stiff as a washboard."

So much for willow branches waving in the wind.

"Maybe you should have taken Mr. Grimmett's advice and ridden astride today."

Astride! Did he honestly think she'd be more comfortable riding in such an unladylike manner, especially in front of other men? At least she knew how to ride sidesaddle. In theory, anyway.

"I don't have the proper attire for riding astride," she said. A shallow excuse at best. She and Jenny had seen the split skirts used by so many women here in the West in the mercantile on Saturday. Jenny had snatched one up and encouraged Maddie to do the same, but she could never have been so bold.

"We have a long day of riding ahead of us. I hope you don't wear out."

"I'll be fine. Really. I just need to get used to riding again, that's all."

He quirked an eyebrow at her but let the subject drop. As they crested a small rise, Rob pointed to a small cluster of buildings off in the distance. "That should be Baldwin's ranch over there," he said. "We won't have time to stop and visit today. We have too much ground to cover if we're going to set up camp by nightfall. But Jackson says our flock is just up the valley from the home ranch. You'll have a chance to rest there while we round up the sheep for moving."

They turned their horses away from the ranch and followed

Jackson in the sheep wagon, over a small stream, and up another butte. There in the valley below them stretched a flock of sheep. Their sheep. Maddie gazed in wonder at the size of the grayish-white mass in front of her. How were the two of them possibly going to keep track of so many?

As if he sensed her question, Rob turned toward her. "Don't worry," he said. "The dogs will do most of the work. You'll see."

Hmmph. If dogs truly did all the work, why was there a need for a shepherd? Ahead of them, Jackson stopped the wagon and jumped down to talk with the young man sitting in the grass off to one side of the sheep. She spurred her mount down the gentle slope, eager for the opportunity to get off her horse and stretch her legs.

As they drew near, a few of the sheep lifted their heads to stare at them, but the majority went right on grazing, paying them no heed. The animals were larger than she imagined, not anything like the soft, fluffy blobs she'd seen in many pastoral paintings. Instead, these creatures were more gray than white, their wool clipped close. Maddie remembered the many freighters on the road from Rawlins, wagons piled high with sacks of wool heading for the railway. Doubtless, their soft, fluffiness would return with time. But time would probably never remedy their smell or the dust.

Maddie brought her mount to a halt behind the wagon, lifted her right leg over the pommel on her saddle, and waited for Rob to dismount so he could help her down. A sharp pain throbbed through her right knee from having been bent for so long. She couldn't wait to get off this horse. Once on firm ground again, she turned and patted the mare's neck. The mare *was* sweet and gentle and had brought her this far safely despite her abysmal riding skills. She only wished this were the end of the ride and not just their first stop.

Jackson and the young herder walked over to where they were standing.

"This is my brother Gabe," he said.

Maddie smiled at the boy while Rob shook his hand. Though almost as tall as Rob, she could tell by Gabe's thin frame and young face he wasn't much older than Rob's brother Fred. Minutes later, a rider crested the rise from the direction of the ranch and rode down amongst the sheep toward them.

"And here comes my brother Louis." Jackson waved as the man cantered up and reigned to a halt. "Glad you could finally join us."

Louis grinned at his brother's sarcastic greeting, then slid from his horse and drew off his large Western hat while Jackson introduced them. Though stockier than the other two, Louis shared his brothers' curly dark hair and height. Wyoming must grow its native sons to match its landscape—on a grand scale.

Jackson turned toward her and Rob. "It'll take a few minutes to round up the sheep for moving. Why don't you two stretch your legs a bit? When we do pull out, I'll take the lead with the wagon. Mrs. Skivington, you can follow me. Rob, if you'll just stay on this side of the sheep, between them and the creek, I'll put Louis on the other side. Gabe can bring up the rear with the dogs. Shouldn't be too long now, and we'll be on our way."

His words proved true. Far sooner than she wanted, Maddie was back on the mare, following the cloud of dust raised by the sheep wagon. For several hours they made their way through the valley created by the creek bed. As the hours passed, Maddie found her confidence on horseback growing as she became accustomed to her mare's swaying motion. She dropped back to ride beside Rob several times, helping him watch for sheep, especially lambs, who would suddenly break out of the flock to pursue side trails of their own.

They nooned in a pretty spot at a bend in the creek where a profusion of gold and purple wildflowers carpeted the meadow on the opposite bank. In the distance, waves of grass-covered buttes rose to meet the blue of a flat-topped plateau. Maddie drank in the beauty of the scene.

Remembering the pansies in the window boxes of the small

cottage in town, she turned to Jackson who was seated near her on a rock. "Will there be flowers like that near our campsite?"

"Not if I do my job there won't. Those purple ones there are lupine. If the sheep eat too much of it, they could fall into a frenzy and die."

Maddie blinked and looked back at the field of flowers. How could something so beautiful be a menace?

"Do any other plants harm them?"

"Sure. Locoweed, larkspur, deathcamas, sneezeweed . . ." Jackson, who'd been ticking the names off on his fingers, let his words trail off. Her alarm must be mirrored in her face. "No need to worry, ma'am. I won't set you up in an area with a lot of poisonous weed, and as long as there is plenty of good food for the sheep, they won't bother with anything poisonous."

Somehow his words held little comfort. Rob had assured her that their best training was on-the-job training, but if such a simple thing as a flower could wreak such havoc, what of the other hazards that were so prevalent in the wild? How could she and Rob possibly protect this huge band of sheep from so many dangers, especially when they didn't know anything about those dangers themselves? She stood and helped gather the tin cups and plates they'd used for their picnic. If only she could pack away her misgivings as swiftly and efficiently as they packed away their picnic supplies.

∼

AN HOUR LATER, JACKSON DREW THE WAGON TO A HALT AT the edge of a swiftly flowing creek and motioned for her and Rob to move forward.

"We'll cross here and head up into the mountains from the other side," he said. "I'll go first with the wagon. Mrs. Skivington, you can follow me, but I'll need Rob to stay behind with Louis and Gabe to help herd the sheep across."

Looking upstream, Maddie could see why Jackson chose this

crossing. The bank further up became increasingly steeper as the water narrowed through canyon walls that led higher into the mountains. She studied the water in front of her as Jackson guided the wagon across. Though fast-moving, it was neither too wide nor too deep. Even at its deepest, the water barely reached to the hubs of the wagon wheels. Satisfied, she urged her horse forward and followed Jackson across the creek and up the opposite bank.

As Maddie fell in behind the wagon, a shrill whistle from the men behind them brought Jackson to a halt. Reining in, she turned to look back. Massed against the far bank, the sheep bleated and paced but refused to step into the water.

"Blast." Jackson climbed down from the wagon and stood next to her on the path.

"What's wrong with them?"

"They're sheep. That's what's wrong with them. Doesn't matter how shallow a creek is. Sheep hate to cross moving water."

"So, how do we get them across?"

Jackson shrugged. "If one comes, the rest will follow."

Maddie looked back at the quivering, frothing throng. Didn't seem to be any likely volunteers at this moment. Louis backed his horse away from the group and came at the huddle of sheep at a gallop, hollering and waving his hat. The sheep in the back of the herd pressed forward, but instead of pushing the lead sheep into the water, the commotion merely caused them to turn around in a panic and run back through the herd. Small bands of sheep scattered in all directions, and it was several minutes before the men and dogs had them all rounded up again and pressed against the creek's edge.

Once again, the lead sheep refused to step into the water. Whenever the pressure from behind became too intense, the line in front would turn and break for the back, causing chaos to ensue all over again.

After a third attempt to push the sheep from behind

awarded the same results, Jackson called across the creek. "Bring Biddy's lamb over here. We'll tie it up. Maybe we can get her to follow."

Louis guided his horse to the water's edge, where he dropped a lasso around the neck of a young lamb standing beside one of the larger ewes at the head of the herd. Pulling the lamb across his saddle, he crossed to their side of the creek and tied it to a small bush along the bank. The lamb bleated and pulled at the rope, frantically trying to get back to its mother. Biddy paced and called back to her lamb on the opposite bank but made no effort to join it. Suddenly the branch the lamb was tied to snapped, and the lamb sprinted for the creek. Louis, who'd been standing just to the side of the bush, made a lunge to catch the lamb but was an instant too late. He landed on the rocks at the edge of the creek with a thud and an oath. Finding his feet, he sprinted back across the water, pulled his lasso off the lamb and threw it around Biddy's neck instead.

Turning, he pulled the rope up over his shoulder and stomped back into the water. Biddy locked her legs and pulled back against the lasso, but Louis dragged her inexorably into the creek, dirt, and rocks flying. Once she hit the water, Biddy went limp. Louis manhandled her across and carried her up the other bank. Setting her on her feet, he faced her toward the tempting green meadow and released her with a swat to her rump. Biddy ran a few steps up the trail, then turned and dodged back toward the creek. The two men tried to head her off, but she nimbly side-stepped them and was soon splashing her way toward the opposite bank.

Louis threw his rope to the ground and kicked it, letting loose a string of words that reminded Maddie why Mrs. Parkhurst felt a sheep camp was no place for a lady. Jackson punched his brother's shoulder and gestured in her direction. Even from where she sat, Maddie could see Louis's neck and face redden beneath his tan as he turned to face her.

"Sorry, ma'am. I forgot you were there."

"I can certainly understand your frustration," she said. "Will they ever come across?"

Both men looked at the sheep lining the opposite shore. Jackson raked a hand through his hair and shook his head. "Don't look like they'll be coming anytime soon."

"Maybe we should take them back to Halls Gulch and cross them there," Louis said.

Jackson looked up at the sky and shook his head. "We won't have time before the storm hits. Once the rain hits that water, the creek will be running as fast in the gulch as it is here." Maddie followed Jackson's gaze and was surprised to see a wall of thunderheads building over the mountains. A low rumble warned that Jackson could well be right. A storm was brewing. She'd been so busy watching the drama unfold down by the creek, she hadn't even noticed the sky darkening. A cool breeze stirred the hair beneath her hat.

"How long do you think we have before the storm hits?"

A louder crack of thunder reverberated through the canyon, drowning out Jackson's answer. A shout from the opposite shore drew their attention back to the water where a lone sheep had plunged in and was swimming their way. Suddenly, as if a dam had burst, the rest of the sheep came pouring down the side of the bank in a frenzied mass, trampling each other in their haste to hit the water. Louis and Jackson sprinted into the water pulling sheep off one another and throwing them toward the shore to keep them from drowning beneath the frantic wave of bodies.

The wall of sheep continued to flow up the bank and down the trail to where Maddie sat on her horse. As the bodies thundered past, she forgot everything she'd learned at Miss Jenkin's School. Squeezing her eyes shut, she fisted her hands in her horse's mane and simply prayed the mare wouldn't bolt. A few minutes later, the thundering of hooves ceased. She cracked open her eyes to see Gabe and the dogs streak by in pursuit of the sheep. Rob followed at a gallop but soon slowed to a walk.

"Well, I'll be." He looked back at Maddie and grinned.

"What?" Maddie urged her mount forward and around a bend in the path. The sheep had come to a halt a few yards ahead in a meadow of thick, lush grass. Many had already begun to graze. The only evidence of their mad dash across the creek was the smell of damp wool. Jackson walked up beside them, took in the scene, and shook his head.

"Dumb sheep," he muttered. He sat down on a nearby boulder, pulled off a boot and turned it over, letting water pour out on the ground. He repeated the process for the other boot, then peeled off his socks and wrung them out.

Louis rode up beside them. "Might as well have left them on," he called to Jackson. "The rest of you is going to be just as wet soon enough."

Another crack of thunder echoed in the canyon, and a cold drop of rain hit Maddie's cheek. She'd almost forgotten about the approaching storm in the chaos of the sheep crossing.

Jackson pulled his socks and boots back on and stood. "We could wait out the storm in the wagon if you'd like, but I don't recommend it if we're going to make camp before nightfall. I've got a couple of rain slickers in the wagon if you're willing to press on."

Rob gave a quick nod. "Let's do it then."

The raindrops began to fall in earnest as Jackson sprinted toward the wagon for the slickers. By the time he got back, Maddie was glad to pull the rubber garment on over her clothes. It fit like a large yellow tent.

Soon they were on their way again, wagon leading the way, with the sheep, dogs, and horses following behind. The rain was coming down in sheets now. Somehow, when she'd imagined living in the great outdoors, she'd forgotten about the elements. Icy raindrops found a path under her collar and coursed in rivulets down her back. She pulled the slicker higher on her neck and ducked her head, so her hat caught most of the onslaught. The dry mountain air might be good for Rob's lungs, but surely this downpour was not. What had they been thinking to believe any of this was a task they could handle? She knew only one thing for certain. They were in way over their heads here, but there was no going back.

Chapter Thirteen

❦

Something was wrong with this clasp. Had to be. Why else would the pearls keep falling off the string? Rob examined the silver-filigreed clasp and the knot he'd placed at the end of the strand. Nothing. It didn't make sense. Lifting another pearl from the tray, he strung it on the thread only to have it slide off the end and skitter to the floor.

Blast! What was wrong with the clasp? Why wouldn't it hold? And why was it so hot in here? He wiped the sweat from his face and turned down the gas in his jeweler's lamp, but it didn't help. Heat radiated from his body. Harvey must be smelting again. He picked up another bead from the tray. *Come on. Got to get this finished by closing time.* Carefully he threaded another bead on the string. It held. Quickly tying a knot, he added another pearl and another. The strand of grayish, white orbs glistened as he held it up for inspection. But as he reached for the last pearl on his tray, somehow, the clasp gave way once more. One by one, the pearls slid from the necklace and bounced to the floor, each growing four legs and a head as it hit the ground. *No. Blast it. No. No.* Bleating echoed around his workstation as the sheep rocketed around the room before heading in a steady stream out the door.

Rob woke in a pool of sweat. He shook his head to clear the cobwebs of his strange dream, then turned to see if he'd awakened Maddie. She lay curled in a tight ball against the far wall of the wagon. Easing from beneath the covers, Rob slid from the bed and pulled off his sodden union suit. Cool air bathed his heated body. Grabbing the pants and shirt he'd folded on the bench the night before, he slipped them on and tiptoed to the door, shutting it gently behind him once he'd stepped out onto the wagon's tongue.

Goosebumps pebbled on his arms, and a shiver ran down his neck where the cold night breeze lifted his sweat-drenched hair. He welcomed the cold blast like he would a cold drink on a hot summer's day. The cool was sweet as an elixir to his dry, hot skin. He drank it in, then hopped to the ground.

Threading his way around clumps of sleeping sheep, he made his way to a large rock a few feet away and lowered his body to the ground, resting his back against it. One of the dogs who'd been sleeping under the wagon got up and made its way to his side. In the starlight, he could barely make out the white patches on her forehead and front. Rosie, the pretty black-and-white border collie.

"Hey, girl. Come to keep me company?" He scratched behind her ears as she settled in beside him.

Leaning back, he closed his eyes. So, the fever was back. Not surprising, given the drenching he'd had today. Even with a rain slicker, he'd been mighty damp by the time they'd reached camp. And it wasn't like he hadn't been pushing himself pretty hard these last few weeks, what with the move out here and the desire to get them settled. Still, fever was never a good sign. *Please, God, don't let this be a relapse.*

At least Gabe was still here. Opening his eyes, he turned his head toward the shadowy outline of the canvas tent they'd set up a few yards to the left of the wagon. When Jackson offered to leave his younger brother with them for a few weeks, just until they got a feel for the job, he'd jumped at the chance. Learning by doing was one thing but learning without someone to teach him the ropes was just too big a gamble. This way, if he were to have a relapse, at least Maddie would have some help. For now.

The crisp air that had felt so refreshing a few minutes ago began to lose its comfort now that his body had cooled. He drew Rosie in close, hoping to draw from her warmth. He should go back in, but he couldn't summon the energy somehow. Night sweats always left him this way—limp and wrung out like one of Maddie's washrags.

He turned his attention to the stars above him, like diamonds displayed on black velvet. The sky here in the west held a beauty that never ceased to surprise him. Brilliant multicolored sunrises and sunsets, vast expanses of blue that stretched for miles, and now, the stars. He'd seen starlit skies before but never like this. Instead of the tiny pricks of light in the distance that he was used to, these stars hung low and luminous, and in layers so deep that he became lost in the magnitude of it all.

When I consider thy heavens, the work of thy fingers, the moon and the stars, which thou hast ordained; What is man, that thou art mindful of him? and the son of man, that thou visitest him?

Had it been a night such as this when the poet David first sang those words? He closed his eyes and allowed time to slip away. The hard rock beneath his head, the soft bleat of a lamb. He was David. He was Jacob. He was Abraham. He was Adam.

"Rob?" His wife's soft call catapulted him back to the present. He turned his head to see her silhouetted in the doorway of the wagon, her long braid dark against the white of her nightgown. "Are you all right?"

"I'm fine. I'll be in soon. Just give me a minute."

She disappeared from the doorway only to return a few minutes later, wrapped in a quilt. He couldn't help smiling as he spied her heavy boots peeking from beneath her gown when she climbed down from the wagon. Only his Maddie could don such an outfit and still walk with the grace of a queen. The contrast was fitting somehow, like Maddie herself, a woman as beautiful and delicate as the fine lawn of her nightgown with a streak as practical and sturdy as her heavy brown walking boots.

"What are you grinning about?" She knelt beside him and felt his forehead. "Night sweats back?"

He gave a quick nod. She must have noticed the wet bedsheets.

"You shouldn't be out here without a coat. It's freezing."

"Ah, but my beautiful wife has brought me a quilt, so why would I need a coat?" He pulled her down beside him and wrapped her quilt around them both, relishing the feel of her soft, warm body up against him. Rosie, who'd been momentarily disturbed by their movements, settled down at his other side. He relaxed with a sigh as warmth coursed through his limbs. He could get used to this.

He must have dozed because he was jerked awake again by Maddie, who sat up with a start beside him.

"What was that?"

"What?"

"Didn't you hear that? That scream?" She tipped her head to the side expectantly. "There. Hear it?"

A shiver shot up his spine, bristling the hairs at the back of his neck. Yes, he heard it. A wailing, agonizing scream like someone in utmost pain. He sat up and pulled Maddie closer as the sounds faded away. What on earth? From under the wagon bed, Rebel let out a sharp bark. Sheep bells tinkled as several of the sheep near the outer edges of the flock scattered, then stilled and settled again.

"Rob," Maddie's voice shook. "Someone's out there. Someone in a lot of pain."

"Sure sounds like it, but I'm not so sure it's a person. It could be some kind of animal. I've heard that a mountain lion's call sounds like a woman's screams." Her sharp intake of breath told him this may not be the track he wanted to pursue. "But most likely, it's just a bird of some sort. Owls can make some pretty human-sounding calls. Or rabbits."

"That was no rabbit."

"Shhh. There it is again." The screams were fainter this time but no less unsettling. His mind conjured up scenes of a woman in difficult childbirth or a tortured soul writhing on the rack. Beside him, Rosie lifted her head and cocked an ear before settling down once again with her head between her paws. He forced the scenes from his mind. It was an animal. Had to be. A person in that much pain would not be on the move. They sat for several more minutes in silence, but the screams did not continue.

Rob rose to his feet and gave Maddie a hand up. "We'd better get back to bed. Gabe says the sheep head out to graze pretty early in the morning." He looked out into the darkness, eyes searching the outer edges of the flock. "Whatever it is, it's not headed our way."

This time, anyway. But if, in the future, a mountain lion were to attack their sheep, would he have the skills to protect them? He shrugged away his doubts. He'd have to learn the skills, that's all.

Chapter Fourteen

Maddie pinned her brooch to the delicate lace of her high collar and tilted the small mirror hanging above the bench next to the stove to survey the effect. She brushed her fingers across the red and white starburst. The brooch had been a wedding gift from Rob, and she loved the way the garnets and opals sparkled against the snowy white background of her collar. Unfortunately, she owned very few pieces of Rob's craftsmanship, this brooch and a small locket. What was that saying about cobbler's children often going unshod? Oh, well. She had little use for jewelry these days.

She picked up her straw boater with the jaunty red ribbon that matched the one at her waist and pinned it carefully over her topknot. Another glance in the mirror confirmed her outfit was complete. Turning, she picked up her Bible and made her way out of the door of the wagon, careful not to brush her skirts against the stove as she passed.

White lawn was definitely not the most practical choice for a sheep camp, but it was her best summer dress, and today was Sunday. She and Rob had agreed on their very first Sunday in sheep camp that they would do their best to mark each Sunday as a day separate from the rest. So, she dressed each Sunday in her best dress, and together they'd have a simple service, just the two of them, followed by Sunday dinner.

She jumped from the wagon tongue onto the bedding ground and picked her way over the bare dirt, careful to avoid sheep dung on her way to the small stream that bordered the campsite. With Sunday dinner baking in the oven, she had time to prepare for their service, and she knew just where she wanted to do that. She smiled at the thought of the day ahead.

Yes, she missed her Sunday visits with family and Pastor Sherwood's sermons. Still, she'd come to appreciate the intimacy of their own private services here on the mountain. On that first Sunday, they'd decided to study a psalm each week, in addition to any other Bible reading they might do on their own. First, Rob would read the psalm aloud, and they would both seek ways to apply it to other passages they knew. Then they'd each pick out a hymn to sing, something to go with the scripture. Some weeks they would spend part of the afternoon memorizing the psalm they'd picked or at least a portion of it.

Wending her way through a grove of aspen, she came to a large boulder that flanked their small stream. She brushed the dirt from its flat surface and climbed atop, settling her skirts around her. Peace settled on her soul as she drank in the beauty of the morning. The shallow water of the stream trickled over rocks and past a small patch of columbine, its blue glory dappled by the sunlight that filtered through the aspen leaves above them. She tipped her head to watch the leaves flutter and dance in the soft breeze, a shimmer of green and gold. She'd found this spot a few days ago and was glad for the opportunity to enjoy its beauty again. Truth be told, it was this beauty that drew her from the wagon, not the need to prepare.

She laughed now at her naïveté with their first campsite when she had all but begged Jackson to park the wagon amidst a field of pretty, yellow wildflowers. At the time, she hadn't understood his cryptic "Guess it wouldn't hurt to enjoy the flowers for a few hours." By the next evening, the flowers were gone, either trampled or eaten by the sheep, and by the third day, the ground around the wagon was bare and wasted.

Now, when Jackson parked the wagon on rocky bed ground, she offered no complaint. Instead, she looked for beauty in the hidden spots off the sheep trail and relished each patch of flowers she found as the gift it was—a love gift from her heavenly Father hidden away for just her to see.

She opened her Bible to today's psalm, though there was little need. Nor would she be spending any time today on memorization. She'd committed its six short verses to memory long ago. Still, she was glad they'd chosen this psalm for today. In fact, she'd looked forward to discussing it with Rob all week. Their current situation was sure to lend new insight.

Men's voices and the sound of horses' hooves cut through the stillness of the morning. Her heart stuttered a beat. Who could that be? Rob wasn't due back at camp yet. Besides, they'd sent their horses back with Gabe when Jackson last moved their camp. Other than the Garrity brothers, they'd seen no one else since moving out here.

She froze in place, hoping the trees would hide her from view, at least until she could ascertain who the men were. She certainly didn't want to entertain strangers, especially men, when Rob wasn't in camp.

"Halloo! Anyone here? Mrs. Skivington?"

Tension drained from her shoulders. Jackson and Gabe. She caught a glimpse of the dark-haired man and boy through a parting in the trees. She hadn't expected them on a Sunday. On a Sunday! Her relief was replaced by disappointment when she realized what those words meant. All her plans for the day would be replaced with the arduous task of moving camp. And on a Sunday.

"Maddie?"

She could see them both over by the wagon now. Gabe had climbed up to glance in the open part of the Dutch door. She slid from her perch atop the boulder and went to greet them.

"She must be out with Rob," Gabe was saying as she stepped into the clearing.

"No, I'm here." Maddie pasted what she hoped was a welcoming smile on her face. Both brothers turned at her voice, Jackson's answering smile fading into a puzzled stare. What in the world? She glanced down. Was there a bug on her? Had she soiled her gown with dirt after all?

Oh. Heat built in her cheeks. Her best dress probably seemed a bit out of place here in the wilderness.

She looked up to see Gabe whisper something in Jackson's ear. Her own embarrassment was soon mirrored in the flush that darkened the big man's face beneath his tan.

"Sorry, ma'am. Gabe here tells me you and your husband are Sabbath observers. I . . . we . . . I guess we don't keep much track of days out here." He had taken off his hat and was kneading its brim with his fingers. "We'd be glad to stay over and move you tomorrow. Or we could come back."

"Don't be silly." Her embarrassment dissipated in the face of his obvious discomfort. "We wouldn't think of causing you any extra trouble. Didn't Jesus himself say something about not muzzling the ox on the Sabbath? Or was that Paul? No matter. I'm sure the same applies to sheep." The discomfort did not ease from his face, and no wonder with her babbling on this way. She'd have to try another approach. "We'd love to share our Sunday dinner with you, and if you have even one letter for me in that pack of yours, all will be forgiven."

A slow smile eased Jackson's worried features. "Not just one letter, ma'am, but three."

Three letters! Any disappointment she'd felt at the day's interruption quickly fled at the thought of letters from home.

"And I got the milk and eggs you asked for. Brought some butter along too," he said.

"Eggs, milk, and butter? Oh, Jackson, I could kiss you." Too late, she realized her words had brought the embarrassed flush back to his cheeks. She'd learned early on that their camp tender was not nearly as used to her teasing as her brothers. "Don't worry." She smiled up at him, hoping to put him at ease. "I'll save my kisses for Rob, but you might find an extra piece of pie on your plate at dinner."

"I'd be happy to take the pie, ma'am." He swung down off his horse and walked over to the packhorse, pulling two quart-sized bottles of milk out of the saddlebag. "We won't unpack everything since we'll be moving camp in a few hours, but you might want to put these in the stream until we leave."

Maddie hurried forward to take the precious bottles from him. He turned and took two more out of the bag on the other side. A gallon of milk. Maddie felt like dancing as she headed toward a small pool in the stream where they kept their perishables.

"Mrs. Baldwin says she'll be glad to send a gallon of milk and a dozen eggs whenever I bring supplies. Do you think that will be enough?"

"It's wonderful. Thank you so much for arranging that for us." A gallon a week fell far short of Dr. Waite's recommended two quarts a day, but it was so much more than she had expected to get being so far from town. Surely any quantity of eggs and milk would be better than nothing. And with all the fresh air and exercise lately, Rob's appetite had improved. Hopefully, he would have no trouble keeping them down.

A tinkling of bells in the distance announced that Rob was on his way, and soon sheep began spilling through the trees that rimmed the campsite. A minute later, Rob and the dogs came into sight. He waved a hand and wove his way through the pooling sheep to reach their side.

Rob greeted Jackson with a hearty handclasp. "Didn't expect you today, though I guess I should have. Pasture's been harder and harder to find these past few days."

"Sorry to disturb your Sunday, sir." Jackson looked over at Maddie, then back at Rob. "I told Mrs. Skivington I'd be glad to stay over or come back if need be. The days pretty much run together for us out here, so I . . ."

A twinkle came into Rob's eyes. "So you weren't expecting to find my wife all decked out in her going-to-meeting clothes?" He shot a grin at her, and she could feel the heat coming back into her face as she remembered the looks on Jackson and Gabe had given her when they'd first seen her step from the trees. "No need to apologize. If Maddie didn't keep close track on her calendar in the wagon, I don't know if we'd even know what month it was, let alone the day of the week. Tell you what. The sheep'll need to rest before we start off again. If you and Gabe wouldn't mind joining us for a little Bible reading and dinner, we'll get packed up right after that. Should have plenty of time to get the move in today without your needing to stay over."

"You'll like the service, Jack. Especially if Mrs. Skivington sings." Gabe had walked over from where he'd been greeting the dogs. "She's got the prettiest singing voice I've ever heard."

"I've thought the same thing myself, many a time." Rob clapped the boy on the shoulder. "Good to see you again, Gabe. In fact, I was kind of wishing you were still around this morning when the sheep decided to take off well before the crack of dawn."

Gabe grinned and shook his head. "And I'm kinda glad I wasn't." During the two weeks he had stayed with them, Gabe and Rob had often ribbed each other about which of them would chase the sheep that wanted to leave the bedding ground early. Maddie smiled to see the two picking up where they'd left off.

"Well, we'd better get to it then. Give me a few minutes to wash up and grab my Bible, then I'll join you by the campfire."

Soon the four of them were gathered around the outdoor firepit. She and Rob occupied a crude bench made from a plank of wood balanced between two rocks. Gabe sat cross-legged in the grass, and Jackson found a seat on her upended washtub.

An awkward silence descended on the group. Beside her, Rob

cleared his throat and leaned forward, elbows on his knees, Bible dangling from one hand with his forefinger marking his place.

"Uh . . ." he cleared his throat again. "I know we've called this a service." He glanced over at Jackson. "But really, it's a lot more informal than that. Maddie and I, when we first got out here, well, we wanted to do something to make Sunday stand out from the rest of the week. So we've gotten into the habit of meeting here before we eat our Sunday dinner. We'll read a scripture, pray and sometimes sing a hymn. Nothing special, really, not anything like a real church service, just something we like to do."

"Don't worry about that on our account," Jackson said. "Living out on Pa's ranch like we do, Gabe and I haven't been to church much. Anything's fine by us."

"Well, then, how about I start with a prayer, and we'll go from there?"

Maddie bowed her head, trying to focus on the words of Rob's prayer and not on her shock over Jackson's admission. If she and Rob were to continue to be ranchers and have children, would they grow up like Jackson and Gabe, never going to church? She was reconciled to not meeting regularly with other believers for now because she considered it temporary, but what if it wasn't? Could she really go years without attending a real church?

" . . . acceptable in your sight, Lord. Amen."

Rob's 'amen' brought her back to the present. He had opened his Bible and was looking at her, a question in his eyes. When she nodded, he began. "Maddie and I have been reading through the psalms since we came out here. Today we've chosen Psalm 23. We've both been looking forward to diving into it with a fresh perspective. Maybe you two can relate?"

When the Garrity brothers didn't say anything, he cleared his throat and began to read. "The Lord is my Shepherd. I shall not want. . . ."

Maddie listened to the familiar words, trying to hear them as if for the first time. The past six weeks of tending to the needs of 2500 unpredictable sheep had certainly taught her something about the heart of God. The level of tender care described in the psalm made her all the more aware of God's love for her. He was her provider. She could trust He would provide for them here. Hadn't He already provided the milk and eggs Rob so desperately needed?

They each offered a few observations on God's character based on the words of the psalm. Then Maddie smiled at Jackson. "And I now understand why David specifically says God leads his flocks by *still* waters."

Jackson grinned. "You haven't been trying to get them dumb sheep to cross any more rivers, have you?"

"We wouldn't dream of trying anything so foolish without you and Gabe around. And now, how about some dinner?"

"Aren't you going to sing for us, Mrs. Skivington?"

Maddie paused, not knowing how to answer Gabe's question. She had planned to sing earlier when it had just been her and Rob, but with both Gabe and Jackson as part of the audience, she suddenly felt shy.

"Maybe we could sing a duet," Rob said.

"Are you sure? Your voice—"

"Has been much stronger since we've been out here. I'd really like to give it a try. You were thinking of singing our favorite, right?"

She nodded. "The Lord's My Shepherd" was the obvious choice. With its lilting melody and gentle harmony, it had been one of their favorite duets during their courting years, so they both knew the words by heart. The thought of singing it together again was a joy she couldn't deny either herself or Rob.

At Rob's go-ahead, she took a deep breath and sang alone through the first verse.

> *"The Lord's my Shepherd, I'll not want.*
> *He makes me down to lie.*

> *In pastures green, he leadeth me*
> *The quiet waters by."*

As Rob's baritone joined in on the second verse, she closed her eyes, savoring the harmony of their blended voices. It had been so long.

The third verse had always been Rob's. She dropped off to let him sing. His voice was hoarse and not as strong as it had once been, but he was singing again.

> *"Yea, though I walk in death's dark vale,*
> *yet will I fear no ill;*
> *for thou art with me; and thy rod*
> *and staff my comfort still."*

How blithely they'd sung those words during those early days, never suspecting death's shadow would soon darken their lives. Her throat seized, and her notes wobbled when she tried to join in again. Clenching her jaw, she willed herself to focus only on the notes but still could not sing again until Rob reached the last stanza.

> *"Goodness and mercy all my life*
> *shall surely follow me;*
> *and in God's house forevermore*
> *my dwelling place shall be."*

She sat a moment with her eyes closed, letting the peace of those words wash over her. Goodness and mercy and hope of heaven. Truly they were blessed no matter what life brought them.

"I told ya, you'd like the singing."

Gabe's words broke into her thoughts. She'd completely forgotten their audience.

"You're right. I don't think I've ever heard a prettier singing voice, Mrs. Skivington. Other than Ma's, that is."

"Your mother sings?"

Jackson shrugged. "She used to. Haven't seen her since I was ten, so I wouldn't know if she still does."

There was a story there that begged telling, but something in the set of Jackson's face told her not to pry.

"Well," Rob said. "I don't know how pretty *my* singing was, but it sure felt good to sing again." He stood up and held out a hand to help her to her feet. "There's a prairie chicken in the oven that's just begging to be eaten, boys. Let's get to it, and then we can pack up."

Chapter Fifteen

That night Maddie lit the oil lamp that hung above the table in their wagon and pulled out the packet of letters Jackson had brought. She'd purposely left reading them until this moment, so she'd have time to savor each one. Her anticipation had been building all day.

Three thick envelopes. Three connections to family and friends. Her fingers trembled slightly as she slit into the first one and pulled out several sheets of paper filled to the corners with the flowing script of Rob's sister Alice. She glanced at Rob, who lay stretched out on the bunk above her.

"Do you want me to read these to you, or do you want to wait and read them yourself?"

He lay with his arm thrown over his eyes and made no movement in response to her question. Asleep already? He'd only now laid down.

Finally, his words came out slow and low. "Better save them for me. I'm too tired to listen tonight."

No matter. She'd enjoy sharing them with him again later. Letters from home were like conversations with the ones they loved, only better. Unlike spoken words, these could be pulled out and enjoyed again and again. She picked up Alice's letter and began to read:

Dear Rob and Maddie,

Mum has asked that I pen a letter from all of us. Maddie smiled. Though Mother Skivington could read anything set in front of her, she'd never learned to write so much as her own name. Of course, Alice would do the writing.

We received your letter of the 15th and were surprised to hear of your decision to become sheep ranchers, though it does seem an ideal way for Rob to spend time in the open air. Are you able to get into town very often?

Often? Ha. How about not at all? Alice would be shocked to hear she had not so much as seen another woman in the past five weeks.

How is Rob responding to the climate and work? Have you seen an improvement in his health? Maddie glanced at her husband's prone form. Truthfully, despite his exhaustion, he was holding up quite well. His cough, of course, was ever-present, but certainly not any worse. And tonight's fatigue was not surprising given the amount of work they'd done today moving the camp and getting settled. Surely, his singing this morning was proof that at least his voice was getting stronger. She was hopeful. Yes. Hopeful.

Mum wants to know if the tonic she sent with Rob is helping? She says she can send another bottle as often as he needs. Oh, dear. How was she to tell Mum that her son had taken one sniff of Dr. Wilson's Cough Elixir and poured the whole bottle out into the grass?

"About the only thing that concoction will provide me is a pounding headache," he had said.

Even if they told Mother Skivington the elixir didn't help, she'd just find another pill or potion to throw her money after. She couldn't blame Mum for trying, but she hated to see her waste her money, especially when she had so little to waste.

The weather has been so hot here, we've not wanted to do much of anything that wasn't absolutely necessary. Seems we do nothing more of an evening but sit out on the porch and fan ourselves. The boys took a half-holiday last Saturday and went down to Asbury Park to swim. They plan to go again on the fourth and want us to come and make a day of it, but Mum, Peachie, and I will probably save the rail fare and go to Military Park instead for the parade and brass band. George wants to know if you've seen any Indians or outlaws yet.

Maddie smiled. Rob's younger brothers would be surprised at how tame their life was out here. Other than the landscape, which was truly spectacular, Wyoming bore little resemblance to the West described in the dime novels the boys found so intriguing. She quickly scanned the last few lines of Alice's letter, folded it away, and reached for the letter from Jenny.

Dear Maddie,

I was so pleased to get your letter and to hear that you and Rob are becoming seasoned sheepherders. I am working with Ted and a few friends to plan a camping trip to the mountains. If it works out, maybe we can come visit your camp on our way. I hope you don't think I am forward by inviting myself, but I have missed you so much since you've left.

Grace is still not the sister/friend I had hoped she would be, but I have met some new friends I know you will like, Will Dickinson and his sister Sara. They are the younger sister and brother of Emma and Julia, whom we met at the quilting. Will used to work at the bank with Teddy and has been his friend since he came to Wyoming. When he and Teddy get together, they are so much fun. They make my sides hurt with laughter.

His sister Sara is such a sweetheart. Some days I find myself wishing Ted had married her instead of Grace. She is just the type of girl I imagined Grace to be. (Please don't think ill of me for having said that. My pen seems to run ahead of me and say all the things I was determined not to say.)

Lest you think there is something brewing between Will and me, I must admit he only pays attention to me in an effort to make Stella Jones jealous. That knowledge at first was quite lowering to my self-esteem, but since I feel for him nothing stronger than the love I feel for Teddy, I don't really mind. I enjoy being squired around by a handsome man, and truth be told, I don't mind making Stella squirm, though she's never given me the slightest sign she notices. It's only the increase in frostiness I get from Grace whenever I'm with Will that gives me the impression his ploy may be working.

Oh, Maddie, I do wish you could have been here for the fourth of July festivities. I'm not sure I can even describe the fun we had during that day. Ranch families came in from miles around, and cowboys from all over the state came to compete in the rodeo events. (Yes, I've finally seen my handsome cowboys, and cowboys in all other shapes, forms, and sizes as well.)

And I've seen Indians too! A large group came down from the reservation and set up their teepees at the rodeo site.

I could try to describe the events to you, but my words wouldn't do them justice. We watched steer roping and rope tricks, and all types of horse races. Will and Ted competed against each other in the buggy races, and Sara and I were at a loss as to which brother we wanted most to win. Ted won that one, but since Will won in a later race, all was forgiven.

Mrs. Parkhurst just about had a conniption fit when I said I wanted to compete in one of the horse races next year, but I didn't say it to get her hackles up (though heaven help me, it's always a bonus). I really do think women should be allowed to compete, and several others agreed with me. Many of the rancher's daughters can ride just as well as their brothers. A women's relay would be so much fun. Sara, Julia, and I have already agreed to form a team next year.

Oh, but I haven't told you about the most exciting part of the day. Do you remember Mr. Sparrowhawk at the stage stop who stood up for us against those rude boys? Well, he competed in most of the cowboy events, and he's every bit as magnificent as ever, but the best part of all was the wild horse race that closed off the program. I can't begin to describe that race. When the gun went off, the horses leaped every which way. Most of the riders struggled just to stay on their horses, let alone get them to run where they wanted.

Now, I am not normally a betting person, but I bet Sara a whole quarter that Mr. Sparrowhawk would win the race. She was sure Mayor

Farlow's young son would win, and for much of the race, it was neck to neck. It wasn't until the last turn that young Farlow's horse bolted and fell. By the time he was up again, Mr. Sparrowhawk had crossed the finish line. I don't need to tell you I was jumping up and down like a schoolgirl by the time the race was over. Mrs. Parkhurst was most unhappy, but I can't remember when I've had a better time.

I know I've rambled on and on, and I hope I haven't bored you terribly with all my silliness. How I wish we could sit down for tea and share our news like old times. Since we can't, I'll have to satisfy myself with this letter and hope to hear more from you soon.

Your affectionate friend,

Jenny

Maddie set her letter aside with a laugh. Jenny was just as lively by letter as she was in person, and she'd finally seen her Indians. She'd have to remember to tell George and Fred about it next time she wrote home.

The last envelope contained three letters, one from Edie and two shorter ones from Les and little Hazel. She settled back to enjoy the one from Edie first, full of news about the family and their friends from the neighborhood and church. As she read, she imagined herself standing beside Edie at the kitchen sink while they washed and dried dishes. That had always been their time to catch up on daily news. Reading slowly, she savored each line. Sally Rodgers had another new beau. Mrs. Kennedy finally had her girl after six sons. More than any of the previous letters, this one took her back to home territory, back to the life she'd left behind, to all that was familiar and dear, and yes, ordinary. But, oh, how she longed for that ordinary right now.

Les's letter was short, full of the baseball game he'd attended that week and, of course, the inevitable questions about cowboys and Indians. Shaking her head, she picked up the final letter from little Hazel. Tears pooled in her eyes as she read the first words:

Dear Mama Maddie, (Hazel's pet name for her.)

I miss you so much. When can you come home? I like the pictures Rob drew of your dogs, Rosie and Rebel. I wish I could have a dog. We had our Sunday school picnic last week out at Robinson's. Horrid Billy Watkins put a caterpillar down May McMurty's dress. She screamed something awful. He tried to put one down my back, but I run too fast. Edie let me bake a cake for Papa's birthday. It was almost as good as the one I baked for you except without the flowers. I am having a tea party today for Isabella Carlotta and Queen Jezebel under the lilac bushes down by the gate. I wish you could come. I am sending you kisses and a great big hug. Please come home soon.

Love from your little girl,
Hazel

Maddie swallowed hard and blinked against the tears that would come no matter how hard she tried to hold them at bay. How she missed them. All of them.

The Lord is my Shepherd, I shall not want . . . words from the morning's psalm seemed to mock her as the tears dripped down her cheeks. She *did* want. She wanted her little cottage in Morris back. She wanted her weekly visits to Father's to see Edie and the boys. She wanted to hold Hazel and smell her little girl smell and hear all about her day. She wanted her husband whole and healthy. She wanted to look to the future with joy and confidence instead of this daily fear of what each day might bring.

Most of all she wanted to be able to say those words, *I shall not want*, and mean them. But deep inside, she knew she couldn't.

Chapter Sixteen

❧

Two hundred head were too many to ignore, though if Rob had his way he'd leave them to their fate. Seems like all he'd done today was chase wandering bands of sheep up hills, down valleys, over streams, and into crevices. Rob followed Rosie as she led the way down yet another rocky incline. His head was pounding, and, honestly, he couldn't care less if he never saw another of the stupid wooly creatures.

Some shepherd he was. The Good Shepherd of Bible fame left his flock to search for just one stray lamb. Here he was sorely tempted to abandon two hundred.

Well, maybe not the entire two hundred. Two hundred head equaled $800, and tired though he was, he wasn't ready to whistle away $800. Had the shepherd of that story been motivated by money as well? Somehow, he'd always assumed the man had acted purely out of love for that one lost sheep. Guess that's why they dubbed him the "good" shepherd.

Well, anyone with half a brain knew *he* wasn't good. What good husband pretended to sleep while his wife cried over letters from home? For that matter, what good husband dragged his wife into the wilderness just because he couldn't bear the thought of leaving her behind? No. A good husband would make the sacrifice, offer the solace, shield and protect. He was anything but good.

And it was the money and only the money that kept his feet plodding down this path in what was beginning to feel like a futile attempt to find this latest band of wanderers.

What had gotten into his sheep this morning anyway? Usually, a new campsite guaranteed him a few quiet days of grazing close to the wagon. But this morning, the sheep had headed out hours before dawn, and once he'd found the main band, it had taken him the better part of the morning to hunt down the strays.

Hard to tell exactly how many were still missing. Gabe had told him to use his black sheep as counters. Two black sheep missing meant somewhere around two hundred head were still unaccounted for. Hopefully, those last few hundred had at least stuck together.

He and Rosie had been following a stream for the better part of an hour. They'd started out heading into the wind, another trick Gabe had taught him, but as the day wore on, the wind had died down, giving him very little to go on. He hoped they were still headed in the right direction. The stream was wide and fast-moving, so he was pretty sure the sheep had not crossed it on their own, but he was beginning to wonder if he might be wiser to head back to his main band and continue the search after dinner. Would his sheep, like Bo Peep's, come home if he just left them alone? Tempting thought, but not very likely. He was more likely to find them all dead at the foot of some ravine if he didn't find them soon.

Rosie, who'd been loping along a short distance in front of him, stopped short and lifted her nose to sniff the air. With a sharp yelp, she bounded up a rocky outcropping and disappeared through a strand of trees to their left. Rob scrambled up the bank behind her, trusting the dog's instincts, using his staff as a walking stick. He had to stop at the top of the ridge to cough and spit and catch his breath before heading into the trees behind her. A few minutes later, the welcome sound of bleating and tinkling of bells told him she'd been right. Sheep were ahead. Hopefully, *his* sheep and not some other band.

He soon reached a clearing and saw what appeared to be all two hundred wanderers. A quick check of the brand painted into the wool of the nearest sheep confirmed them as his. With any luck, he'd be home in time for dinner after all. He gave a short whistle, but there really was no need. Rosie had already begun the task of rounding the sheep for travel. He leaned on his staff while she worked her magic.

Could a man fall asleep standing up? If it were at all possible, he believed he could master the art if he stood much longer. Closing his eyes, he dragged out a breath through a chest so heavy he could swear a man sat on it. Heavy chest, heavy head, he dreaded what those symptoms could portend. A hemorrhage was the last thing he needed right now. *Please God, not that. Not now.*

Loud bleating brought his attention back to the herd. Rosie was at the far end of the field trying to herd an old ewe back toward the rest of the flock. The dog would no sooner steer the ewe in the right direction before she would break off and return to her former spot, bleating and kicking back at Rosie's sharp nips. He walked over to investigate.

Drawing closer, he recognized the ewe. He'd dubbed her Mrs. Finch in honor of the head schoolmarm back at Ward 9 School. A few months ago, when Tavis told him his sheep were like people, each with distinct personalities, he'd thought the man as daft as his dad. All sheep looked alike. How could anyone possibly tell one from another?

But it hadn't taken him more than a couple of weeks before he too began to see those distinct personalities in his own sheep. Mrs. Finch, like her namesake, was especially given to intimidating stares and lengthy lectures, both of which she was employing on Rosie right now. Calling the dog to his side, he looked around for Fred, Mrs. Finch's lamb, whom he'd also named, this one after his little brother due to his propensity to find trouble. No sign of him.

His heart sank as he realized the old ewe was standing on the edge of a ravine. He walked to her side and looked down, dreading what he'd see.

Sure enough, on a rocky ledge about ten feet down lay a bundle of white stained with red. But only one bundle. Knowing sheep as he did, it could have been a whole lot worse. As many as twenty or thirty sheep could easily have followed young Fred into that ravine. So why did his heart feel so heavy? That'd teach him to name his sheep.

As a wether, Fred's days had been numbered anyway. A few more months, and he'd have been off to market. If he'd made it that long. As adventurous as Fred had been, he could just as easily have become coyote bait. They'd lost several of their lambs and a few of the older ewes to coyotes already. But this one had been special, his antics drawing their attention early on, climbing the older ewes backs while they rested, leapfrogging with other young lambs, nuzzling Maddie's books when she read in the field.

"You gotta let him go." He squatted down beside Mrs. Finch, addressing the words to himself as much as to the old ewe. He might be a city boy, but he knew enough not to grow too attached to the livestock. Or thought he did. He supposed he should take the body home for mutton stew, but the thought turned his stomach. Leaving Fred on the ledge as prey for predators didn't sit right either.

He judged the distance between him and the lamb. If he were to climb onto the narrow rock outcropping jutting out a few feet below the bank, he could probably reach Fred with the hook of his staff. Much too risky an undertaking for a dead lamb, though. Better just to leave him.

He turned to go, nudging Mrs. Finch with the end of his staff. Her plaintive bleating tugged at his heart, but it was the fragile, threadlike answering baa from the ravine that stopped him in his tracks. Turning, he looked down at the wooly bundle. Sure enough, the lamb's head which had been tucked down into his body moments before, was now raised as he tried to answer his mother's call.

Rob hopped down onto the ledge. Though narrow, there was still plenty of room for him to lie on his belly. Reaching out, he stretched the hooked end of his staff until it touched the top of Fred's head. The lamb looked up, giving him the opportunity to get his crook into position. Carefully hooking the lamb under his front legs, he slowly raised him hand over hand. *Please, God, don't let him struggle.*

If Fred fell off the hook now, the ledge might not catch him, and he'd fall to certain death into the rocks and stream far below. But the lamb hung limp, a testament no doubt to its weakened state. How long had he been down there? An hour? Maybe two.

Finally, Rob pulled Fred onto the ledge beside him and began a careful inspection of the animal's injuries. A gash along his side had been the cause of the rusty red streaks on the lamb's wool, but the cut was not deep and had long since stopped its bleeding. More troubling was the lamb's rear left leg that hung at an awkward angle. Definitely broken. No normal bone was meant to bend that way. The little lamb flinched and struggled to get away when he reached to gently touch it.

"Steady there, Fred. No need to hurt it any further." The bone would have to be set, but maybe it could wait until he got the herd back to camp. He'd probably need Maddie to hold the lamb before he could do anything for it anyway. Tucking Fred under his arm, he leaned his weight onto his staff and pushed to his feet. A smattering of pebbles and dirt hit his hat as he rose, and he turned to find himself eye level with the brown legs of a horse.

"Well, well, well," a mocking voice forced his gaze upward. "I thought it was just the scabs we was smelling, but looks like we got ourselves a smelly ole scab herder, as well."

Though he'd only met him once, Rob instantly recognized

the rude cowboy who had accosted Maddie and Jenny at Sparrowhawk's road ranch. Behind him on a gray gelding was another youth, probably one of the cohorts who was with him that day. Great. Just what he needed to make this morning a complete disaster.

"Morning, Jake." He forced himself to be courteous.

The youth's eyes narrowed, then recognition dawned.

"Why, if it ain't the jeweler." He turned to his companion. "Lookee here, Zeke. The jeweler's a scab herder now." He looked down with a leer. "Can't say as I think much of your choice of occupations."

"Can't say as I asked your opinion," Rob shot back.

"Oooo. The scab herder has a sassy tongue. Mighty brave of a man in his position."

The venom in Jake's voice caused a small frisson of fear to snake up Rob's back and lift the hairs on the back of his neck. He hadn't realized until now how vulnerable he was, standing on this narrow ledge five feet below ground level with nothing more to defend himself with than a measly shepherd's staff. Both young men had rifles strapped to their saddles.

Jake glanced away, looking over the small band of errant sheep which Rosie had managed to herd into a compact mass about fifty feet away. "Where are those two pretty jewels you had with you last time we met? I wouldn't mind renewing my acquaintance with them."

Rob struggled to keep a lid on the heat within. Lucky for Jake, he was stuck on this ledge because planting a fist into the boy's obnoxious mouth would feel pretty good about now. It'd also go a long way toward relieving the frustrations of the morning. Instead, he chose to ignore the question.

"So, Jake, what brings you into our neighborhood?" Even he had to admit his own question came out sounding more accusatory than friendly.

"*Your* neighborhood?" The boy's face turned ugly. "Let me tell you something, scabman. My family has ranched in these parts long before you ever got here. Maybe you should tell me what you're doing in *my* neighborhood?"

Rob knew the public lands were open to any rancher, whether of sheep or cattle, so the boy might have a point.

"Oh. I didn't realize. Cy had told me your family's ranch was down on the Sweetwater."

The boy's flush told him he'd hit a nerve. What type of nerve, exactly, he couldn't tell.

"Yeah, well, we're tracking a mountain lion. If you scab herders would take care of the varmints around here, we cattlemen wouldn't have to come up here and do it for you."

"I'll be glad to take care of it if I see it. Truth is, I haven't seen any sign of one near here." He decided not to mention the pawprint Tavis had seen or the screams he and Maddie had heard their first night in the mountains. That was weeks ago. If a mountain lion were still in the area, surely they would have lost some sheep to it by now.

"Smart cat, then. Seems he likes steak better than mutton." Both Zeke and Jake hooted at Jake's lame joke.

He waited for their laughter to subside. "Anything else I can do for you boys?"

"Yeah, you could do something about the stink around here. Hey, Zeke, is it just me, or is that sheep smell getting worse? I almost can't take it." Grinning, Jake whipped a large, red handkerchief from his pocket with a loud crack and waved it toward the huddled flock of sheep.

The animals startled at the first crack of the cloth then scattered as the red banner continued to wave in the breeze. White-hot anger blossomed in his chest as Rob watched the sheep stream off in ten different directions through the trees, Rosie in hot pursuit. Great.

Jake settled the handkerchief under his nose and smirked down at Rob. "That's better. Now I can breathe again."

All Rob's pent-up frustration from the morning came out in one mighty roar. Without thinking, he swung his shepherd's staff at the legs of Jake's horse. The bay reared, hoofs pawing the air in front of him, then took off at a gallop while Jake struggled to keep his seat.

"You shouldn't oughta done that, mister."

Rob looked up to see the barrel of Zeke's rifle pointed straight at his head. He froze. He'd forgotten about Zeke. He'd forgotten about the guns. Seems he'd forgotten a lot of things. Would this boy truly shoot him over something so foolish? He held his breath and waited. He hadn't felt this vulnerable since he tried to take on the school bully on the playground back in grade school. If he remembered right, that hadn't ended well either.

Hoofbeats to the right of him told him Jake was returning, but Rob kept his eyes trained on Zeke's gun.

Jake reined his horse in beside Zeke's. "Not the brightest tool in the shed, is he, Zeke? But then he's a scab herder, so what can you expect?"

"Want me to shoot him for you? I'd be glad to."

"Naw. Another day, maybe. Today I'm feeling right generous. But I'm warning you, jeweler. You keep those scabs of yours out of my way. Next time we meet, I might not be so nice. Come on, Zeke. We got work to do."

Rob waited until the two cowboys were out of sight before slowly releasing his breath. If only he could release his anger just as easily. He hated feeling this weak and defenseless. They were kids, really, boys like Fred and George, but put a gun in their hands, and they thought they were invincible. How he wished he could meet them on even ground, no guns, no wounded sheep to hamper him. Maybe he could pound some manners into them.

Instead, he had two hundred head of sheep to find. Again. And an injured lamb to care for. He placed Fred on the bank and pulled himself up off the ledge before scooping the lamb up again. Standing, he settled Fred on his shoulders and took up his staff, bringing to mind a picture he'd once seen in his family's Bible.

Rob snorted. The resemblance, if any, was purely superficial, as anyone would know, could they but see the murderous thoughts boiling just beneath his surface. Good Shepherd? Hardly. Today he was anything but "good." And the worst part? He didn't even want to be.

Chapter Seventeen

❧❧❧

Maddie folded the last clean dish towel and laid it on the pile with the rest. Digging a fist into the ache in her lower back, she lowered herself onto the wagon bench and ran her eyes over the pile of clean clothes and linens on the table in front of her. She blew out a long sigh. The end of another wash day was always such a relief.

Still, she could remember summer wash days back home that had been far less pleasant. Though primitive, there was certainly something to be said for washing over an open fire in a pretty mountain meadow. And the warm, dry sunshine of the late August afternoon was a perfect recipe for fresh-smelling sheets and quickly dried towels. Of course, winter wash days could be a different story entirely, but she'd deal with that when the time came. "Sufficient unto the day . . .." as the Bible said.

She stretched her legs across to the opposite bench and laid her head back against the wall of the wagon. She wouldn't rest long, just a minute or two. Her day's work wasn't done yet. The clothes needed to be tucked away in the drawers beneath the bed. The large pots of dirty wash water needed to be emptied, supper needed to be tended to. But Rob wouldn't be home for several hours yet, and supper would be simple fare as it always was on wash day. A pot of beans and bacon simmered on the stove beside her. She had time.

A fly droned in the window above the bed. A gentle breeze wafted through the wagon, causing a loose strand of her hair to tickle at her cheek. She reached up to brush it away, feeling the fine strands catch on the rough skin on her hands. She should find the hand salve. Wash days were murder on hands, and the air that allowed the clothes to dry so quickly out here wasn't as beneficial to her skin. But that same dry air had also given her husband improved health. His appetite was better. He'd even gained some weight back since coming here. Best of all, no hemorrhages. She'd sacrifice soft hands for that any day.

She sank into the heaviness that glued her body to the bench. Just a few more minutes, then she'd get up and get that salve.

A faraway peal of laughter seeped into her consciousness, pulling her from her doze. Laughter? She must be dreaming.

Yet, the sound came again. She tipped an ear toward the wagon door. Yes. Those were voices. Women's voices. She sprang to her feet and was halfway to the door before she recalled her appearance. She groaned. Could she never be dressed appropriately for visitors? She pulled off her soiled apron, tucked her shirtwaist into her skirt, and smoothed her hair. It wasn't much, but it would have to do. Whoever was visiting would just have to take her as she was.

Peeking her head around the doorway, she saw several horses coming through the trees on the far side of the meadow. On a pretty roan right in front, blond curls spilling from beneath an enormous hat, sat Jenny, riding astride and grinning from ear to ear.

Maddie jumped to the ground and began to run. Jenny slid from her horse and met her with a squeal halfway, pulling her into a tight embrace. Maddie hugged her back just as tight, tears pricking from behind her eyelids. Goodness. What a watering pot she'd become. Not that she cared. She hadn't seen another woman in almost three months. Three months!

"What are you doing here?"

"I told you I'd come to visit."

Their words tumbled out on top of each other, leaving them laughing and breathless. Jenny pulled out of their embrace but held onto Maddie's hands.

"So, you're not angry with me for not giving you any notice we were coming? Truly, I didn't know we'd be able to come until yesterday and didn't have the time to write and tell you."

Maddie squeezed her friend's fingers and laughed. "Angry? I'm so delighted to see you I could burst. You know you are welcome anytime." She looked over at the growing crowd of riders. "All of you."

My, there were quite a lot of them. Trust Jenny to travel with a crowd. Maddie gave a smile and nod to Ted Westraven, then turned her attention to the ladies in the group, a young woman about Jenny's age with red hair and friendly blue eyes and . . .

"Emma?" Maddie blinked. Was she still dozing? What was their hostess from the quilting bee in Lander doing way out here?

"Oh, you do remember me. I'm so glad." The friendly, easy manner Maddie had enjoyed that long-ago day at the Ladies Aide meeting sparkled from the woman's countenance. "When Mrs. Parkhurst insisted on a chaperone for this camping trip Jenny arranged, I just couldn't resist. Who better to chaperone, I told her, than a bossy, older sister? So Drew and I left the kids and the store in the capable hands of my parents and escaped for a little vacation.

"I don't believe you've met my husband, Drew." She gestured to the stocky man at her side wearing a western hat and a mustache that could rival Rob's. "And this is my sister, Sara. And my brother, Will, is hiding somewhere back there." At her gesture, a young man waved from the back of the group.

"These are the Dickinsons I told you about in my letters. I know you're going to love them as much as I do," Jenny said.

"And, of course, you remember Mr. Sparrowhawk from the stage stop?"

Sure enough, the Buffalo Bill look-alike was there as well, still sporting his buckskins and shoulder-length hair.

"Yes, of course. Mr. Sparrowhawk. So good to see you again," she said.

The last of the group was a handsome young man with a dimple in his chin and warm, brown eyes. Dressed in an eastern, three-piece suit, he looked out of place next to everyone else's more casual western attire.

"Oh, I almost forgot Ben!" Jenny said, waving a hand in his direction. "This is Mr. Bennett. Remember me telling you about my Aunt Bethany in Newark? And my job at the law office? Ben was my boss and also my aunt's neighbor. He and Ted and I spent our summers together back when we were young. He showed up in Lander last week just out of the blue. He said we had promised him a western adventure, so, of course, we had to organize this camping trip. Mr. Sparrowhawk has promised to show us all the best spots for hunting and fishing."

"Well, welcome, everyone. I'd invite you in"—Maddie glanced over at their little wagon, then turned back to the group and gave a shrug—"but we mostly live 'out.' So, please, feel free to tether your horses and make yourselves at home. You are staying the night, aren't you?" She looked anxiously at Jenny. She hoped they hadn't planned on just passing through.

Jenny's nod reassured her. "Tonight and all day tomorrow. But you're not to worry about where we'll sleep. We've brought all our supplies with us. We'll just pitch our tents and have a jolly time camping out."

"And you're not to worry about feeding all of us, either." Emma had dismounted and come over to join them. "As Jenny says, we've brought all our supplies with us. We have enough for ten days of camping, so don't worry about us at all."

"But I have a large pot of beans and bacon you are all

welcome to share. And plenty of bread and some gooseberry pies. You must let me do my part since you are my guests."

"Gooseberry pie? I love gooseberry pie," Sara piped in, having handed her horse off to her brother.

"Then let me show you my wee kitchen, and we'll see what we can scrounge up for supper."

Chapter Eighteen

"So, what do you think?" Rob tried to gauge Sparrowhawk's reaction across the carcass of the dead sheep he'd discovered just after dawn while walking the perimeter of the bedding ground.

Squatting, the man brushed leaves and grass off the body, where the head remained nearly intact. "Yep, it's a mountain lion kill. See those fang marks on the back of its neck? A cat'll go for the head or neck when it attacks. And the way it's been buried is another clue. They like to bury their prey and come back to it later." He sat back on his heels and nodded over at a strand of brush and pine about thirty yards away. "Wouldn't surprise me if she was holed up in there, just watching us. Waiting for us to leave."

Rob fingered his rifle. "Any chance of us hunting her down?"

"Not without a hound or two. A dog would tree her, but if we were to walk over there right now, she'd most likely slip away without our ever seeing her. And you can't follow tracks in this hard dirt."

Great. Another predator he could do nothing about.

"It's possible she'll just move on. Especially if she's seen us. Doesn't hurt that you have such a large crowd around right now, either. Those big cats don't like humans, and if she sees extra activity with all of us milling about today, she may just cut her losses and run for it." Sparrowhawk pushed to his feet and gave the carcass a soft kick. "May as well leave this lie. If the cat comes back for it, it may be enough to satisfy her hunger and keep her from going for more. For now, anyway."

Rob hoped he was right. As far as he could tell, he'd only lost a couple of sheep so far, but if the cat kept it up, the losses could become more substantial before Jackson came back to move them to another area. He stood to his feet and brushed his hands on his trouser leg.

Maybe he'd been wrong to suspect Jake's story about why he'd been in this part of the mountains the other day. Maybe he and Zeke had been hunting this lion. But something about their story still didn't ring true. From what Sparrowhawk said, hunting a mountain lion without a dog or two would be futile. But why else would they be here?

He spared one more glance at the brush behind them, then turned back to where his flock was beginning to stir and mill about. It wouldn't be long now before the lead sheep headed out to pasture. No time really to be chasing a cat who probably couldn't be caught.

Besides, some of their guests had expressed an interest in helping him herd the sheep today. Last night, he'd promised to take them along when the flock left camp. He'd have to deal with this newest threat another time.

∼

AROUND MID-MORNING, MADDIE LED JENNY AND EMMA through a grove of lodgepole pines in the direction Rob, Ben, and Drew had taken shortly after breakfast. Everyone else had followed Sparrowhawk on an angling expedition to a nearby mountain lake. Jenny had opted to spend her day with Maddie.

"I want to live the day as a sheepherder," she'd said. "I may never get another chance to see a sheep camp in action."

Emma asked to join them, insisting she'd get plenty of hiking and fishing in the days to come. The three women had stayed behind to clean up camp after breakfast but were now hoping to catch up with the grazing flock.

"How do you know which way to go?" Jenny asked.

"I don't really. Usually, I'll just take off in the same direction Rob did and try to follow the sheep's trail." She pointed to places in the forest where branches had been broken and dirt packed hard. "A band as large as ours isn't too hard to follow. It's when a few of them break off on their own, especially over rocky patches, that you'll have a hard time tracking them. That's when you need the dogs."

Soon, the trees began to thin, and they stepped out into a meadow where the sheep were spread out, grazing contentedly on the lush, green grass. At the far side of the field on a little rise, they spied the men and the dogs. Maddie waved and started across the grass toward them.

"Oh, Maddie. It's so beautiful. I can't imagine living in this every day." Jenny had stopped short the moment they exited the trees and now stood, hands clasped in front of her, eyes bright with wonder. Maddie smiled at her friend's enchantment.

"It *is* beautiful," she said. "Rob and I hate the thought of leaving these mountains behind soon, but Jackson tells us we won't enjoy them nearly as much in the winter, at least not with sheep to care for."

"When do you have to leave?" Emma asked.

"We move a little lower with each new campsite, but we probably won't be completely out of the mountains until mid to late September. We have a few more weeks anyway."

The rest of the morning passed quickly as the group spent their time swapping sheep camp stories with news of what had happened in Lander since they'd left. After a lunch of cold ham and fresh apples, Maddie leaned against the boulder where she sat beside Rob. She loved this part of their day. Most often, the sheep were their quietest in the early afternoon. On warmer days, many of them dozed in the sunshine, and the setting was so peaceful, she'd often doze a little herself.

She listened with half an ear as Rob and Ben discussed methods of hunting coyotes, wolves, and mountain lions. A few feet away, Emma leafed through a recent issue of *The Ladies Home Journal*. Jenny sat at the edge of the herd of sheep, playing with Rebel, who was always eager for a belly rub. Rosie, who took her position as head sheepdog very seriously, looked on in contempt.

Maddie's gaze drifted, as it often did, to the gray-blue peaks at the head of the valley. Jenny's hunting party would be leaving tomorrow to explore those mountains. How she envied them. The more time she spent in the shadow of those ridges, the more she longed to see them up close. But mountain climbing was not practical with a herd of over two thousand sheep and a sheep wagon.

Jenny gave Rebel a final pat and came over to sit beside her.

"Oh, Maddie. You are so lucky to get to enjoy all this every day," she said.

Maddie laughed. "You wouldn't feel so lucky if you lived out here very long. Do you know that, as of yesterday, you, Emma, and Sara are the first women I've seen or talked to face-to-face in over three months? You couldn't go a week. You couldn't even go a day, without having a friend to talk to."

"Maybe." Jenny's smile grew pensive. "It's all so beautiful, though." She turned her head toward the snow-topped mountains. "Sparrowhawk says we could climb to the top of Wind River Peak if we want to."

"Do you think you will?"

"I don't know. It looks so high. He says the hike would take a full day from the base of the mountain."

"It might be worth the climb. I imagine you could almost see forever from up there."

"You should come with us." Jenny's voice throbbed with excitement.

"What? Oh, no. I couldn't." She *shouldn't*, anyway.

"Why not? We'll only be gone a week at the very most. We could drop you off back here on our way out."

"I can't. Not without Rob. Besides, we'll have moved camp again by then. You wouldn't know where to drop me."

"I'll bet Sparrowhawk could find it. He found you this time, didn't he?" Jenny wasn't backing down.

What if she did go with them? She'd been dreading the thought of them all leaving again tomorrow. How quiet camp life would seem after the excitement of this visit. She'd so enjoyed talking, really talking, with other women again. And Wind River Peak. She stared again at the mountain's alluring beauty.

But no. She couldn't. She wouldn't. Not without Rob. They hadn't come here for sightseeing. Besides, Wind River Peak wasn't going anywhere. When Rob got better, they'd climb it together.

Chapter Nineteen

※

Eye on his target, Rob slowly released his breath and pulled the trigger on his rifle. Dirt sprayed into the air six inches behind the tin can he'd aimed for. Blast. Missed again. He lowered his gun and surveyed the row of cans he'd lined up on a log about forty yards away. He'd hit three out of six. Not great, but better than some of his earlier attempts.

He was tempted to try one more shot, but he'd used all but one of the bullets he'd brought with him today. "Never carry an unloaded gun. Not out here," Jackson had told him when he'd set up their first camp. Though he wasn't the best shot and had never yet needed to use his gun for anything more than target practice, Rob had always heeded his advice. After seeing the bear Sparrowhawk brought down last month, he'd been even more careful. Not that he could bring down a bear with the same kind of accuracy as the hunting guide, especially given his poor showing with these targets today, but a bear was a lot bigger than a tin can. He figured he could at least do some damage.

Picking up his knapsack, he turned toward the meadow where he'd left Maddie and the sheep. They wouldn't be staying in the mountains much longer. Jackson told them their next move would bring them into the foothills and eventually out onto the high plains where they would make their winter camps. He would miss the beauty of these mountains and the long, lazy summer days. The days were already getting shorter and the nights cooler. All the more reason to get back to the meadow. Maddie would need to head back to camp if she were to get supper ready before he brought the sheep in for the night.

He set out through the patch of forest that separated this clearing from the bigger meadow. The pine needle carpet was soft beneath his feet. He breathed in deeply of the crisp, pine-scented air. The air on the plains would still be as dry but not nearly as fragrant. He'd miss that too.

Stepping out into the open meadow, he took a minute to enjoy the peace of the scene spread before him. The sheep were calm, contented. Some were eating, some resting at the end of a long day. The lambs were now as big as their mothers, though still far more energetic. He watched as two of them chased each other around a large boulder. Maddie sat against a rocky outcropping on the far side of the meadow. He threaded his way through the mass of sheep toward her. She was reading, head bent toward the book in her lap. Knowing her, she wouldn't notice him approach, probably wouldn't even look up until he stood beside her and called her name.

Something fluttered in the rocks above her. A bird? He glanced up and froze. A large cat crouched on a ledge twenty-five feet above Maddie, its tawny fur blending almost completely with the rocks around it. If it hadn't been for the twitching of its tail, he never would have noticed it. The mountain lion. In their last two campsites, they'd seen no sign of the animal. He thought they'd left it behind, higher in the mountains. He'd thought wrong.

Inching his rifle onto his shoulder, he sighted in on its head. He'd seen enough house cats to know this one was in hunting mode, its attention trained on Maddie below. Dear God. Should he shoot? He only had one bullet. What if he missed? Would it scare the animal away or precipitate an attack? Before he could come to a decision, the cat launched itself into the air. Rob pulled the trigger, then broke into a run.

"Maddie." He bellowed her name as the tumbling, spitting mass of angry cat hurtled toward her. He would never reach her in time. *Dear God, help.*

Maddie looked up just as the cat hit the ground only yards from where she sat. Her scream echoed through the canyon. The cat rolled to its feet, launching itself toward Maddie. A blur of white and tan cut it off.

Rebel. The two animals came together in a mass of biting, barking, hissing flesh. From across the meadow, Rosie also came running, barking ferociously. Rob made it to Maddie's side seconds later. She had jumped to her feet and stood pressed up against the rock wall, hands clamped across her nose and mouth as if to corral her screams.

He stood over the fighting dog and cat, barrel of his gun raised like a club, hoping for a chance to strike at the cat without hurting Rebel, but before he could find an opening, the cat went limp and dropped onto its side. Rebel lunged at its throat, but Rob pulled him back. The cat lay still, eyes glazed in death. A bullet hole in its chest oozed blood.

He'd hit it. Took a while for the varmint to die, but God help him, he'd hit it.

Leaning his rifle against the rocks, he pulled Maddie into his arms. She sobbed into his shirt.

"Hush. It's okay." He rubbed his hand slowly up and down her back. "It's going to be okay. It's dead. The cat's dead." He said the words to comfort himself as much as her.

What if he'd been a few minutes late coming into the meadow? What if he had used that last bullet in target practice? What if he had missed that shot? He shook his head to stop that line of thinking. "What ifs" could drive a man crazy.

The fact was he had come in time, and his shot had proved true. God had been with them today. He breathed a prayer of thanksgiving and clung to his wife.

"Hush, now. Hold still." Maddie clipped the fur around the wound on Rebel's shoulder. The cat's teeth had sunk in deep, leaving four nasty bite marks where it had latched onto the dog. Other than that, he was a little worse for wear after his tussle with the mountain lion. Maddie wished she could say the same for herself. Her fingers trembled as she worked.

Focus. Don't think about it. Though how she was ever going to forget the shock of a hundred pounds of snarling wildcat falling from the sky at her feet was more than she could fathom. She'd be having nightmares about it for weeks. She drew in a deep breath and slowly released it before examining each wound more closely.

If it weren't for Rebel's intervention, this could be her flesh, punctured and oozing blood.

"Good boy, Rebel. You're such a good boy." Rebel turned his head and licked her hand as she worked. She smiled down into his sweet brown eyes. "Give me a minute to fix you up, bud, and I'll get you a treat. Yes, I will."

The meaty ham bone she'd set aside to make soup would be his reward. He deserved it. But first, she needed to make sure these wounds were treated. Taking one of the dosing syringes they used for the sheep, she flushed each of the punctures until she was satisfied they were clean. Then, she pulled out the jar of ointment Emma Johnson had left her when she'd treated Mr. Bennett's bear wounds last month. She still wasn't sure what was in it. Honey, for sure, and maybe some comfrey or witch hazel. Whatever the ingredients, they'd worked like magic on Mr. Bennett. It should be just as effective for a cat bite.

If someone had told her before she'd left Lander that she'd soon become proficient at treating wild animal bites, she'd never have left town. Some days, today especially, she wondered why she stayed. But the answer was obvious. Rob. If all of this—the loneliness, the animal attacks, the camping in all types of weather. If that was what it took for Rob to get better, she would stay. Of course, she would stay.

A tap sounded at the door of the wagon. Turning, she saw an older man looking at her through the open top of the Dutch door. Lank gray hair hung about his shoulders, and a long gray beard gave him a wild appearance. Where was Rob? She'd thought he was just outside.

"Excuse me, ma'am," he said, a soft Scottish burr lacing his words. "I'm Tavis. Rob tells me our Rebel is hurt. Mind if I take a look?"

Tavis. Of course. Rob and Jackson had mentioned him before. He was another of the herders Jackson tended, the one Rob had visited before deciding to take up sheepherding.

"Yes, of course. Come in, Mr.—" She let her words trail off, not knowing if Tavis was his first or last name.

"Just Tavis, lass. No one's called me Mr. MacKenzie in longer than I can remember."

She stepped to the side to let him see the table where she'd laid Rebel. As he came close, Rebel wagged his tail and struggled to get up.

"Whoa, there, laddie. Best stay put." Tavis stroked the dog with a gentle hand and scratched him under the chin. "Rebel was the whelp off my best dog, Lassie, so we know each other well. I'm glad to hear he's left his puppy days behind and is doing his job like a mon." He bent closer to inspect the wounds on Rebel's shoulder.

"I washed them with a syringe and used that ointment Mrs. Johnson gave us. Is there anything else you'd suggest I do?"

Straightening, he smiled down at her, deep laugh lines bracketing the kindest blue eyes she'd ever seen. "No, lass. Looks like Rebel's in good hands. He's lucky to have such a good nurse."

"We're lucky to have him. He . . . he saved me today."

Tavis nodded. "A good sheepdog will always protect. That was some cat your mon killed. He's done us all a service. Now that I know Rebel's in good hands, I'll go help him skin it so he can earn his bounty."

"How did you know to drop by?"

"I heard the gunshots earlier and thought I should check-in. Jackson told me ye were my neighbors when he set up my camp last week. All the sheep camps will be a might closer now that we're heading out of the mountains. Makes it easier to check on each other and such through the winter, especially after a storm. I suspect ye'll be seeing more of me than ye'll be wanting soon enough."

"I doubt that, Mr.—um, Tavis. I, for one, will be glad to have you as our neighbor. Now, after you help Rob, be sure to stop by, and I'll send you home with some cookies I baked yesterday."

Chapter Twenty

Rob brought the hammer down on the large metal link from the wagon's stay chain. The trip down from the mountains into the upper foothills had wreaked havoc with his equipment. There'd been a time he would have gone to a blacksmith for repairs of this nature, but he was quickly learning to make do on his own since coming west. Other than the size of the link, this task wasn't much different than fixing a broken watch guard. He returned the damaged link to the fire and sank back on his haunches to wait for the metal to heat.

As was often the case these days, his gaze drifted westward where the sun was turning the snowy patches on the Atlantic and Wind River Peaks a deep coral. He loved this time of the evening. The sheep bleated softly as they settled into their bedding ground. A yeasty smell of biscuits mingled with wood smoke wafted from the wagon where Maddie was preparing their evening meal. He heard her humming softly as she worked.

They'd taken to cooking inside again now that the days were shorter and nights cooler. Fall came early in these mountains, and though the days were still warm here in the foothills, most mornings, he'd find frost blanketing the grass when he got up to follow the sheep. Sure was beautiful, though. He'd always been partial to fall with its mellow sunshine and crisp, cool air. Colors were different here in the West, though. None of the blazing oranges or deep burgundies he was used to in the oak and maple-lined streets of Newark, but bright yellow willows lit up the streams and riverbeds, and aspens ran like streams of molten gold amid the fir-covered slopes in the distance. Color hid in the grasses as well, subtle streaks of red and yellow mixed with the tans and browns.

His gaze settled on a large cloud of dust rising in the southwest. A group of horsemen was heading their way at a fast clip. They were still too far off for him to make out how many. An advantage of camping in the foothills was, once you set up camp at the top of one of the rises, you could see for miles. He'd run into other sheepherders now and again in the mountains, but most of the time he'd felt like he and Maddie were in a world of their own. Out here, he realized just how many other herders there were. Columns of smoke rose from campfires in all directions.

Rob threaded a metal rod into the link he'd set on the fire, pulled it out, and carried it back to the anvil. No use wasting time contemplating some faraway riders. Most likely, they weren't on their way to see him, and the red-hot metal was now the perfect temperature for repairing the link.

He had just thrust the restored link into a pail of cold water to hiss and sputter as it cooled when the horsemen crested the rise next to theirs and made their way toward his camp. Seven men altogether and all moving at a break-neck pace. Rather than turning and riding around the outskirts of the flock, the group dove right into the middle of the herd, scattering sheep as they came. They skidded to a halt on the far side of his campfire.

"Why, lookee who it is," one of the men said, pushing back the wide brim of his hat so Rob could see his face. "It's our friend, the joo-ler." The irritating drawl was all too familiar. Jake. How was it the people you'd least like to ever see again kept turning up like a bad penny?

He rode the same brown mare he'd ridden that day in the mountains, but the saddle was new. Fancy. Black with brightly colored saddle strings and silver conchos. How did a kid like Jake afford a saddle like that?

Jake let loose a whistle. "Oooh. He's got one of his jewels with him this time."

Maddie, looking flushed and beautiful from the heat of the cook stove, stood in the open doorway of the sheep wagon, her smile of welcome quickly dying on her lips.

"Is the little blonde in there too?" Jake turned to Rob, an ugly leer on his face.

The men broke out into a chorus of groans and cat calls as Maddie melted back into the shadows of the wagon's interior. Rob's hand tightened around the handle of the hammer he still held in his hand. He was sorely outnumbered. In addition to Jake's usual company of uncouth youths, the group included two older men. One, the size of a small mountain, would give Jackson a run for his money if a fight should occur. The other, a well-dressed, middle-aged man with a waxed mustache, had eyes as hard and cold as gun metal. A shotgun was placed prominently across his saddle horn.

Rob willed his voice to stay neutral. "What can I do for you, Jake?"

"Do for me? What makes you think a scab herder such as yourself could do anything for the likes of me?" Jake looked around at his fellow riders with a smirk and let loose an expletive. "The only thing I can think of that you could do for me is to get your disease-ridden vermin off my land."

"*Your* land? Your family's ranch is down on the Sweetwater, isn't it? All the land around here is public land."

Jake narrowed his eyes and was about to reply when the older gentleman cut him short.

"Jake." The man tipped his head to the east.

"Lucky for you, we've got a card game to attend, or I'd be inclined to teach you another lesson in respect. Just keep those scab bearers of yours away from the Sweetwater, ya hear? We sure as heck don't need them stinking up perfectly good ranch land." With that, he wheeled his horse around and followed the group as they headed east, scattering sheep again as they rode out.

∿

Rob mentioned the run-in to Jackson the next week when he brought his herd to Baldwin's ranch to take part in the annual culling.

Jackson shook his head. "McCreedy, you say? He's a rough one. His father's not too bad. Has a nice ranch down near Rongis. Good businessman, but not much in the way of a father. His wife's been gone as long as I can remember. I'd say Jake pretty much raised himself. Emmett's bent on building the biggest cattle ranch in the county and doesn't seem to care much what Jake does.

"I hear Jake's taken to running with a pretty rough crowd. Spends a lot of time gambling in the saloons in South Pass and Atlantic City. Sounds like he was probably heading into Derby to do some gambling with the oilmen there. Miners and oilmen are cut from the same cloth. Want to get their money quick and spend it even quicker."

Rob smoothed a hand down his mustache to hide his smile. He'd heard the same said of sheep men, but Jackson was as far from the stereotypical sheepherder as a man could be. Only a few years older than Jake, the young giant seemed decades older in wisdom and responsibility. Baldwin was lucky to have him as foreman. And he and Maddie had benefited greatly from his services.

Today was no exception. Rob welcomed this opportunity to learn the next step in the ranching process, culling his herd for market. All the herders of Baldwin's summer bands were gathered today with their sheep. Once the wethers and older ewes were sorted from each herd, the herders would be left with smaller winter bands kept back for breeding and next season's wool harvest.

Jackson and several other sheepherders would drive the market lambs to the railroad in Casper for shipment to Omaha. They'd agreed to take Rob's lambs along with Baldwin's, leaving him free to stay with his winter band and Maddie.

"Best get at those lambs if we're going to get the entire flock done today," Baldwin called from over by the sheep pens.

Rob looked at Maddie, who was sitting to his left. "You want to come watch?"

She shook her head. "You go ahead. I'll help Mr. Lee clean up here."

He knew she'd been disappointed when they'd arrived at the ranch yesterday to find no women in residence. Mrs. Baldwin and her daughters were living in Lander for the school year, leaving Maddie the lone woman in their group this week. After a lukewarm welcome from the other herders yesterday morning, Maddie had opted to stay in the kitchen with the camp cook.

At first, Cookie hadn't seemed too anxious for her company either, but by suppertime, she'd won him over. Rob wasn't sure if it was her sweet nature or her flaky biscuits that did the trick, but the two seemed to have established enough of a rapport that Maddie had continued to help the man prepare meals and clean up the kitchen. Regardless, he knew this week hadn't been the social reprieve Maddie had been anticipating. He leaned over and dropped a kiss on her cheek.

He fell in beside Tavis on his way toward the corral that held his group of spring lambs. They would be culling his sheep first today.

"We'll sell all the wethers?" He asked Tavis.

"Most of them. We'll mark a few of the smaller ones to keep back as yearlings. That gives them a chance to put on weight over the winter and lets you harvest their wool come spring."

They'd reached the edge of the pen where his lambs had been

gathered overnight. At their approach, Fred broke loose from the herd and trotted over to the gate with his usual bleat of greeting. Squatting, Rob reached through the slats in the fence to pat his soft, wooly head, noting with regret that this young lamb was anything but small.

"Who's your friend?"

Rob felt a flush creep up his neck. The seasoned shepherd must think him every inch a fool, making pets out of his livestock. He stood up and stuffed his hands in his pockets.

"That's Fred." Great. Make it worse by admitting he'd named him. "He had a broken leg earlier this summer. With all the extra care, he's somehow come to look on me like another mother. Follows me around a bit, I guess. So should I get the dogs?" He needed to change the subject quickly if the man wasn't going to think him the greenest of all greenhorns.

"Sure, I'll head on over to help with the marking. Just guide the lambs toward that chute. Once the lead lamb enters, the rest will follow. Should be done in no time."

Rob whistled for Rosie and Rebel, who soon came trotting over from the barn. He opened the gate to the holding pen, and with a few quick commands, he had the sheep flowing out of the pen and down the hill toward the chute. Fred fell into his usual spot beside him as he walked behind the herd.

Up to this point, he hadn't allowed himself to think about what it would be like to send Fred with the other wethers to market. He'd just assumed when the time came to cull the sheep for market, he'd find an excuse to hold Fred back. Now he feared the decision would not be his to make. The herd was already pouring into the two corrals as the experienced herders quickly marked the lambs flooding into the chute.

He looked down at Fred. The lamb had recovered well from his injury and was now a healthy, well-fed wether. No herder, looking at the lamb, would find any reason to hold him back. He wished he'd thought about the ear notch. He'd have made a ewe out of him before they got here.

Some kind of rancher he was, plotting ways to keep his lambs from market. Still, a lump formed in his throat as he nudged Fred toward the end of the chute. Maybe he could come back later and put Fred into the other pen when the other herders weren't around.

Or maybe he just needed to let him go.

He watched Fred enter the chute, bobbed tail held high, the last of the sheep heading trustingly to slaughter. Poor, dumb lamb had no idea what lay ahead of him. As Fred came abreast of Tavis, Rob saw the grizzled herder reach out and mark the lamb's head with a blue X. Fred trotted into the pen with the ewes and smaller wethers, and Tavis turned his head and winked at him.

Rob walked over to stand beside the man.

Tavis shrugged. "He looked a little puny to me. Sometimes happens when they've been hurt."

Rob shook his head. "You must think me a pretty sorry shepherd."

"No, laddie. Ye're a good shepherd. Ye love your sheep. Ye just make a lousy businessman, that's all."

Rob chuckled. "Fair enough."

"Now, bring us your ewes so we can cull the old ones. Got any in that group you need to tell me about?"

"No, we're good." Unless he counted Mrs. Finch. But as lead sheep and a good breeder, he figured she was safe. At least for a few more years.

Chapter Twenty-One

The sheep wagon rocked as another blast of icy wind hit its exterior. Maddie shivered and pulled the blanket tighter around her shoulders. This was definitely not how she pictured spending her Christmas Eve. It had all seemed so simple when they'd made their plans. Plans she hadn't allowed herself to dream until Rob had joined the scheming.

"Come to town for Christmas," Jenny had written in her last letter. Maddie had read the words to Rob with a chuckle, quickly dismissing the possibility, but Rob had not laughed.

"Why not?" he'd said. "We could get Gabe to watch the sheep for a few days. You deserve a break, Maddie. It's been forever since you've seen other women. And Jenny could use a friend right now."

Yes, she could. What that horrid man had done to her was unconscionable. Had Maddie known what her friend was facing, she would have been there for her earlier this month, but by the time they heard about the trial, it was all over and done. But she had promised to be there for Christmas. And now, even that was impossible.

They should never have made any plans at all. But now, since they had, she couldn't help but wallow in what might have been.

What might have been was a trip into town this morning and a chance to worship with friends at the M.E. Christmas Eve program tonight. How she would have loved watching the children's faces as they received their gifts from the Sunday School's Christmas tree.

Then tomorrow, they had planned to spend Christmas dinner with Jenny, Ted, and Grace at the Parkhurst's. She had been so looking forward to seeing everyone, even Mrs. Parkhurst.

She turned to stare for the fiftieth time out the small window above their bunk. Still nothing but white. The snow had started sometime in the middle of the night and had not let up all day. The combination of wind and snow made it impossible to see more than a foot or two in the distance. There would be no one traveling today. Rob couldn't even check on the sheep. She hoped they had stayed put and not wandered before the storm hit as they were apt to do. Even if they had wandered, there was nothing she or Rob could do about it right now. For that much, she was grateful. The winter weather had not been kind to Rob's health thus far. A walk in a blizzard could only make it worse.

Which was another reason she regretted not being able to make it to town. She had hoped he'd be able to stop by Dr. Calloway's before they returned to the range. She didn't like the sound of Rob's cough the last few days. His disease made him prone to bouts of bronchitis and pneumonia, and they'd long since run through the cough tonic Dr. Waite had prescribed them back in Newark.

She looked down at the *Ladies Home Journal* she'd been pretending to read for the last half hour. What was the use? She'd read all the articles many times before. Another problem with being snowbound right when they were expecting a load of new camp supplies was a lack of new reading material. She let out a sigh and stood up.

"Would you like a cup of tea?" She directed her question at the bed sheet Rob had hung down the center of the wagon to close off his side of the table from hers. A few weeks ago, Rob had pulled out his bag of jeweler's tools and supplies and hung the make-shift partition.

"I'm making your Christmas present," he'd said. Since then, she'd made a few half-hearted, laughing attempts to peek behind the curtain, but he'd rebuffed them all. Today, he'd spent the better part of the afternoon hiding behind his wall, whistling occasionally and coughing, but for the most part, deeply engrossed in what he was making. It almost made her wish she still had something left to work on, but her gifts were all made and packed in the traveling valise beneath the bed, all set for their trip into town. The trip that wasn't going to happen.

"Sounds good," Rob answered.

She took down two teacups from the shelf above the stove and set the water on to boil. With a sigh, she pushed aside the curtain over the small window in the door. Still white. Blowing, whirling sheets of snow whipped past the window, blocking any view of the world outside. She felt as if they were suspended in time in this cocoon of a wagon, cut off from reality forever. With a shiver, she let the curtain drop and turned back to her task.

She measured tea leaves into the bottom of her tea pot, poured the boiling water on them, then turned to dig the strainer out of a drawer behind her. One nice thing about close quarters, everything was within an arm's reach of where she stood.

The trouble was, she was missing home . . . again. She could picture her family gathered around the dining room table after Christmas Eve service. Little Hazel and Les would be brimming with excitement. Father would have his stories. And Edie. Edie and Walter would be showing off their new baby. Albert James would be two months old by now. How she wished she could be there to hold him. She shook away the thought. No use wishing for what couldn't be.

Pouring the tea into the teacups, she added one lump of sugar to hers and a teaspoon of honey to Rob's to calm his throat.

"Where would you like this?"

"Hmmm?"

"Your tea? Do you want me to bring it to you?"

"Just set it there."

His distracted tone warned her she was on her own for a while. Really, what was the use of being trapped in a small wagon with someone if they weren't even going to acknowledge your presence? She was almost tempted to kick Rob's feet as she stepped over them and sat down again on her side of the curtained-off table but couldn't quite bring herself to do something so petty. After all, the man was making her a Christmas present. She just wished he would talk to her while he did it.

She picked up the *Wind River Mountaineer* and opened it with a snap. Surely there was something in the four-page broadsheet she had not yet read. A quick perusal of the local happenings told her this was a mistake. Every other line reminded her of all she was missing—advertisements for Christmas hams, last-minute Christmas gifts at Mrs. Stacia Allen's, and reminders of all the church programs scheduled for tonight. She quickly turned back to the national news on the first page but found nothing there of interest. She checked her watch pinned to her shirtwaist. Three o'clock. Would this day never end?

Rob poked his head out from behind the curtain, eyebrows raised, mustache twitching.

"What?"

"Bored, are we?"

"Not at all. I'm reading the paper."

Rob laughed and pushed to his feet. Picking up his tea from the stove, he came to her side of the table and squeezed onto the bench beside her.

"Must be some pretty heavy reading to cause all those sighs."

"I haven't been sighing." Had she?

"No? I could have sworn the air is almost as blustery in here as it is outside."

Setting down his teacup, he took the paper from her and

began scanning the headlines. "Let's see . . . the railroads have placed more orders than at this time a year ago. Not much to sigh about there. Senate is arguing a ship subsidy bill. Yawns, maybe, but still nothing to sigh about. Oh. Here we go. The English suffered heavy losses in their engagement at Wonderfontein on the eighth. I didn't realize you were so caught up in the Boer War."

"All war is sad." She plucked the paper out of his hand, folded it, and placed it on her stack of magazines and books. "But you're right. That's not why I'm blue."

He pulled her toward him, wrapping his arms around her and resting his chin on her head. "I know you're disappointed about today. I'm disappointed too. But we'll get into town. I promise. As soon as the weather clears."

Yes. But it wouldn't be the same. Christmas would be over, and all the programs and festivities with it. She didn't mind spending the everyday, normal days alone. She was used to their solitude, enjoyed the time they spent together, in fact. But the holidays were different. Holidays were meant to be celebrated with family and friends. They were times to come together, renew friendships, catch up on life. To spend a holiday alone, doing nothing different than they did every other day of the year, was wrong somehow. She couldn't remember a Christmas ever where she hadn't spent the day with buggy-loads of family and friends.

"What we need is a distraction. Something to get our minds off today and the weather."

"Like what?" She turned in his arms to look up at him.

Rob waggled his eyebrows at her like a villain in a poorly acted melodrama.

She laughed and swatted at his shoulder. "Be serious."

"What makes you think I'm not serious?"

She shook her head, giggling as he pulled her close again and began nuzzling her ear.

"How about I give you your Christmas present now?"

"It's done?"

"It is."

"But I don't have anything to give you." She'd asked Jenny to buy Roosevelt's *Ranch Life and the Hunting Trail* for her to give to Rob, expecting to get it from her when they went into town today. Now his present would have to wait until they could get into Lander or have Jackson bring it out to them.

"That doesn't matter. I'll get mine when I get it, but I'd like to give you yours right now. Hold on a minute."

Rob popped back behind his side of the curtain and came back holding a small parcel in the palm of his hand. It looked like he'd used one of her white lawn handkerchiefs to wrap whatever he'd made and tied it with one of her red hair ribbons.

"When did you wrap this?"

"Just now when you were making us tea. Open it."

Maddie untied the ribbon and slowly unfolded the handkerchief. Buried deep inside was a small pin for her lace collars, delicate and beautiful. The yellow-gold oval featured a smaller, oval-shaped red rhinestone in its very center. Flanking each side were three dainty flowers whose stems formed two delicate, filigree hearts. On the top, bottom, and both sides of the larger oval, Rob had attached four larger, heart-shaped leaves.

"It's beautiful," she said.

"The flowers are to remind you of our days in the mountains with the wildflowers. The hearts symbolize my love for you. I tried to make it small and delicate and beautiful, just like you, Maddie. Merry Christmas."

She lifted her face to receive his kiss.

"Merry Christmas, love," she murmured as his lips claimed hers.

This. This was why she could move thousands of miles away from home and family. This was why she could sacrifice Christmases spent with friends. This love. This man. As she fell into the passion of his kiss and his touch, the world outside faded. Nothing else mattered besides the two of them.

Rob woke to silence and sat up to cough. After thirty hours of hearing the wind shriek and howl, silence lay heavy around him. Christmas Day. Somehow the calm seemed fitting. He spat into the glass he'd placed next to his bunk and gave the sputa his morning scrutiny. The streaks of brown had been more pronounced since his last head cold. Probably nothing to worry about. Maybe. Whatever the case, he needed to get up and check on the sheep.

The cold hit like a wall of ice as he threw back the covers. Maddie stirred in her sleep but didn't wake as he hopped to the floor and quickly pulled his pants and shirts over his woolen union suit. Mornings were always cold in the wagon, but this one took the prize.

A few minutes later, having stoked the fire and put a kettle on to boil, he blew a hole in the frost on the window of the door and peeped out into the blinding brilliance of a snow-covered morning. Off to the right, he saw several groups of sheep huddled like mounds of butter against the milky white snow. *Thank you, Lord.* They hadn't wandered.

Before the storm hit, he and the dogs had bedded them on the leeward side of the hill, hoping they'd stay put, but sheep were unpredictable. He had no way of telling during the storm whether one of them had taken the notion to run, and, as he well knew, if one went, many would follow. The fact he could see any sheep at all from in his limited field of vision was a good sign.

Maddie stirred in the bed behind him and sat up. Her long brown curls were tousled around her shoulders, reminding him of the intimacy of the night before. He was more than tempted to jump back into bed and spend the day there in her arms.

"Has the storm stopped?" Her breath puffed white in the air around her.

"Yup. Cold in here, though. You might want to stay put until the fire has a chance to heat things up a bit."

She pulled the quilt around her shoulders, seeming more than willing to follow his suggestion.

"Want some coffee?"

At her nod, he poured two cups of coffee, adding a scoop of sugar to both before coming to perch on the bunk beside her. Handing her a cup, he reached out to cup her chin, lingering to caress the silky-smooth skin on her cheek.

"Merry Christmas, beautiful." The minute the words left his mouth, he wished he could call them back. The regret that flickered briefly in her golden eyes reminded him of the disappointment this day brought her. He watched her muster an overly bright smile.

"Merry Christmas, love. I don't suppose Saint Nicolas managed to visit in the night and drop off your present?"

"Don't you worry about my present. Saint Jackson is sure to bring it as soon as he can get through. It will give us something to look forward to."

"Did we get much snow?"

"Hard to tell from what I could see through the window. I need to get out to see if there's any grass uncovered for the sheep to eat."

"You sound hoarse this morning. Is your cough worse?"

"Not particularly." No need to tell her of the new abscesses he was certain had formed in his larynx. She would only worry, and there was no remedy.

"Well, be sure to dress warmly before you go out."

"Yes, Mum." He grinned at her, then finished off the last few sips of coffee, willing himself to swallow normally as the hot liquid poured past the sores in his throat.

Standing, he buttoned an extra woolen shirt over his flannel one, then dug two pairs of woolen socks from the drawer beneath the bed. He knew once he donned his blanket-lined overcoat and pulled on his boots, he'd feel ten pounds heavier, but judging from the temperature inside the wagon, he was going to need all the layers he could get this morning.

He turned to Maddie, still huddled under the quilt. "I shouldn't be gone too long."

She nodded. "I'll get breakfast started while you're gone."

"No hurry. Let the wagon heat up a bit first."

He grabbed his coat and hat from the peg by the door and headed out. The sun reflecting off the snow brought tears to his eyes. He could feel the fabric in his canvas pants begin to stiffen. Pulling a pair of leather gauntlets over his woolen mittens, he leaped down from the tongue of the wagon and whistled for the dogs. Rebel scrambled out from beneath the wagon. Rosie was already at work, keeping a vigilant eye on the sheep from atop the ridge.

A quick scan of the area told him though some of the sheep had gathered in the area around the wagon, most were still down in the sheltered valley where he'd left them. Huddled in groups, they showed little interest in feeding. Probably just as well since the ground there looked to be covered with a good foot or more of snow. Food was limited to the spots where the snow had blown to reveal the taller grasses and sage bushes. With these frigid temperatures, no telling how long it would be before they had any substantial snow melt.

He walked to the top of the ridge and checked the opposite side of the hill where the wind had unleashed its full fury during the long hours of the storm. Sure enough, there were plenty of places where the sheep would have little trouble digging away the snow to find grass. He'd lead them there after breakfast. Maybe by then, they'd be willing to feed.

He turned back to assess the flock, absently counting the black sheep as he did. Hold on. Thirteen? If that was correct, almost a quarter of his flock was missing. He quickly counted again, arriving once more at thirteen. Great. Part of the band must have wandered with the storm after all. His easy morning had suddenly become complicated.

An hour later, belly full of bacon and hot cakes, he ordered

Rebel to stand guard over the main herd and called Rosie to his side.

"Let's go find the stragglers, girl."

He studied the bedding ground for a minute but could see no tracks leading through the snow in any direction. The missing band must have left ahead of the storm. Typical, but not especially helpful for tracking. He scrutinized the area for a minute, then struck up the valley toward the southeast. Sheep always traveled with the wind before a storm. Judging by the drifts, he guessed the wind had blown primarily from the northeast. His best bet was to head southwest and see what he found.

The snow was deeper in the valley than he'd expected. After sinking into drifts up to his knees several times, he began to test the path ahead of him with his shepherd's hook to avoid the deeper pitfalls. Good thing he'd worn his leather gaiters this morning and that extra pair of woolen socks. He pulled his muffler over his nose, leaving just his eyes exposed. Rosie ran a few steps in front of him, leaping in and out of drifts, her tail a black plume against the white backdrop.

The valley soon veered sharply to the right, and Rob trudged around the corner after the little black and white dog to find his stray sheep quietly grazing on sage and tall grasses. Ridges of snow spiked high against the red walls of the canyon here, leaving the middle ground bare. The wind must have barreled through the chasm like a freight train during the storm. For the most part, his sheep ignored him, but the lead sheep raised her head and leveled an implacable stare his direction. Mrs. Finch. Her blue-collared bell verified her identity, but Rob would know that stare anywhere. Trust her to lead the sheep to the largest stretch of bare ground he'd seen yet today.

Best of all, they were only a short distance from the rest of the sheep. He could lead the others here to graze. He'd been dreading the thought of spending the majority of his day traipsing through the snow, but now, with a sheltered spot in the sun and chance for a few short breaks inside the wagon, his day had suddenly taken a turn for the better.

He turned to head back the way he had come, only to stop short in his tracks. Where was Fred? If Mrs. Finch were here, then Fred should be nearby. He'd never known the lamb to stray too far from his mother unless he was at his heels. Come to think of it, Rob had not seen the friendly little lamb all morning. He turned to count the sheep in the valley. A hundred and sixty-three, only about half of the three hundred head he'd been expecting. Drat. He might have known it wouldn't be that easy. Of course, his count could be off, or Fred could still be back with the main flock. He'd bring them down here and get them settled before setting off on another search.

Chapter Twenty-Two

His count wasn't off. He'd found no sign of Fred back with the main herd, and once he'd led the flock into the valley to feed, he'd come up short by one black counter. Some of the sheep were still missing, whether fifty or a hundred and fifty, he couldn't say, but enough to send him out searching once again.

He'd left Rebel and Maddie in charge of the main band, though he'd hated that she had to sit out in this cold. She'd offered no complaint, though, promising to split her time between the sheep and wagon as she prepared stewed chicken and apple pie for their Christmas dinner. Christmas. Had he ever spent a stranger Christmas? Who would have ever thought he'd spend a Christmas morning tramping around in the snow looking for a bunch of lost sheep? Though now he thought about it, Christmas did have something to do with lost sheep after all.

Had Jesus ever felt like giving up on his lost sheep, leaving them to their fate? He sure did. If Fred hadn't been among the band, he might well have given up long ago. He was glad the effort of climbing hill after hill kept the blood flowing, and his body heated at least a little against the frigid air. Even Rosie seemed to have none of her usual enthusiasm for finding the lost. Once they'd brought the larger band into the valley with the others, she'd paced nervously back and forth along the cliff wall as if expecting some calamity to befall the grazing herd. He'd had to whistle several times to get her to follow him, and even then, she'd walked a good five paces behind instead of bounding ahead as was her wont.

"What's got into you today, Rosie?" He bent to scratch her behind her ears. "It's not like you to get distracted from work. Come on, don't play the Rebel with me now. I need you. It's far too cold to stay out here any longer than necessary."

Although, he was beginning to wonder how much longer *would* be necessary. They'd already been searching for almost an hour and still had seen no sign of the missing sheep. Should he continue the search or head back and try again in another direction?

As if in answer to his question, Rosie lifted her head to sniff the air, then bounded up the path in front of him. At the crest of the hill, she began to bark excitedly.

Rob jogged up behind her and found sheep. But not his sheep. A sheep wagon perched on the top of the neighboring hill, a plume of smoke waving a welcome from its smokestack. A tan and white sheep dog separated itself from the edge of the herd and ran toward Rosie, barking and snarling.

"Halloo," He called out a greeting over the noise but saw no herder guarding the sheep. Eyeing the strange dog with caution, he called out again. His fingers and toes had been numb for the last half hour. A rest by a cozy wood stove would be most appreciated.

Finally, the door to the sheep wagon swung open, and a grizzled head peeked around the corner. Tavis! Rob waved a hand at his old friend.

"Merry Christmas, Tavis."

The older man shaded his eyes with his hand, then returned his wave. "Och, laddie. Are ye daft wondering aboot in this weather? Come in out of the cauld." He whistled to the dog, who backed away but still watched warily while he and Rosie passed.

"Trouble?"

"Lost some sheep."

"How many?"

"I'm guessing a hundred head or more. I found one band not far from camp but haven't been able to find hide nor hair of the others."

Rob grabbed Tavis' outstretched hand and let him pull him up into the wagon. The wagon's dim interior seemed dark as night after the brilliance of sunshine on snow, but the warmth from the man's stove radiated summer sunshine to his chilled fingers and toes. Gratefully, he dropped onto the bench beside it and stretched his hands close.

"I'm frying some tatties and onions. Ye'd be welcome to join me."

The growling response of his stomach reminded him he'd walked many miles since breakfast. "Thanks. I'd appreciate that. And coffee, if you have it."

Tavis poured liquid black as river mud into a chipped tin mug and handed it to him. The first sip was as strong as its color, but the warmth lit a welcome path of fire down his throat. He tightened his fingers around the hot cylinder, content to merely breathe in the heat.

"Ye've walked a fair piece today. No sign of your sheep at all?"

"No. None."

Tavis set a plate of fried potatoes on the table in front of him, then dished himself a plate and sat down on the opposite bench. Rob knew the man well enough to not expect any more talk until the meal was finished, so he dug into his plate with gusto. Nothing like a long walk on a cold morning to stimulate the appetite. Dr. Waite would be proud to see how his fresh air cure was working. Not even the pain in his throat inhibited his desire for food these days.

A few silent minutes later, his companion pushed back his plate and cleared his throat. "Could be, they're buried."

Rob struggled to recall the thread of their latest conversation. "The sheep?"

"Aye. Happens if the snow be deep enough. Sheep dinna ken the danger 'til it's too late."

"How do you find them?"

The man shrugged. "A good dog can sometimes sniff them out. Otherwise, ye willna find them till the snow melts unless ye ken where to look. Where'd ye find the other band?"

"In a narrow canyon not far from camp."

"Muckle snow?"

"Very little. The wind had swept it bare. I have my sheep grazing there today."

"Drifts?"

Rob remembered the white peaks drifting up the red canyon walls. "Deep ones against cliffs."

Tavis nodded. "We'll look there, then. Mayhap Rosie will be of help." The man was on his feet and shrugging into a heavy coat before Rob had a chance to reply.

He followed Tavis out of the wagon, pulling the flaps down on his cap and tugging on his gauntlets. He knew he should protest Tavis's need to go with him but somehow couldn't resist the luxury of his help.

"Will your sheep be all right in your absence?"

He glanced over at Tavis's band, some busily working the snow to lay bare patches of grass but most content to huddle together in small groups to ward off the cold.

"Lassie'll see to them. Nae anybody going anywhere in this cauld."

He grabbed his shepherd's crook and a small shovel from under the wagon and set off at a brisk pace in the direction Rob had come. Rob whistled for Rosie and followed.

∽

THEY FOUND MADDIE WITH THE SHEEP, WRAPPED IN A QUILT and seated on a large rock, Rebel hunkered at her side. At their approach, she looked up from a well-worn volume she'd been reading. Dickens's *A Christmas Carol*, he'd be willing to bet. She'd read it every Christmas since he'd known her.

"Mr. Tavis. So good to see you." She greeted the older shepherd with a smile, then turned to Rob. "No sign of the sheep?"

"Tavis thinks they might be buried."

Her eyes widened. "Buried? How?" She looked around. "Where?"

He gestured to the drifts against the canyon walls. "There. Under the snow."

"Oh, the poor things. Are they all dead, then?" She turned a worried face toward Tavis.

"Aye, some mayhap. But not all. I've ken of sheep that have survived up to two weeks under snow before they be found. Last night's snowfall was light and dry. Ye may be surprised at how many will make it."

Rob hoped the man was right. He studied the drifts in question. He hadn't really noticed them before, but the snow was certainly deep enough along the edge of the cliffs to hide a good number of sheep. Rosie, who'd returned to her strange behavior of pacing nervously back and forth along the canyon walls, let out three sharp barks and began digging furiously into the snow.

"Looks like Rosie's sniffed some out for ye. Thought she might be of help." Tavis shouldered his shovel and hobbled over to where she was digging.

Suddenly, the dog's odd behavior earlier that morning made sense. She must have smelled the sheep under the snow before they left. No wonder he had so much trouble getting her to follow. If he'd only known how to interpret the signs, he could have saved them both a lot of walking.

The thought of Fred and the others trapped beneath the snow only made their wild goose chase that much more disturbing. No time to waste now. He turned and sprinted up the trail to find a shovel. Back at the wagon, Maddie, who had followed him, climbed inside and returned with her dishpan.

At his raised eyebrow, she flushed but wrapped the large pan to her chest somewhat defensively. "Last time I checked, we only had the one shovel," she said.

"And you plan to dig with that?" He let his amusement tip the edge of his mouth in a smile.

"This will work just fine. You'll see."

"Suit yourself."

He'd prefer she didn't have to help at all, but with the number of sheep still missing and the large area of snow to cover, he knew he'd need all the help he could get.

By the time they got back to Tavis and Rosie, the two had located three of the sheep. His heart sank to see their stiff, frozen forms thrown in a pile next to where Tavis was digging. He jogged to where Tavis was searching and began shoveling snow beside him. Their shovels soon hit the body of another frozen sheep. Blast. Would they have survived if he had known to look for them sooner?

The snow in this area lay about two feet deep. Each of the carcasses they uncovered was of single sheep, cut off from the rest of the herd. As they dug deeper into the drifts, they began to uncover small groups of sheep whose combined warmth as they'd huddled together against the storm had managed to keep them alive. Once freed, they'd shake off the excess snow that clung to their wool and leap to join the rest of the flock as if they'd never been trapped.

He, Maddie, and Tavis soon fell into a rhythm with their work. Rosie would sniff the snow, then scratch at an area until one of them came over to dig. Once they took over, she'd move to another spot and start again. She was so quick and accurate in her role they'd soon uncovered close to fifty sheep, over half of which were still alive. Apparently, only the single sheep trapped in the snow by themselves had succumbed to the frigid temperatures and died.

The snow grew deeper and the work more difficult as they shoveled their way toward the canyon walls. Rosie, who'd climbed the drift ahead of them, suddenly became agitated, sniffing along the edge of the cliff and barking as she ran back and forth across the pile of snow in front of them.

"Must be a pile of them in there, lad. Help me dig an opening." Instead of climbing up beside Rosie and burrowing down into the snow as they'd done before, Tavis tunneled his way forward from where they stood.

Rob shoveled into the drift at his side. After several minutes, Tavis gave a shout and dropped to his knees. Over his shoulder, Rob could make out a black nose and a pair of dark eyes. Tavis dropped his shovel, digging around the sheep with his hands. Rob shoveled a few more scoopfuls of snow, uncovering the head and shoulders of another sheep standing beside the first. After scooping away more snow, he realized they both were standing shoulder-deep in a shallow gully that probably ran the length of the cliff.

"Give me a hand, lad, and we'll lift this one out."

Each taking a shoulder, the men hefted the ewe's upper quarter until her front legs gained purchase on the bank in front of it. Another push on her hindquarters, and the animal leaped free, trotting out of the snow tunnel to join the rest of the flock. They employed the same method to free the second sheep. Rob watched it leap to freedom, then turned back to find two more sheep filling the gap they'd uncovered. Once those were released, two more filled their space.

"Looks like we've hit the mother lode," he said to Tavis.

"Aye. Most likely, they all climbed down to take shelter from the wind, then couldn't get out once the snow grew too deep."

For a quarter of an hour, they hefted and pushed sheep up onto the bank and out of the tunnel, working as fast as they could to keep the ones in the back from trampling the others in their rush to get out. Rob's shoulders and forearms burned, but his heart lightened with each live sheep that pushed its way into the gap, especially one with a bedraggled red ribbon that licked his face as he hefted him to the surface.

"Fred, you scamp. Get on with you. I'll deal with you later." He carefully avoided the older shepherd's gaze as he watched his favorite trot over to greet his mother.

All in all, he counted sixty-seven sheep before he turned to find the opening bare. Tavis poked his head down the gully in both directions. "Looks like that's the lot, lad."

Even Rosie seemed satisfied the recovery mission was complete. After thrusting her head in beside Tavis and giving the channel one more sniff, she backed away and trotted over to join Rebel in his vigil over the flock.

"I can't thank you enough for your help today." Rob reached out to pull Tavis to his feet, giving the man's hand a hearty shake before releasing it.

Maddie, who'd been standing at the opening to the snow cave, cheering each released sheep, echoed his thanks. "Would you be able to stay for a little Christmas dinner? Nothing fancy, I'm afraid. But we do have pie."

A twinkle lit the man's blue eyes. "Och, that pie would sure be tempting, but I have me own sheep to tend to. I'd best be away home now."

"Wait just a minute, then, and I'll send some with you." She sped off toward the wagon to return a few minutes later with a pie tin covered with a checked blue cloth which he suspected contained more than just a sliver of pie. She'd been baking Christmas delicacies for the better part of the week, and though he loved her cookies and pastries, he was more than willing to share the bounty.

"Thanks again, Mr. Tavis," she said, handing him the loaded pie tin. "I don't know how we would ever have gotten all those sheep dug out without your help."

"That's nae bother. I'm glad tae help whin I kin." Tucking the tin into the crook of his arm, Tavis shouldered his staff and shovel and headed off at a fast clip up the canyon.

Rob envied the older man's spry gait. He felt his own strength drain from his body as he sank to a seat on a nearby rock, rolling his neck and shoulders to loosen the kinks. It wasn't right, somehow, when a man thirty years his senior could best him in strength and endurance.

Curse this disease. The burning in his throat and dull ache in his chest promised the day's exertion would cost him—dearly.

"Are you all right?"

He dug deep to muster a smile that would wipe the concern from his wife's face but had little success.

"You look all done in. Why don't you head up to the wagon and rest awhile before dinner? The dogs and I can see that the sheep are bedded down for the night."

He knew he should argue, man up, and finish his responsibilities, but for the second time today, his need was greater than his pride.

He forced himself to his feet and pulled Maddie into a quick embrace before staggering up the hill to the wagon.

Chapter Twenty-Three

❦

Maddie dipped her cleaning rag in the disinfectant and wiped the bench next to Rob's side of the bunk. The formalin in the solution stung her nose and throat. Keeping house in a sheep wagon was light work compared to their New Jersey cottage, but keeping house for a consumptive was never easy. Luckily the day, though cold, was fair, like most days here in Wyoming. As soon as she finished with the wipe down, she would open wide the window and door and join Rob with the sheep. The wagon would have plenty of time to air before dinner.

They'd never made it to town for New Year's. Never made it to town at all, though Jackson arrived a few days after the Christmas blizzard with Jenny in tow laden with gifts and letters from Edie and Mother Skivington. By the time Jenny left, Rob's heavy work in the frigid temperatures of Christmas Day had taken their toll. He'd developed a horrendous chest cold which, compounded with his tuberculosis, had left him weak as a baby lamb and barely able to raise his head even to cough.

How he'd frightened her. Jackson too, no doubt, since he returned to their camp the next day with the young doctor from Dallas. The poor man was obviously more used to mining accidents than tuberculosis patients, but he was able to prescribe a mustard poultice that turned the trick of loosening the congestion in Rob's overworked lungs and some morphine that finally allowed Rob to get the rest he so desperately needed.

She still wasn't sure he should be up and around, but she had little say in the matter. One week of bed rest was all she could get out of the man, though she'd proven herself more than capable of handling the sheep on her own. Well, with the help of Rosie and Rebel, of course. Lord knows, they'd both be lost without the help of those two.

Giving the bench one last swipe, she dropped the rag back into the basin. A quick sweep of the floor and her cleaning would be done. She reached above her to pull her broom from the hooks, which fastened it to the domed roof of the wagon. Squeezing the solution from the rag, she wrapped it over the straw bristles of her broom and tied the ends in a knot around its handle. Sprinkling the small patch of linoleum with more of the disinfectant, she quickly swept up the dampened dirt, careful not to raise any of the dust that was the bane of consumptives. Or so the doctors said.

Thank goodness the wagon was so small. Just a few minutes of cleaning was making her head pound from the fumes. She probably should have opened the top of the dutch door and the window to create a cross current while she worked, but she hadn't wanted to let in the cold of the February morning. No matter. She'd be out in the wind soon enough. Time enough then to clear her head.

She pulled off her rubber gloves and untied her apron. Now to bank the stove and set the beans on to simmer, and she'd be on her way.

She'd just lifted the lid to stir the pot of beans when she heard them. Hoofbeats! Who could that be? Jackson had been out to move them two days ago, so she was sure it wasn't him. Could someone be coming to visit? Not likely in the depth of winter. Jenny had just been to visit, or she might suspect her.

171

Pulling back the curtain on the small window in the dutch door, she scanned the horizon, hoping for signs of company, but her breath caught and froze at what she saw cresting the rise to the left of the wagon. Men. Armed men. With hoods, billowing black with holes cut for the eyes and mouth. She let the curtain drop back into place and backed away from the door, thankful now that she hadn't opened it wide for cleaning. Would they stop here? What could they want? One thing was certain. Guns and hoods were not a good thing.

She quickly flipped the night latch on the door and melted into the shadows of the wagon's interior. With curtains on both the door and window, there was little chance of anyone seeing her from the outside. Yet, she still felt vulnerable standing in the middle of the wagon. She dropped to the bench beside the stove and pulled her knees up against her chest, willing herself invisible. Maybe if they found no one home, they would just go away. If not, there was always Rob's rifle.

She glanced over to where it hung off the brackets above their bed. He rarely took it with him during the daytime since they'd moved down to the plains. The sight of it hanging there brought her some comfort, though she'd only used it herself one time. Rob had insisted on teaching her to use it one day early last summer. But the kick had been enough to knock her backward, and she'd sported a bruise on her shoulder for days after that. She'd not been tempted to ask for more lessons, and Rob hadn't pushed. Now she wished she at least remembered how to load the thing.

"Hey, scab herder! Anyone home?"

Her head whipped around at the sound just to the other side of the door. The wagon dipped as someone stepped onto the ladder and jiggled at the doorknob.

"He's got it locked."

"Is someone in there?"

"Not likely if the sheep aren't here."

"Unless he's sleeping on the job." This comment was greeted

with laughter and a few crude comments.

"Hey, boss." The man at the door yelled above their chatter. "Want I should fire it for you? If he's in there, we could smoke him out."

"Naw. Leave it for now. Let's find the sheep, and then we can come back. I'd like to look through it first. If it's locked, must be something in there he doesn't want to lose."

The wagon lurched again as the man outside jumped down. A few minutes later, she heard the men's horses leave. She let out the breath she'd been holding since they'd talked of firing the wagon and wiped shaking hands on the broadcloth of her skirt. *Dear God. Now what?*

The men's last words finally registered. The sheep! If they found the sheep, then they would find Rob and . . . her eyes cut to where his gun still hung, useless, over their bed.

A sob strangled in her throat. Throwing herself across the bunk, she pulled back the window curtain just in time to see the horses disappear over a rise, heading straight for the grazing area. Rob! Kneeling, she pulled the heavy rifle off its perch and fumbled for the pouch of shot on the shelf above the window. Breathing one last desperate prayer, she flew to the door of the wagon.

～

Rob leaned against the hillside, eyes closed, absently stroking Rosie's fur. How he hated this infernal disease and the energy it sapped from his body. He squinted through half-closed eyelids at the sketch pad and book that lay on the ground beside him. Last summer, he'd filled the pad with images of the sheep, the dogs, birds, bugs, flowers. Now he couldn't even summon up the energy to pick up a pencil or flip a page.

He sucked a deep breath into his lungs, held it, and slowly released. Eight months they'd spent in this new, dry climate. Eight months! Yet here, he was no better off than a year ago at this time. He could fool Maddie into thinking his weakness was due to the cold that laid him low right after Christmas, but he knew better. She probably did too, but they weren't talking about it. Neither wanted to admit to the other that this desperate journey they'd taken might well be futile.

He knew the signs, though. His afternoon fevers, the ache in his chest, and the fullness in his head—all signs that had nothing to do with a cold and everything to do with diseased lungs and hemorrhages. Hadn't he had exactly these same symptoms last winter before that first hemorrhage that had thrown them into the panic and landed them here, fifteen hundred miles away from anything familiar? And with what gain?

A coughing spasm wracked his body, forcing him to sit up and draw out the large paper napkin from his pocket. When he pulled it away, he studied the tell-tale streaks of blood that marred its pristine whiteness. Another one he'd have to burn before Maddie could see it. He folded over the stains and tucked it back in his pocket. Lying back, he drew in another deep breath. He held it as if this breath would suddenly be the one to make the difference, to tip the scales and set the diseased material it touched on the pathway to health and vitality.

Releasing slowly, he scanned the sheep spread out around him, feeding on brownish-gray grasses and sage that looked about as dead as he felt. How could they even find sustenance? At least the snow was sparse here. Merely a thick dusting of powder that would surely be gone by midday. And, as Jackson was quick to tell him, the snow was a blessing. It allowed the sheep the moisture they needed without finding a stream or a river, both hard to come by in this lower winter range.

At least the sheep were surviving, flourishing even. Judging by the round bellies on most of the ewes, their stint with Baldwin's buck band back in late November had its intended result. Six more weeks, and they'd be welcoming new lambs to the flock. He should be pleased, but the thought only made him nervous. If he hadn't enough energy to put pencil to paper, how in the world would he manage the lambing season? By all accounts, he'd heard from the other shepherds, the spring season with its lambing and sheering was the busiest of all in a shepherd's year. He had no idea how he and Maddie were going to handle it.

Well, he'd worry about that another day. Who knew? In six weeks, he might be a new man ready to take on the world again. Yeah, and the Sahara might just become a rain forest too.

He wasn't sure when it first registered that the pounding in his head was hoofbeats and not merely his headache intensifying. Probably not until he heard the whinny of a horse and looked up to see them—lined up across the ridge, black hoods billowing in the wind. Five horsemen. All armed. And him with nothing more than his shepherd's crook to protect him.

The pounding of his heart now matched that of his head. He struggled to his feet, hoping his legs would hold him. Whatever the men intended—and from the looks of it, it wasn't good—he'd be deuced if he'd take it lying down.

The men began wending their way through the sheep toward him. When they were less than a hundred feet from him, they stopped.

"Why, lookee here, boys. If it isn't the joool—" A jab from his neighbor's gun butt stopped the words short, but not before Rob recognized both the voice and the saddle on the rider's bay. No one else he knew had one as fancy.

"Hello, Jake." He wasn't sure if acknowledging his recognition would serve to his advantage or disadvantage, but it was too late to recall the words now. They were barely more than a raspy whisper anyway. He couldn't even face the enemy with the strength of voice.

"Fool." A stocky man on a testy black stallion barked at Jake. "Shut up and let me do the talking."

He turned to Rob, dark eyes glinting through the holes of his hood. "You've crossed a deadline, scab herder. This here's cattle country. Your scab carriers aren't welcome here."

"I've never heard of any deadline. Far as I know, this is all government range land, open to anyone."

"Shows how much you know, then, scabber. Now, if you want to live to tell about today, you'd best stand back and not interfere with what we're about to do." The man wheeled his horse toward the grazing sheep and shouted to the other men. "Have at 'em, boys."

Guns blazing, the men sat in their saddles and began mowing down sheep by the dozens. Rob closed his eyes, willing himself to think of something, anything, he could do to stop the slaughter. But he had nothing. No gun. No weapon of any kind. He could whack at one of them with his shepherd's hook, but what would that accomplish? Probably nothing more than getting himself killed. No, for Maddie's sake, much as it galled him, he'd best sit tight and let them do their worst.

Rosie wasn't inclined to be so passive. At the first sound of gunfire, she'd shot after the men's horses, growling and nipping at their hooves. The men paid little attention to her until she leaped under the legs of Jake's big bay, causing it to stumble.

Cursing, Jake sighted his gun on the little dog and pulled the trigger. The bullet's impact sent her rolling.

"No!" The roar burst from somewhere deep inside him. He sprang toward Jake, swinging his shepherd's crook with all his might. The blow landed square on the bay's backside. At its impact, the horse bucked, pitching Jake off, then stampeded into the milling sheep, scattering them as he ran. The flock took off as if a pack of coyotes was on their tail.

But that roar was too much for his pathetic lungs. The minute it left his lungs, he felt the burst. The hemorrhage no longer announced itself in small droplets but burst forth in force, gushing from both his mouth and throat. Coughing and spewing blood, Rob felt the darkness closing in as the ground rushed up to meet him. And just before the black took over, he thought he heard a woman scream.

I'm sorry, Maddie. So, so sorry.

Chapter Twenty-Four

The first gunshot stopped her cold in her tracks, then sent her sprinting the last few yards to the top of the ridge. She was too late. *Please, God. No. Don't let them hurt Rob.*

She'd been imagining all sorts of dire scenarios since setting off from the wagon but hadn't really expected the men to resort to gunfire. She'd been wrong.

Panting, she threw herself to the ground just at the top of the hill and peered over. What she saw exceeded even her worst nightmares. Sheep lay in piles, bleating in agony and terror as the hooded men mowed them down with round after round from their rifles. The dogs raced amongst the horses' hooves, barking frantically. One of the horses whinnied and reared, sending the rest of the flock racing in streams of white terror up and over the neighboring hill. But the terror that caught and held her eyes was the sight of Rob pitching forward, blood pouring from his mouth and pooling in the snow around him as his head hit the ground.

No. No. No. She shut her eyes, willing this to be some horrible dream, then opened them again to see the scene unchanged. They'd shot her husband. These monsters. These hooded, beastly cowards had shot an unarmed man in cold blood.

"No!" Her scream was deep and primal. Rising to her feet, she pulled the rifle to her shoulder, leveling her aim on the nearest horseman. She wanted to shoot, hurt as she'd been hurt, but wasn't even sure the gun was loaded. Instead, she let her anger and frustration out in a scream so piercing, all five men turned in her direction.

The one she held in her sights slowly raised his hands in surrender, rifle held loosely at arm's length.

"Whoa, there, ma'am. No need for bloodshed."

Too late for that.

"Get out." The words came out in a low guttural snarl she barely recognized as her own voice. "Get out, or I'll shoot. I swear I will."

She swung her gun, pointing at each man, in turn, causing each to lower their guns and back away.

"Lady, we don't want no trouble," the first man continued. "Just put down your gun so we can talk."

She wanted so badly to pull the trigger but knew she couldn't risk it. If the gun wasn't loaded, then they'd know she was unarmed and as helpless as Rob had been. No telling what they'd do then. Her best bet was to stick to her bluff.

"I don't want to talk. I just want you to leave."

"Now, see here, ma'am. That's where we have the problem. Like I told your man here before he started coughing up blood . . ."

Coughing blood? A hemorrhage? Then Rob wasn't shot? Her relief was so intense she almost lowered her gun. She had to get to him. If only these men would go away. She forced herself to focus on what the hooded man was saying.

" . . . so you see, ma'am, it's not us that needs to leave. We'll give you forty-eight hours, and then we'll be back. If you and your man and what's left of your stinking scab bearers aren't out of here, then we'll escort you out of here—without your wagon and without your sheep. And no amount of rifle waving is gonna stop us. Do I make myself clear?"

She gave the man a quick nod, hoping her agreement would do what her threats had been unable to accomplish.

"Then our work here is done. Come on, boys. Let's go." He raised a hand to his hooded forehead as if to tip an imaginary hat at her, then wheeled his horse and thundered off over the rise, the rest of his gang trailing behind him.

Maddie watched until the last horse disappeared over the horizon, then stumbled down the hill to Rob's side.

"Rob. Rob." Dropping to her knees beside him, she felt desperately at his throat for a pulse. A faint flutter sparked her hope. *Please, God. Let him be alive.* Quickly, she rolled him over on his back and loosened the collar button on his shirt, still wet and sticky from his blood.

"Rob. Can you hear me? It's Maddie. I'm here."

She ran her fingers through his hair, feeling his scalp for signs of a gunshot, then over his neck, shoulders, chest. Nothing. Could the armed man have been telling the truth? Had he truly not been shot? The blood caked his mustache and beard and covered the front of his shirt but came from no other source that she could see.

She shook him gently and lightly patted his cheeks. They were so very pale.

"Please, Rob. Wake up. Talk to me. Please."

His eyelids flickered but stayed closed. Then he mumbled incoherently.

"What is it?" she leaned in to catch the sound.

"Rosie." The word was faint but audible. Rosie? Why was he so worried about that dog? The last she'd seen, the dogs had been tearing around amongst the horses. She hadn't paid any attention to them once she saw Rob fall.

"Rosie and Rebel are fine. Probably off gathering the rest of the sheep for us right now. I'll see to them later. But first, we need to get you back to the wagon." Though she had no idea how she was going to accomplish that. It would almost be easier to bring the wagon to Rob. General, the mule Jackson had left them, was tied up by the wagon. But without Jackson's horse to help, General wasn't strong enough to pull it.

But he could pull Rob.

Her brother Percy had a picture book that showed Indian warriors pulling their wounded behind a horse in a carrier. A travois she thought it was called. Surely she could fashion something from material they had back at the wagon.

Only she hated to leave Rob alone. Feeling in the pocket of Rob's heavy overcoat, she located his canteen. Thank goodness, it still held plenty of water. She pulled off her own coat and wadded it behind him to prop up his head and shoulders.

"Rob, I have some water for you. Can you drink it for me?" Cupping the back of his head, she placed the neck of the canteen against his lips and let the water dribble against them. Obediently, he opened his lips and swallowed.

"Once more."

He swallowed again. Heartened by his response, she screwed the lid back on the canteen and placed it beneath his right hand.

"Rob, I have to go back to the wagon to get General. I won't be long. If you need more to drink, your canteen is right here. Don't try to get up on your own. I'll be right back. Do you hear me?"

An almost imperceptible nod, and then a murmur. "Rosie."

Again? Reluctantly, she turned to the piles of dead and dying sheep she'd been able to ignore in her concern for Rob. Scanning the slaughter, her heart sank when her gaze snagged a small black and white mound just a few yards away. Oh, no. No. Not Rosie, too.

Heart in her throat, she rose and walked slowly toward the little bundle, softly calling the dog's name. The mound did not move, but a flutter of the dog's tail sent Maddie racing to her side. Like Rob, Rosie lay motionless in a pool of her own blood. Dropping to her knees, Maddie quickly located a bullet hole just above the little dog's right shoulder. Blood oozed from the wound.

As Maddie stroked Rosie's silky fur, the dog raised her head and weakly licked Maddie's fingers.

"Hush, now. Don't try to move, girl." Pulling off her apron, Maddie folded it into a pad to staunch the wound, then used the apron strings to tie it tight. Gently, she lifted the wounded animal and carried her over to Rob where she settled her by his side in the crook of his arm.

"You two sit tight now. I'll be back with General as quick as I can."

With a last stroke of Rosie's fur and a kiss to Rob's cheek, Maddie stood, lifted her skirts, and ran toward the wagon.

Chapter Twenty-Five

How she managed to get the two of them into the wagon, Maddie never was certain. The afternoon became a blur of strained muscles, worry, tears, and despair. The makeshift travois she fashioned from a blanket, a shovel, and a broom worked relatively well. Without it, she would never have been able to transport Rob the quarter-mile to the wagon. However, she feared he'd suffered more damage from the rocks along the way than if she'd left him lying where he was. But with daylight waning and the temperatures falling again, she didn't have that option.

Once back at the wagon, she used every ounce of her strength to heft him up into the doorway, then drag him into the wagon and up onto the bunk. Now settled into the bed, a warm mustard poultice on his chest, he had regained a little of his color but still had not opened his eyes. She knew she faced an impossible decision. With night fast approaching, should she risk the darkness and colder temperatures to ride for help, or should she waste precious hours and minutes to wait for morning? One look at her husband's pale, white face told her she could not wait. He needed more care than she could give him.

She quickly stoked the stove, then began to prepare herself

for the cold, dark ride ahead. Shrugging out of her dress, she pulled on a flannel shirt and donned a pair of Rob's thick canvas britches, rolling up the legs and cinching them tight around her waist with a belt. A woolen muffler, a thick duster, and gauntlets completed the outfit. Finally, she grabbed Rob's wool cap and pulled the flaps down over her ears.

Winter days were short, and she would need to get on her way as quickly as possible to take advantage of the daylight she had left. As it was, the sun was already sinking low over the mountains to her west.

Whistling for General, she quickly threw Rob's saddle on the mule's back and adjusted the stirrups. She'd never ridden astride before in her life but had no choice tonight. The lady's horse and sidesaddle she'd rented for her ride out to camp last summer had been returned to town long ago. She led General over to the wagon and used the wagon's tongue as a mounting block.

Grabbing the saddle horn, she pulled herself into the saddle. Mother would be spinning in her grave to see her now, sitting astraddle in a man's britches. She couldn't think about that now, or about how high she was off the ground, or how nervous horseback riding of any kind made her. She had to concentrate on moving and moving quickly. Rob's life depended on it.

Kicking General's sides, she set out at a brisk trot, heading northeast. Keeping the Wind River mountains to her left and setting her sights on a spot slightly to the right of Table Rock Mountain, she knew she was heading in the right direction. As long as daylight held, she would be fine. Once night fell, she had no idea how she would navigate. She'd worry about that when the time came. She'd take it one worry at a time. For now, she had all she could handle to keep her speed up and stay on the horse.

The thought of Rob's still, white face spurred her on. By now, she was convinced he had indeed suffered a hemorrhage. She'd found no gunshot wounds, and he'd had no more bleeding. She had no way of knowing how much blood he had lost, though.

She'd heard of hemorrhages so severe they were fatal. If it were to happen again while she was gone . . .

I can't lose him, Lord. I can't. Her words pounded in rhythm with General's hoofbeats. She knew it would be close to four hours before she could even hope to be back at his side. And that was if she were able to find a doctor in Dallas. If she had to go all the way to Lander for help, the time away would be even longer. What if the hooded men returned before she could? Would they burn the wagon with Rob still in it?

She spurred General again, urging him faster and faster. The sun dropped below the mountains to her west, creating a rosy glow on the snow ahead of her. Any other time, she would have reveled in its beauty, but tonight she only shuddered, knowing its loss meant a dark, lonely ride ahead. The cold nipped at her nose and numbed her fingers even through the thick leather gauntlets.

Had she been a fool to leave Rob? If she got lost on the trail or froze to death during the night, it might be days or even weeks before someone found them. *Lord, keep me on the trail. Lead me to some help.*

She felt General's labored breathing beneath her and knew she'd have to slow her pace. The old mule could not keep up her breakneck speed for long. Somehow, she'd have to calm herself if they were to survive this.

Slowing her pace, she searched her memory for words of promise to still her thoughts.

He that dwelleth in the secret place of the most High shall abide under the shadow of the Almighty . . . . Thou shalt not be afraid for the terror by night; nor for the arrow that flieth by day . . . For he shall give his angels charge over thee, to keep thee in all thy ways. They shall bear thee up in their hands, lest thou dash thy foot against a stone. . . .

Soon other verses sprang to mind.

My help cometh from the LORD, which made heaven and earth. He will not suffer thy foot to be moved: he that keepeth thee will not slumber. . . . The LORD is thy keeper: the LORD is thy shade upon thy right hand. *The sun shall not smite thee by day, nor the moon by night. The LORD shall preserve thee from all evil: he shall preserve thy soul.*

As the sky darkened, a full moon rose in the northeast ahead of her, like a beacon sent from God to light her way. Breathing a prayer of thanks, she cantered on in its path.

∼

SHE'D BEEN RIDING FOR ABOUT AN HOUR WHEN SHE SAW THEM, riders cresting the next rise. Heart racing, she searched the landscape around her. No trees, no coves, not even a ditch deep enough to hide both her and General. Had they seen her? Doubtful in this light, since the moon was at their backs. Still, if they came much closer, she would have no way to avoid them.

What if they were the hooded men coming back? She could think of no good reason for anyone to be traveling this time of night. The harmless traveler would have camped for the night by now. Unless they had an emergency like she did. But in that case, they should be heading the other direction. No town of any size lay behind her.

They rode steadily toward her as if drawn by an invisible line. Pulling General to a walk, she eased him closer to the scarlet cliffs, praying the shadows would conceal her presence. As the riders drew near, she could see there were three of them, all men, the lead horseman looming far larger in height and breadth than the other two.

On they came up a path that would take them within a few feet of where she stood. She covered General's nose to keep him from whinnying a welcome to the oncoming horses, then held her own breath as they trotted by. Wait. There was something so familiar about the lead horseman.

"Jackson!" At her call, all three men pulled their horses to a stop and turned in her direction.

Oh, Lord. Please don't let me be wrong. But it had to be him.

She'd met no one else other than the Garrity brothers, who even came close to sitting so tall in the saddle.

"Who's there?" The man turned into the shaft of moonlight, giving her a clear look at his face.

With a sigh of relief, Maddie stepped from the shadows. "It's me, Jackson. Mrs. Skivington."

"Maddie?" One of the other riders jumped from his horse and ran toward her. From his size, she thought it might be Gabe, but the voice was all wrong. "What are you doing out here in the dark? Where's Rob?"

Maddie blinked as the boy stepped into the moonlight. Was this a hallucination? Had she become so cold and tired she drifted off and was now dreaming? She saw his face, *knew* that face, but nothing made sense.

"George?" She looked to Jackson for answers.

"I found these two by the stage office in Lander this morning. They wouldn't rest until I agreed to lead them out here. Ran into a problem with the shoe on one of the horses we hired and had to stop off at Baldwin's to repair it, or we would have been out to your camp by now."

These two? Maddie peered around Jackson at the face of the third rider, also familiar, also unexpected.

"Fred, too?"

She threw herself into George's arms and, to her dismay, and most likely his as well, burst into tears. His arms came around her, and she could hear the panic in his voice.

"Maddie. What is it? Why are you here? Has something happened to Rob?"

"He's fine. Well, not fine, but not shot anyway."

"Shot!"

Goodness, she needed to pull herself together, or she'd have them all in a panic.

She pulled out of George's arms and wiped her eyes. Taking a deep breath, she started again.

"A band of armed men raided our camp this morning." Was it really only this morning? It seemed a lifetime ago.

"They shot up the sheep, told us we'd crossed their deadline, warned us to move our camp, or they'd be back and burn our wagon . . . take everything." Hard as she tried, the last words still came out in a sob.

Taking another deep breath, she tried again. "Rob had a hemorrhage, lost a lot of blood. I was on my way to find a doctor. He's bad, George. Worse than I've ever seen him. I don't know . . ." The tears would come, no matter how hard she tried to stop them.

George pulled her close again. "Hush, now. We're here. You're no longer alone."

When had this boy become a man she could lean on? She didn't know but was so very thankful God had sent him and Fred when she most needed them. Jackson too.

"Can you get your brothers back to camp?" Jackson's voice was tight with anger.

"Yes, I'm sure I can find the way."

"I'll ride to Dallas and fetch Doc Reynolds. I should be back by morning, but if I'm not, go ahead and hitch your brothers' horses to the wagon and start pulling it this way. I'll meet you with help as soon as I'm able. After we've seen to Rob, I'll notify Baldwin and Bunce. We'll get this sorted out. They won't get away with this, I promise you."

"Thank you, Jackson. Please, just get the doctor. George and Fred can help me with everything else."

With a nod, he turned his horse and galloped away.

Chapter Twenty-Six

Something warm and heavy lay on his chest, making it hard to breathe and impossible to move. He struggled to lift a finger, move an eyelid, but the effort that took was beyond him. Where had all his strength gone? If he could just open his eyes, maybe he could make sense of where he was, what it was that held him down.

He must have drifted off because when he woke again, he heard voices, hushed and worried. Familiar voices. Voices of home. He must be dreaming. He was in Wyoming. That much he knew, but he could swear he heard his brothers' voices.

With a monumental effort he dragged his eyes open, taking in the worried, white face of Maddie and there behind her, George, and was that Fred? Maybe he wasn't in Wyoming after all, and yet above him, he could see the arched ribs of the wagon's roof boards dark against its white canvas top. Faces from home in a Wyoming setting. Why could he not make sense of this? And who was sitting on his chest?

Struggling, he lifted his head to peer down at his body.

"Don't try to move, Rob. You've had a hemorrhage and must stay still. The doctor will be here shortly." Maddie pushed gently against his chest until he acquiesced.

A hemorrhage. Now he remembered. The dull ache in his chest, the torrent of blood that seemed to burst from his nose and throat. Other memories flooded back.

"Rosie."

"She's here. On the bed beside you. I've bandaged her wound the best I could. I think she'll be all right, but we'll let the doctor tend to her too when he arrives."

His recovered memory made his brothers' faces behind her even more incomprehensible. They seemed real. George and Fred, pale and more shaken than he'd ever seen them, yet there all the same. He almost hated to ask.

"George? Fred?" What if they were hallucinations? Some trick his mind was playing on him. Maybe he was farther gone than he thought.

"Yes, Rob. It's George and Fred. They're here with us. They came all the way from New Jersey just when we needed them most."

Relief coursed through him. He tried to smile, but the effort afforded him little more than a slight lift to his mustache. His attempt to stretch out his right arm to the boys was almost as futile, but enough to bring George to his side to clasp it and give his shoulder a pat.

"Mum sent us out. Said we should come help with the sheep before lambing season begins."

George's words almost drew forth another smile. Wasn't that just like their mum? For as long as he could remember, she'd been sending these two out to help him. Why should his moving clear across the country make a difference? Actually, the only difference he could see was that they were finally big enough to be a help.

"Thank . . . you." He wished he could express himself in more than a low, raspy whisper, but the words themselves were almost more than he could manage.

The squeeze from his brother's fingers told him they were more than enough. He closed his eyes and must have drifted off again because the next thing he felt was the cold pressure of metal against his chest.

Dragging his eyes open again, he saw the sandy-haired doctor who'd visited their camp a few weeks ago peering down at him, stethoscope to his ears.

"Ah, you are awake. Splendid. If you can do so without coughing, I'd like you to take a deep breath for me and hold it."

The man seemed competent enough, though young. He certainly knew the standard routine. If Rob had a nickel for the times a doctor had listened to his breathing in the last two years, well, he certainly wouldn't need to chase a bunch of dumb sheep around for a living.

Ignoring the burning in his lungs and throat, he pulled a breath in deep and held it, slowly releasing at the doctor's nod.

"Now, again."

The second breath caught in a tickle at the edge of his throat, and try as he might, he could not hold back the cough.

The doctor held up a hand. "Enough for now. We don't want to initiate any more bleeding. But I'd like a look at your throat. Mrs. Skivington, if you would, hold that lantern just above his face, and if you'd just open up and say 'ah' for me, sir, I'll take a quick peek. A little lower, ma'am. Yes. There." His words trailed off as he peered close for a minute, then took a step back.

Turning to his doctor's bag, he pulled out a syringe and vial. "Well, Mr. Skivington. I'm sure I don't need to tell you, you've suffered a severe hemorrhage, probably due to those abscesses in your larynx. There could possibly be others in your lungs as well. All natural occurrences, given your disease. However, we'd like to stem any further bleeding if possible. I recommend complete bedrest. At least until the bleeding stops completely. No talking. No exertion of any kind. I'm going to give you an injection of morphine to help you rest, and we'll do all we can to make sure you are comfortable."

As if he could get up and move around if he felt like it. After all that blood loss, he was too weak to even lift his little finger.

He hated the fuzzy-headed feeling morphine gave him but allowed the doctor to administer the shot without protest. He'd learned early on that doctors liked their medicines. And until he gained a modicum of his former strength back, he knew he was at the mercy of the doctor and his wife and all the other well-meaning people who filled the wagon. When he'd turned his head earlier, he'd caught a glimpse of Jackson, and his brothers huddled just inside the door. Six people in their tiny wagon. He'd thought it crowded with two.

Rob let his mind wander as the doctor handed Maddie another vial from his bag and continued his instructions. Managing the details of his daily care would fall into his wife's capable hands and not his own. His main concern was getting on his feet again as soon as possible. He had no idea the state of his flock. He knew the gunmen had decimated a good number of them, but he'd watched the majority of the herd take off amid all the chaos. If he could locate them, he might still salvage some of their livelihood. With lambing season in the offing, haste was imperative.

He turned his head in an effort to capture Jackson's attention, but the man seemed intent on what the doctor was telling Maddie. He wished he could clear his throat, cough, talk, anything but didn't want to risk the possibility of another onslaught of blood like the last one. And drat it all, that confounded morphine was already taking effect. He could feel the languor steeling up his body, turning his limbs to lead and his brain to mush. His talk with Jackson would have to wait.

～

MADDIE FELT THE BILE RISE IN HER THROAT AT THE SIGHT OF all the sheep carcasses lying in frozen heaps on the open plain, streaks of rust marring the white of their thick wool. She blinked away tears at the sheer waste of it all. All those pregnant mothers. All the unborn lambs.

Jackson, who'd left with the doctor the night before, had returned this morning with an entire band of men in tow. Herders Tavis, Gabe, and Louis, had come to help them round up their errant flock. A Mr. Spence, who Jackson introduced as one of the best shearers in Fremont county, planned to salvage whatever wool he could from the piles of sheep carcasses. Ranchers Baldwin and Bunce came as representatives of the Fremont County Wool Growers Association. Sheriff Charlie Stough had also come to survey the damage.

They all stood on the crest of the ridge where Maddie had confronted the hooded men the day before. In her worry for Rob yesterday, she'd barely registered the destruction they'd left in their wake. Now her heart ached at the sight of so many slaughtered sheep.

Beside her, Tavis pulled his cap from his head and slapped it against his thigh. "It's a shame, lassie. That it is. A crying shame."

"It's more than a shame. It's an outrage. Those cattle ranchers have no more right to this land than we do." Louis paced the edge of the ridge, face dark with anger.

"You say we're nowhere near their deadline?" Sheriff Stough asked him.

"You know as well as I do, those ranchers set the Sweetwater as their deadline ten years ago. That's fifteen miles south of here. Jackson's anger was more controlled than his brother's but no less evident. "Besides, Emmett and the others have never ranched this far north before. We've been using this ground for sheep for years. Doesn't make a lick of sense."

"You're sure it was Emmett?"

"Can't be sure of anything. The men were all masked, but Rob swears that one of them was Emmett's kid Jake. Recognized his horse, plus the boy was foolish enough to address Rob by name," Baldwin answered.

Sheriff Stough turned toward her. "Can you verify this ma'am?"

If Rob said it, then it had to be true, but she had no knowledge of it. "I didn't come upon the men until later, and I only spoke to one of them. He was their leader, I think. Short, stocky, and riding a black horse."

"Could it have been Finley?" Jackson said.

"Could have been any number of men. Heck, could a been Bunce here, though somehow I doubt that." Baldwin's words drew all their gazes to the second rancher, who was indeed short and stocky. He patted the mane of his black gelding and gave them all a sheepish smile.

"The fact is," Baldwin continued. "The men were masked and other than Mr. Skivington recognizing Jake, we have no idea who any of them were. The best we can do is put out a reward for information and wait to see what happens."

"So, we just sit back and let them get away with this?" Louis's voice oozed incredulity.

"I didn't say that. I said we wait. Won't do us any good to be pointing blame without proof. When we get our proof, then we act."

Sheriff Stough seemed to be pondering Baldwin's words. Turning her way again, he said. "Can you tell us again what the man said to you?"

"He said we'd crossed their deadline and would have to move our sheep. He said he'd give us forty-eight hours to leave the area, and if we weren't gone by then, they'd come back and destroy everything. Wagon, sheep, everything."

"Forty-eight hours, huh? And about what time was that, ma'am?"

She thought back. It had been late morning when the men first rode into their camp and probably mid-afternoon before she was able to drag Rob back to the wagon. "Somewhere around noon, maybe?"

"So, we have 'til around noon tomorrow." The sheriff stroked his mustache and looked out over the bloody heaps of sheep.

Louis turned to Baldwin, excitement lighting his face. "We

could always call their bluff. Hide in the wagon with plenty of men and firepower, and when they come back, we'd catch 'em red-handed."

"No!" The men turned at her sudden outburst. "I'm sorry, Louis, but I cannot, *will not*, use my home as bait. Rob is unwell, and I have his two young brothers to consider." She ignored George's cry of protest. "If at all possible, I'd like to be miles away from this spot before noon tomorrow."

The sheriff nodded. "I understand, ma'am. And I certainly have no intention of putting you or your husband in the path of further danger. Besides, more than likely, the men who did this are watching us right now. Not much chance of our catching them by surprise. They won't be coming back unless they know they have the manpower to outgun us. I don't know about the rest of you, but I'm not in the mood for an all-out war."

He turned to Baldwin and Bunce. "Your best bet, the way I see it, is to put out word of the reward you mentioned earlier. Then, if that doesn't bring any results, you could try to spark a confrontation by bringing in another herder and his flock in a few weeks. Hide men in his wagon before you ever cross their supposed deadline and wait and see if they attack. I'm not recommending it, mind you. That's a sure-fire way to get someone killed, but if you're looking to spark a fight, it would be your best option. In the meantime, I'll poke around a bit, see if I can unearth any clues. Then, I'll head on over to the Sweetwater and visit with some of the ranchers."

With a tip of his hat in her direction, the sheriff made his way down the embankment toward the masses of dead sheep.

Tavis cleared his throat. "If you're wantin' a mon to be the bait for these blackguards, I'd be a willin', sir."

"Thanks, Tavis. I appreciate the offer, but I'm not sure I'm willing to risk my men or my sheep at this point. Let's see what Charlie digs up in his investigation before we try anything drastic."

Maddie could tell Louis wasn't pleased with Baldwin's decision, but the young man was wise enough not to continue arguing with his boss. For her part, she was relieved that the sheepman had chosen to react with a cool head. She had enough on her plate to not want to add a range war to the mix.

∽

"That should do it, ma'am." Mr. Baldwin threw the last bale of wool into his wagon. "I'll store these at the ranch for you until we send our shipments out next month. Spence counted a little over six hundred head. I'd say you'll earn around $700 or $750 off the wool depending on the price they set this spring."

Unspoken between them was the loss six hundred head would cost in the long run. Of the six hundred, they could add to the count at least four to five hundred lambs that would not be born this spring. A devastating loss, no matter how you looked at it.

"Thank you, Mr. Baldwin. I can't tell you how much I appreciate your help today. I don't know what we'd have done without you and Mr. Spence and the others."

"No need to thank me, ma'am. We sheepherders stick together. You tell Rob we'll do all we can to find the men responsible for this. We won't let this rest, I promise you."

"I appreciate that."

"What would you like me to do with these, Miz Skivington?" Mr. Spence came around the wagon, holding out a pile of collars and bells he'd taken from the necks of almost a dozen of the slaughtered sheep. Her throat constricted, and eyes stung when she caught sight of the bedraggled red ribbon in their midst. Oh no.

She remembered the December day she'd tied that ribbon around Fred's neck, tiny gold bell attached. How sweet he'd looked in his jaunty red bow. Their Christmas lamb, she'd called him.

Pressing her lips tight, she reached out to take the bundle from Mr. Pence, pausing at the sight of the blue-collar with the largest bell. Mrs. Finch too? Her fingers trembled as he placed them in her hand. Taking a deep breath, she pasted a fake smile on her face.

"Now, gentlemen. Is there anything I can get you before you leave?"

"No, thank you, ma'am. We'd best be on our way." Mr. Baldwin pulled himself into his saddle, then shaded his eyes as he looked to the southern horizon. "Jackson should be back soon with any of your flock he's been able to find. I told him I wanted you moved out of this area before sundown tonight. You should have no need to worry about a second visit from those outlaws."

Maddie nodded and waved to the men as they headed away, then turning, she climbed the ladder of the sheep wagon, still clutching her handful of sheep bells. Either Rob was already awake, or the bells woke him because he turned his head to look at her as she set the clanging bells on the bench near the stove.

"Mr. Baldwin and Mr. Spence have finished skinning the sheep. Mr. Baldwin said he'd store the wool at his ranch until we can work out the details of having them shipped to market." She wished she could ignore the unspoken question in his eyes but knew no reason to delay the inevitable. "A little over six hundred, Mr. Spence said. That's only a third of the flock."

Rob's gaze drifted to the bundle of bells, then back to her face, more questions in his deep brown eyes. Each bell represented more than a faceless sheep among thousands.

The bell sheep were all known, many named, chosen for their ability to lead or tendency to move about more than the other sheep.

"So, if Jackson and the others are successful, we should still be able to recoup our losses over time." She stepped between him and the pile of bells, hoping to distract him, at least for a time, but the intensity of his gaze never wavered. With a nod to the bench, he asked the wordless question again.

Sighing, she gave in. "Blackie, Spot, Ruby, Black-face, Flossie, Bossy . . ." She ticked off the names, feeling as if she were landing a blow with each one. The last two were the hardest. Swallowing, she choked them out in almost a whisper. "Mrs. Finch and . . . Fred." But he heard. Oh, he most definitely heard.

Turning away, he stared up at the roof of the wagon, jaw tight, muscles in his throat working. Closing the distance between them, she clasped his hand and sank down on the bench beside him.

"I'm sorry, Rob. I'm so, so sorry." The tears she'd been holding in all morning spilled out and over. He reached out with his free hand to wipe them away. How long they sat in their shared misery, she couldn't say. Minutes ticked by unnoticed until Rosie, who'd been sleeping on the bed beside Rob, suddenly lifted her head, ears twitching, and let out a sharp bark.

"What is it, girl?"

An answering bark from outside the wagon sent Maddie running for the door. At that moment, she couldn't recall a sight more beautiful than what she beheld. Hundreds of smelly, stupid sheep flowed in thick white bunches up and over the horizon, Rebel nipping at their heels.

"They're back, Rob! They've found the sheep."

She unlatched the door and hopped down, hitting the ground at a run. Laughing, she threw her arms around the first sheep she came to, startling the animal, who bleated frantically and pulled away. Rebel wasn't nearly as reticent. Seeing her, he bounded over and leaped up, barking a welcome. She bent to hug his quivering body and scratch the soft fur behind his ears.

"Hey, buddy. Did you keep our sheep safe for us?"

From the wagon behind her, she could hear Rosie's answering barks and imagined it was taking all Rob's strength to keep the little dog caged on the bed beside him. Rising, she scanned the horizon until she was rewarded with the sight of Tavis, George, and Fred topping the rise. Grinning like a child on Christmas morning, she waved them in.

"You've found them," she called as the group drew closer.

"A good number of them, aye. All spread in a valley, with our Rebel on guard. By my count, this should be the most of them, aroond a thousand head."

A few hours later, Jackson and Gabe rode in herding several hundred more, followed closely by Louis, who was able to find a few stragglers.

"Found about fifty or so that'd run themselves right off a cliff," he said. "But, given how fast and far they ran, you're lucky to have so many survivors."

He was right. The damage could have been so much worse. As it was, they'd ended up with almost two-thirds of their flock still intact. Truly they had much to be thankful for.

"Is there still time to move camp tonight?" Maddie held her breath as she waited for Jackson to answer. She hated to play the coward, but she wanted nothing more than to pack up what they had and leave this area far behind. The thought of the sheep carcasses piled just over the next rise filled her with a sense of foreboding.

With a quick glance at the late day sun, Jackson nodded. "If we all step to it, we should have you moved by sundown."

The men dispersed, each taking on a different task, and two hours later, Maddie found herself settled into a new camp three miles north and east of the previous one.

"Those men down by the Sweetwater should have no reason to bother you here," Jackson said. "I know of at least four other outfits that are camped closer to them than you are. Tavis, here, being one of them."

She glanced over at the grizzled sheepherder, who gave her his slow smile.

"Louis and I will head over to Tavis' camp tonight and stay with him a few days to see whether those men cause any further trouble. I'll leave Gabe here with you. He can show your brothers the ropes. All you'll need to concentrate on is getting that husband of yours well."

"I will. And Jackson, thank you. Thank you all so much."

The men mounted their horses and set off into the fading light. *Be with them, Lord.* The thought of any of those dear friends having to confront the raiders sent a chill down her spine. *Be with us all.*

Chapter Twenty-Seven

❦

"Baldwin said to tell you he's having a shearing crew in next week. We'll probably be ready for your band by Thursday, barring any rain."

Jackson pushed back his empty pie plate and leaned back, coffee cup cradled in one large hand. The camp tender had arrived with Gabe that morning to help him and the boys dock the tails on the new lambs and castrate all the males. Maddie had spent the day baking in the sheep wagon, and they were all benefiting from her labor. She'd had her hands full, providing enough to feed the lot of them. George and Fred were hearty eaters, but he didn't think he'd ever seen anyone eat so much and so fast as the Garrity brothers.

Gabe, George, and Fred were eating their meal out by the campfire, leaving the small table in the wagon for him and Jackson and Maddie.

Rob cut into the flaky crust of his own piece of apple pie and savored the mixture of tangy and sweet in his mouth. His appetite was finally returning after that hemorrhage two months ago. His strength was returning too.

"Tell Baldwin we'll plan to be there. I sure appreciate all you and he have done for us. I don't know what we'd have done this past year without you and Gabe helping us out. Especially with the lambing."

Thank goodness Mum had sent the boys when she did, or the Garrity brothers would have had to do his entire lambing season on their own. Rob certainly had been no help, bedridden as he was that first month. But the boys had pitched in and done a great job.

Even the job today, unpleasant as it was, after the first few demonstrations by Jackson, George had taken to the work like a duck to water. That boy had the makings of a rancher. Not much fazed him.

He and Fred weren't quite as handy, but they were learning. Thankfully, his ewes and the ones he was herding for Baldwin had come through lambing season successfully.

After that debacle with the hooded cattle ranchers, he hated to lose any more of Baldwin's sheep than he had to, though Jackson had assured him the loss was minimal. Not any worse than what might have been lost had the winter been a hard one. Still, the brutality and senselessness of it all still stuck in his craw.

"Any news from Stough on the investigation?"

Jackson's face darkened. "Nothing new. I don't know why the Association decided to leave it in the sheriff's hands, instead of initiating their own investigation. Everybody knows Charlie's more on the side of the cattlemen than he is us sheep ranchers. Even if he does find out who's behind it, I imagine they'll get away with little more than a slap on the hand."

After this many months, Jackson was probably right. Not that Rob wanted an escalation of enmity between the cattlemen and sheepmen. He hadn't come out here to fight any battles, at least not that kind. Yet, the thought of how he'd ended the confrontation, face down in a pool of his own blood, didn't sit well either. The less he thought of it, the better.

"Besides, Charlie seems to have his hands full with all the robberies these days."

Maddie gave a small gasp. "Robberies?"

"Nothing major. Not like that big bank job over in Casper last month. Just a run of petty jobs. Enough to keep Charlie hopping, though."

"We hadn't heard," Rob said.

"No, I guess you wouldn't since I just brought the latest papers today. A rancher and his wife down near Hailey were attacked about a week ago by a couple of men with black hoods on their heads. Same as you and Maddie. This time the victims were cattle ranchers. The men tied the couple up and left with a sack of valuables. Seems the rancher had just sold some of his steers and still had the money with him at the ranch. The men didn't kill anyone, but they made off with about a thousand in cash.

"And then last Wednesday, a lone gunman held up the stage between Rongis and Meyersville. Mr. Murphy was carrying about five hundred dollars on him from a sale he'd made down in Rawlins. They took that, plus the mail and a few more trinkets and valuables from the schoolteacher for the Twin Creek School who was also on the stage that day."

"Oh, the poor woman. Was anyone hurt?" Maddie was looking decidedly pale.

"The driver was shot in the leg. They were able to get him to the doctor in Rongis, and it looks like he's going to be all right. Like I said, the jobs weren't real big ones. But there's been enough of them in a short span of time to put everyone on edge. The stage has hired an extra outrigger to ride alongside their driver on all their trips now."

Rob placed a hand over Maddie's, which were now clinched tightly in her lap. February's attack was still too fresh. "I'm sure we'll be fine. Those robberies were miles from here."

"Might not hurt to be on the lookout, though," Jackson said. "Keep the wagon door locked at nights and keep your rifle loaded. Do you want me to buy rifles for your brothers? With what you folks went through last winter, it never hurts to be prepared."

"Thanks, Jackson. It might not hurt to have at least one more gun between the lot of us. We'll be headed back into the mountains soon and could use them for predators and game at the very least. I'm hoping the trouble we had with those cattle ranchers was a one-time thing."

Jackson pushed to his feet. "Let's hope. Thanks again for supper, Miz Skivington. Gabe and I better be off if we're to make Baldwin's by sundown. We'll see you there next week?"

"We'll be there."

∼

Rob stood at the edge of an open corral where the crew of shearers was already hard at work. Baldwin had hired a crew of ten men, each able to shear between one and two hundred sheep a day. They should easily be finished with his band before sundown.

The day was hot and dry. The dust from the corral stirred up his cough, but he was reluctant to stand any farther away from the action. He'd never seen a shearing before and was fascinated with the efficiency with which the men worked. Thank goodness Maddie was with the other women in the ranch house today, or she'd be at him like a mother hen to get out of the dust. She meant well, he knew, but he'd be glad when she stopped treating him with kid gloves. Though the hemorrhage had been months ago, she couldn't seem to let it go. Guess he shouldn't complain, but he sure wished she'd start acting less like a mother and more like a wife again.

He coughed into the paper napkin he kept in his pocket, then rested his arms against the top rail of the corral to watch the action. Once a shearer finished with a sheep, he'd set it on its feet, and one of Baldwin's wranglers would direct it into a large pen to the right of the corral where it would be painted with Baldwin's mark.

An unshorn sheep would be released from one of the nearby holding pens, and the shearer would wrestle it into position on its back haunches. The sheep would come into the corral bleating and skittish but go limp and quiet once turned on its back. The shearer would then set to work on the sheep's belly and work his way around the animal until a pile of wool lay at his feet, and the sheep looked as thin and naked as a man in his union suit. The entire process took only minutes to accomplish.

A shout drew Rob's attention to a cloud of dust heading up the road toward the ranch house. A lone horseman was riding hellbent up the drive. Jackson straightened from where he'd been lounging against the corral fence next to Rob, shading his eyes with his hand as he peered in that direction. The rider came to a clattering halt near the barn. Baldwin waved a hand in greeting and detached himself from the group of wranglers out by the pens.

"Looks like Pattie McPherson, camp tender for Bunce's outfit. Better find out what's up," Jackson said.

By the time they reached the man, quite a crowd had gathered. Though the shearing continued in the corrals behind them, the wranglers who weren't busy in the pens hurried over. George, Fred, and Gabe came running over from the horse corral. Baldwin's nine-year-old daughter, who'd been underfoot most of the morning, poked her head up under her father's arm, braids swinging.

"A freight train carrying wool to Rawlins was attacked south of Meyersville yesterday." The young man's words came out in a rush.

"What! By who?"

"Three men on horseback wearing black hoods, the driver says. Attacked him about sundown just as he was stopping to set up camp for the night. One of the men held him at gunpoint while the other two set the wagon on fire. They hit the freighter on the head with the butt of one of their guns and tied him up after that. Just left him there. Another freighter found him this morning, but the wagon was a complete loss by then."

"Whose wool was it?"

"Ours, sir. Bunce and Delfelder's."

"Just one wagon?"

"Yes, sir. We had a freighting train of five wagonloads. That wagon had a bad wheel and had a late start out of the shearing sheds at Hailey, so the freighter wasn't traveling with the rest of the shipment."

"How much did you lose?"

"About 15,000 pounds. The deputy in Meyersville and a posse of sheep men tried to track the raiders this morning, but the trail was already cold by then. Bunce's holding a meeting for any wool growers who can make it to his place this evening. Six o'clock. Charlie Stough and Carmody went down to investigate. Tom said he'd be at the meeting with any information he can find."

"You can bet we'll be there," Baldwin's words were tinged with steel. "Come on up to the house, now. I'll get you a drink."

"No, sir. I better not. I told Bunce I'd make it to as many ranches as I could before six."

"Where all do you need to go? Some of our boys could help take the message."

"I'd appreciate that. If you could get word to Sanderson and Williams, I'll head west and get Vidal and Werlin."

At Baldwin's nod, McPherson turned his mount and urged it at a gallop back down the drive.

"I can go, Mr. Baldwin."

"No, Jackson. I'll need you here to help finish the shearing. Louis, Gabe, saddle up and get the word to Sanderson and Williams."

"Yes, sir." The two brothers were already on their way to the barn, George and Fred on their heels. He supposed he should call his brothers back to help with his own shearing, but since they knew as little about the process as he did, he figured they wouldn't be missed.

Fifteen hundred pounds might only be a small portion of the proceeds for a large operation like Bunce and Delfelder, but for him, a loss like that would take his entire profit. Much as he didn't want to get involved in this range war, he'd be at that meeting tonight with the rest of them.

Chapter Twenty-Eight

"Little Gracie Harris is doing much better. She had such a bout of tonsilitis last month, but I talked to her mother last week. She says she's finally on the mend."

"Did you hear about Mrs. O'Neil? Poor thing. She's been laid up almost all winter after her accident."

"I heard Tom Lowe finally found himself a wife. He went to visit his cousin in Iowa last summer and met a lady there. He's been writing her ever since and left just last week to marry her."

Maddie sank her hands deep into the warm suds of the dish basin and let loose a sigh of contentment. Woman-talk. Though she had no knowledge of any of the people mentioned, she was happy just to be here in the presence of women, listening to the easy cadence of their conversation. After how many months? She did a mental count. Gracious, could it really be nine?

No wonder today felt like a vacation, even though she'd worked like a fiend all day. The last time she'd been on this ranch, she'd been the sole woman. She'd had no idea what to expect when she arrived here this morning. To her delight, she was not only welcomed by the familiar face of Cookie, the camp cook, but several women as well. Beatrice Baldwin, the rancher's wife, her sister, Blanche, and sister-in-law, Nell, had come in from town to help cook for the shearing crew. The women had brought with them a bevy of daughters ranging in age from nine to nineteen. A whole army of women! They'd needed that army.

When she'd arrived just after breakfast cleanup, Cookie greeted her with a smile and a mixing bowl and set her to work on biscuits. A great compliment, Mrs. Baldwin had informed her. Cookie didn't allow just anyone to make biscuits in his kitchen. She didn't know if it were a compliment or merely necessity, but after watching the men go through the noontime meal like a company of locusts, she was inclined to believe it was the latter.

Now, after a full day on her feet, mixing, measuring, stirring, cutting, kneading, washing, and drying, she was still content to be here. That's why she hadn't been at all disappointed when Rob asked if she'd stay at the house until he came back from the meeting. She had little inclination to return to the sheep wagon just yet, and now she had a perfect excuse to stay. She let the women's words flow over her like a balm.

"Jane," Mrs. Baldwin called to her oldest daughter. "Have you seen Mary? She was supposed to churn the butter for me. We won't have enough for breakfast tomorrow if she doesn't get it done soon."

Jane looked up from where she and her cousin Florence were poring over the latest issue of *The Delineator*.

"I haven't seen her all afternoon."

"She told me she was going for a horseback ride," Emily, another of the Baldwin daughters, piped up. "But that was ages ago."

"Maybe Charlotte's seen her." Mrs. Baldwin opened the front door and called to her youngest daughter who was playing with one of the puppies in the yard. "Charlotte, have you seen Mary?"

"She came to the barn earlier and took Duchess out."

"When was that?"

"I dunno. After lunch?"

"Didn't anyone see her at supper?"

They'd all been so busy trying to get all the men fed before the meeting at Bunce's, Maddie couldn't remember who was at supper. They'd eaten in shifts between cooking, serving, and cleaning up.

"Charlotte, check and see if she's in the barn." Mrs. Baldwin turned to her sister with a shake of her head. "That girl is so horse crazy, I can barely keep her in the house."

A few minutes later, Charlotte came running back, her braids flying out behind her. "She's not in the barn, but Duchess is gone. Her saddle's gone too."

"Didn't you say she rode out after lunch?"

Charlotte nodded.

"But that was hours ago. She wouldn't have ridden for that long, especially when she knew she was needed here." Mrs. Baldwin sent a worried glance toward the horizon. Twilight was quickly fading to darkness. "Did she say which way she planned to ride?"

"Naw. She just said she was going for a ride, and I wasn't welcome."

Beatrice drew in a deep breath and firmed her chin. "Girls, I need you to spread out and search all of the buildings. See if she's somewhere on the property. I'm going down to the shearing sheds to speak to the men who didn't go to the meeting. If we can't find her here on the ranch, I'll head up a search party."

~

ROB SHIFTED IN HIS POSITION AT THE BACK OF THE SMOKE-filled room. Too many bodies, too little ventilation, and too many cigars made it difficult for him to breathe without coughing. Another spasm caught him, forcing him once again to step outside into the crisp night air. Just as well. He took a deep breath and held it. Not much being accomplished in there anyway. Not as far as he could tell. Slowly exhaling, he drew in one more cleansing breath and the cough stilled.

Should he attempt to rejoin the meeting? He cast a dubious eye toward the doorway, then walked over to a small corral, leaning his back against its railing. He tipped his head to the night sky, marveling once again at the layers of stars that filled the heavens out here. The quiet and the view stilled the churning in his gut that had started with the first fiery speech of the night.

He hadn't come to this country to get involved in a war. Fighting this disease was enough of a battle for him right now. And yet, he felt himself drawn into the fury despite it all. The thought of little Fred, Mrs. Finch, and all the other nameless sheep the armed men had so brutally slaughtered last winter still brought a bitter taste to his mouth. And now the senseless burning of another man's livelihood!

Part of him joined with Louis and the others in a desire to exact justice on whoever was to blame for the outrage. Another part felt like giving up. Cashing in on his losses and leaving this business behind. After all, he wasn't interested in building a sheep dynasty like so many of the men here tonight. He only wanted his health back. But with the loss of so many sheep last winter, he couldn't afford to sell out now. He needed at least another year to recoup his losses and hopefully regain his health.

Someone stepped out of the building, looked around, and headed his way when he spotted him. Jackson, he guessed, by the man's build and walk.

"You all right?" The young man's concern touched a chord inside Rob. Friends like this man would be hard to leave.

"Yeah. My sorry lungs don't take well to the tobacco smoke, but I'll be fine."

Jackson nodded, then leaned on the rail beside him. "What do you think of all that?" He gestured with his chin toward the crowd inside.

"I think if the cattlemen were trying to get the sheepherders organized into a cohesive group, they might have succeeded with this last stunt."

"Delfelder's got 'em going, all right."

Rob had to agree. He hadn't met the man until tonight, but he'd realized right off the sheepman had all the makings of a politician. A handsome, middle-aged man with salt and pepper hair and a trim mustache, John Delfelder was one of the most successful sheep ranchers in Fremont County. A partner with Bunce, the two of them ran well over 36,000 head of sheep. When Baldwin had introduced him to the man earlier in the evening, Delfelder had taken him around the room, presenting him to the other sheepmen as the one who'd had his camp raided last winter.

Yes, the man knew what he was doing, stirring the embers of past outrages to help fan the flame of the current one. Rob had become a bit of a celebrity tonight as sheepman after sheepman extended him their sympathy and regret. He couldn't help feeling the regard came a little too late, though. The reward the Association had put up last winter to help find the culprits had been nominal at best.

Maybe Delfelder's fiery oratory tonight would help raise the pot. Maybe. He'd learned it was easier to express words of sympathy to a neighbor than it was to back those words up with deeds, especially monetary ones.

Galloping hoof beats drew his and Jackson's attention to a rider off in the distance, clearly headed their way. Now what? Rob felt Jackson tense beside him.

"It's Cookie," Jackson said as the man drew closer.

Cookie reined his horse to a stop beside them. Unease stole up the back of Rob's neck at the sight of the man's anxious expression.

"Mary Baldwin's gone missing. We've searched the ranch, but no one can find her. Mrs. Baldwin thinks she might have gotten hurt when she took her horse out riding earlier today. She told me to come here to get her father and some of you men to help us look."

While Jackson sprinted back inside to round up the others, Rob looked out into the night around him. That poor girl. If she was hurt, how would they possibly find her in the dark?

Chapter Twenty-Nine

Maddie pulled herself up the steps into the wagon and sank to a seat on the hard bench beside the stove. She should try to sleep. She'd come back to the wagon for just that purpose but knew any attempt would be futile. At least not until someone . . . *anyone* returned with news regarding Mary. Waiting was so impossibly hard. The men doing the searching had it easier. She was sure of it.

She could endure the waiting, the not knowing if only she felt as if she were doing something to help find her. Getting breakfast for the few groups of men who had straggled in this morning was all she'd been allowed to do. Not that she would know where to look for her. In all the open wilderness out there, she'd probably end up getting herself lost. Still, this waiting was killing her.

Be anxious for nothing, but in everything, with prayer and petition, make your requests know unto God . . . she repeated once again the words that had been on her heart all night. *I'm asking, Lord. Keep her safe. Please, keep her safe.* She'd long ago given up any effort for her prayers to be more eloquent.

Of all the groups that had gone out last night, she had held out the most hope for Beatrice and the men from the shearing crew. They had been the first to take up the hunt and had the advantage of the ranch's hunting dogs. But shortly after daylight, they had made their way back to the ranch. Cold and exhausted, they'd lost Mary's trail at Beaver Creek and were never able to pick it up again on the other side.

The grim-faced mother had stopped barely long enough to force down a few bites of food and saddle a fresh mount before setting out again. Her husband's group had yet to return to the ranch, nor, according to Beatrice, had the two crossed paths during the night. But Maddie had to believe with daylight and the sheer number of people and dogs out searching, news would be coming soon.

The sound of gunfire and shouting drew her to the door of the wagon. Men were dismounting over by the barn and sheep sheds. Even from this distance, she could pick out Gabe and George, and there, on a slight rise, about fifty yards from the barn stood Jackson, rifle raised in the air. He fired two more shots, a signal to anyone within earshot that the search was over.

Maddie threw open the wagon door and turned to go down the ladder.

"Maddie. Wait."

Looking over her shoulder, she caught sight of Rob coming from the barn at a trot. She dropped to the ground, hiked up her skirts, and ran to meet him.

"Have they found her?"

"Her father found her. In an old miner's shack not far from Beaver Creek. We must have passed by her a dozen times last night but couldn't see it in the dark." The grim set of his mouth told her the news was not all good.

"What? What is it? Is she . . . ? She's not . . ."

Rob put an arm about her shoulder and steered her back toward the wagon. "No, she's not dead. But . . ." His jaw tightened. She could see the muscles in his throat working as he tried to form his next words. "A group of those hooded men found her when she was out riding yesterday. They beat her up pretty badly, Maddie. And each of the men . . . well, they each had a turn at her."

"A turn . . . you don't mean . . . ?"

His curt nod told her all she needed to know.

"Oh, God. No." A vision of Mary's sweet young face, blushing at something her aunt said less than twenty-four hours ago, sprang to her mind. How could they? She was barely sixteen! Maddie started to pull out from under Rob's arm, but he held her firm.

"I should go to them."

"Not now. Not yet. She needs time with her family now."

She knew he was right. Besides, what could she possibly do that would make anything better?

"My God, Rob. How could they . . . why?" She struggled to keep her tears at bay.

"I don't know, Maddie. I don't know." He pulled her into a full embrace, rocking her gently from side to side. There was no help for it. Maddie let the tears flow—weeping for the loss of girlhood, for the loss of innocence, for the loss of everything good and pure and right.

∽

THE NEXT DAY, MADDIE TRUDGED UP THE DIRT PATH TO THE Baldwin ranch house. Buggies and horses had been coming and going all day as word spread to the neighboring ranches and farms. People like herself who wanted to lend support, offer condolences, or whatever else one said in such a situation had forged a path to the Baldwin's front door.

She clutched the two small packages she'd brought with her. Paltry offerings in the face of such a heinous offense, but she couldn't come empty-handed. Somehow she had to do something.

Nell greeted her at the door with a hug.

"So good of you to come, dear. Are you doing better?"

They'd all been exhausted when they'd parted yesterday morning. The dark circles under Nell's eyes testified to the fact that Maddie wasn't the only one who'd found it hard to sleep, but she managed a nod and a weak smile.

"I brought some sweet bread . . ."

"How thoughtful. Just set it on the table, dear, with the others."

Maddie glanced toward the kitchen table piled high with breads, pies, cakes, and sundry other food items. Like a funeral spread. Why was it people felt the need to bring food in the wake of disaster? She was sure no one here felt the least bit like eating, yet she offered her own parcels to the growing pile.

The atmosphere in the room felt funereal as well. A scattering of women gathered in small clusters murmuring to one another in hushed voices. Truly, there had been a death of sorts. A death of innocence and girlhood dreams.

"How is she?"

"Resting now. She was pretty badly battered, but the doctor says she should be on the mend in a couple of days. Beatrice is with her. Come, I'll take you to see her."

"Oh . . . no. I don't want to intrude."

"Nonsense. Beatrice would be upset with me if I didn't let her know you were here. You and your husband are leaving in the morning, right?"

"Yes. Jackson's moving us to our summer pasture."

"Then, come along." Nell led her past the groups of women and down a short hallway. "It's not like you're one of the curious neighbors come to gawk and gossip," she told Maddie in a whisper. "You were there with us that night. You need to see for yourself that Mary is all right."

She opened the closed door on their left and motioned her inside.

As far as reassuring measures went, this one fell hopelessly short. Maddie could not believe the figure sleeping in the bed was the same vibrant young girl she'd met two days ago. Bruised and swollen, Mary's face was a patchwork of purples and greens. An angry cut slit her bottom lip, a white bandage circled her forehead. If her face showed this much damage, Maddie could only imagine what injuries the rest of her had sustained.

She swallowed the bile that rose in her throat at the thought of those brutal hands on this poor child's body. Blinking back tears, she turned to Beatrice, who had risen from a chair in the corner at their entrance.

"I'm sorry. So very, very sorry."

Within seconds, Maddie found herself wrapped in Beatrice's soft, ample embrace. "I know, child. I know. That first sight of her is mighty hard, but we have her back with us. And she will heal. Things could have been worse."

Not much worse.

With an effort, she pulled back out of Beatrice's embrace and forced herself to look at Mary. She'd come to comfort, not be comforted.

"I just can't understand why. Why did it have to be Mary?" She was so young, so innocent. "Isn't God supposed to protect His own? I was praying and praying . . ." Maddie's voice broke on the words. Obviously, her prayers were reaching no higher than the padded canvas on her sheep wagon's roof.

"Oh, honey. God's people are no more exempt from life's storms than the ungodly are exempt from God's blessing. Didn't Jesus himself say, the Father 'maketh his sun to rise on the evil and on the good, and sendeth rain on the just and on the unjust?' Remember Job?"

Yes, she had read Job, but the book had never been one of her favorites. Somehow the thought of God bartering the well-being of one of his faithful servants in some sort of contest with Satan had never set well with her. Nothing about that book ever answered her questions of why?

"Trusting in the Good Lord doesn't mean we'll live a life of ease," Beatrice continued. "But if we let Him, He can teach us to sing in the midst of the storms. There are sweet songs to be learned solely from resting in His arms." The quiet peace on Beatrice's face lent truth to her words, yet Maddie knew she'd rather not learn that kind of song, no matter how sweet it might be.

A change of subject would be good. Reaching into the pocket of her skirt, she brought out a small beribboned package. "I brought this for Mary. For when she wakes up. It's not much, really. Just a bookmark I made. She'd admired one I had like it on Monday . . ." Had it truly only been two days since that carefree day they all had spent together?

Beatrice smiled and took the package. "I'll be sure to give it to her."

"Will you stay here at the ranch, do you think? For the summer?"

"No. Joseph and I have decided it might be best if I take the girls to Denver for a few months. My sister, Bridgett, lives there. A change of scenery might do us all a world of good. Then when school starts up again in the fall, well . . . we'll see."

All her encounters with the women out here seemed destined to end just as they were beginning. Though now she and Rob were heading to summer pasture again, the chances of their paths crossing any time soon were slim anyway.

She reached out and gave the older woman another quick hug. "Tell Mary I've enjoyed getting to know her. If she wants to write to someone, I'm an avid letter writer. I'd be glad to correspond."

"Bless you, dear. I'll be sure to tell her."

Chapter Thirty

❦

"What do you think, Maddie. Shall we make this our home for the winter?"

Maddie surveyed the log cabin in front of her. Compared to town standards, it was tiny and quite primitive. It consisted of one sixteen-by-twenty-foot room. However, compared to the sheep wagon, it was expansive. Their living quarters would increase threefold.

"Wait. Before you say anything, let me give you the grand tour." Taking her arm, Rob led her into the cabin's single room. "First, I give you the kitchen." He gestured to the right. "Here we have the latest in wood cooking stoves. A dish cupboard to hold our pans and dishes, and hanging on the wall just outside the cabin, you will find our sink, the very latest in elegant wash basins."

Maddie laughed.

"Over here, is the dining room." Rob swept an arm to the other side of the room, where a simple pine table and four chairs sat. "And straight ahead, if you'll follow me, you'll find the living area." She took a few steps forward toward the back of the room where he'd set two rocking chairs, a small bookcase, and a table with a lamp.

"Charming." Maddie's brow wrinkled as she surveyed the room. "But methinks something is awry. Did I somehow miss the bedroom in our tour?"

"Ah, yes. The bedroom. Step this way." Rob turned and walked a few more steps to the right, coming to a stop in front of a large armoire on the far wall of the cabin. A dresser stood beside it in the corner. "And here, my dear, we have the bedroom."

"But there is no bed."

"*Au contraire, mon ami.* You just aren't looking close enough." With a flourish, he pulled down on a handle on the armoire to expose a hidden double bed.

"Of course! A Murphy bed. How clever."

"So, you like it?"

"I think it's going to work."

They'd recently returned from the mountains to the winter camping grounds in the Red Canyon. The summer months had left Rob feeling much better. Definitely better than he was last winter. If they could move into this cabin, she wouldn't be worried that he'd have a relapse like he did in January. Fred and George could handle the majority of the outdoor work, and they wouldn't have to rely on the flimsy, canvas walls of the sheep wagon for their warmth.

"This cabin looks wonderful, Rob. Truly, it does. Where did you find the furniture? Especially that bed?"

"Most of it came with the cabin. The bed and dresser are from the Baldwins. Mrs. Baldwin insisted we use it as long as we need. She and Mr. Baldwin had it early in their marriage before they built the ranch house, but she says they have no real need for it these days. Of course, she and the girls will be living in town now that school has started again."

"They're back from Denver, then?"

"Yes. They got back on Thursday. All of them but Mary, of course."

Maddie had corresponded through letters with both Mary

and Beatrice all summer. Though Mary's physical wounds had healed fairly quickly, Beatrice was afraid the mental and emotional wounds would take much longer to heal. She'd decided to leave Mary with her aunt in Denver for a least a few more months.

Pounding hooves drew their attention outside the cabin. "Halloo! Anyone home? Rob? Maddie?"

"It's Jackson," Rob said.

Maddie released the breath she'd caught at the sound of an unexpected visitor. Would she ever feel truly safe again?

Jackson sprang from his horse, and Rob met him at the door.

"We weren't expecting visitors quite this soon," he said.

Jackson didn't smile. Instead, he pulled an envelope from his pocket and cleared his throat. "A telegram came for you this morning. Mr. Stavers said I should get it to you as soon as possible."

A telegram. A tremor started in Maddie's fingers. Neither Mother Skivington nor Father would pay the extra it cost to send a telegram unless the news was urgent. She looked to Rob, whose face turned grave as he read the return address.

"Who?"

"Your father."

Dear, God. No. Not Hazel. Not Edie's baby.

Rob tore open the envelope and read the message. Color drained from his face. Not waiting, she snatched the telegraph from his hand and read the words herself.

EDIE IS DEAD STOP SCARLET FEVER STOP FUNERAL SATURDAY STOP

She read the line again, as if somehow, in reading, the message would change. Edie. Dead. Funeral. She saw the words but could not comprehend them.

This could not be real. God would not be so cruel. Delicate, fragile Edie gone? No. She had a baby to care for. A full life ahead. *No. God. No.*

Rob's arm came around her waist, and she turned into his chest and wept.

Chapter Thirty-One

Death surrounded her, from the moldering marble at her feet to the towering oak, maple, and elm above, their skeletal branches black against the rusty reds and yellows of their leaves. Beautiful now, maybe, but soon they'd join the other leaves that lay scattered across the expansive lawn or huddled in dry, decaying heaps against headstones and mausoleums.

Why had she ever thought autumn to be beautiful? It was the season of death, and she hated it.

Nor would she escape death's image when she left the graveyard. It hung all over the city in black bunting and half-masted flags. It screamed from headlines and whispered in conversations. On the heels of Edie's death came news of President McKinley's. "It was God's way," the poor man's dying words were on the lips of every tragical matron and schoolgirl. As if God's way ever included death, disease, and murder.

She turned from the mound of new earth that marked Edie's grave and scanned the thousands of grave markers around her—each representing someone's mother, sister, father, friend. To her left lay the graves of Mother and Katie Alice. All gone now. In heaven, yes, but gone to her.

"I hate this. Hate it." Her voice came out strangled and ugly.

"I know, lovey. I know." Mother Skivington's arm came around her shoulders, drawing her close. Rob had not made this third trip to the cemetery with her. The day was damp, promising rain, and he had an appointment with Dr. Waite. She would have been happy to come alone, but Rob's mother wouldn't hear of it. A tiny portion of her soul responded to the woman's loving touch, but for the most part, her inner being was as cold and hard as the stone angel that graced the end of the row of graves in front of her.

"I can't understand any of this." Why would God take Edie? Why her? Why now? A young wife and mother who hadn't even lived long enough to finish her second decade.

"I'm not sure we're meant to understand it. God's ways are not our ways."

She'd heard that phrase more times than she cared to count. What did it even mean? Of one thing she was certain, if God's way really included a young mother's death, then His way truly was not her way. If she had *her* way, Edie wouldn't be cold and buried in this graveyard. She'd be safe at home, happy in the love of her husband and delighting in the joys of her precious baby boy.

Maddie pulled from Mother Skivington's embrace and set off down one of the cemetery's winding paths. Each gravestone she passed gave mocking testimony to the myriad of God's ways she did not understand—a young soldier boy cut down by war, a small child wrested from his mother's arms by disease, lives cut short, bodies ravaged by the ugly hand of death.

She finally came to a halt on the eastern edge of the park where the cemetery overlooked the Passaic. Brushing away some leaves, she took a seat on the marble steps of a mausoleum and leaned back against the cold marble of a fluted stone pillar. In front of her, the Passaic made its sluggish way south past factories, beneath bridges, blithely unconcerned whether its course passed the living or the dead.

Her memories transported her to that beautiful May afternoon she and Edie had sat on the opposite bank and watched this same river meander by. Had she known then what she knew now, would she have ever left home? But if they hadn't gone to Wyoming, would she be visiting Rob's grave today as well? A tear crept down her cheek, followed by another. She let them fall unhindered onto the bodice of her black serge gown.

She sensed rather than saw Mother Skivington come up to stand beside her.

"Why does God keep taking from me all the ones I love?" The words tore from her in a soft wail.

"Oh, lovey," Mother Skivington dropped to the step beside her and took her hand. "God is a generous God. He doesn't *take* anything from you. But you can be sure He's *keeping* your loved ones for you. Safe in His loving arms they are."

"Are they?" Was that horror or sympathy that sparked in Mother Skivington's eyes at her words? Blasphemous, she supposed, but she couldn't find the need to retract them. Pulling her hand loose from the woman's kind grasp, she plucked up a fallen leaf and shredded it between her fingers.

"Oh, I know what the Bible says, and on most days, I believe it. I do. But there are times when it's just so hard to have that faith. Look around you." Maddie waved her arm toward the cemetery behind them. "How am I to believe God has conquered death when all around me everything I see . . . all I *know* . . . is either dead or dying?"

For a few minutes, Mother Skivington said nothing. Then, she bent and picked up an acorn that lay half-buried in the leaves at their feet. "Not quite everything, lovey." She held the acorn in the palm of her gloved hand and poked at it with her finger. "There's life in this, though we can't see it. If I was to plant this in the ground, this hard, dry shell would die and decay, but the life inside would not, and in God's time, something new would burst forth, more glorious and stronger than anyone could ever imagine this seed would ever be."

She stood and walked over to a sturdy oak that stood a few

feet away, placing her hand on its trunk. "And there's life in here, though the leaves may make us think it's dead. In the springtime, each of these dead, dry leaves will be replaced with glorious new life." She looked back at Maddie and smiled. "Now, lovey, the reason you don't see the life around you is because you're only seeing what's on the outside. But life is there. As true as the promise of springtime, it's there."

She walked slowly back and dropped down beside her. Taking her hand, Mother Skivington dropped the acorn into her palm and closed Maddie's fingers tightly around it. "Hold tight to your faith, Maddie dear. Though God's promises may seem hidden, they are all around us. You need only open your eyes to see."

She squeezed the acorn in her hand until its sharp point bit through the thin layer of her glove. Hold tight to your faith. But would that be enough? Her faith felt about as thin as her gloves right now.

Father, I believe. The words reminded her of the father of the sick boy in the gospel of Mark who made the same statement but followed it with the words, "Help thou mine unbelief." Because faith was fragile. Faith was hard.

Oh, Lord. Help thou mine unbelief.

At her prayer, something cold and hard that had begun inside her with the words of Father's telegram—no even earlier than that—with the first shot of the raider's guns, melted and broke, flowing out from within in a series of wracking sobs. Throwing herself into Mother Skivington's waiting arms, she let the tears flow. How long they sat there, clutched in each other's arms, she did not know. Long enough to soak the front of Mother Skivington's black cloak and leave Maddie feeling as weak and limp as a newborn lamb.

Finally, she lifted her head and pulled back. "I'm sorry. I've made a mess of your cloak."

"Now, deary, don't you fret. I'm thinking that was a long time coming and just what you needed." Mother Skivington handed her a handkerchief, then cupped her chin with her fingers. "I know life looks very bleak for you right now, Maddie, but always remember, 'earth hath no sorrow that heaven cannot heal.'"

The words from the song they sang at Edie's funeral. Did she believe that? Could she believe that?

Help thou mine unbelief.

Chapter Thirty-Two

"So, you wish to take the last of my girls from me?" Father's words, though spoken lightly, held an undercurrent of pain.

If it weren't for the silent plea in Hazel's eyes, Maddie might have set down her paring knife and headed into the next room to put a stop to the men's conversation. As it was, she continued to work on peeling the potatoes in front of her as she and Hazel silently listened.

"Not permanently, sir." Rob's measured tones held a plea of their own. "We would bring her home whenever you felt it necessary. I'm just thinking about what might be best for her."

"Being away from us would be best?" Father asked.

"I didn't mean it that way. We were thinking more along the lines of what would be the most *healthful* environment . . ." Rob's words trailed off. "What I mean is—"

"I know what you mean." The sigh that followed was heart-deep. "Don't you think I can't see what this city has done to my family? It's taken two daughters, my first wife . . ." His voice broke on the words.

Both Maddie and Rob had been shocked at the change in Hazel when she'd come with Father to meet their train in October. The healthy little girl they'd left behind was gone, replaced instead by a tall, thin waif with a pale face and huge eyes. The fever which had taken Edie had felled Hazel as well. Hazel had recovered, but her body was still weak.

But scarier to Maddie was the haunted look that now lurked in the shadows of Hazel's large brown eyes. She knew well the pain and guilt of being the surviving sister. She'd felt the same when typhoid had taken Katie Alice, but not her. If they could take Hazel out of the city, with its poisonous air and constant reminders of Edie, maybe the zest that had been so much a part of her baby sister would once again return.

"I don't suppose you'd consider staying through Christmas?" At Father's words, Hazel's expression grew hopeful.

"I don't see how we can," Rob said. "We've been gone far too long already. I must see to the breeding of the ewes before December is out, or the lambs will come too late to fatten up for market. Besides, we plan to stop in Denver on our way back. Dr. Waite wants me to meet with an open-air treatment specialist who practices there. After what happened last February, he wants me to get his opinion before heading into this winter."

"Then we must make the best of our Thanksgiving together."

"She can accompany us then?"

"Yes, she may go."

With a squeal, Hazel threw down the potato she was working on and ran into the next room.

"Do you mean it, Papa? Truly? I can go?"

Maddie wiped her hands on her apron and followed, coming into the room in time to see Hazel launch herself into Father's arms.

He placed a kiss on her soft, brown hair, shorn close to her head after the fever, and said, "Yes, Poppet, you can go, as long as you promise to come back to me with roses in these cheeks of yours." He pinched one of her cheeks softly, then set her on the floor.

Blinking back tears, Maddie crossed the room and gave Father a hug as well. His embrace was fierce.

"I promise we'll take good care of her."

"I don't have any doubts on that score."

"Doubts about what?" Fanny, who'd been upstairs putting baby Albie down for a nap, entered the room.

"Rob and Maddie will be taking Hazel with them when they go back to Wyoming."

Fanny pressed her lips together, then gave a quick nod. "Might be best. She's not recovered as well as I would like to see." They all turned to look at Hazel, who stared quietly back at them. Fanny turned to Rob. "Are you still planning to leave next week?"

"Yes." Rob's monosyllabic answer brooked no argument.

"Then we'll have to step lively to get her ready."

"But not until tomorrow. Today we'll enjoy our Thanksgiving together," Father said.

"Of course," Maddie said. "And speaking of Thanksgiving, we'd best get back to preparing the meal, or we won't have anything ready when Herb and Annie get here."

∽

MADDIE PULLED HER BABY NEPHEW CLOSER INTO HER LAP AND offered him another bite of pumpkin pie. His chubby fists helped guide the fork into his mouth. She cherished the moments each day when he allowed her to hold him, limited as they were to a few sleepy moments in the early mornings or right after his nap. Now that he was walking, a skill he'd mastered within a few weeks of their return, he didn't want to be held by anyone. She wasn't above bribing him for a few minutes of his company.

Albie swallowed his bite of pie and reached out for another. She was barely in time to catch his fingers from pulling the pie plate off the table. "You're a greedy little love, aren't you? Hold on. I'll cut you another bite."

He was a beautiful baby with soft golden curls and huge blue eyes. Edie had had every right to be proud of her sweet baby boy. The thought of all the moments Edie would miss in her little son's life made her heart seize, but she wouldn't dwell on it today. Couldn't dwell on it. She'd dwell on all God's blessings instead. It was a day to be thankful, after all.

She looked around the table at all the ones she held so dear. All here. All together at last. Even Walter, whose waking hours since his wife's death had been spent either at work or at Duggan's Pub, had made it to Thanksgiving dinner, though he'd skipped the church service this morning. Other than Edie's empty chair, the scene was all she'd imagined on those lonely days and long nights in the sheep wagon last winter.

"We should play parlor games and sing together later," she said.

"And everyone must participate," Hazel chimed in.

Maddie laughed when Percy and Les groaned. The Long sisters had always loved an evening of parlor games and singing. They had instituted the participation rule to guarantee their brothers' involvement. The brothers often complained but usually enjoyed the games as much as anyone.

"Yes, everyone must participate, but it can be something as simple as just stating something you are thankful for. It is Thanksgiving, after all," she said.

"Oh," Hazel bounced in her chair and raised her hand as if she were in the classroom. "I know one. I'm thankful I get to go with Maddie to Wyoming."

"And *I'm* thankful you're going with Maddie to Wyoming. I won't have to put up with you pestering me anymore." Les was still smarting over the fact that he had to stay home while his little sister enjoyed a Western adventure.

Hazel stuck her tongue out at him from across the table, but Father quelled any further retaliation with a stern look at both of them. A loud scraping brought everyone's attention to Walter, who pushed his chair back and stood, face mottled.

"I'm sorry, Maddie," he said, voice laced with sarcasm. "I won't be participating in any of your fun and games tonight. Try as I might, I can't think of a single thing to be thankful for." He stalked from the room, leaving a silence behind him that was broken only by the slamming of the front door.

Not a single blessing? Not one? Maddie kissed the soft curls on her nephew's head, her heart breaking for him and his hurting father. "I'm sorry." She looked around the table at the rest of her family. "I didn't mean to be insensitive. It's just that with everyone here, it's so easy to pretend that Edie's still with us. Somehow. Someway. She always did love parlor games . . ." Her voice broke on the words.

"I think Maddie's idea is a great one. Edie *did* love those games, and what better way to honor her memory than to play some together tonight?" Herb's wife Anne said. "I say we all meet in the parlor as soon as we've cleaned up here. And everyone must participate." She directed a warning glare at Percy and Herb, who both seemed about to protest.

Maddie shot her a grateful look. Anne was ever one to try to smooth the troubled family waters.

"But only if you want to," she said. Much as she appreciated Anne's efforts, she wasn't about to force anyone into something that might cause them pain.

But half an hour later, when the women entered the parlor, all the men were there waiting for them. Even Father. They enjoyed a lively evening of Forfeits, Blind Man's Bluff, and Charades. They finished up around the piano, singing many of their favorite tunes and ending with a few Christmas carols.

"On account of our not being able to sing them together at Christmas," said Hazel.

Though the gathering didn't break up until almost midnight, Maddie didn't see Walter again until she found him in the kitchen the next morning when she came down to get Albie his early morning bottle.

One look at his bleary, bloodshot eyes told her all she needed to know about the type of evening he'd had. She bade him good morning, then headed for the ice box to get the milk. Should she apologize for yesterday? She wasn't the one who had stormed out, but then she couldn't help but feel that she should have been more sensitive. Not sure how to broach the topic, she looked up to see him watching her fill Albie's bottle.

"You're quite the little mother, aren't you? What's the matter, Maddie? You can't have kids of your own, so you think you have to take everyone else's? You gonna want to take Albie with you to Wyoming, too?" His bitter words hit her like a slap to the face.

"Don't be ridiculous. Of course, I don't want to take him from you." In the weeks they'd been home, she'd never seen Walter lift a finger to care for his son. Fran had been his caregiver, and whenever Fran was busy, Maddie had gladly stepped in to help out. Had they been wrong to take on Edie's duties? Should they have left those to his father, instead? But how could they? Walter was rarely home, and someone had to care for his child.

But maybe, if they hadn't been so quick to take over Albie's care, Walter would have stayed home to give it. Had they been cheating Albie out of a father as well as a mother?

"You don't think I'm capable of being a good father, do you?"

"I never said that."

"You don't have to say it. Just like your sister, your eyes do your speaking for you."

"You have no idea what I'm thinking." She set the bottle down in front of him with more force than was necessary. "Here. If you want to be a father to your son, here's his bottle. Go feed him."

Walter dropped his head into his hands and groaned. Grabbing fistfuls of his hair, he shook his head back and forth. "I can't." The words sounded as if they were being drug from him. "I can't. I can't hold him without thinking of her. And when I think of her, I don't know how to go on. Don't you think I want to be a good father? But I can't. I can't."

Maddie laid a hand on Walter's head, his curls a darker gold than his son's but achingly familiar. Tears clogged her throat. She forced her words around them. "I know you're hurting, Walter. We all are. But you *can* be a father to Albie. With God's help, you can."

Walter bolted to his feet, flinging her hand away. "God? What does God have to do with any of this? I asked for his help months ago, and look what it got me. A dead wife. If that's the kind of help God's gonna give me, then I don't want it."

He pushed past her, grabbing his lunch pail off the counter. Without another word, he strode from the kitchen, down the hallway, and out the front door. She winced as the door slammed behind him. Great. For the second time in less than twenty-four hours, she'd sent her brother-in-law slamming out the door. It was probably a good thing they were leaving soon. But could she blame him? His words seemed achingly familiar to the words she'd said to Mother Skivington just days ago. *I'm trying, Lord. I am. But trusting you are good, when everything around me is so bad, is just so hard.*

Chapter Thirty-Three

Rob took in a deep breath of the crisp morning air and held it before slowly exhaling. It was good to be back in the West again. They'd been greeted in Denver with a snow shower when they'd arrived late last evening and, subsequently, had not lingered to take in their surroundings. Instead, they'd collected their bags and dashed up the street to the nearest hotel.

Given the cold, they'd probably taken any lodging the city afforded them as long as it was close to Union Station. Luckily for them, the Oxford, just a few hundred yards away had lived up to its billing as an elegant, yet affordable hotel.

He'd even paid the extra dollar per night to ensure them a private bath. After three days of sharing a convenience room the size of a postage stamp with every other gentleman on the train, he felt they had earned the right to that luxury. The girls agreed with him.

In contrast to yesterday's inhospitable welcome, this morning had dawned bright and clear. A layer of new snow draped awnings, lamp posts, and sidewalks, glistening like trays of diamonds in the blinding sunshine. He was glad he'd chosen to walk to his doctor's appointment. The snow was not deep enough to impede his progress. In fact, given the strength of the sunshine, he wouldn't be surprised if it were gone by evening. Yet, it gave the city a mantle of cleanliness that was sadly lacking in Newark.

He cast an eye over the surrounding buildings. Of course, the sheer newness of most of the structures could also be responsible for this sense of purity and good hygiene. In Newark, the buildings sagged under layers of soot and grime brought about by years of teeming industry. Yet on this block of city alone, he'd be hard-pressed to find a building as old as he was. Yes. There was certainly something to be said for new.

He reached the corner of Broadway and took a left until he reached Sixteenth Street. As the doorman had predicted, the Majestic Building stood before him, seven stories of imposing red brick topping a base of pale granite. Speaking of new, he'd be astonished if this building had seen so much as a decade of life.

He climbed the front steps and entered through an arched doorway. Looking around, he soon located a directory in the building's front lobby and searched for the words H. Sewall, M.D. Rooms 433-4. Could be worse. Could be the eighth floor. Four flights of steps were daunting enough. His lungs were already feeling the effects of the thinner air of this higher altitude after the fourteen-block trek from the hotel. It wouldn't do to show up at the good doctor's doorstep in a puddle of exhaustion.

In room 433, he gave his name to a lady in a white shirtwaist and black skirt, who stepped into the next room and returned to tell him, "Dr. Sewall will be with you shortly, Mr. Skivington. Please take a seat."

He took a chair opposite the room's windows, which looked out upon the Rocky Mountains, in all their purple, white-topped glory. A magnificent view. Made him long to be back in his sheep wagon amongst the Wind Rivers, though he had to admit, this mountain range put the Winds to shame.

Dr. Sewall must either be very fortunate or very good to

afford rooms with such a view. Surely the rent on rooms facing west was much higher than those to the east, or, for that matter, interior rooms with no view at all. But then Dr. Sewall was a tuberculosis specialist in a city where, if the brochures were to be believed, nearly one-third of the population suffered from the disease. Business was bound to be good.

"Dr. Sewall will see you now, Mr. Skivington."

Rob was ushered into the next room, where a short, middle-aged man in a black frock coat greeted him and proceeded with the examination.

For the next twenty minutes, he was put through the now-familiar paces of poking, prodding, and chest tapping. He calmly answered a battery of questions that two years ago he would have stated were no one's business but his own and obligingly procured for the man a specimen of sputum that the good doctor then studied for several minutes under his microscope. Strange how quickly one became accustomed to certain medical procedures.

Turning from his microscope, the doctor bade him to get dressed, then motioned for him to take a seat in the empty chair beside him at his desk. Leaning back, he gazed at him over steepled fingers.

"Since your extensive hemorrhage last February, have you experienced any others?"

"There were spots of blood for several months after that, but none since June or July, I think."

"And what is it you said you do in Wyoming?"

"I'm a sheepherder, sir."

"Strenuous work?"

"Not especially. Some days there's a lot of walking."

"And what's the weather like in the winter?"

"I'd say it's a lot like here. Cold, but sunny. Snow at times, but not too heavy in the lower elevations. The wind blows a lot of it, so the grass is accessible to the sheep." Though he supposed the doctor wasn't too interested in the care of the sheep.

"Do you get a lot of wind?"

"Most days, yes."

"And you live in a sheep wagon?"

"Last winter, we did. We're living in a cabin now."

"Tell me, Mr. Skivington. How many days a week would you say you ran a fever last winter?"

"Two or three, maybe." That was a lie. For many weeks, he'd run a fever every single day. Especially right before and after that hemorrhage.

"And did you stay off your feet each of those days?"

"That would be impossible, sir. Someone has to see to the sheep at all times."

"Day and night? Am I correct?"

"Yes, sir."

"Were there many nights, then, where you would say your sleep was interrupted on behalf of the sheep?"

The doctor must have read the answer on his face because he didn't wait for a reply.

"I'm sorry, Mr. Skivington, but I cannot like this prescribed cure for you. I concur with the idea that you need plenty of fresh air and sunshine, but I cannot like the profession you have chosen. Sheepherding may be beneficial short term, say during the summer and fall, but that type of exposure to harsh winter elements, day and night . . . frankly, sir, in light of that last hemorrhage, you are lucky to still be alive today."

"I anticipate things will be much better this winter, sir. My brothers have joined me and have taken over a large portion of the sheepherding. Also, as I mentioned, we've moved to a cabin, so I won't be exposed to the elements nearly as much as last winter."

"And diet? Good doctor care? From what you've told me, your location is quite isolated. I can't help but believe your circumstances in both those areas are less than ideal."

"So, what are you recommending?"

"My first suggestion for anyone in your position would be a sanitarium." He held up a hand when Rob opened his mouth to protest. "Yes. I know. Dr. Waite informed me that you would not be open to that line of treatment. I'm not adverse to imitating the sanitarium treatment in the home. But in order to be effective, you must be able to imitate it on all six fronts. I do not see how that is to happen in your current situation."

"Six fronts?"

"General hygiene, special hygiene, excellent diet . . ." the doctor began counting off points on his fingers. "Open-air treatment, hydrotherapy, and constant supervision by a physician. Can you honestly tell me you can provide yourself with each of those elements in your occupation as a sheepherder?"

He didn't even know what most of those elements meant. Hydrotherapy? Constant supervision by a physician? Why, if he didn't count the last two months, he'd seen a physician exactly once in the year he'd been in Wyoming, and that was a mining camp doctor who probably didn't know the first thing about treating tuberculosis. No, his current plan of care was falling miserably short of Dr. Sewall's expectations.

"I don't know if I can follow all of those things in Wyoming."

"I'm fairly certain you cannot. My advice to you would be to get out of sheepherding as soon as possible and move here to Denver. Put yourself under my care or the care of any of my colleagues. I think you would soon find your condition considerably improved. You have the care of your two brothers?"

"My brothers work for me but are no longer under my care. But there is my wife and her younger sister. I will need to seek other employment were we to move." Again. Though he supposed he was better able to find work in a city than he'd ever been on a ranch.

"You are married, then?"

"Yes."

"Children?"

"We have not been blessed so far."

"You misunderstand, Mr. Skivington. Your lack of children *is* a blessing." Dr. Sewall leaned forward, features stern. "I'm surprised Dr. Waite did not warn you against the possibility of having children. Though tuberculosis is not an inherited disease, research tells us that children born to a consumptive parent are most certainly tainted with a predisposition to the disease. If you and your wife have not conceived, you should be thankful, and you must do everything in your power to see that it never happens."

No children. Ever? An image of Maddie's face, full of joy and contentment, when she held baby Albie flashed across his memory. What of their dreams? He knew the scads of babies he'd once promised her were probably not realistic, but none? Would God take that from them too?

"But if I were to be cured . . ."

"I still could not recommend it. Tell me, Mr. Skivington. This cabin you have built. Does it provide you with separate sleeping quarters from the rest of your family? A younger sister, you said, as well as a wife and two brothers, I believe? If it does not, then I suggest you make arrangements for one as soon as possible. Until you do, you are endangering all of their lives."

Rob thought about their small cabin and the even smaller sheep wagon. He thought of little Hazel still frail from the ravages of the fever. *You are endangering all their lives.* Good Lord. Could the man be more brutal?

"But I've been especially careful in the disposal of my sputum, as Dr. Waite instructed, and Maddie has followed all the cleaning regimens he recommended."

"I'm glad to hear it." Dr. Sewall rifled through some papers in one of the cubbies of his roll-top desk. He pulled out a small pamphlet and handed it to Rob. "Here's a copy of a paper that was read before the New York Medical Society last year. In it, you will find the in-home regimen I described to you earlier. Take it with you. You and your wife should read through it and see to it that you incorporate as many of its principles into your care as soon as possible. I don't think I need to tell you. Another hemorrhage like the one you suffered last February could well be your last."

A quarter of an hour later, Rob found himself on the sidewalk outside the Majestic Building, feeling like he'd just been sucker-punched. In a way, he had. He'd gone into Dr. Sewall's office this morning feeling mighty good about the progress he'd made this summer. After all, hadn't Dr. Waite been pleased when he'd seen him last month? A little grave maybe, when he'd heard about his troubles from last winter, but overall the doctor was pleased. Rob had gained back at least ten of the pounds he'd lost last winter and was able to walk two to three miles easily without tiring. Surely that counted for something.

Rob walked blindly for a few minutes, finding himself in a park where he dropped onto a bench and buried his head in his hands. They'd have to move again. No matter, he supposed. He'd never expected the sheep-raising business to be permanent. It had been a means to an end—an avenue for him to regain his health and live the outdoor life Dr. Waite had recommended. But he couldn't sell out just yet. Not after what the masked raiders had done to his herd. He couldn't bear the thought of ending on a loss.

This spring's batch of lambs should put them in the black again. If they had a promising enough crop, someone might be willing to pay him a good price on speculation of them bringing a profit come fall. If not. They'd see them through the summer themselves, then sell the whole flock in the fall.

Summers were never his problem. And from what Dr. Sewall said, this winter would be a good test at how long he could survive in Wyoming. If he had a repeat of last winter, then he'd have no choice but to sell out.

He sat up and pulled the pamphlet Dr. Sewall had given him from his inside coat pocket. He flipped through the pages, skimming its contents. Much of the hygiene and cleaning methods they'd already incorporated into their daily life. But much as Maddie had tried, he had to admit they'd fallen far short on the requirements of diet.

Some weeks last winter, their diet had consisted of little more than mutton stew and canned beans. Living in the sheep wagon had made it impossible to get the amount of milk, cream, butter, and eggs the diet called for.

But things should improve with their move to the cabin. They could keep a cellar for vegetables and buy a cow and some chickens. That didn't solve the problem of sleeping arrangements, though.

"The tuberculosis patient should always sleep alone, if possible, in a room of his own," the pamphlet read. A room of his own? When had he ever had a room of his own? Even as a bachelor, he'd always had a younger brother or two underfoot. The small, one-room cabin they had built offered no such luxury.

He sighed. He could erect a camping tent next to the cabin, with enough clothing and blankets that would serve him for all but the coldest of nights. But to sleep alone? His mind turned to the pleasure he'd come to cherish of pulling his wife close in his arms each night of their marriage. On all but his very worst days, they'd slept that way. Must he give that up too? It had been over two years, and she'd suffered no ill effects so far. Which brought him to the doctor's comments about children.

Sleeping in separate beds would certainly go a long way toward solving that problem. But could he do it? How could he live with Maddie, day after day, having lived intimately with her for almost four years, and not want to be with her? When he was very ill, it was never a problem, but as soon as he felt better, like this summer, he could think of little else than wanting to hold her, touch her, love her.

He turned back to that section of the pamphlet:

"On the other hand, when it comes to the prevention of conception in a tuberculous man or woman, I believe it is the sacred duty of the physician to teach these people legitimate means that they may not bring into life a being tainted with the predisposition to this disease."

These people. Tainted. Being. The words made him feel like some leprous monster liable to spawn other monsters of his kind. Surely a child born of his and Maddie's love would not be some tainted being. And yes, he knew there were so-called legitimate ways to prevent a pregnancy but were they truly legitimate? How did God feel about them? They all felt so wrong, somehow.

And what about Hazel? Was it fair, knowing what he now knew, to enclose her in a small, one-room cabin over the winter where the possibility of infection would be great? My God. He'd promised her father this trip would bring her health.

He pushed to his feet and started his slow trek up Sixteenth Street, dodging puddles and piles of gray slush. The day which had started out so pristine and beautiful had taken on a sordid hue. He knew he needed to get back to the hotel. Maddie would be worried if he tarried too long. And yet, he was reluctant to return without some plan in hand. They didn't have much time. Their train left for Wyoming in the morning, and he needed to get back.

But Hazel and Maddie didn't.

That was the thought he hadn't wanted to put into words, the plan he didn't want to make, yet he knew it had merit. If Maddie and Hazel were to stay the winter in Denver, that would keep Hazel protected and allow him time to come to terms with his beliefs about contraception. He would join them in the spring after the lambing was done. Maddie wouldn't like it. Neither would he, but he saw no other solution.

A sign swinging from a building in front of him seemed designed to test his resolution: **Rooms for rent. Inquire within**.

Well, it couldn't hurt to ask. He turned in at the gate and knocked at the door.

Chapter Thirty-Four

She was tired of being sick. For that matter, she was sick of being tired. Oh, let's face it, she was just sick and tired.

Maddie let the sock she was darning drop into her lap and leaned her head against the back of her rocker, closing her eyes for a minute. She just wished this constant bilious feeling would subside. It might help if their room wasn't situated right above the kitchen and if Mrs. O'Dougherty wasn't quite so fond of fried foods.

She just wasn't herself today. Hadn't been herself since they arrived in Denver over a month ago. In fact, if she'd been herself on that day when Rob returned from his doctor's appointment all grim-faced and hollow-eyed, instead of sick in bed with a thundering head cold, then she probably wouldn't be sitting here in Miss Whitcomb's boarding house smelling the first wafts of what promised to be liver and onions for the noon meal, instead of in her own cozy cabin in Wyoming able to choose her own menu which most certainly would not include liver and onions . . . or anything fried.

Another waft of onion-laden air assailed her senses, rising the gorge to the back of her throat and causing her to break out in a cold sweat. And if it hadn't been for that nasty oyster stew she'd consumed New Year's Eve, she wouldn't have had that horrible bout of food poisoning, the aftereffects of which still wouldn't leave her.

"Would you like to take a walk?" She asked in a voice that sounded weak even to her ears.

Hazel looked up from the desk where she had set her to working some sums. "Are you going to be sick again?"

She didn't even try to answer, but instead made a dash for the window. Pulling up the sash, she stuck her head out and gulped in a large draught of cold January air. She took in another large breath, then another, before pulling her head back in and leaning her forehead against the window's cool pane. Thank goodness their bedroom window faced the back of the house. What a fine spectacle she'd be to anyone walking by on the street.

She turned her head to see Hazel standing beside her, holding the chamber pot. She waved it away.

"I'm fine."

"You're still white as a sheet."

"It's the liver and onions. You know I never could abide them. But I'll be fine. I just needed a bit of fresh air."

"Should we take a walk then?"

"Yes. Definitely."

"Can we have lunch at the Brown Palace?"

"The Brown Palace? What? Are we rich as Croesus now?" She'd treated Hazel to lunch at the Brown Palace at Christmas as a way to make the day special and take their minds off Rob and the rest of the family celebrating so far away. Hazel had talked of little else since.

To be truthful, she had enjoyed the treat as much as Hazel. The meal had been sumptuous, and the surroundings tastefully elegant. But even as a Christmas treat, the cost had been far above their budget. They could not make a habit of it. Especially since their meals here were already covered in their monthly boarding fee of thirty-two dollars.

And yet, the thought of facing down Mrs. Dougherty's liver and onions in less than an hour was anything but pleasing.

"Maybe the lunch counter over by the capitol?" She might not be able to swing a dollar a piece for a luncheon at Brown's, but she'd willingly sacrifice ten cents to escape those liver and onions.

With an excited nod, Hazel pulled her coat off the hook by the door and ran out into the hallway. Maddie pulled on her own coat, then finding her hat, gloves, and reticule, she shut the open window before heading out of the room behind Hazel and down the front stairs. Miss Whitcomb stood by the door in the front hallway sorting through the day's mail.

"Going out so close to the lunch hour?"

Why did this woman always make her feel like a recalcitrant child? "Yes, Miss Whitcomb. In fact, we won't be back for lunch at all. We . . ." she glanced over at Hazel, "have another engagement."

"I see. You do know, I cannot refund you for the cost of any meals you miss."

"Yes, I know. Nor do I expect you to."

With a nod and a sniff, Miss Whitcomb turned back to her pile of mail.

"Are there any letters for Hazel or me today?"

Miss Whitcomb leafed through the remaining envelopes, then shook her head. "Seems to have been quite some time since you've heard from your husband." Her gray eyes pierced at Maddie over the top frame of her spectacles. "He does know the rent is due at the first of each month?"

"Of course, he does."

With nearly three weeks left in the month, she had no doubt Rob would send February's payment in plenty of time. She'd learned early on to ignore Miss Whitcomb's jibes. The woman was no sooner paid than she began worrying her boarders about their next month's rent.

A whiff of liver and onions floated down the hallway. Maddie pressed her gloved fingers to her nostrils and moved to step around her landlady.

"Are you sure you are all right, Mrs. Skivington? You are looking very pale."

"Yes, I'm fine. I merely need a bit of fresh air."

"Hmmph. If you ask me, you haven't been fine since you got here. If I had known you were sick, I'd never have allowed you to board in this house. I told you and your husband at the outset that I do not take in consumptives."

The irony of that statement would have made Maddie laugh had she not been fighting another wave of nausea. As it was, she was able to do little more than nod and push Hazel ahead of her out the door.

Half a block later, she was finally able to give the woman's words some thought. She had heard the sentiment many times since coming to Denver. No consumptives. No lungers. She knew there were boarding houses that specifically catered to the many health seekers who chose to make Denver their home, but twice as many, it seemed, did not. And the ones that did often charged exorbitant fees. Something they would have to deal with should they take Dr. Sewall's advice and move to Denver. Though she was still not convinced a move was necessary.

Was Hazel truly better off here than she would have been in Wyoming? Much as Miss Whitcomb insisted she did not house consumptives, the cough of Mr. Butler, in the room two doors down from them, sounded so familiar that many nights she wakened thinking Rob was still with them. Not all health seekers were as truthful as she and Rob might be.

And if Mr. Butler were tuberculous, could she trust that Mrs. O'Dougherty and the housemaid, Betty, were as conscientious with the cleaning of his utensils and bedding as she had been with Rob's? Well, of course, they weren't if they didn't even know the man was sick.

She looked down at her little sister, who looked back with a smile. "What?"

She shook her head. "I was just thinking. Are you feeling better here?"

"Much better than you are."

She was right. Though Hazel had suffered from the same head cold she had when they first came to Denver, she had recovered far more quickly than Maddie had. To look at her now, cheeks and nose red from the cold winter air, eyes bright with laughter, no one would be able to tell she had almost died from scarlet fever four months ago.

Maddie, on the other hand, couldn't seem to shake any of it. Couldn't shake the cough, couldn't shake the nausea, couldn't shake the headaches and the intense fatigue. Dear Lord. What if she were consumptive?

Oh, she was being such a goose. Of course, she didn't have tuberculosis. A cough, yes, but only at night now and merely a leftover from last month's cold.

But hadn't that been what they'd said about Rob's cough for weeks, even months, before he ever visited a doctor? And there was the persistent nausea. Would a bout with bad oysters truly keep her stomach unsettled for two weeks? And she *had* lost weight. She'd mentioned to Hazel only this morning that she'd have to think about taking in the waists of her skirts should this keep up. And what of the fatigue? Seems she didn't have the energy for anything these days.

"Maddie, why do you think he hasn't written?" Hazel's question broke through her racing thoughts.

"Who?" She looked down into Hazel's worried eyes. "Rob?" Goodness. Miss Whitcomb's comments had done a number on both of them. "But he *has* written. Remember? He sent us the draft for this month's rent and the extra money for Christmas. And he told us that funny story about Rosie and the rams."

"But that was ages ago."

"Ages? Why it's not been even so much as a month!"

"But you've written him almost every day since he's been

gone. Seems to me we should have had more than just the one letter."

True. She had written him a fair number of letters. Most of them were filled with reasons she should be with him, rather than here in Denver—reasons she'd thought of only after he'd left them so precipitously. She, too, had been hoping for word from him to see if she might have convinced him with all her logical reasoning that their waiting until spring to join him was quite unnecessary. But she hadn't expected an answer yet. There simply had not been enough time.

"Even if Rob had written me every day, we wouldn't have received his letters yet. Remember how it was when you got our letters back in Newark? How they'd come in bundles all at once? In Wyoming, it's not like Newark or Denver, where we have mail carriers who bring mail to our doors every day. Rob has to wait as long as ten days between mail deliveries. Sometimes two weeks, if Jackson is waylaid. And it might take almost as long for Jackson to return to town to see that our letters are mailed out. One of these days, probably very soon, we're going to get a whole pile of letters from Rob. You'll see. It'll be like Christmas all over again. Now, no more worrying. It's such a nice day. What do you say we take the long walk over to Broadway?"

"Up Grant Street?"

"Of course, up Grant Street."

She and Hazel loved to walk by the huge mansions that lined that street, marveling at the towers and turrets and the stained glass that sparkled under arched window frames. They weaved stories about the families who lived in such palaces and wished for just one glimpse of their opulent interiors.

Crossing Sherman, she lifted her skirts to avoid the puddles of icy water gathered in the wheel ruts. Hazel skipped happily across in front of her. It was a nice day. Though cold, the sun shone brightly in the cloudless sky so common to Denver. No more worries. The fresh air had chased away her biliousness. A brisk walk and a warm bowl of soup should set her to rights again. And if she were still to have the same symptoms next week, why she'd look up the name and address of Doctor Sewall and pay him a call. No use worrying over something that could easily be dismissed with a simple visit to the doctor.

~

MADDIE WAS GLAD HAZEL WAS ICE SKATING TODAY WITH SOME new friends and hadn't needed to accompany her on this visit. Though she'd spent plenty of time in the company of doctors in her life, even had a brother who practiced the profession, she'd never been party to an office visit before, at least not one where she was an active participant. In fact, now she thought on it, she'd rarely had a doctor in to see her either.

Oh, she'd spent countless hours in consultation with Dr. Waite over the years, but always on behalf of her mother or siblings, and in recent years, Rob. But, other than the typhoid fever she'd shared with Katie Alice so long ago, she, herself, had been as healthy as a horse. Which made these last few weeks so troubling. She was never sick. Yet, since reaching Denver, she hadn't known a day where she could say she truly felt well.

Hopefully, Dr. Sewall would be able to find a reason for that. She rebuttoned the collar and sleeves of her shirtwaist and slid off the examining table, gathering the shreds of her dignity around her. Who knew a simple doctor's visit would require so much prodding and poking?

Taking a seat in a high-backed chair situated to the left of the doctor's roll-top desk, she waited for the doctor to reappear from behind a screen where he'd disappeared a few minutes earlier with a slide of her sputum.

This part of the exam was far too familiar, though she hadn't been able to provide a specimen anywhere near the likes of what Rob would cough up. Her own cough had faded so as to hardly bother her this past week, recurring only on rare occasions when the dry air would catch at her throat and send her into a spasm.

What hadn't subsided was the nausea. It was that, more than the cough, that brought her here today.

Dr. Sewall stepped out from behind the screen and made his way to his desk chair. She could read little from his expression, a trait common to his profession, she'd found. She waited while he settled back in his chair.

"Well, Mrs. Skivington, as you may have learned through your husband's experience, tuberculosis can be difficult to diagnose, especially in its early stages. Frankly, though you show several symptoms of the disease and have certainly cause to suspect probable infection based on your close living proximity with your husband these past few years, I would be very hesitant to make any type of positive diagnosis at this early date.

"Your sputum certainly shows no sign of the disease, though that can often be the case in incipient stages. I find the stomach upset and fatigue a bit more troubling. However, they too, could certainly be attributed to other causes. Tell me. What was the date of your last menses?"

Her monthlies? Why, she couldn't even remember. What with Edie's death, all their travel, and then her illness since arriving in Denver, she'd not even thought about her monthly sickness. Let's see. There was the time right before their trip to Newark, then again, in Newark, she vaguely remembered it as being a part of her pain during those early weeks of sorrow and loss, but since then, had there been another? Why that was way before Thanksgiving!

"I . . . I don't recall. November, maybe?" Try as she might, she could not remember having her courses anytime since they arrived in Denver.

"And are you usually quite regular?"

"Yes. Yes, I am." The nausea, the fatigue, could that mean . . .? "Are you saying—?"

Dr. Sewall held up a hand to cut her short. "Though the cessation of menses is not unusual in cases of extreme illness and even with tuberculosis, I don't think that is the case here. Yes, I would say, Mrs. Skivington, given the comparatively short duration of your illness, we can most likely conclude the cause to be the most obvious one. You are pregnant."

Maddie forced down the laughter that was building inside her. Morning sickness. Of course. She must be dense to have missed it. Hadn't she helped her mother through the early part of four pregnancies? She knew all the signs. How could she have missed them? Tuberculosis indeed. She really had been a goose.

But she and Rob had been married almost three years with never so much as a hint of pregnancy. Somehow, she'd come to believe they were never meant to have children. Yet, here, amidst months of sorrow and death, finally, a baby.

"The Lord giveth and the Lord taketh away." She could almost hear Mother Skivington reminding her that the Lord hadn't really taken anyone. He was keeping them for that grand reunion by and by. And now, a new, precious baby to join their midst. He giveth and giveth. *Dear, Lord, thank you.* She closed her eyes against the tears that threatened to spill.

"I wish I could offer my congratulations, ma'am, but in light of the circumstances, I fear I cannot. As I told your husband, a pregnancy was what I had hoped to avoid."

Maddie's eyes flew open as the doctor's words hit her like a pail of cold water. "What? You told Rob what?"

"Yes. I see now that it was much like barring the barn door after the cows got out, but when he told me the two of you were childless, I had hoped to be in time to prevent such an event happening."

"Why ever for?"

"Did he not share the pamphlet I gave him with you?"

She didn't remember any pamphlet, though maybe he had. Their last hours together were somewhat of a blur, what with her illness and the haste of his moving them to the boarding house and his departure.

"What did it say?"

"Merely what I have told you. A household that houses a tubercular person is no place for a child."

"I believe he did mention some sentiments along that line on behalf of my sister."

"But the likelihood for the disease is even more pronounced in a child of his own. Though recent science has proven tuberculosis to be a contagious disease, many in the medical community believe that certain physical dispositions are more inclined to contract the disease than others.

"I know of many cases of people who have lived and worked among the tubercular for years yet have never contracted it. On the other hand, I've known of other instances of entire families who, generation after generation, lose members to it. We can only assume that these families possess a type of hereditary taint that makes them more prone to contracting the disease. Tell me, Mrs. Skivington, do you have a history of tuberculosis within your own family?"

"No. Not that I know of."

"Good, good. Then there is still a fine chance this child will be quite without taint, as well. Though the chances it will not are still high enough that I can't quite like it. Didn't Dr. Waite warn you of this possibility?"

That their children would somehow be "tainted"? Gentle Dr. Waite would never think to say anything so unkind. Rob had an illness. He was not tainted, nor would their child be. She had known of this baby's existence less than a quarter-hour, and yet she felt as proud and protective of it as a mother bear. No one was going to label her baby "tainted" or unfit in any way.

She pushed to her feet. "I won't take up any more of your time, sir. I appreciate what you've tried to express today and will certainly keep it in mind. However, since God chose to bless us with this baby, I have to believe that He most definitely has a purpose for its life, whether it be a long life of health or one cut short by disease. God does not make mistakes."

"No. No, of course not. I didn't mean to infer that this child is a mistake, per se—" His words trailed off under her level stare. He cleared his throat and began again. "At any rate, should you wish for my services during your confinement, please don't hesitate to come to me. And I would be most happy to advise you at any time on the proper care for a child with a predisposition for tuberculosis."

She swept by Dr. Sewall without giving him an answer. She'd had quite enough of this particular man's advice. He may have all the knowledge in the world, but his manner of imparting it lacked compassion. It was all so clear to her now. Rob's stricken face when he'd returned from the man's office that day could only be due to the doctor's odious arrogance. "Tainted" indeed.

Her indignation lasted until she alighted from the streetcar at the corner of Sixteenth and Larimer Streets. Dodging a bicycle and a horseless carriage, she had just gained purchase on the sidewalk in front of the imposing First National Bank of Denver when a young mother and her son breezed by, brushing against her skirts as they passed. The little boy's chubby legs, encased in sturdy boots and thick black hose, churned to keep up with his mother's longer strides. Soft, baby curls bobbed beneath his jaunty sailor hat.

"Maw maw. When can I see Papa?" she heard him lisp as he trundled along at his mother's heels.

"Soon, baby, soon. Just one more stop."

She placed a hand to her stomach as she watched them go by. A baby. The wonder of Dr. Sewall's diagnosis struck her anew, wiping away the last vestiges of her anger. She and Rob were going to be parents. She couldn't wait to tell him.

But how could she tell him? The thought caught her up short. A letter seemed hardly appropriate for news of such import. Yet how could she wait until spring? By then, one look at her would give away her secret. He would have to know before then.

"Are you going in, ma'am?"

A gentleman held open the heavy glass door of the bank's entrance in front of her.

"Oh. Yes. Of course. Thank you." Cheeks burning, she swept by him with what she hoped was some modicum of dignity. How long had she been standing there like a ninny?

She stepped into the nearest teller's line and pulled a bank draft from her reticule, determined to focus on the business at hand. True to her prediction to Hazel, a packet of letters had arrived from Wyoming just yesterday, and with it, a draft that would pay for next month's rent and leave her and Hazel a little spending money besides. But, truth be told, the "packet" of letters had only been three woefully short missives, one from each of the Skivington brothers.

Rob's letter had been the shortest and said little in response to her long, eloquent arguments to join him, other than the weather was miserable, the sheep as stupid as ever, and she should stay put until spring. Not ever having the need to correspond with Rob by letter before, she had no gauge to judge this one by. His brother's letters were hardly any more expressive, though the postscript to George's letter had given her many hours of worry the past few days.

Have you and Rob had a falling out? He's as cross as an old bear these days.

Until her interview with Dr. Sewall, she didn't know what to make of his question. Now, having met the doctor and heard his views, she had a pretty good indication of what might be bothering Rob. How she wished she could talk to him. Dr. Sewall had done much damage, but she knew she could reassure Rob if only she could see him face-to-face. Letters took too long and were too susceptible to miscommunication. She needed to see him for so many reasons, and spring was just too far away.

She stepped up to the window and handed the draft to the teller.

"Do you want to deposit or cash this, Mrs. Skivington?"

The man's question sparked an idea. "Cash it, please. And I would like to close the account."

"I'm afraid I can't do that, ma'am. The account is listed under your husband's name. He would need to come in and close out the account himself."

"You don't understand. My husband is in Wyoming, sir, and I will be leaving soon to join him. We have no more need of an account here in Denver."

"Well then, have him send written confirmation, and we'll have the funds transferred to a bank of his choice in Wyoming."

"Can I still withdraw funds from the account?"

"You will need to keep a balance of at least five dollars."

"Very well. Give me the remainder of the account, with the exception of five dollars."

As he counted out the bills, she began to make her plans. The money Rob had sent for next month's board would more than cover train and stage fare to Wyoming, and the rest of the cash would help with any additional travel expenses.

The teller stuffed the pile of bills in an envelope and handed it to her.

"Thank you, Mrs. Skivington. I hope we can be of help to you and your husband again someday."

With a nod, she turned to the door, unable to quench the smile that began to spread across her face. Pack your bags, Hazel dear. We're going to Wyoming.

Chapter Thirty-Five

Maddie tucked her gloved hands into the sleeves of her fur-lined wool coat and buried her face in its collar. Would she ever be warm again? She glanced down at the shadowy lump that was her sister, asleep on the coach floor, snug under the buffalo robe Mr. Allen had placed around her at the last coach stop.

Early in their journey, Hazel had opted for a seat atop the pile of mail sacks on the floor rather than one on the hard bench seats. But with each stop, her perch grew shorter as Mr. Allen pulled one sack after another from beneath her. Soon she'd be left with nothing but the bare floor. Maybe, with the thickness of the buffalo fur, she might not notice.

She envied Hazel her oblivion. She should sleep too, but in the cold found she could not. Even with the canvas curtains drawn and six bodies crammed into the small interior, the coach was icy cold. Had she been able to see in the darkness, she knew she'd see her breath and that of the other passengers curling white into the air around them. She tried to wiggle her toes, numb within her high-top boots.

The hostess at the last stage stop had given them each a hot brick for their feet, but the welcome warmth had worn off hours ago. How much farther before they would have a chance to stop again, if only to move around, bring some blood back into their frozen appendages?

She shifted in her seat and glanced again at her sleeping sister. She was so tired, she was almost tempted to join her on the floor. How Mother would spin in her grave to see her grown daughter attempt anything so undignified. And Edie . . . Oh. Edie. The wave of pain and loss hit unexpectedly, seizing her throat and pricking her eyelids with tears.

Funny thing about grief. She never knew when a new wave would hit her. A thought would come out of the blue and level her in a flash. If she had been alone, she would have allowed herself a good cry. As it was, she couldn't stop the tears that flowed silently down her cheeks in the darkness. She missed her sister so. She let the tears flow for a few minutes before wiping them with her handkerchief.

"Do you grieve a husband?" A soft voice whispered in the darkness.

She turned to the lady seated next to her on the bench. "No. A sister."

"A recent loss?"

"Yes."

"It gets better with time."

Something in the woman's voice made her ask. "And you? Do you grieve someone too?"

"My husband."

"I'm sorry." And then, prompted perhaps by the darkness, she added, "Is it harder when it's a husband?"

"Some say as it is. I wouldn't know. I've only had the one loss."

One loss or many, the pain of death was universal. She tried to remember what the woman looked like but could only recall a brief impression of a small, middle-aged woman in a well-worn black cloak. She'd boarded the stage at Crook's Gap, one stop past their supper break, and though Maddie had been glad to have another woman join their group, which until then had consisted of three men in addition to her and Hazel, they had not spoken to each other until now.

"And his loss. Is it recent?"

"Been over a year now since I lost my John. Some days it seems like just yesterday, though." Her voice broke a little on the last words.

Maddie could think of nothing to say, so she reached out in the darkness and squeezed the woman's hand. The woman squeezed back. They lapsed back into silence, and Maddie must have dozed off because the next thing she knew, she was wakened by a sharp blast of icy air. Through a fog of sleep, she realized the coach had stopped its incessant rocking and bouncing. Mr. Allen stood at the open coach door.

"Sorry to have to wake you, folks, but I'm going to need you to get out."

Were they at another stage stop? She peered past Mr. Allen but could see no lights or buildings in the distance.

"We've come to Rocky Hill. The road's pretty icy, and the wind's come up. This coach has been known to blow over here before. I don't want to chance it. I'm going to put the chains on, but I'll need all of you to walk down to the bottom of the hill."

Walk? Here? In the middle of the night? She bent to wake up Hazel, who still slept at her feet. The girl whimpered as she pulled the buffalo robe off her and helped her to her feet. Wrapping a blanket around her shoulders, she directed her toward the door where Mr. Allen lifted her down. Following, she stumbled a little as her numb feet hit the snow-covered ground.

"Careful there, ma'am. You all right?" Mr. Allen steadied her with a hand to her elbow.

"I'm fine. Thank you."

The widow disembarked next, followed by the three male passengers. She was glad to see she wasn't the only one with unsteady legs.

. . .

"If you folks would just follow the road there, it'll take you to the bottom of the hill. I'll follow with the stage as soon as I get these chains on," Mr. Allen said.

One of the men, a blacksmith from Rongis, stayed behind to help Mr. Allen and the stage guard with the chains. The rest of them stumbled ahead down the road lit dimly by the headlamps of the stage.

"Maddie, I'm cold."

"I know, honey. We all are. But the sooner we get down this hill, the sooner we can get back on the stagecoach."

She started at a brisk pace until her foot hit an icy patch. Arms flailing like windmills, she struggled to regain her balance, only narrowly escaping a fall. Getting to the bottom of this hill was going to be harder than it looked.

Taking Hazel's hand, she picked her way slowly over the rocks, the icy wind stinging at her cheeks and nose and threatening to blow her hat to kingdom come. This was definitely a first. Never before had she paid for transportation only to be told to get out and walk.

They'd made it about halfway down the hill when a shout and a rumble behind them told them the coach was on its way. Pulling Hazel into the deeper snow on the side of the road, she watched the coach sway by, rocking and pitching and picking up a dangerous amount of speed. Hitting a small boulder, the coach careened on two wheels for a minute flinging Mr. Allen up against the rails of the box. Just when she thought the stage was going over, it righted itself and hurtled to a stop at the foot of the hill.

"Guess it's a good thing we walked, huh?" Hazel's eyes were round.

"Looks like it. Watch your step now, or we'll be sliding down after it."

Ten minutes later, their small group of passengers made it back into the coach. Maddie regained her seat next to the widow lady and pulled Hazel onto her lap. Drawing the buffalo robe up off the floor, she wrapped it around the three of them.

"There, now. We'll be warm again in no time," she said, with more conviction than she felt. She might never be warm again. What a fool she was to have taken this trip in January. Somehow, in her excitement over seeing Rob again and sharing her news about the baby, she'd entirely forgotten the horrors of this thirty-six-hour stage ride. If she ever made it back to their cabin, she was staying put for a very long time. And never, ever again would anyone convince her to travel this route in the winter.

Her shaking gradually subsided beneath the combined warmth of the heavy robe and Hazel's small body. Hazel leaned her head against her shoulder and soon fell back asleep, but sleep remained elusive for Maddie. Dawn was breaking, filling the interior of the stage with a warm, rosy glow.

Tonight she'd be home and could sleep in her own bed for the first time in months. She wouldn't think of the cold or her aching bones or the persistent nausea that threatened to break loose again. Soon. Soon. She'd see Rob again soon.

Turning, she caught her seatmate's eyes on her and returned the woman's tentative smile. "I feel as if we know each other, but we've not been introduced. My name is Maddie Skivington."

"Jane Wells." The woman's faded blue eyes were friendly and kind.

"Do you travel much farther today?"

"As far as Hailey. My sister lives on a ranch near there. She's in the 'family way' again, and I promised to be there for her lying in."

"She's lucky to have you near enough to help out. She has other children, then?"

"Three. The oldest is just turned seven. A regular hand full they are. I told her I'd stay until spring roundup. My boys are near grown and can handle the ranch while I'm gone. Between them and our ranch foreman, they'll do just fine. May not eat as well"—she chuckled—"but they'll do just fine with the ranching. And you? Are you bound for Lander?"

"Dallas. We—my husband and I—have a cabin near there. My husband's a sheepherder."

A look of surprise flitted across the woman's face. "You don't say. I'd a never taken you for a sheepherder's wife. I reckoned you for an easterner out here on a visit."

"Well, you're not far off. Rob and I moved here from the east a year ago last June. For my husband's health."

"I see. And he's been better?"

"Some better, yes. We're hopeful."

"Glad to hear it." The woman reached over and patted her hand. "And how do you like living here so far?"

"It's been interesting. And full of new experiences. Take last night, for instance. Now I can say I've walked behind a stagecoach through the desert in the middle of the night."

Mrs. Wells chuckled. "Truth be told, that's a new one for me as well. I'm mighty glad it was just a walk, though. When the stage door opened, I was certain we were in for trouble like they had near Meyersville back last November."

"What kind of trouble?"

"You didn't hear of it?"

"No. We've been back east since October."

"There was a rash of stagecoach hold-ups, three of them in the space of a month. They all happened just south of Myersville, where the stage crosses the Sweetwater. A group of hooded, armed men would attack the stage, take the mail and any valuables they could find on the passengers. During the last one, Billy Cobb—he was the driver—decided to fight back. Ended up with a bullet in his leg and near died from the blood loss before he could get the stage into the Myersville station."

"Oh, my. The poor man. Is he all right?"

"I saw him just last week." The blacksmith from Rongis took up the story. "He's still hobbling around, but he's doing fine. It was a close one, though. The only passenger on that stage was a schoolmarm come to teach at the Hailey school. She fainted dead away during the gun battle and was no help. If the horses hadn't been so used to the road, he might not have made it to Myersville in time. The station master said Billy was slumped over unconscious on the box when the stage pulled in. And the schoolmarm? Well, word has it she'd a' packed up and left the county that day if she weren't so afraid to get back on the stage."

The rancher and his son laughed at that, along with the blacksmith, but for Maddie, who well remembered her encounter with hooded outlaws, the fear was still too real. She pulled Hazel tight against her. Myersville? Wasn't that their breakfast stop? If the brightening daylight outside the canvas-covered window was any indication, they should be crossing the Sweetwater at any minute.

"Did they ever catch the robbers?"

"Not yet. But after Billy was shot, the stage line's taken to hiring a guard to ride shotgun on all its runs. There hasn't been any trouble since."

Maddie recalled the grim-looking man dressed all in black who'd helped Mr. Allen and the blacksmith put chains on the wheels last night. She prayed his presence would continue to deter all robbers, at least until this particular stage reached Dallas. *Please, Lord.* Was it too much to ask?

Her months in the east must have turned her soft. She'd forgotten how hard life was here in the west, though it was all coming back to her now with a vengeance—from the grueling, thirty-six-hour stage ride to the renewed threat of menacing, masked men. Maybe she should have stayed in Denver after all.

The stage slowed, causing everyone inside to tense. The rancher drew his pistol and used the tip of the gun to ease back the canvas curtain. Through the gap, Maddie could see the waters of the Sweetwater River glistening in the morning sunshine. Soon, the horses' hooves clattered on the bridge's wooden planks as the stage swayed across, then lurched up the opposite bank. No one spoke.

Within minutes the stage had regained its speed and was hurtling down the road toward Myersville. Maddie let out her pent-up breath. The rancher let the curtain drop back into place and reholstered his pistol. Maddie felt the tension oozing from the inside of the coach like air from a balloon.

Not long after, the coach pulled into the Myersville station. They'd barely rolled to a stop before the tender was busy at the harnesses, unleashing the horses. Maddie woke Hazel and guided her toward the door of the coach. They'd have to step lively if they were to grab a bite to eat for breakfast.

"A bit late this morning, aren't ya, Tom?" She heard the tender say to Mr. Allen as she climbed down behind Hazel. "We was beginning to think you might a' had some trouble."

"Just an icy patch at Rock Hill. Slowed us up a bit, I reckon."

"No road agents?"

"No. Why? Have you heard something?"

"Posse rode by about an hour ago. Guess a freighter bound for Fort Washakie was attacked just east of here last night. The bandits made off with a consignment of rifles and the officers' payroll. The freighters put up a fight, though. Sounds like it was quite a gun battle. One freighter was shot dead. Another was shot in the shoulder, but the doc says he'll be all right. And at least one of the outlaws was hit. The posse followed a blood trail this morning but lost it at the Sweetwater."

By this time, all the passengers had gathered around, intent on the stage tender's news. The guard hopped down from his perch on the box and began to pepper the man with questions.

"How many outlaws? Did they say?"

"Five or six. The freighters said they were outnumbered two to one."

"And the posse came through this way?"

"One group did. Said they were headed northwest toward the Winds. The other stayed down by the Sweetwater. Planned to follow it down toward Brownsville to see if they could pick up the trail."

Maddie exchanged an uneasy glance with Mrs. Wells while the rancher and the blacksmith listened with grave expressions. Their path toward Lander lay to the north and west.

The tender must have sensed their unease. "Don't reckon you folks'll have any trouble, though. If those outlaws came this way, they were through here hours ago. Most likely, they stayed down near the river anyway. Especially if one of them was hurt."

A shiver coursed down Maddie's back. Had the outlaws watched them cross the bridge from some hiding spot by the river? Silly thought. If they'd come that way at all, they'd be long gone by now. Still, breakfast had somehow lost its lure. All she wanted was to get back on that stage and get home.

Chapter Thirty-Six

This day's leaden skies matched Rob's mood, which is probably why he'd sent the boys back to the ranch with the rest of the sheep, opting to stay behind to chase an errant band of about two hundred head by himself. A storm was brewing, no doubt of that. If the heavy, snow-laden clouds and sharp north wind weren't proof enough, he had only to note the behavior of his flock to verify it. He'd lived with sheep long enough to know the signs.

Blasted sheep! Why they couldn't stay put before an approaching storm and trust their shepherd to see to their care was beyond him. But, no. The first sign of an ill-favored wind and one of them was off, followed by a whole passel of the mindless ninnies with no more sense than to come in out of the rain. Wouldn't be so bad if they could truly take care of themselves, but nine times out of ten, they'd rush headlong into the one spot they should never be—over the side of a cliff or into a creek bed where they'd be caught and buried. There was a lesson for himself in their behavior, he supposed, but he was in no mood to admit it.

He wasn't in the mood for much that was good for him these days and no fit company for man nor beast, as his brothers were sure to attest. A niggling guilt deep down told him he hadn't been fair to Maddie. He should have stayed and talked things over with her instead of rushing off as he did. She'd have had her arguments, valid ones too, from the sound of her letters, but it wouldn't have changed anything. Besides, she didn't know all the doctor had told him. And he knew he couldn't live with her as her husband and protect her the way he needed to. He didn't have it in him. It was better for all of them if he kept to himself—better for Maddie, better for Hazel, and better for the boys. At least until he was well again.

And he *was* improving. He'd been following the doctor's orders since he'd come back. For the most part, he lived at the cabin and let George and Fred follow the sheep with the wagon while he served as their camp tender. He was only out today on account of the approaching storm. He wanted to get the sheep in closer to the ranch where he'd stockpiled a bunch of hay. That way, should the snowfall prove heavy, they would still be able to feed the sheep. And though he had chosen to follow this wayward band today, he was doing so on horseback, not on foot as he would have done last winter.

When he'd come back in December, he'd asked Jackson to help him find a horse. A week later, the man had shown up with Trapper, a pretty paint with a willing disposition. Leaning forward, he stroked the horse's soft neck. He and Trapper had bonded immediately. Which is more than he could say for his other new addition. He glanced down at the silky black and white coat of the dog trotting at his side.

He'd brought on a new dog this winter also, giving each of his brothers and him a dog to use when they herded the sheep. Though sired by the same dog and birthed from the same bitch as Rosie, Rowdy had inherited few of the other dog's abilities.

To be fair, even Rebel was no match for Rosie. Few dogs were. But Rowdy fell far short of even Rebel's abilities. Could be his age. He wasn't yet a year. Maybe in time, he'd settle down and work the sheep at least as well as Rebel.

He probably should have brought Rosie with him on this hunt, but he felt more comfortable leaving her with the large band. Rowdy should do fine with the job they had ahead of them today. It wasn't as if he needed him to track the sheep. Though the weather had been mild the last few weeks, there was still enough snow on the ground. He'd have to be blind not to know which way the sheep had gone. As long as he kept on their well-marked trail, he should eventually find them. And Rowdy was lively enough to keep any band moving once they were headed in the right direction.

But they needed to find the sheep soon. A snowflake drifted down, followed closely by another. If he didn't locate them within the next half hour, he'd probably have to leave without them. He might still be a greenhorn, but even he wasn't fool enough to tarry when a storm was blowing in.

He scanned the horizon but still could see no sign of them. They were near the spot where he and Maddie had been attacked last winter. He was sure of it. Just ahead, he could see the rocky outcroppings of the Freak Mountains and the trail that led through the foothills into the Winds. If that were the case, then he had little time to lose. Judging by the direction of the sheep trail, the band was heading toward a steep drop-off that had taken a small portion of his flock last winter when they'd been spooked by the raiders. How ironic it would be to lose another group at that same spot.

Rob set his jaw and spurred Trapper to a trot. Not this year. Not if he could help it.

~

MADDIE BREATHED A SIGH OF RELIEF AS THE BUCKBOARD rounded the last bend, and she finally could see their little cabin tucked into the hillside midway up the valley in front of them. Home at last. Even tinier than she remembered, the cabin looked dark, cold, and vulnerable against the barren hills. Or maybe the heavy, gray clouds were responsible for the bleakness of the scene.

Whatever the case, the place looked deserted. No smoke rose from the chimney. No men or dogs were evident in the yard. The men must all be out with the sheep. No matter. Her grueling trip was over. She was home.

She'd been fortunate to find young Petie Garrity at the stage stop in Dallas picking up supplies for his family's ranch. The youngest member of the Garrity family had proved every bit as helpful as his brothers. Within minutes of her offer to hire him to drive them home, he had his family's buckboard harnessed to the team and her and Hazel's belongings stowed in the back of the wagon.

At twelve, Petie lacked the height and breadth of his older brothers but judging from the size of his hands and feet, he'd have them matched, if not beaten, someday. All elbows and knees, he moved with the grace of a newborn colt, but once behind the reins, he drove the team with the confidence of any grown man.

Unlike Jackson, this boy could talk. He'd enlivened the hour and a half trip with a steady stream of all the news and events that had happened in the area in the last few months. By the time they reached the cabin, Maddie felt more in the loop of local happenings than she had when they'd left. The last few miles were full of speculation on the whereabouts of the most recent outlaws. Petie was convinced they'd traveled north and could be hiding at any point down the trail ahead.

"But don't you worry none, Miz Skivington," he'd said. "I kin shoot this here rifle as good as Jackson. Won't be nobody bothering us."

Thankfully, he hadn't had to prove himself. He soon pulled the team to a halt in front of the cabin door. She hopped down from the buckboard and shook out her skirts. Though her wool traveling suit didn't wrinkle as badly as her cotton one, she knew she looked worse for wear after three days of travel. Maybe it was best no one seemed to be home. She'd have time to freshen up a bit before greeting Rob.

Trying the door, she found it locked and began fishing in her reticule for the key she had placed there on the outset of their journey. Hazel dropped to a seat on the stone doorstep. Poor child. She must be exhausted.

Petie came around the back of the wagon, hauling her valise. "I'll get that trunk in just a minute, Miz Skivington." He stopped short at the sight of her fumbling with the lock. "Well I'll be. All locked up in the daytime? I never heard of such a fool thing."

Maddie laughed. "Oh, we city folk do all manner of fool things." Personally, she was glad Rob had locked it. The thought of this lonely cabin sitting open to any who passed by was unsettling, given all the talk about outlaws she'd heard today.

Once inside the cabin, she found evidence that Rob or one of the boys meant to return soon. The fire was banked but not out completely. A few dirty dishes sat in the dry sink, and a pot of beans sat soaking on the stove. As soon as she got things settled a bit, she'd set to and fix them a nice, big supper. Wouldn't Rob be surprised to come home to find both her and a warm meal?

A thump made her turn toward the door. "Oh goodness, Petie." The boy was wrestling her horsehair trunk in the front door. "Let me help you with that."

"No need, Miz Skivington. I'm stronger than I look."

He must be, for his arms looked no bigger around than twigs. Still, he managed to lift the heavy trunk through the doorway and drag it to the middle of the cabin floor.

"Anything else you need, ma'am? Want I should stick around until Mr. Skivington gets back?"

"Oh, that won't be necessary. He may not come back until tomorrow, and your mother would be sure to worry if you weren't home by dark."

"My ma hasn't been around since I was a baby, but if you don't need anything, I guess I'd best be going. Looks like a storm's a'brewing, and I'd like to get them horses back before it hits."

That's right. She'd forgotten the Garrity family were men only. Fishing in her reticule once again, she dug out the half dollar she'd promised him. "Thanks so much for your help. And when you see Jackson, tell him to stop by. We'd love to see him again."

She watched until the creaking wagon disappeared around the bend, then turned back to survey the cabin. Hazel sat at the kitchen table, head down on her folded arms.

"Come, sweetheart. Let's get you to bed."

She remembered how tired she'd been the day they'd first arrived in Lander, how she and Rob had slept the whole afternoon and night through. She should be tired too, even more so than Hazel, who had actually gotten some sleep last night, but she wasn't. She knew she was running on excitement alone. After putting Hazel to bed, she set about cleaning up the cabin and preparing supper like a woman possessed.

She was just pulling a pan of fluffy biscuits from the oven when she heard sheep bells tinkling in the distance. Flying to the door, she caught a glimpse of a sheep wagon following a line of sheep into the valley. As the animals and men drew nearer, she recognized George driving the wagon and Fred walking along beside it.

The late afternoon light was fading, and snow was beginning to fall in earnest. But where was Rob? Could he be riding in the wagon? She called out a greeting and waved as they cut through the line of chokecherry trees that grew along the stream. At her call, Fred looked over and stopped short before letting out an answering shout and breaking into a run. But George whipped up the horses on the wagon and beat him into the yard.

"What are you doing here?" He asked as he sprang from the wagon. "Does Rob know?"

"No, of course, he doesn't." Fred gave his brother a disgusted look as he jogged up beside him. "Do you think he'd a been such a bear today if he knew she was coming?"

"Where *is* Rob?"

"Oh, he should be along soon. He stayed back to find a band that'd wandered off last night. He can't be more than an hour behind us."

So she'd have to wait. Still, it was wonderful to see the boys. Tears sprang to her eyes as George bounded onto the doorstep and pulled her into a hug. Fred was right behind, claiming a hug of his own while Rosie and Rebel barked and ran circles around their happy group. Left to themselves, the sheep milled about the yard, baaing and bleating.

"You've brought the whole flock in, then?" Maddie said, surprised at how happy she was to see the animals.

"Rob wanted them near the cabin before the storm hits. He's got hay stacked out in the barn in case the snow's too deep for them to forage. We'll get them bedded down for the night, then be right in." George said.

Fred poked his head through the doorway and sniffed. "Are those biscuits I smell?"

"Yes. I've made a whole pan of them, so hurry along so you can have some while they're hot."

"You don't have to ask us twice. Come along, Rosie. Let's get these sheep to bed. We're gonna eat good tonight!"

Maddie laughed as the boys ran back out into the yard, whistling for the dogs and driving the sheep toward the pens back behind the barn. Turning, she stepped back into the kitchen and pulled the door shut behind her. She hoped Rob wouldn't be too long. That north wind had a bite to it, and she hated the thought of his being out in it.

Chapter Thirty-Seven

A flash of movement to the right of him caught Rob's eye as he rounded a bend in the valley. His hand moved to the rifle strapped across his saddle. Was that an antelope? Deer? The animal disappeared for a moment behind a strand of pines, then reappeared heading down through the pass that led from the canyon toward the Wind River Mountains. As it drew nearer, Rob could make out a streaming mane and tail. A horse, but not a wild one. Someone's mount, judging from the empty saddle atop its back.

He pulled Trapper to a stop. The runaway was headed straight for them. If he could keep from spooking it, he might have a chance of capturing the animal.

"Sit, Rowdy. Stay," he called, in a low voice, thankful that the dog obeyed at least those simple commands. He held his breath as the horse pounded nearer, willing himself, his horse, and the dog not to move. When it was about thirty yards away, the riderless horse suddenly sensed them, checking itself midstride, then veering away from them to the south. With a touch to his spurs, Rob gave chase.

"Come on, Trapper. Let's catch her."

The young paint didn't have to be told twice. Trapper began

to slowly gain on the larger animal, hitting full stride until the two were running side by side. Giving Trapper his head, Rob held tight his saddle horn with one hand while reaching out to grab the reins on the runaway with his other. The horse lunged to the right, but Rob was able to catch onto the leather straps minutes before they slipped away.

He pulled back on them with all his might.

"Whoa, there. Whoa."

Gradually, both horses slowed to a trot, then a walk, and finally to a halt. Keeping a tight grip on the other horse's reins, Rob slid from his saddle. The horse was a fine brown mare, wild-eyed and winded. He reached up to stroke the animal's strong neck.

She gentled at his touch but flung her head and sidled backward as Rowdy, who'd been left behind in the chase, came running up.

"Hush, now, girl. Hush. Nobody's going to hurt you. What's got you so spooked?" A streak of blood on the saddle caught his eye. "Are you hurt?" He searched for cuts along the horse's neck and flank, then moved to the other side. What he saw there stopped him short. That side of the saddle was coated with blood, some still wet. It had run down the saddle and soaked into the blanket beneath. Worst of all, saddle strings of braided red and black latigo hung from shiny silver conchos on the saddle.

He knew this saddle. Its fancy markings were hard to forget. He'd seen it first that October day beside his campfire when he fixed his broken stay chain. He'd seen it again on a cold February day when he lay bleeding in the snow watching its hooded rider canter on by.

Jake's horse. And most likely, Jake's blood.

He wanted nothing more than to give the horse a mighty slap on its flank and send it back on its heedless flight. Let it be someone else's problem. He had sheep to find. He'd wasted enough time as it was if he were still going to find them and get them home before the storm hit. He lifted his hand to deliver the swat, then balled his fist and let it drop to his side.

He couldn't do it. Jake or no Jake, that much blood meant someone was in terrible trouble. Going to his saddle, he pulled out a length of rope to use as a leading wire. Tying it to Jake's horse, he climbed atop Trapper and headed both horses back toward the pass. The sheep would have to wait.

Chapter Thirty-Eight

Maddie and the boys were halfway through their meal when the jangle of sheep bells and bleating of lambs reached their ears.

"There's Rob," Fred said, around the biscuit he'd just stuffed in his mouth. "Must'a found that bunch right off."

Maddie leaped to her feet, but George grabbed her arm before she could head to the door.

"Let's not tell him you're here, right off. Hide back there behind the screen, and then you can hop out and surprise him. I want to see his face when he sees you are here."

Maddie laughed but did what he suggested, slipping behind the screen in the corner where Hazel lay sleeping on a cot. What would Rob say when he saw her? Would he be angry that she came when he'd specifically told her to stay put? Or would he truly be happy to see her as the boys believed? Two months ago, she would not have doubted, but the time apart had left her feeling shy and unsure. Her heart beat a rapid tattoo as she waited.

Finally, she heard boots stamp on the doorstep, then a rap at the door. A blast of wind rocked the screen in front of her as the door flew open.

"Hope you boys don't mind some unexpected company tonight. If it'll help, I brought a band of sheep in payment for my room and board." Jackson's voice, not Rob's.

Feeling foolish, Maddie stepped out from her hiding place. "Mrs. Skivington! I didn't know you were back."

"We just got back today. In fact, your brother Petie drove us out from Dallas." Her hand was soon swallowed in his hearty handshake. She'd forgotten what a big man he was. Bearlike, he took up most of the kitchen area, his shaggy black hair and beard wet with thawing snowflakes.

He glanced around. "Rob's not here?"

"No. In fact, we thought you might be Rob. The boys came in about an hour ago with the main bunch. Rob stayed behind to look for a band that had gone missing."

"That's the one I brought. Found 'em just east of Tavis's camp, huddled against a canyon wall." He turned toward the table where George and Fred sat, still shoveling in their meal. "I planned to drop them off at your camp but found you'd already left. I followed your tracks here."

"It's a wonder you didn't run across Rob on your way. He was headed that direction when we left him."

"Must'a just missed him. He'll probably be along soon. If not, he'll most likely hole up with Tavis or Pedro until the storm passes. I was planning to bunk with you boys tonight. Ain't fit weather for man nor beast out there, but I didn't realize Mrs. Skivington was back."

"No matter. You can stay out in the sheep wagon with me," George said. "Fred can stay in here with the girls."

"Of course," Maddie said. "You know you're always welcome." Where were her manners? She'd been so caught up in her worry over Rob, she'd forgotten to play hostess. "Let me take your coat. And please, sit and eat. There's plenty for everyone."

∽

His trek up the valley to the pass was a battle. Like Jonah of old, Rob wanted nothing more than to turn around and run. But the Lord had commanded him to love his enemies and do good to his persecutors. Running would avail him no more than it had Jonah.

But deep inside, he knew he was obeying the letter of the law at best. There was no love in him for Jake. None. Nor did he want there to be. He would do his duty. That was all.

Once he entered the pass, the trail of blood was as easy to follow as the sheep's trail had been through the snow in the valley. Dark, reddish-brown spots marked the path into the mountains, splashed across rocks and staining patches of old snow. Jake, or whoever it was, was hurt and hurt bad. He'd gone about a hundred yards when the trail of blood came to an abrupt halt. He'd lost it in a stretch of bare dirt, expecting to pick it up again in the next snowy patch as he had before, but when he reached it, he found nothing.

The snow was old and hard-packed, leaving little trace of any tracks, but up ahead where the snow lay deeper, he thought he could see a path a horse had made through the snow. As he started toward it, Rowdy, who'd been alternating between running ahead and dropping behind him as they trailed up the mountain, set up barking from behind. He turned to see the little dog, front haunches down, neck fur bristling and barking with all his might at a strand of juniper lining the trail. Probably a rabbit or some other critter back in there.

He whistled for the dog to 'come by,' then turned back up the trail. The last thing he needed was for Rowdy to take off chasing rabbits. Daylight was wasting, and a light snow was beginning to fall. If he didn't find something soon, he'd have to give up his search.

He came around a bend in the trail and pulled Trapper to a stop. The path ran ahead into a canyon, deep with snow. No tracks had been through there in weeks. He turned back down the trail to find Rowdy still pacing in front of the strand of junipers. Seeing him, the little dog came running over to his horse, barking furiously.

Curious, Rob eyed the strand of bushes growing close against the side of the mountain. Couldn't be anything much bigger than a rabbit hidden in there, could there? Then his eye caught a drop of blood on the snow just beneath the fringe of evergreens. What in the world?

He jumped from his saddle and walked to where the trail of blood ended. How was it possible for anything as large as a man to be hidden in there? With a short bark, Rowdy dove into the branches and disappeared from sight.

"Rowdy!" Bending, Rob pulled back the nearest branch and peered into the darkness. Understanding dawned. The bushes hid the entrance to a small cave carved into the rocky ledge of the hillside behind it. Rob let the branch fall and backed away. A cave that size would be a perfect lair for a mountain lion or even a bear. "Rowdy," he called. "Get back here."

A low moan emanated from within, reminding him of the blood and his reason for being here. Feeling a little foolish, he pulled the branches aside again and peered inside. He could see nothing in the darkness ahead of him, but if Rowdy and Jake were both in there, he supposed it was free of any other inhabitants.

You're not making this easy for me, are you, Lord? He hated caves and small spaces—anything that made him feel confined. At least this cave seemed shallow, and its entrance, though low, was broad. With a last look at the waning daylight, he dropped to his knees and crawled into its inky recesses.

His eyes took a moment to adjust to the darkness, but soon he could see Rowdy over by the shadowy outline of a body lying face down of the cave floor a few feet in front of him. Was the man dead? But no, he'd heard a moan just a minute ago. Rob crawled over and touched the man's shoulder.

"Jake?"

At his question, the boy turned his head. "I know'd you'd

come back for me, Zeke. I know'd you wouldn't leave your old friend to die, all by his lonesome."

"I'm not Zeke."

Jake didn't seem to hear his answer. "Gimme some of that whiskey, Zeke. I'm powerful thirsty. Powerful . . . thirsty."

His words trailed off, and his eyes fluttered shut. Rob watched him for a moment, waiting for him to respond again, but could see no further signs of consciousness. No doubt about it. The boy was hurt and hurt badly, but in the darkness of the cave, he could see no visible injuries. What he needed was some light.

Rocking back on his haunches, he took stock of his surroundings. Not likely Jake just stumbled on this cave, especially hurt as he was. The place was probably a hide-out of sorts, and if so, might be stocked in some manner, but as he scanned the shadowy room, measuring some eight by ten feet, he could see little evidence to support his theory.

The cavern's roof was low, only about four feet at the mouth, then gradually tapering to around two feet at the back. Two or three full-grown men could sleep comfortably enough in here, but there was no way they'd be able to stand up and walk around. Not much of a hide-out.

A shadowy shape near the back of the cave caught his attention. Crawling over, he found what he needed—a small wooden crate containing about a dozen candles. He dug one out and lit it with one of the matches he kept in his front coat pocket. The light immediately illuminated the area around him, revealing a narrow opening in the wall not much bigger around than a man's body.

Now this made more sense. He'd heard of small passageways that led to bigger rooms and caverns within the bowels of the earth. The cave must extend much farther into the mountain than he'd thought, meaning the room they were in was little more than an anteroom. No wonder it held so few supplies.

Lying flat on his stomach, he shined the candle into the

opening but could see no further than a few feet. He shuddered at the thought of anyone voluntarily pushing themselves into that little tunnel. Not for him, thank you. This outer room was all he was willing to stomach, and even then, he didn't plan to stay any longer than he had to.

Candle in hand, he crawled back over to Jake and let the light roam across the boy's legs, arms, torso, and head but could see no blood. Gently, he rolled the boy over. Jake's duster draped open, revealing a dark red stain that spread from the boy's abdomen to his upper thigh. He loosened Jake's belt and pulled up his shirt to find a hole, about the size of a quarter, right above Jake's hip bone on the right side. Bullet wound, no doubt. What had the boy been up to now?

Taking a knife from his belt, he cut Jake's union suit away from the hole and surveyed the damage. The angry red hole oozed a small trickle of blood. Rolling Jake to his side, Rob searched his back for an exit wound but could see none, which meant the bullet was probably lodged somewhere inside him. So, where had all the blood come from? Further investigation unearthed another wound along Jake's right hip. Here the bullet had grazed the skin rather than entering the body but, judging from the condition of the clothing around it, was probably the source of the blood trail he had followed.

Sighing, Rob stripped off his coat and flannel shirt to get to the soft cotton shirt he'd worn over his long johns. Luckily, he'd dressed in layers this morning. Taking up his knife, he cut the shirt into bandages which he wadded up and placed against the leg wound, then used several longer strips to tie the pad securely into place.

With the worst of the bleeding stopped, he could now concentrate on the hole in the abdomen. Not much chance of his finding the bullet. Not much chance of him doing anything at all that would help Jake in the long run. A wound like that needed a doctor's care, and they were miles away from help of that kind.

Even if he were able to somehow manhandle Jake onto the back of his horse and tie him down, they'd never get to a doctor in time to do Jake any good. He looked toward the cave opening where the snow was coming down in earnest now. Who was he fooling? They'd probably not even make it as far as Tavis's camp, which he knew to be about six miles to the south and east of here. He could try to make it to Tavis's on his own, but that would mean leaving Jake to certain death. Even if he survived his wounds, he'd have very little chance of surviving the night's cold temperatures, given his condition.

There was no help for it then. He'd have to stay with Jake at least until morning. The cave would serve as a good shelter from the storm once he got a fire started, and in the morning, he'd go for help.

Chapter Thirty-Nine

Rob threw two more logs on the fire, then sank down next to Jake, with his back against the cave wall. Rowdy lay in between them, head on his paws. With any luck, they'd have enough heat to last the night. Firewood was hard to come by in these canyons. He'd been lucky to find that dead cottonwood laying just off the trail when he'd gone searching earlier. Using the small ax he kept in his saddlebag, he'd spent the better part of his evening hours chopping the tree into smaller logs.

Despite the snow swirling outside and the wind howling through the nearby canyon, the cave was surprisingly warm, thanks to that fire. He'd built it close to the cave's entrance to keep most of the smoke at bay. Occasionally, a gust of wind would blow the smoke back into the cave, provoking his ever-present cough. Still, for the most part, he and Rowdy were comfortable.

He wished he could say the same for Jake. It had been a rough night for the boy, yet Rob had a feeling the battle was far from over. He'd tried to make the young man as comfortable as possible, resting his head against one of the saddles and wrapping him in the two horse blankets. Still, Jake would have periods where he'd shake almost uncontrollably. During the last bout, Rowdy had padded over and lain beside the boy. Whether it was the dog's extra warmth or just the comfort of his company, Jake's shaking had gradually subsided, but the moans and wild ramblings had not.

"Zeke . . . buddy . . . Zeke . . . gimme some whiskey, will ya? I need a drink bad."

Rob covered his ears with his hands, wishing he could block out Jake's plaintive cries. Early on, he'd responded to a similar plea by giving the boy a drink of water from his canteen. What a mistake that had been. Jake had no sooner swallowed the water when he retched violently and vomited, again and again, clutching at his gut and moaning piteously. Rob was thankful when the boy finally fell back and lapsed into a semi-conscious state.

Rob stared into the flames of the fire, watching the snow swirl and blow behind it. How long did it take a man to die? He had no doubt Jake was dying. A shot like that to the gut was a death sentence without a doctor close by. Jake would be long past helping by the time any doctor came near here. It's not like he wanted Jake to die, but if his fate were inevitable, then he wished God would take him. Listening to the boy's agony was almost more than he could bear.

"Get 'em off me! They're tearing at my gut, man. Get 'em off me!" Jake sent Rowdy flying with a sweep of an arm. The little dog skittered to a stop against the far side of the cave and lay down, eying Jake warily. Cursing, Jake struggled to sit up.

Rob reached over and pushed him back down. "Lay down, Jake. Getting up will only make it worse."

At his words, Jake turned his head and looked at him as if seeing him for the first time. "Joo-ler? Is that you? What are you doing here?"

"You've been shot. I'm just trying to help you out."

An ugly sneer twisted Jake's face. "No, you're not. You're just trying to help yourself to the gold, most likely. Well, you're not gonna get it. You try to go down that rat's hole, and I'll kill ya.

Don't think I won't neither. I'll kill ya, sure as you're sitting there. Ain't nobody gonna take . . ."

Jake clutched at his stomach and let out an unearthly moan as another spasm of pain cut off any further words. Rob waited until the pain subsided, then bathed Jake's face with a cool, wet cloth and tucked the blankets back around his legs.

Jake glared at him. "Ya don't think I could do it, do ya? I could. I've killed a man before." When Rob didn't answer, the boy's eyes turned cloudy and confused. "Remember, Zeke? You remember, don't ya? That train engineer? Shot him clean through the forehead, and he just looked so startled like. Remember how we laughed?" The cackle Jake let out was pure evil.

Rob sat back and covered his ears once again. He didn't want to hear any of this. Had heard too much already this night—tales of robbery, rape, violence, and now, murder. Surely a boy so young could not have lived a life this vile.

Why am I even here, Lord? What good could possibly come of this midnight vigil? Of course, nobody should have to die alone, but if anyone deserved to, it would have to be someone like Jake who laughed at cold-blooded murder, even when he himself lay dying.

Rob breathed a sigh of relief when the wild talk finally subsided, and the boy fell into a fitful sleep. Jake's labored breathing echoed off the cave walls. Rowdy crept back over and lay down between them again. Rob scratched behind the dog's ears, glad for the company of another living being during this dark deathwatch. Eerie shadows danced on the walls in the flickering firelight. He could almost feel the hand of death resting on his shoulder. He shuddered.

Yea, though I walk through the valley of the shadow of death, I will fear no evil, for Thou art with me.

The familiar words wrapped around him like a blanket of comfort. *Thou art with me.* His eyes fell on the restless body of the dying boy. What would it be like to walk that valley without the presence of the Savior?

Maybe that's why he was here.

Slowly, deliberately, he began to recite the words of the entire psalm out loud, starting from the beginning. "The Lord is my shepherd, I shall not want . . ."

Once finished, he repeated it, then moved on to another. "He that dwelleth in the secret place of the most High shall abide under the shadow of the Almighty. I will say of the LORD, He is my refuge and my fortress: my God; in him will I trust. . . . He shall cover thee with his feathers, and under his wings shalt thou trust: his truth shall be thy shield and buckler. Thou shalt not be afraid for the terror by night. . . ."

The words flowed around the cave, dispelling the heaviness of the shadows and replacing the echoes of the moans and evil ramblings that had filled it before. Maybe it was his imagination, but even Jake's breathing seemed to quiet, his movements to calm under the influence of the sacred promises. Rob continued reciting psalms and hymns until his throat grew sore and his voice too hoarse to continue. How Maddie would scold him were she here.

He let his mind dwell on thoughts of his wife. How he missed her. He missed the feel of her, the smell of her, all of her. How long had it been? Seven, eight weeks? Almost two months and still the gaping hole her absence left in him had never closed. Probably never would. And yet, she was better off without him. He knew that.

Here in the darkness with death hanging close, he almost couldn't bear the pain of their separation. Ha. Who was he kidding? He hadn't born their separation well ever. His brothers would be the first to testify to that. He leaned his head back against the rocky wall behind him and closed his eyes. For the first time in two months, he allowed himself to dream of holding her again.

He must have slept for several hours, for when he woke, the fire had burned to a small heap of glowing coals. The sky had lightened outside the cave entrance, but the storm had not abated. Snow blew so fast and furiously, he could see nothing outside the cave but a moving sheet of white.

Labored breathing at his side told him Jake was still with them, but Rowdy was nowhere to be seen. Forcing his aching joints to move, he crawled over and fed kindling, then logs, to the fire until he once again had a roaring blaze. He looked at their dwindling supply of firewood. Hopefully, the storm would give out before their fuel did.

His activity kicked off his morning coughing jag, the burning in his throat reminding him of the abuse he had given it last night. A little hot water should soothe it. Rob filled his empty canteen with some of the snow that had drifted against the cave's outer wall, then set it on one of the rocks that rimmed the fire pit. What he wouldn't give for a few coffee grounds or tea leaves about now.

Digging through his pack, he pulled out all that was left of the lunch he'd packed before leaving the cabin yesterday. Half a slice of cornbread, a hard-boiled egg, and a small slab of cold bacon. Not much of a breakfast, but possibly all the food he would get today. He finished cornbread and bacon off in two bites, then packed the egg away for later. No telling how much longer he'd be stuck here.

He returned to his seat beside Jake and searched the back recesses of the cave for Rowdy. Where had that dog got to? Cupping his mouth, he whistled and peered out into the storm. He couldn't see more than a few feet in front of the cave's entrance. Hopefully, the dog hadn't tried to go out in the snow, but where else could he be?

A rustling near the back of the cave made him turn in time to see Rowdy scrambling out of the small tunnel. The dog raced over, tail wagging, body writhing, holding something in his mouth.

"Whatcha got there, boy? Drop it." He reached toward the dog's mouth.

Obediently, Rowdy deposited a raw potato into his palm,

half-chewed and dripping with slobber. Rob looked back toward the small hole. He had a feeling there was much more to this cave than met the eye but still had no desire to investigate any further. Not if it meant traveling down that narrow tunnel. Rowdy might fit through it, but there were no guarantees he would. He wasn't going to find out. Not if he could help it.

Rob gave the potato back to Rowdy and wiped his hand on his trouser leg. The dog set to work finishing it off. Just as well. Lord knows, he had nothing left to feed him. In fact, had the potato been in better condition, he might have been tempted to fight him for it and bake it in the hot coals of the fire, but he wasn't that desperate. Yet.

Instead, he retrieved his canteen from the stones near the fire. Testing the water, he found it hot but cool enough to drink and sat back to enjoy the feel of the warm liquid on his raw throat.

"Got any whiskey in there, joo-ler?"

Rob turned to see Jake looking at him, eyes lucid.

"No. Just water. I'd give you some, but that didn't turn out so well last time."

Jake grimaced. "Water's for preachers and sissies. Give me some whiskey, will ya?"

"I don't have any whiskey."

Jake jerked his chin toward the back of the cave. "There's whiskey down the rat's hole. I'd let you go down there if you'd get me some."

He must mean the tunnel. Rat's hole would be a pretty fair name for that thing. "No thanks." Something in the name sparked a memory. "Didn't you say you'd kill me if I went down there?"

Jake looked up at him, eyes narrowed. "Probably still would. But not until *after* you gave me the whiskey."

Rob let out a snort which Jake answered with a shadow of a smile.

"How long do you think it'll take?" Jake said after a few minutes of silence.

"What? To get out of here?"

"This dying business. How long will it take?"

So, he *did* know he was dying. It didn't make the question any easier to answer. "I don't know. Maybe you won't die. You seem a lot better this morning."

"No. They're still there."

"Who's still there?"

"Them demons. They've been skulking back there in the corner ever since you began spouting all them words last night. But they're still there, just waiting to take me."

A shiver skittered down Rob's spine. Jake stared into the shadows of the cave as if something really were there.

"How'd they happen?" Rob asked, hoping to distract the boy. "The gunshots. Do you remember? Do you even know how you got here?"

"Sure, I know how I got here. Zeke and I rode here after the robbery."

"Robbery?"

"Yeah. You think I got shot at some Sunday school picnic? We robbed a freighter just before dawn. Turned into a regular gun battle. We got outta there all right but had to split up. Tom and the rest of 'em took off up the Sweetwater. Zeke and I rode up here."

Right before dawn. Yesterday? Had to have been. The blood trail was still pretty fresh when he'd found it.

"So what happened to Zeke?"

"I dunno. Must'a got skeered and run off. What I can't figure is what you're doing here."

"I found your horse and followed your blood trail."

"That was a darn fool thing to do."

"Probably."

Jake shook his head from side to side. "Poor, scab lover. Always showing up where you're not wanted. You know we never would have attacked your old sheep last winter if you hadn't camped right in the pathway to this here hideaway. Weren't no way to get up here without going through your camp"—Jake gave a slight shrug—"so we moved your camp."

He said it all so matter-of-factly as if what they had done that day was inconsequential, with as little import as one would give to the brushing away of a fly. That day's work had cost Rob a large portion of his livelihood—had almost cost him his life.

Bitterness churned at the memory of that day—the fear, the horror, the senseless killing—and through all of it his sense of utter helplessness. Jake had left him to die that day in a pool of his own blood, yet here he sat, trapped in this cave of his own volition because he believed no one should be left to die alone. Jake was right. He was a fool.

One thing was certain. He was done. As soon as the storm lifted, he'd be up and out of here on Trapper. Jake be hanged.

Bless those that curse you. Do good to those who persecute you.

The admonition that had brought him here in the first place haunted and mocked him.

No, Lord. No more. He didn't have it in him anymore.

Chapter Forty

Rob flicked open the lid on his pocket watch, clicked it shut, and flicked it open again as if the mere checking of the time would somehow force it to move more quickly. If it were not for his watch ticking off the minutes and hours, he would have thought himself suspended in time. The storm continued to rage outside the mouth of the cave. Inside, the cycle of death continued. Jake rotated between bouts of vomiting and pain and periods of delirium and fitful sleep.

Through it all, Rob waited and continued to minister to Jake, holding him steady when he vomited into the only receptacle Rob could find—Jake's battered hat—wiping his brow with a cool rag, and reciting verses when the sounds of pain and delirium became more than he could take.

The only signs of any change at all were the ticking of his watch and the dwindling of their pile of firewood. To conserve fuel, Rob kept the fire so low it barely heated the cave. Still, one log at a time, their stockpile had diminished. About an hour ago, he'd cut up the only wood he could find in the cave, the small crate that had held the candles and their holders. The way he figured it, they had only a few hours of wood left. If the storm didn't abate soon, he and Rowdy were going to be shivering as badly as Jake, who constantly shook from the chills of a raging fever.

He heaved a sigh so heavy it sparked a coughing jag. He dug into his coat pocket for his sputum flask, wincing at the burning in his throat as he cleared it and spat. He would pay dearly for the work of the last twenty-four hours.

A low chuckle at his side turned his attention back to Jake. The boy's eyes were bright with fever but clear, so the laughter wasn't spurred by delirium.

"Something funny?"

"Look at the two of us—a couple'a dying fools—too darn stubborn to die." His voice was a mere thread, but the mockery was still there. "Last time I seen you, scab lover, I'da bet you'd be dead within a week. But here you sit, still hacking up your lungs, and I'm the one who's dying. Taking my time at it, though, just like you are."

Rob didn't say anything. Didn't know what to say. There was truth to Jake's words, but he didn't see anything funny about them.

"Funny thing is," Jake continued. "I always sort'a pitied you. Poor scabman, just living to die . . . didn't realize I'd be the first to go."

"Aren't we all just living to die? From the minute we draw our first breaths, we're on the path to death. No one knows the day or the hour except for God. That's why how we choose to live is so important, so we'll be ready to die whenever the time comes." The words sounded as flat and sanctimonious as a Sunday School pamphlet. Even he knew, he didn't come close to living what he preached.

"You ready to die, scab man?"

He paused before answering. "Yes."

"Then why are you fighting so hard to live?"

A valid question, and one he'd asked himself several times these past six weeks when the future without Maddie looked so bleak. He shrugged and quoted. "Thus conscience doth make cowards of us all."

"Huh?"

"Shakespeare. You know, 'to be, or not to be?' Hamlet's soliloquy?" Jake's blank look told him explanations were pointless. "Never mind. I guess it's inborn; this need to cling to life no matter how hard it is. I have the confidence of my faith. I believe what is to come is far better than here—no more sickness, no more pain, no more tears—but I also know what I have here. I can see it, touch it, hold it—and what I have is very good." He closed his eyes and envisioned Maddie's face smiling back at him, love shining from her beautiful eyes. "When I think of saying goodbye to the ones I love—my wife, my family—" his throat seized. He let the words trail off. What was he doing, baring his soul to this mocking boy? He cleared his throat and shrugged. "That's why I fight, I guess. For a few more hours, a few more days, and God-willing, a few more years with the ones I love."

Jake was so silent he thought the boy had fallen back into semi-consciousness until he heard the words, faint as a whisper, "I never had nobody to love."

He didn't know what to say to that. "Maybe not a wife, but there's your family . . ."

Jake shook his head. "Ma runned off when I was four. Got tired of Pa beating the devil outta her, I guess. When she left, he set in on me. Said he wanted to put the fear of God into me, so I wouldn't end up like my Ma. Funny thing. The more he beat, the more the devil stayed with me. That's why those demons are sitting over there. They're just waiting to take me down where I belong." He reached out to grab Rob's hand, eyes wild and full of fear. "Don't let them take me. I don't want to go yet. I don't."

Jake's fear was so real, Rob couldn't help glancing over toward the empty corner. "You don't have to go with them, Jake. God made a way of escape."

"Didn't you hear me, scabman? I haven't lived a good life.

I've broke every single one of them ten commandments—every . . . single . . . one. No way am I gonna make it up there." He pointed to the roof of the cave, but Rob knew what he meant.

"Isn't that the point? If we could save ourselves, why would God need to send us a Savior? None of us are good enough to make it up there. That's why Christ came to die. He's already fought those demons for you and won."

"Why would he do that?"

"Because he loves you."

"I told you, ain't nobody ever loved me."

"You're wrong. God loves you. Loved you enough to die for you."

"How do you know that?"

"He told us. In the Bible. 'For God so loved the world he gave his only begotten son that whosoever believeth in Him will not perish but have everlasting life.'"

"Them's just a bunch of words. Where's your proof, scab man? My own Pa and Ma didn't love me. I'm evil through and through. If Pa couldn't beat the evil out of me and set me on the straight and narrow, I don't see how all this love business could."

Frustrated, Rob leaned his head back and closed his eyes. *Lord, how do you reach someone who's never even known what love is? Why am I even here? I can't cure his wounds. I can't calm his fears.*

A sudden thought made him turn back to Jake. "He must love you some. He sent me to you."

"*You're* the proof God loves me?" Sarcasm dripped from each word.

"You think I'd be here if He hadn't sent me? When I came across your horse out there in the valley, the last thing I wanted to do was follow its tracks to find you. I knew it was your horse, and I wanted nothing to do with it. But God wouldn't let me go. I had to come, and once I got here, He hasn't let me leave." Rob nodded out at the blowing storm. "Seems to me He went to a lot of trouble to keep me trapped here with you. Guess He must care more than you think He does."

"If that's the case, I dunno why He wouldn't have sent me a doctor instead of some Bible-spouting, blood-coughing scab herder."

"I guess He knew your soul needed healing more than your body. If your body dies, so what? Everyone's body will die someday. But if your soul dies? That's eternal. That's what your demons over there are hoping for."

Jake glanced over into the corner and shuddered. He gazed into the darkness for a few minutes before turning back to face Rob. "So, let's say I believe all this you're saying—that God really does love me, then what?"

"Then you have a choice, just like you do with any love that's offered. You can either accept God's love and forgiveness or turn your back and walk away. God doesn't force His love on anybody. It's up to you."

"And if I accept?"

"He welcomes you back with open arms."

"And if I don't?"

"There'll be some mighty happy demons in this cave tonight."

"You're crazy, you know that?"

"What can I say? I'm a sheepherder."

"Yeah. Ya got that right."

Jake closed his eyes, and a few minutes later, his steady breathing told Rob the boy had fallen asleep again. Rob sighed. Had anything he'd said made a difference?

Jake didn't wake again until later that night when Rob was adding his last scrap of wood to the meager fire. Even then, he didn't open his eyes. When Rob took his seat beside him, he could hear him muttering under his breath. Leaning low, he listened.

"It's so dang cold in here. Why don't you build up the fire? I'm freezing."

Rob tucked the horse blankets closer to Jake's shivering body. "I can't. We're about out of firewood."

"Stupid, scab man . . . plenty of wood . . . down the rat's hole."

Rob eyed the dark tunnel one more time. Seems as if that tunnel must lead to a veritable storehouse of riches. There was food down there, he knew. In addition to the potato, Rowdy had brought back a strip of deer jerky from one of his trips down the tunnel. This time, Rob had grabbed Rowdy's prize and torn off a portion for himself. Yes, he was desperate enough now to eat food from a dog's mouth, but still not desperate enough to enter that tunnel.

He might have been had the snow not stopped falling about an hour ago. The way he figured it, between the residual heat from the fire, the horse blankets, and their shared body heat, they should be able to survive the night. In the morning, he'd go for help.

"Sing to me, scab man. One of them songs . . . sing." Jake plucked at his blankets, eyes closed, head rolling in agitation.

Rob remembered how the night before he'd fought against Jake's demons with verses and hymns. His voice would never stand for that now. It had been raw and hoarse all day. But something within told him he had to at least try.

Throat burning, voice cracking, he forced out the words, "Amazing grace, how sweet the sound, that saved a wretch like me . . ."

He made it through three verses until the rasp of Jake's labored breathing told him the boy was asleep again. The harsh rattles echoed off the walls of the cave. He studied the glowing coals of the fire and followed each breath in and out, in and out, in . . . . He waited, bating his own breath, then. . . out. The dying continued. Any optimism over Jake's possible recovery faded with each ragged breath. The coals in the fire would be dead by morning. No doubt Jake would be too.

Chapter Forty-One

❦

Sunshine. Was there ever anything more beautiful? Maddie stood at the cabin's east window, cradling a cup of hot tea and drinking in the deep red glow off the cliffs on the horizon. The white drifts at their base sparkled in the rays of the early morning sun. Finally, after more than thirty hours of continuous snow and wind, today dawned clear and full of promise. Today Rob would be home.

A stamping of boots on the front doorstep signaled that the boys and Jackson had completed their morning chores and were coming in for breakfast. Maddie moved to the stove and began heaping their plates with mounds of scrambled eggs, stacks of pancakes, and strips of bacon.

"Smells good," Jackson said as he came through the door, George and Fred on his heels.

"I'll take two plates." George stole a slice of bacon as he walked by the stove to deposit his pail of fresh milk on the nearby counter.

Maddie swatted at his hand as he reached for another. "There's plenty here for everyone, but you need to wash up first."

He reached by her and grabbed another anyway, then headed

for the sink. Fred set a basket of fresh eggs beside the milk and followed him. One of the blessings of living in the cabin was they now could keep a milking cow and chickens. Rob's diet could include enough fresh milk and eggs to satisfy any doctor.

She turned to where Jackson stood by the door. "How are the sheep?"

"Good. None of them wandered. Looks like they huddled up close to the barn and sheds for their shelter. We got about two feet of snow, but with the wind, there's still plenty of bare grass out in the open areas. After breakfast, I'll help George and Fred move them so they can graze. Then I'll probably head over toward Tavis' to see if either he or Pedro need help finding strays."

She hadn't thought of that. Rob would probably stay to help also. She handed the men their plates, then filled two for her and Hazel before joining them all at the table.

"Well, when you see Rob, tell him to be home before sunset," she said.

George grinned. "If we tell him you're here, he'll probably be back long before sunset."

Maddie felt the heat rise in her cheeks. She hoped so. Given the brusk nature of his last letter and her hasty decision to come without telling him, she wasn't so sure. No matter. She couldn't wait to see him. She was tired of the waiting.

∼

ROB WOKE TO SILENCE. BRIGHT SUNLIGHT STREAMED IN THE mouth of the cave, yet the room seemed eerie. Too still. No howling wind. No crackling fire. No labored breathing. He turned to look at Jake, white, cold and . . . silent.

Limbs stiff with cold, Rob struggled to sit up. Reaching out, he felt Jake's neck for a pulse. The boy's flesh was ice-cold beneath his fingers. No pulse. No breath. No life.

The wait was over.

He studied Jake's features for a minute before pulling the horse blanket up to cover his face. What a waste. A life so young. Why the hair on his chin and upper lip was little more than peach fuzz. The finality of the boy's death hit him harder than he ever would have expected. Sometime within their time together, Jake had ceased to be his enemy and had become a human being, much of an age with his brothers. Had Jake's demons had the victory last night or had Jake somehow found his way to grace?

Only God knew for certain. Rob closed his eyes in silent prayer, then, with a final look at Jake's still body, crawled out the entrance of the cave.

The brilliance of the sun against the new snow brought tears to his eyes. He'd need to make use of the soot from the fire to guard against snow blindness before setting off for home. But first, he wanted to check on the horses.

Hobbling on legs stiff from sitting hours in the close quarters of the cave, he set off down the path for the strand of pine where he'd tethered the horses. Given the force of the wind during the storm, it was hard to tell how much snow they'd had. Judging by the size of some of the drifts, though, he'd guess they'd had over two feet.

Trapper neighed a greeting as Rob floundered through one of the drifts to release him from his tether. The grass to the south of the pines had long since been covered by the snow, but as he'd hoped, both horses had found sustenance by gnawing strips of bark off the trees.

He patted the paint's flank. "Just a couple more hours, boy, and you'll be in a nice warm stall with a pile of hay. How does that sound?"

Trapper whinnied his approval. He untied the two horses and led them back to the cave, where he soon had them saddled and ready to travel. Rowdy, eager to be on the move, ran joyous circles around the horses while he worked.

He decided to leave Jake's body until he could notify Sheriff

Stough of the outlaw's hideout. No sense in making the trip home any harder than it already was. With a whistle for Rowdy, he set off down the trail.

The going was slow. In some places, the path was bare where the wind had whipped it clean. Other spots had drifted as high as three feet. He hoped for easier going once they gained the more level ground in the open plain ahead. But, at the next bend, his heart sank.

The narrow pass into this mountain valley was blocked by a wall of snow at least six feet high and probably as long as the pass itself. There would be no getting through it any time soon.

Rob pulled Trapper to a stop and stared at the barrier in front of him, the jeopardy of his situation slowing sinking in. If there were another way into this valley, he didn't know it. He could head out in search of one, but that option was nothing more than a gamble. Though the day had started out fine, a brisk wind had already come up, blowing the soft snow in swirls around him. He knew from experience that storms such as the one they'd had were often followed by a cold snap. Temperatures could drop well below zero at night.

What he needed was a cabin or a sheep wagon where he could shelter until the weather warmed up. Someplace with provisions and a source of heat. He knew of nothing like that this side of the pass. In fact, he knew of no shelter of any kind nearby.

Except for the cave.

But, without a fire, even the cave would provide little protection from the cold. He scanned the path behind him, mentally cataloging the surrounding terrain, but he knew it was hopeless. He'd commandeered all the available firewood before the storm hit. Any he might have missed was, more than likely, buried by the snow.

There's plenty of wood in the rat's hole. Jake's words mocked him. Could he trust the boy? And even if he did, could he fit down that narrow tunnel? The outlaws had, apparently. And thanks to his disease, he was not a heavy man. His chances of finding shelter there were far better than anything he might find in this canyon. The thought of that dark tunnel sent chills up his spine.

Slowly, he turned the horses and headed back up the trail. At the mouth of the cave, he freed both animals of their tether ropes and set them free. They'd have a far better chance of survival foraging on their own. Once the weather warmed, and the snow melted, he'd have to walk out. Tavis's winter camp wasn't too far from the other side of the pass.

With a last look at the cloudless blue sky, he ducked under the rocky overhang and crawled back into the cave. Ignoring Jake's body, he made his way to the back wall and peered into the dark of the tunnel. Lighting one of the candles piled next to the opening, he lay on his stomach and looked in. The candle flame illuminated a few feet of tunnel, but beyond that was darkness.

He rolled to his side as Rowdy pushed up beside him. "You gonna lead the way, boy? You've been down there before. I haven't. Go on. Show me the way."

The little dog didn't need a second invitation. Tail wagging, he trotted into the tunnel and soon disappeared from sight. Rob took a deep breath and followed, pushing his head and chest into the narrow opening. Don't think. Just move.

Using his elbows and forearms to propel him, he inched his way forward, the sharp rock of the cave's walls biting into his flesh. His movements were hampered by the candle he still clutched in his right fist, but he wasn't about to let go of it. Flame light flickered on the dark walls in front of him

He'd crawled about ten yards when he heard the click of Rowdy's claws in the tunnel ahead of him, the dog's pants growing louder as he headed back his way.

"No, Rowdy. Stay."

Too late. The dog bounded out of the darkness ahead, tail waving. In horror, Rob saw the flame on his candle dance wildly in the onslaught of air currents. He reached up to shield it just as Rowdy skittered to a stop in front of him. The dog's body collided with his hand, sending the candle flying. As it hit the cave wall, its flame flickered, then died.

Rob smelled Rowdy's warm breath of his face, felt the swipe of his wet tongue, then the dog was off again, leaving him alone in the utter darkness. He squeezed his eyes shut, hoping to blot out the reality of the blackness around him. He struggled to get air. The panic he'd managed to hold at bay with the feeble flame of his candle caught him in a stranglehold.

The walls of the cave bore down on him, creeping closer, ever closer. He was going to die here under the weight of the mountain, and no one would ever know.

Chapter Forty-Two

❦

Maddie placed another tiny stitch in the square of flannel she was hemming. She longed to pull out the packet of soft, white lawn she had tucked in the bottom of her trunk. How fun it would be to start cutting and piecing tiny garments, but she'd promised herself she'd tackle the mundane sewing first. The storm had given her plenty of time to catch up on all Rob's mending. Amazing the quantity of missing buttons and small tears that occurred in a six-week period of time. Ranch work was hard on clothes.

Beside her, Hazel heaved a deep sigh and jabbed her needle into her sampler.

"Something wrong?" Maddie hid a smile at the sight of her sister's martyred face.

"When do you think we can go outside?"

Maddie followed Hazel's gaze to a patch of sunlight streaming in the cabin's west window. "It looks a lot warmer out there than it is."

Despite the hours they'd been forced to stay inside during the storm, Maddie was more than content to keep to her warm spot beside the stove. Though far warmer than the sheep wagon with its canvas roof, the cabin was nowhere near as cozy as Mrs.

Whitcomb's boarding house. Wind and snow blew through chinks in the walls, and they'd kept busy during the storm covering the largest cracks with paper.

She glanced up to see the wistful pleading in Hazel's soft brown eyes and relented. "Tell you what, you finish the row you're working on, and I'll take you out to the barn to meet Bessie."

Hazel attacked her sampler with a vengeance.

"Mind your stitches now. If they're too crooked, you'll have to do the whole line over."

Fifteen minutes later, they were bundled against the cold and sloughing their way through the deep snowdrifts to the barn. During the storm, the men had marked a triangular path between the barn, the cabin, and the sheep wagon with lengths of rope tied to each of the buildings. Maddie held onto the rope and did her best to stay in the footprints made by George and Fred.

"We should build a snowman or a snow fort," Hazel said.

"Maybe in a few days if it warms up a little. The snow's too light and dry to do much packing today. Look, here's our chicken coop." She opened the wire door an inch or two, causing the chickens to flutter and squawk. "Tomorrow, I'll have Fred show you how to gather their eggs. Now that you live on a ranch, we'll have to set you to doing some chores."

Hazel peered in at the chickens from the doorway. "Will they bite?"

"They might peck at you a little, but for the most part, they'll keep out of your way."

They continued on toward the barn. Maddie pushed open its wide doors breathing in the smell of wood and hay and horses. With the horses all out with the men, Bessie was its only occupant. She looked up when they entered, studying them for a minute with her velvety brown eyes, then turned back to her feed trough.

"And this is Bessie. She's the one we have to thank for all our fresh milk and butter." Maddie walked over and patted the cow's hindquarters. "What do you think of her?"

"She's awfully big."

"But gentle as a baby lamb. Speaking of lambs, we'll have to take you out to meet the sheep soon. We don't have any lambs yet, but in a couple of months our flocks will be full of them again. Oh, and there's Rebel and Rosie. You'll like them. Though they're working dogs and not pets, that doesn't mean they're above climbing in your lap on occasion and licking your face."

Hazel laughed.

A shout and the pounding of hooves drew them back to the doorway of the barn. Squinting against the bright sunlight, she spotted George riding neck or nothing up the path the sheep wagon had made in the snow this morning. When he spied them, he pulled his mount to a trot and then a walk, before pulling to a halt in front of them.

"Has Rob come back yet?"

"No."

"Drat. I'd hoped . . ."

"What is it? Did you see him this morning?"

George shook his head. "He wasn't with Tavis or Pedro."

Fear washed over her, kicking her in the stomach and buckling her knees. She grasped the door jam for support.

"Maddie!" George sprang from his horse. "Don't look like that." He braced her under her elbow. "Come on. You should sit down. Hazel, go see if you can find some witch hazel or smelling salts."

"No. I'm fine." Her voice sounded weak and strangled, even to her ears.

Hazel took off at a run for the cabin. George led her into the barn and pushed her down onto a hay bale. Squatting before her, he began chafing her hands.

"Come on, Maddie. No need to be imagining the worst. He probably went another direction than we expected and is holed up with one of Bunce's men. We'll find him, or he'll come home on his own before sundown. You'll see."

Maddie wanted to believe his words, but a deep sense of dread held her in its grip. The fears she hadn't let surface over the past two days bounded to the forefront of her mind. What if he hadn't found shelter? What if he'd been caught, all alone, out in the open during that terrible storm? How could he have survived that?

She'd heard the stories. Sheepmen lost and frozen to death in storms. Their bodies never found until spring. She pulled her hands out of George's grasp and buried her face in them. *Oh, God, please. Not this. Not now. Not so close after Edie.* She hadn't even had the chance to see him again, to feel his arms around her, to tell him about their baby.

Dear, God. The baby.

She moaned, rocking herself back and forth. *I can't take this now, Lord. I can't.*

The barn door slammed as Hazel ran back in.

"Here, Maddie, take a whiff of this," George pulled her hands away from her face and waved the bottle of smelling salts beneath her nose.

The pungent odor made her nose burn and her eyes sting. She pushed the bottle away. "I'm fine. Really." Looking up, she caught George's concerned gaze, his dark eyes so like his brother's she wanted to cry. But she wouldn't. She had to be strong now. For Rob's sake. "What can we do to find him?"

"Jackson and Tavis have already started a search. I'm on my way to Baldwin's to find Louis and Gabe. The more men we have looking, the quicker we can cover the area."

"Do you want me to watch the sheep, so Fred can go with you?"

George considered for a minute, then shook his head. "No. We need someone here at the cabin in case Rob comes home on his own. If he does, shoot the gun two times to let us know he's been found. If we don't return an answering shot, wait a few minutes and shoot again."

He stood and handed Hazel the bottle of smelling salts. Then, turning back to Maddie, he said, "Are you sure you're going to be all right?"

"I'm fine. Go. Oh, and George?"

He turned to face her, his body silhouetted against the doorway of the barn.

"If . . . *when* you find him, give him my love."

Chapter Forty-Three

Rob couldn't move, couldn't think . . . couldn't breathe. He was trapped within the walls of this cave like a mouse in the jaws of a boa constrictor. He opened his eyes, straining into the blackness that surrounded him to see a shadow, a shape . . . something . . . anything. Was this what the Scripture meant when it talked about souls being cast into utter darkness?

Oh, God. Oh, God. Help me!

Yea, though I walk through the valley of the shadow of death . . .

There were no shadows here, only a black so thick he could feel it seeping into his pores, into his soul. And yet.

"Thou art with me." He spoke the words aloud, their certainty pushing back the waves of panic. "Thou art with me." Even here, in the bowels of the earth where no one could see him and no one knew where he was, God saw. God knew. God was here.

I will never leave you nor forsake you.

The words calmed his breathing and released the pressure from the walls around him. Closing his eyes again, he concentrated on his surroundings. Ahead, in the distance, he could hear the drip of water hitting water. He could feel the small rocks on the surface of the cave floor biting into his chest and legs. Turning over, he reached up to touch the ceiling of the tunnel. The opening was tight, but not so tight he couldn't move freely within its confines. He just needed to keep moving, to find Rowdy and whatever lay at the end of this Rat's Hole. He could do this.

Feeling for handholds in the rocky surface above him, he pushed himself forward with his feet. Inch by inch, foot by foot, he pushed himself along the tunnel, not allowing his mind to dwell on anything other than his forward progress. Gradually, the tunnel opened up around him until finally, after what seemed like an eternity but was probably only a few minutes, his head and shoulders pushed out of the tunnel and into an open room.

He stretched a hand into the blackness around him and collided with Rowdy. The little dog's wet tongue bathed his hand. Laughing and sitting up, Rob pulled the writhing body onto his lap.

"About time I made it, huh, boy?" He'd never been so happy to hold another living creature. He stroked the dog's silky fur. "Don't happen to have a light on you, do you? No? Guess I'll have to find one for myself, then."

He put the dog down and began groping around the opening to the tunnel. On the other side, they'd had a crate full of candles. Would it be too much to ask for the same thing on this side? Apparently so. He could feel nothing but empty space on either side of the hole, but as his fingers explored further up the cave wall, they connected with something cold and hard. A lantern. Could he light it in the dark? He didn't even know if it had any oil in it.

Digging in his pocket, he pulled out his waning box of matches. Lighting one, he held it up. Yes. Plenty of oil. Quickly, he primed the wick but had to let the match go out before it burned his fingers. Groping in the dark, he lifted the lantern down from its hook and pulled off the glass chimney. A second match caught the wick, bathing the area around him in a circle of light. Turning, he shined the light into the room ahead of him, then stopped cold in his tracks.

A man sat braced against the opposite wall. The barrel of his shotgun pointed straight at Rob's heart.

Chapter Forty-Four

His first instinct was to extinguish the flame in his lamp and dive back into the Rat's Hole, but something made him hesitate. Something in the way the man was sitting. Something in his gaze. After all, if he wanted to shoot at Rob, why hadn't he done so already? He'd had plenty of time while Rob was fooling around trying to light the lantern. For that matter, why was the man sitting all alone in the dark?

Cautiously, Rob stepped closer and raised his lantern, letting its soft glow trail up the man's body and settle on his face. Blank eyes stared back at him. He flicked the lantern light down to the right, where an inky stain covered the man's white shirt in front of him. Well. The mystery of Zeke was solved.

Zeke hadn't abandoned his friend, after all. His fate and Jake's fate had been the same. Though, from the looks of all the blood, Zeke had probably bled out long before Jake had died.Rob shuddered. Flashing the light from the lantern around the room, he found a tarp folded in the corner and used it to cover Zeke's body. He needed to explore this end of the Rat's Hole but knew he wouldn't be able to do it with Zeke's lifeless stare gazing out at him.

He tucked the ends of the tarp around Zeke's boots and

straightened. Plowing his fingers through his hair, he shook his head. What a waste. Two young men—kids really—not much older than George and Fred, cut down in the prime of life. And for what? He lifted his lantern and scanned the dark crevices of the cave. For whatever lay hidden down here, no doubt.

His shaft of light uncovered boxes and tarp-covered bundles against the back wall of the room, but what he really wanted to find was the wood Jake had promised. And food. His stomach growled at the mere thought of more of that jerky Rowdy had discovered.

He glanced down at the little dog seated on the floor beside him. At his look, Rowdy stood, tail wagging, as if waiting for a command from him.

"How about it, boy? You going to show me where the food is?"

Rowdy took off at a trot toward a narrow passage off the main room. Great. More dark, narrow passages. Another quick scan of the room unearthed the promised pile of wood and kindling stacked neatly beside a woodburning stove in the corner, plus a full crate of coal, but no food supplies were evident.

Guess he'd have to trust the dog. This interior room was chilly but nothing like the frigid temperatures of the outer cave. A fire could wait for now.

He followed Rowdy into the passageway, glad for the sturdy glow from his lantern and the fact that the ceilings in this area were high above his head. He didn't have far to go. Rowdy sat at the entrance to an alcove some ten feet away. Ducking inside, he found a small storage area packed with a wide assortment of fruits and vegetables: sacks of potatoes, turnips, carrots, onions, crates of apples, and a shelf of canned preserves, plus several tins of baked beans.

Hanging from the ceiling were strings of sausages, a couple of ham hocks, and strips of jerky. From the looks of the ends of sausage and jerky, Rowdy had helped himself to all that was within jumping distance.

Rob tore off a piece of jerky, threw a small chunk to Rowdy, and stuffed the rest into his mouth. "My turn now, bud. Looks like you've had more than your fair share already."

The dripping water he'd heard while in the Rat's Hole sounded louder here. Poking his head back out of the alcove, he decided to investigate. He followed the passageway a little farther until he reached a fork. He stuck to the right, led on by the constant dripping in the distance.

A few minutes more brought him to a bend in the corridor. He turned the corner and stopped short.

A deep pool of water lay at his feet, stretching down smaller channels into the dark ahead of him. Stalactites dripped from the ceiling like waxy fingers hovering above the pool. At each fingertip, a drop formed, pillowed, and then plummeted into the water below. Shining his lantern into the water, Rob could see the rocks that formed the lip of the drop-off.

Water. Food. Fire and shelter. He had everything he needed to survive for days, months even. Certainly, long enough for the snow to melt from the pass into the canyon. He breathed a prayer of gratitude then chuckled. If someone had told him two days ago that he'd be thanking God for dark, enclosed spaces, he'd have called them crazy.

Rob picked up the pail he found sitting on a rock shelf beside the pool and filled it. The outlaws most likely left it there for that purpose. He'd take a look at that stove now and maybe cook himself a meal. Any other exploring would have to wait until he had a belly full.

Once back in the main cavern, he inspected the stove. A smaller model, about the size of the one in their sheep wagon, the stove was vented through a pipe that extended up through the rock in the ceiling. Opening the lid, Rob could feel a draft of cold air coming in through the flue. The outlaws had either blasted a hole to the outside or found a natural one. Either way, they'd gone to a lot of work to make this hideout livable.

Bringing the stove in through the Rat's Hole had to have been a challenge. They must have brought it in in pieces and built it from inside. Still, as heavy as the stove pieces were and as narrow a passage as the Rat's Hole, that was no mean feat. Somehow, knowing the trouble they'd gone through to stock and furnish this cave made him uneasy.

Zeke and Jake were only two of a whole gang of men who knew the location of this cave, desperate men, men on the run from their last robbery. Staying here for any length of time could prove dangerous. His only hope was that the snow that kept him trapped would also keep them out, provided they were already on the outside of the canyon when the storm hit. The fact that no men had joined them in the past two days gave him hope.

Whatever the case, he wasn't letting his fears stop him from taking advantage of the stores they'd stockpiled. He had eaten little to nothing in the past forty-eight hours, and no threat, no matter how probable, was going to keep him from eating well tonight. He grabbed a handful of kindling and several small pieces of wood and arranged them in the stove's firebox.

As soon as he had the fire burning, he filled the tea kettle sitting on the stove's back burner with the water he'd brought from the underground pool. Once the water boiled, he'd be ready to cook, but until then, he needed to do something with Zeke.

The thought of sharing his living quarters for the next day or two with a dead body gave him the willies. If it weren't for the Rat's Hole, he'd take Zeke to rest beside his friend in the outer cave, but he had no desire to push or pull a dead body through that tight corridor. He'd need a different plan.

He tied one end of his leading rope around Zeke's feet and the other around his waist. Picking up the lantern, he headed back down the larger passageway toward the water pool, dragging Zeke's body behind him. When he came to the fork in the tunnel, instead of taking the right-hand bend toward the water, he followed the pathway to the left for about one hundred feet. Then he untied his burden and tucked the canvas-wrapped body up against a crevice in the cave wall. Not the best of graves, but it would do until he had a chance to notify Zeke's people about his death.

He supposed the boy had a family somewhere. Jake had a father, though given what Jake had told him as he lay dying, that relationship was none too pretty. Could Zeke's family life be just as barren? Whatever the case, someone should be notified. When he got out of this canyon, he'd send word to the McCreedy ranch. They could decide how to bury their dead.

He turned to walk back to the main cavern, then stopped. Didn't seem right somehow to leave the body without some sort of acknowledgment. Turning back, he squatted down beside Zeke and bowed his head.

Lord, he began. But what do you say about a boy so young, a life so wasted? He had little memory of Zeke at all other than a shadowy figure behind Jake, aiding and abetting in the boy's arrogance and irreverence. Not knowing what else to say, he recited the Lord's Prayer, then rose and walked away.

An hour later, Rob set what was left of his supper of potatoes, beans, and ham on the floor for Rowdy to finish. He leaned back against the cave wall, surprised at how comfortable he felt here in the dark recesses of the cave.

A wry grin raised one corner of his mouth. That was hardly the only irony here. Who would have thought that he, who had been living like a dead man for months, would be sitting here, belly full and very much alive, while two healthy young men ten years his junior lay cold and dead a mere hundred feet or more from his side.

It all seemed so futile. Life. So short. In reality, weren't they all just living to die? Whether eighteen or eighty, the end was the same for all men. Like the Bible said, man was like a blade of grass, flourishing in the morning only to be cut down by nightfall.

And what had these two boys gained in their brief sojourn in this world? He glanced at the shrouded stacks in the far corner of the room. While he'd waited for the stove to heat and his potatoes to cook, he'd satisfied his curiosity as to their contents. What he found came as no surprise. Cash boxes filled with bills and coins, a stack of gold bars, a varied assortment of jewels and gold watches, enough guns and ammunition to outfit a small army: spoils from all the robberies that had plagued their area for the past eighteen months. What good were all those earthly riches to Jake and Zeke now?

They'd certainly laid up nothing of value for themselves in the life to come. The one the Bible told them would be everlasting. And what of his own life? *Teach us to number our days,* the Psalm said, *that we may apply our hearts unto wisdom.* Had he learned to number his days? To use each of them to the fullest? Not lately.

Seemed like the last few years, the sole focus of his life had been chasing a cure. He'd put all his effort and energy toward getting better, so he could get back to the life this disease had interrupted. And for what? He wasn't guaranteed that life any more than he was guaranteed his next breath. Had he wasted all those days? What if God's plan for his life was not for him to live well *after* the disease but to live a fruitful life *within* the disease?

A fruitful life. What did that even look like? Certainly not anything like the life he'd led the past few months, caught in a perpetual pity party, pushing away the people who loved him the most. He hadn't even asked God what to do about Maddie and Hazel. Instead, he'd pushed ahead on his own. Playing God. Trying to control the situation all by himself.

Was that the reason God gave him breath each morning? To live like that? To focus only on his own needs and what he wanted? He was no better than the outlaw gang, squandering the precious gift of life on himself and his own interests.

Father, forgive me. Forgive my need to control my life and the outcome of my disease. I know it's not mine to control. Help me to live each day to the fullest and serve you in the midst of the struggle. I can't do it by myself.

But with God's help, he could. For hadn't the Lord used him to reach out in love to Jake? If the boy had received redemption, had felt the power of God's love in his last moments, it had been all because of God, not him. Lord knows, he'd come into the situation kicking and fighting, as reluctant as the prophet Jonah to let God's love flow out to his enemies. Yet, the Lord had used him anyway. Any demons that were chased away last night had run from God's power, not his.

But how wonderful to be a part of that, to be the tool God used. And how much more amazing would it be if he were a willing participant. A man who rose each morning ready and willing to do God's will for the day, not his own.

Excitement sparked within. He hadn't felt this alive, this filled with purpose in months. He had the foolish urge to head out right now and attack the snow in the pass with his bare hands. Instead, he'd have to wait, at least until morning.

Chapter Forty-Five

Waiting. Oh, how she hated this waiting. Maddie paced between the table and the stove for what had to be the hundredth time, yet somehow, she couldn't stop. She needed to walk, to move, to do something . . . anything, but wait.

Why was it always the women's role to wait? For centuries men had gone off to war or to hunt, leaving the women behind to wait. She supposed they meant to protect the women, save them from the hardships. But didn't they know waiting was hardest of all?

In a way, she wished she had Mrs. Baldwin's confidence the night Mary had been lost. She hadn't waited for the men to find her daughter. She'd grabbed a rifle and set off on her own. But Maddie knew any such action on her own part would be futile. The men would soon be looking for two lost souls, not just one. Still, how she longed to be looking . . . doing . . . anything but waiting.

Not that she hadn't been doing something while she waited. She surveyed the pies and loaves of bread that lined the shelf above the kitchen cupboard and spilled over onto the table. Unable to sit quietly and sew, she had spent the afternoon baking. Ostensibly, she'd been teaching Hazel to bake, but in reality she had needed something to keep her hands and mind busy. That she'd gotten a little carried away went without saying.

Oh, well. If—no, *when*—Rob finally came home, at least he would not go hungry. But when would that be? George had stopped by in the early evening to tell her they'd searched all the nearby sheep camps and still had not found him. How could he possibly have survived the last few days in that storm? How would he survive the night?

She glanced at the clock on the bureau, then over at Hazel asleep on the bed. No chance she would be sleeping tonight. It was well past midnight. But how could she possibly sleep with Rob out there somewhere in the frigid night? How she envied Hazel's oblivion.

She dropped to a seat at the table and buried her head in her arms. She couldn't do this. She couldn't lose Rob. She couldn't. Not now, with the wound of Edie's death so raw and a baby on the way. *Lord, how can I possibly handle this now?* How could she *ever* handle this?

Trust Me. The words, soft and sure, echoed in her soul. Trust? Could she? She'd seen what God allowed—the death of a young mother, the rape of an innocent girl. Trust? How could she trust when disease, death, and evil seemingly triumphed all around her?

I'm not asking you to trust that the worst won't happen. I'm asking you to trust Me. If the very worst were to happen, then what?

Then she'd be all alone.

I will never leave you nor forsake you.

She wouldn't be able to cope. She simply couldn't handle any more loss, any more grief.

My grace is sufficient . . .

But how could she possibly carry on? How could she raise this baby all by herself?

You can do all things through Me. I will give you strength.

Her arguments stuttered to a stop. Could she trust Him? Did she?

It is of the Lord's mercies that we are not consumed, because his compassions fail not. They are new every morning; great is thy faithfulness.

He *was* faithful. Hadn't she witnessed that over and over? In those months after Mother's death and again these last few months after Edie's, hadn't He always been there, holding, comforting, providing new joy in the midst of the sorrow? And hadn't He already provided all she would ever need by making a way for her to be with Him and all the ones she loved for eternity?

Lord, help me with my fear. Help me surrender to your will and trust that no matter what happens, your way is best.

Peace flooded her soul. A deep weariness crept through her, settling in her limbs. She should sleep. Yes. And she *could* sleep, like Hazel. Like a child resting in the care of Her Father.

Tomorrow . . . well, tomorrow, she and God would deal with whatever the day might bring. She rose from the table and began readying herself for bed.

∽

ROB WOKE TO VOICES. MEN'S VOICES FILTERED THROUGH THE Rat's Hole into his area of the cave. Rob sat up and reached for Zeke's gun. Had the outlaws finally made it back to their hideout? If so, what was he prepared to do about it? He could try hiding deeper in the cave, hope they didn't find him, but for how long?

He studied the rifle in his hands. Was it even loaded? If it were, did he really want to use it? Would he pick off the outlaws as they exited the tunnel in front of him? Somehow such a method felt too much like cold-blooded murder. He might be able to kill a man in self-defense or in defense of Maddie or Hazel, but to pick them off without ever knowing their intent?

Shouldn't be too hard to guess their intent, though. He was

an intruder in their domain. He'd seen their stash. He knew their secrets, and, unlike him, *they* had killed before.

He bent his ear toward the Rat's Hole, straining to hear any movement. Should he extinguish his lantern? He'd left one lantern burning while he slept, unwilling to plunge himself into total darkness. His fingers hovered over the knob.

"Rob. Rob. Are you down there?"

His name echoed off the walls of the Rat's Hole as clear as a clarion bell. *His* name. The outlaws wouldn't know his name. Besides, he recognized the voice.

"George?" he called.

"Rob! Is that you?"

"I'm here. Hold on, I'm coming out." He shouted his answer into the dark recesses of the tunnel before extinguishing the lantern light and pushing his body into the small opening. The complete darkness was no longer a threat. After only a minute or two, he could see the pale light signifying the opening in the distance.

Had the Rat's Hole been this short on the way in? Somehow it had felt like a mile or more. In actuality, it was probably as short as fifty yards. Homing in on the circle of light in the distance, he continued to inch his way forward until he could see George's face, grinning at him like Rowdy with his eye on a bone. As he pushed his way out of the hole, his brother pulled him to his knees and into a tight embrace.

"Man, am I glad to see you. We'd about given up ever finding you."

Rob returned his brother's hug, then reached behind him to shake Jackson's hand. "How did you find me? I figured I might have to wait for the spring thaw to get out of here."

"We found your horse out on the plains and followed his trail. I'd have probably walked on by this cave, but Jackson spotted a boot track in the snow just on the other side of the bushes. Not the easiest place to find."

"No. That's what makes it such a great hideout." He gestured toward the body in the corner, a few feet from where Jackson was crouched. "I take it you saw Jake."

The big man nodded. "Freight train robbery?"

"From what I gather. His friend Zeke's on the other side of this hole. Same condition. You'll find their booty down there too. All the evidence anybody'd ever need to convict them of just about all the crimes that have occurred around here in the past year or more. They weren't in it alone, though. Jake told me the rest of their gang escaped down the Sweetwater after they robbed that freighter, but I'm betting they'll make their way back here to gather their loot sometime soon. Probably could catch the whole gang if you were to set a trap for them here."

"Whoa. Are you telling me this is some outlaw gang's hideout?" George's face told him just how incredulous that sounded.

"See for yourself. That is if you don't mind crawling through about fifty yards of total darkness. They've got quite a setup down there. Plenty of food supplies, fresh water, heat . . . I probably could have been set until spring if you hadn't found me. How'd you know I was down there?"

"We didn't. In fact, we found Jake's body and were about to leave, thinking it was his boot track we'd followed. I was already out of the cave with Jackson right behind me when we heard a bark. We turned around, and there came Rowdy bounding out of the back of the cave like he'd been there all along when we knew he hadn't been there a minute ago. So, we set about investigating and that's when we found the hole. Even then, I couldn't imagine you'd ever go down there."

"Believe me, I never would have if I'd had a choice. Jake had said some things that made me think there might be supplies down there, so when I found the pass blocked with snow, I figured it was either trying my luck with the tunnel or staying out here and freezing to death. Turned out to be a good decision." He looked over at Jackson. "But how'd you get through the pass? There's no way all that snow's melted already. Unless I'm like Rip Van Winkle and slept a lot longer than I thought."

Jackson chuckled. "We didn't come through the pass. We came down the valley through Hall's Gulch the same way your horses did."

"I figured there might be another way out of here. I guess I should have stuck with the horses and given them their head, but I didn't want to chance it in the cold."

"Probably best you didn't. We didn't find them until this morning. As cold as it is, you wouldn't have made it through the night last night without some sort of shelter." Jackson turned to crawl out the front entrance of the cave.

Rob and George followed suit. The bright sunlight stung at Rob's eyes, but he was glad to be able to stand upright again. Jackson stepped a few paces off the path and fired his shotgun two times in the air.

"Gabe and Louis aren't too far from here," he said. "I sent them to search the path up ahead. Tavis should hear that also and spread the word to the other herders."

Rob looked back at the cave opening, hidden again by the junipers. "So, what do you think we should do? I hate to leave here and let those outlaws have free access to the cave again. They might never be caught."

"I'll send Gabe to find Sheriff Stough. We'll let him and his men decide how to handle it. Louis and I can stay here until he gets here, though I doubt the gang will try to come here any time soon. If they're hanging out down near the Sweetwater, there's no way they can get back in here from that direction with that pass blocked."

"I could stay with you until the sheriff comes if you'd like. You'll need me to show you where I left Zeke's body."

Jackson exchanged a look with George and shook his head. "That's not necessary. I'm sure you'll be wanting to get home."

Rob knew what that look meant. They didn't think he was well enough to stay in the cold much longer. Twenty-four hours ago, they might have been right, but after a good meal and a full night's sleep, he felt more alive than he had in months. He barely noticed the burning in his throat.

"I know my voice sounds rough, but I feel great. Really. I probably got more sleep last night than you did."

Jackson shrugged. "I'd feel better if you went home with George. You'll be needing to get back to your sheep."

His sheep. He'd completely forgotten about the lost band. He turned to George. "I never found that band I was after. Any chance they might have made it through the storm?"

"Jackson brought them in just before the storm broke. That's how he knew you were missing. He stayed with us during the blizzard."

"Guess, as usual, you've saved my hide. I'm sorry you were repaid with two-days worth of suffering through my brothers' cooking."

Jackson exchanged another cryptic look with George. "Actually, the cooking was better than you might expect." A twinkle lurked in the depths of the man's dark blue eyes. There was something they weren't telling him.

He had no chance to explore the issue because, at that moment, Louis and Gabe came around the bend ahead of them, cutting off all further conversation. The next few minutes were spent filling Jackson's brothers in on the situation. Rob drew a map in the snow, showing Jackson and Louis the layout of the inner caves and where he had left Zeke's body.

Then, he crawled into the cave one last time to retrieve his saddle. It was time to go home.

Chapter Forty-Six

They had gone as far as Halls Gulch before he realized why he was so reluctant to go home. Those hours in the cave when he had dreamed of home, of safety, of rescue, those dreams had all included Maddie. Somehow going home without her there was anticlimactic. He'd been such a fool to think he could make a life without her. He would send for her as soon as he was able to get a letter out, but knowing it would still be weeks, maybe a month before he saw her again, was almost too hard to bear.

At the Canyon Road, Gabe continued north towards Lander to find Sheriff Stough while he and George turned back south. Five more miles would bring them to the cabin. It wouldn't be the homecoming he wanted, but he'd still be glad to get out of this cold. His fingers were stiff and numb beneath the heavy leather of his gloves. His cheeks burned from an hour of facing the cold north wind.

"Did we lose many sheep to the blizzard?"

"None. Jackson helped us bed them down before the worst of the snow began. Luckily, they stayed put because we went about twenty-four hours not being able to see more than a foot in front of us. Not much chance of any of us checking up on them. Once the snow stopped, we were able to move them right away to better feeding ground, so we didn't need to use any of the hay we'd stockpiled. Fred's got them camped just south of the cabin in the pasture there."

Tomorrow he'd head out there and let Fred return to the cabin for a few days. Both his brothers deserved a break after weathering this storm. From what he could tell, Fred had had constant care of the sheep while George spent the past day and a half searching for him. It wouldn't hurt for them all to take a turn at resting up.

They rounded the bend at the head of the valley. He could see the cabin now, dark against the snow-covered hill at its back. The scarlet cliffs that edged the valley glowed in the afternoon sun. A plume of smoke from the cabin's chimney waved its flag of welcome to his frozen appendages. But wait.

"I thought you said Fred was with the sheep. You didn't leave a fire going, did you?"

Before George could answer, a figure came to the door and stepped out onto the doorstep, shading her eyes with her hand as she peered down the valley toward them. The scene was so like the one in his dreams that it took him a moment to realize the figure was real.

He turned to look at George, an unspoken question in his eyes.

"She and Hazel came in by stage just before the storm hit," George said.

"Why didn't you tell me?"

George gave him a shrug and a rueful grin. "She wanted it to be a surprise."

No wonder Jackson wouldn't let him stay behind. All those cryptic looks the two had exchanged now made perfect sense. He spurred his horse to a gallop and headed toward his wife like a homing pigeon headed for its nest.

He leaped from the saddle before Trapper even came to a complete stop and pulled Maddie into his arms, reveling in the feel of her body, real and solid, in his arms. He breathed in the scent of her. Bent his head to find her lips with his. Here, in this moment, was all he needed. He had no desire to ever let her go.

A soft clearing of a throat behind him reminded him of his surroundings. Breaking off the kiss, he saw George standing awkwardly in the yard behind them.

"Don't mind me," he said. "It's just, well, it's a little cold out here."

Laughing, Maddie pulled out of his arms and drew him after her into the kitchen, leaving the doorway free. Hazel, who must have been standing just inside the door, threw her arms around him.

"Did George find you? We thought you'd never come home," she said.

"He did find me, hiding in a cave. And, believe me, if I'd have known you two were here, I would have been here long before this."

His eyes returned to Maddie, who stood smiling at them just a few feet away. Had she always been this beautiful? He drank in her loveliness, the curve of her cheek, the soft, lushness of her lips, the love shining from her gorgeous golden eyes. He longed to pull her to him and kiss each feature, but that would have to wait until they were alone.

"Tell you what, Hazel," George said from behind him. "Why don't you and I go tell Fred that the prodigal brother has returned? I don't think you've had a chance to see the sheep camp yet, have you?"

Bless the boy. He'd owe his brother more than just a few days of rest after this. Hazel was bundled up within minutes, and the two were out the door, leaving him alone with Maddie. He opened his arms, and she was soon nestled against him once more.

"I've missed you so much," he breathed the words into her hair.

She lifted her face for his kiss, tears glistening on her eyelashes. "I thought I'd never see you again."

He kissed away the tears, tasting their saltiness, his lips brushing the satin silkiness of her skin. "Don't cry, Maddie-girl. We're together now." He felt his own throat constrict, his eyelids sting with unshed tears.

"You aren't angry with me? That I came back to Wyoming without telling you?"

"Angry! I've never been so happy as I was when I saw you standing in that doorway. Maddie-girl. I've been such a fool. Pushing you and everyone else away. Can you forgive me?"

"There's nothing to forgive." She cupped his face in her hands, stroking his beard with her fingers. "Rob, I know why you left. Or at least, I think I do. I know what the doctor said to you."

"What do you mean?"

"I went to see Dr. Sewall. Remember when you left? I had that terrible cold? Well, the cough wouldn't go away, and everything I ate was disagreeing with me. I got to thinking I might . . . well, that I might have tuberculosis."

He felt the blood drain from his face.

"No, now don't look that way, Rob. I was just being foolish. I don't have anything, at least not anything to worry about. But while I was there, he told me many of the things he must have told you, how children whose parents are tubercular and those who are frail and weak from recent illness are particularly susceptible to developing the disease. I don't need to forgive you, Rob. I know you were only thinking of Hazel and of me when you left us in Denver.

"But Dr. Sewall is wrong. You aren't a threat to us, nor will you be a threat to our children. Not if we continue to be careful, to follow the guidelines Dr. Waite recommended."

"But Dr. Sewall said—"

Maddie placed her fingers over his mouth. "I don't care what Dr. Sewall said. Did you read all of the pamphlet he gave you?

Because if you did, you'd have seen there are plenty of other doctors out there who don't agree. Doctors like Dr. Waite believe if we're careful with your sputum and follow the cleaning recommendations, we have nothing to worry about."

"All right, my little tigress. I won't send you away again. Is that what you want to hear?"

"And you won't worry about Hazel and our children?"

"Our children? Aren't you getting a little ahead of yourself there?"

"Actually, no. Just the opposite. I think the way Dr. Sewall put it was, 'We shut the barn door after the horses got out.'"

"What do you mean?"

"What I mean is, by the end of the summer, you're going to be a father. The reason I was feeling so poorly is because I am pregnant."

Pregnant? Pregnant!

"Maybe you should sit down."

He sank into one of the chairs by the table and stared blindly into space. Pregnant. A baby. A child. *His* child.

"Rob? Are you all right? Talk to me. At least, let me know if you're happy."

Happy? He tested the idea. Happy? He was ecstatic. He reached out and pulled Maddie down onto his lap. He knew he was grinning like a fool, but he couldn't help it.

"We're having a baby."

"Yes. Oh, Rob, you *are* happy."

"Of course, I'm happy." How could he not be happy? "Maddie, you have no idea. Twenty-four hours ago, I didn't know if I'd live to see your face again. I swore if I ever got out of that cave alive, I would send for you. And here I come home, and you're already here, and I'm going to be a father . . ." his voice broke, and he swallowed, struggling for control. "God is so good. He's just so good."

Tears streamed down Maddie's face. "I know."

"I haven't had time to tell you all that happened in the last two days. I won't go into it all now, but there were three of us in that cave. Two healthy young men, who as far as they knew three days ago, had their whole lives stretched before them, and me, a walking-dead man. Today, both of them are dead, but I'm here . . . alive and holding you. God taught me something as I waited out that storm. I don't know how many days He has allotted for me.

"I don't know if I have tomorrow or next week, but I do know each new day I have is a gift. I don't want to squander another minute of the days He gives me worrying about whether tomorrow I'll be rid of this disease or if tomorrow will bring another storm. I want to live each day to its fullest because I know if He's given me another day, then it's one more opportunity to live my life for Him."

He laid a hand on Maddie's belly. "I don't know His plans for this child—whether it will have a long life or a short one. I don't even know if I'll live to see him or her grow up, but I do know one thing. If God created this child, then He has a purpose for its life. And He has a purpose for whatever's left of mine. So I need to stop worrying about the way my life might end and start living the life I have, right here, right now."

"Because we can trust Him," Maddie said.

"Yes. We can trust Him." He pulled her close and dropped a kiss on her soft brown curls. Everything he needed, everything he wanted, was right here in his arms. God was good.

Author's Note & Acknowledgments

As a child, one of my favorite activities was browsing through the old picture albums and boxes of family photos that hung out in my mom and dad's closet. A couple of those boxes came from my maternal grandmother. I'd sit for hours sifting through these moments of captured time, wondering about the people and places they depicted. Some I recognized as relatives in their younger days. Many, though, had passed long before my time.

Their stories intrigued me. The older the story the better. As I sifted through a box full of scenes from my grandmother's and her brother's childhood, I happened across what I considered a treasure trove—a little packet of sepia-toned photographs pasted on small gray and tan sheets of cardboard. I could tell they were once part of a miniature photo album, but the binding had long since been lost. Some of the pictures had pulled loose, leaving behind merely a caption.

The first photo in the small album showed a man with a black beard and mustache seated on a sage-covered hill. He wore a tweed Newsboy cap, a heavy coat, and knee-high leather gaiters. Tucked up under his right arm was a black dog, its head and front paws resting on the man's lap. The caption read, "Watching the Sheep." A companion picture showed a young woman seated in the same spot. She also was warmly dressed in a heavy wool jacket, a broadcloth skirt, and leather gauntlet gloves. Atop her head was a jaunty boater complete with ribbon and a flower. Tucked up against her left side was another dog—this one lighter in color with white spots. That caption read, "A Seat in the Sage Brush." This was to be my first introduction to Rob and Maddie (Maudie) Skivington, my great-grandparents.

I'd heard their story from my mother many times before. I knew they had traveled from New Jersey to Wyoming and become sheep ranchers in a quest to cure Rob's tuberculosis. I knew they were the reason I had so many relatives living in Colorado. Their story had always intrigued me, but those sepia-toned snapshots made them real. Not long after this, I read an account of their Wyoming adventure written by my great-uncle Stanley. In it, he said their story was unique enough that it deserved to be the plot of some best-selling novel. In the hubris of youth, I determined I would be the one to write that story.

I've gained a lot of years and, hopefully, a little wisdom since that time. I'm no longer naïve enough to imagine my rendition of their story will be a bestseller, but I am ecstatic to finally see it in print. Don't get me wrong. This *is* a work of fiction. Much of what you read is simply the product of my over-active imagination. But the skeleton of the story is theirs. I hope I was able to accurately portray the faith and character with which they lived that story. This is not a romance like I typically write, but it *is* a love story. Though I love writing about the excitement and angst of that first bud of romance, there's something to be said for the beauty of the mature bloom of a love tested by time and the storms of life.

Authors often compare the publishing of a book to the birth of a baby. There's truth to that analogy. An author labors for months before presenting their precious bundle to the world. With this book, however, it feels more to me like launching a grown child into the world. This story has been a part of me for so many years, it is woven into the very fabric of my life. Have I done enough? Is it ready? Am *I* ready? But whether it is, or I am, or not, it's time to let it go. It's time.

I hope Rob and Maddie's story inspires you much as it did me those many years ago as I sifted through the old family photographs. Thank you for reading it.

∽

I want to thank my Father God for the legacy of faith that made this story possible. I have been blessed by many generations of faithful Christ-followers whom I'm privileged to call family.

To my husband Kurt, I'd never do any of this writing business without your constant support. Living with an author is not always easy. Thanks for doing it so well.

To my editor, Kristin Avila—once again, your insight helped me grapple with the theme of this book and make the story arc so much stronger.

To my sister Marjorie, whose copy-editing skills help make my writing shine, thanks for all the time you put into my stories.

To Evelyne LaBelle at Carpe Librum Book Design, thanks again for another beautiful cover.

To my MBT Huddle group—Pattie, Linda, Dalyn, Mary, and Geri—your daily prayers and encouragement are priceless.

To my kids, Jared and Megan, and all my extended family, your support means the world to me.

To my readers, thank you for coming along on Rob and Maddie's journey. I hope you enjoyed the ride.

About the Author

A south-Texas transplant to the good life of Nebraska, Kathy Geary Anderson has a passion for story and all things historical. Over the years, she has been an English teacher, a newsletter and ad writer, and a stay-at-home mom. When she's not reading or writing novels, she can be found cheering (far too loudly) for her favorite football team, traveling the country with her husband, or spending time with her adult children. For more information on upcoming releases, visit www.kathygearyanderson.com.

Also by Kathy Geary Anderson

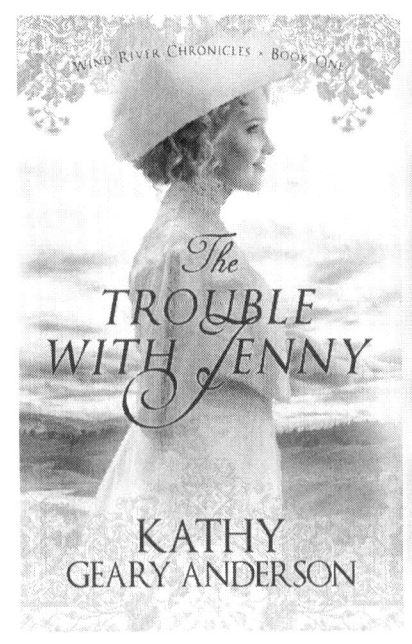

The Trouble with Jenny — Wind River Chronicles, Book One

She's always getting into trouble. He's always getting hurt.

At the turn of the 20th century, New York socialite Jenny Westraven is in trouble ... again. An orphaned heiress from a large banking family, she's expected to follow the rules of society and marry according to her wealth and status. But Jenny craves adventure and anything BUT the ordinary. So, when her guardian aunt and uncle return from a European vacation to find Jenny working as a typewriter girl in a Newark law office, they are appalled. Worse yet, they interrupt a kiss between her and her young boss Mr. "Ben" Bennett.

Jenny has been getting Ben in trouble since he was ten, so he's secretly relieved when her guardians reject him as a suitor. He has other plans for his life, and they don't include his troublesome childhood friend. When Jenny uses outrageous methods to reject the suitors her family does approve for her, her aunt and uncle decide to send her to her brother in Wyoming.

Then, a family tragedy takes Ben out west as well, and his path crosses with Jenny's once again. As they work together to end an injustice, what was merely an attraction between them develops into something more. Unfortunately, Jenny's involvement with another man comes between them and puts her in the worst trouble of her life.

Now Ben must decide whether to risk his heart to rescue her once again or cut his losses and let her go.